FIRESTARTER is the latest magnificent horror novel from Stephen King whose powers as a storyteller have established him as the master of the genre. Still in his early thirties he has written five previous novels and a collection of short stories, all of which have been bestsellers. He lives in America with his wife, Tabitha, and their three children.

Also by Stephen King:

Stephen King

Firestarter

'It was a pleasure to burn.'
 – Ray Bradbury, FAHRENHEIT 451

Futura

A Futura Book

First published in Great Britain in 1980 by
Macdonald & Co (Publishers) Ltd
London & Sydney

First Futura edition 1981
Reprinted 1981, 1982, 1983, 1984 (twice), 1985,
1986 (twice), 1987, 1988

Copyright © Stephen King 1980

ISBN 0 7088 2101 4

A limited first edition of this book
has been published by Phantasia Press

Filmset, printed and bound in Great Britain by
Hazell Watson & Viney Limited
Member of BPCC plc
Aylesbury, Bucks, England

Futura Publications
A Division of
Macdonald & Co (Publishers) Ltd
Greater London House
Hampstead Road
London NW1 7QX
A member of Maxwell Pergamon Publishing Corporation plc

In memory of Shirley Jackson,
who never needed to raise her voice.

The Haunting of Hill House
The Lottery
We Have Always Lived in the Castle
The Sundial

New York/Albany

1

'Daddy, I'm tired,' the little girl in the red pants and the green blouse said fretfully. 'Can't we stop?'

'Not yet, honey.'

He was a big, broad-shouldered man in a worn and scuffed corduroy jacket and plain brown twill slacks. He and the little girl were holding hands and walking up Third Avenue in New York City, walking fast, almost running. He looked back over his shoulder and the green car was still there, crawling along slowly in the curbside lane.

'Please, Daddy. *Please.*'

He looked at her and saw how pale her face was. There were dark circles under her eyes. He picked her up and sat her in the crook of his arm, but he didn't know how long he could go on like that. He was tired, too, and Charlie was no lightweight anymore.

It was five-thirty in the afternoon and Third Avenue was clogged. They were crossing streets in the upper Sixties now, and these cross streets were both darker and less populated. . . . But that was what he was afraid of.

They bumped into a lady pushing a walker full of groceries. 'Look where you're goin, whyn't ya?' she said, and was gone, swallowed in the hurrying crowds.

His arm was getting tired, and he switched Charlie to the other one. He snatched another look behind, and the green car was still there, still pacing them, about half a block behind. There were two men in the front seat and, he thought, a third in the back.

What do I do now?

He didn't know the answer to that. He was tired and scared and it was hard to think. They had caught him at a bad time, and the bastards probably knew it. What he wanted to do was just sit down on the dirty curbing and cry out his frustration and fear. But that was no answer. He was the grownup. He would have to think for both of them.

What do we do now?

No money. That was maybe the biggest problem, after the fact of the men in the green car. You couldn't do anything with no money in New York. People with no money disappeared in New York; they dropped into the sidewalks, never to be seen again.

He looked back over his shoulder, saw the green car was a little closer, and the sweat began to run down his back and his arms a little faster. If they knew as much as he suspected they did – if they knew how little of the push he actually had left – they might try to take him right here and now. Never mind all the people, either. In New York, if it's not happening to you, you develop this funny blindness. Have they been charting me? Andy wondered desperately. If they have, they know, and it's all over but the shouting. If they had, they knew the pattern. After Andy got some money, the strange things stopped happening for a while. The things they were interested in.

Keep walking.

Sho, boss. Yassuh, boss. Where?

He had gone into the bank at noon because his radar had been alerted – that funny hunch that they were getting close again. There was money in the bank, and he and Charlie could run on it if they had to. And wasn't that funny? Andrew McGee no longer had an account at the Chemical Allied Bank of New York, not personal checking, not business checking, not savings. They had all disappeared into thin air, and that was when he knew they really meant to bring the hammer down this time. Had all of that really been only five and a half hours ago?

But maybe there was a tickle left. Just one little tickle. It had been nearly a week since the last time – that presuicidal man at Confidence Associates who had come to the regular Thursday-night counseling session and then begun to talk with an eerie calmness about how Hemingway had committed suicide. And on the way out, his arm casually around the presuicidal man's shoulders, Andy had given him a push. Now, bitterly, he hoped it had been worth it. Because it looked very much as if he and Charlie were going to be the ones to pay. He almost hoped an echo—

But no. He pushed that away, horrified and disgusted with himself. That was nothing to wish on *anybody*.

One little tickle, he prayed. That's all, God, just one little tickle. Enough to get me and Charlie out of this jam.

And oh God, how you'll pay . . . plus the fact that you'll be dead for a month afterward, just like a radio with a blown tube. Maybe six weeks. Or maybe really dead, with your worthless brains leaking out your ears. What would happen to Charlie then?

They were coming up on Seventieth Street and the light was against them. Traffic was pouring across and pedestrians were building up at the corner in a bottleneck. And suddenly he knew this was where the men in the green car would take them. Alive if they could, of course, but if it looked like trouble . . . well, they had probably been briefed on Charlie, too.

Maybe they don't even want us alive anymore. Maybe they've decided just to maintain the status quo. What do you do with a faulty equation? Erase it from the board.

A knife in the back, a silenced pistol, quite possibly something more arcane – a drop of rare poison on the end of a needle. Convulsions at the corner of Third and Seventieth. Officer, this man appears to have suffered a heart attack.

He would have to try for that tickle. There was just nothing else.

They reached the waiting pedestrians at the corner. Across the way, DON'T WALK held steady and seemingly eternal. He looked back. The green car had stopped. The curbside doors opened and two men in business suits got out. They were young and smooth-cheeked. They looked considerably fresher than Andy McGee felt.

He began elbowing his way through the clog of pedestrians, eyes searching frantically for a vacant cab.

'Hey, man—'

'For Christ' sake, fella!'

'Please, mister, you're stepping on my *dog*—'

'Excuse me . . . excuse me . . .' Andy said desperately. He searched for a cab. There were none. At any other time the street would have been stuffed with them. He could feel the men from the green car coming for them, wanting to lay hands on him and Charlie, to take them with them God knew where, the Shop, some damn place, or do something even worse—

Charlie laid her head on his shoulder and yawned.

Andy saw a vacant cab.

'Taxi! Taxi!' he yelled, flagging madly with his free hand.

Behind him, the two men dropped all pretense and ran. The taxi pulled over.

'Hold it!' one of the men yelled. 'Police! Police!'

A woman near the back of the crowd at the corner screamed, and then they all began to scatter.

Andy opened the cab's back door and handed Charlie in. He dived in after her. 'La Guardia, step on it,' he said.

'*Hold it, cabby. Police!*'

The cab driver turned his head toward the voice and

Andy pushed – very gently. A dagger of pain was planted squarely in the center of Andy's forehead and then quickly withdrawn, leaving a vague locus of pain, like a morning headache – the kind you get from sleeping on your neck.

'They're after that black guy in the checkered cap, I think,' he said to the cabby.

'Right,' the driver said, and pulled serenely away from the curb. They moved down East Seventieth.

Andy looked back. The two men were standing alone at the curb. The rest of the pedestrians wanted nothing to do with them. One of the men took a walkie-talkie from his belt and began to speak into it. Then they were gone.

'That black guy,' the driver said, 'whadde do? Rob a liquor store or somethin, you think?'

'I don't know,' Andy said, trying to think how to go on with this, how to get the most out of this cab driver for the least push. Had they got the cab's plate number? He would have to assume they had. But they wouldn't want to go to the city or state cops, and they would be surprised and scrambling, for a while at least.

'They're all a bunch of junkies, the blacks in this city,' the driver said. 'Don't tell me, I'll tell you.'

Charlie was going to sleep. Andy took off his corduroy jacket, folded it, and slipped it under her head. He had begun to feel a thin hope. If he could play this right, it might work. Lady Luck had sent him what Andy thought of (with no prejudice at all) as a pushover. He was the sort that seemed the easiest to push, right down the line: he was white (Orientals were the toughest, for some reason); he was quite young (old people were nearly impossible) and of medium intelligence (bright people were the easiest pushes, stupid ones harder, and with the mentally retarded it was impossible).

'I've changed my mind,' Andy said. 'Take us to Albany, please.'

'*Where?*' The driver stared at him in the rearview mirror. 'Man, I can't take a fare to Albany, you out of your mind?'

Andy pulled his wallet, which contained a single dollar bill. He thanked God that this was not one of those cabs with a bulletproof partition and no way to contact the driver except through a money slot. Open contact always made it easier to push. He had been unable to figure out if that was a psychological thing or not, and right now it was immaterial.

'I'm going to give you a five-hundred-dollar bill,' Andy said quietly, 'to take me and my daughter to Albany. Okay?'

'Jeee-*sus*, mister— '

Andy stuck the bill into the cabby's hand, and as the cabby looked down at it, Andy pushed . . . and pushed hard. For a terrible second he was afraid it wasn't going to work, that there was simply nothing left, that he had scraped the bottom of the barrel when he had made the driver see the nonexistent black man in the checkered cap.

Then the feeling came – as always accompanied by that steel dagger of pain. At the same moment, his stomach seemed to take on weight and his bowels locked in sick, griping agony. He put an unsteady hand to his face and wondered if he was going to throw up . . . or die. For that one moment he *wanted* to die, as he always did when he overused it – *use it, don't abuse it*, the sign-off slogan of some long-ago disc jockey echoing sickly in his mind – whatever 'it' was. If at that very moment someone had slipped a gun into his hand—

Then he looked sideways at Charlie, Charlie sleeping, Charlie trusting him to get them out of this mess as he had all the others, Charlie confident he would be there when she woke up. Yes, all the messes, except it was all the same mess, the same fucking mess, and all they were doing was running again. Black despair pressed behind his eyes.

The feeling passed . . . but not the headache. The headache would get worse and worse until it was a smashing weight, sending red pain through his head and neck with every pulsebeat. Bright lights would make his eyes water helplessly and send darts of agony into the flesh just behind his eyes. His sinuses would close and he would have to breathe through his mouth. Drill bits in his temples. Small noises magnified, ordinary noises as loud as jackhammers, loud noises insupportable. The headache would worsen until it felt as if his head were being crushed inside an inquisitor's lovecap. Then it would even off at that level for six hours, or eight, or maybe ten. This time he didn't know. He had never pushed it so far when he was so close to drained. For whatever length of time he was in the grip of the headache, he would be next to helpless. Charlie would have to take care of him. God knew she had done it before . . . but they had been lucky. How many times could you be lucky?

'Gee, mister, I don't know—'

Which meant he thought it was law trouble.

'The deal only goes as long as you don't mention it to my little girl,' Andy said. 'The last two weeks she's been with me. Has to be back with her mother tomorrow morning.'

'Visitation rights,' the cabby said. 'I know all about it.'

'You see, I was supposed to fly her up.'

'To Albany? Probably Ozark, am I right?'

'Right. Now, the thing is, I'm scared to death of flying. I know how crazy that sounds, but it's true. Usually I drive her back up, but this time my ex-wife started in on me, and . . . I don't know.' In truth, Andy didn't. He had made up the story on the spur of the moment and now it seemed to be headed straight down a blind alley. Most of it was pure exhaustion.

'So I drop you at the old Albany airport, and as far as Moms knows, you flew, right?'

'Sure.' His head was thudding.

'Also, as far as Moms knows, you're no plucka-plucka-plucka, am I four-oh?'

'Yes.' Plucka-plucka-plucka? What was that supposed to mean? The pain was getting bad.

'Five hundred bucks to skip a plane ride,' the driver mused.

'It's worth it to me,' Andy said, and gave one last little shove. In a very quiet voice, speaking almost into the cabby's ear, he added, 'And it ought to be worth it to you.'

'Listen,' the driver said in a dreamy voice. 'I ain't turning down no five hundred dollars. Don't tell me, I'll tell you.'

'Okay,' Andy said, and settled back. The cab driver was satisfied. He wasn't wondering about Andy's half-baked story. He wasn't wondering what a seven-year-old girl was doing visiting her father for two weeks in October with school in. He wasn't wondering about the fact that neither of them had so much as an overnight bag. He wasn't worried about anything. He had been pushed.

Now Andy would go ahead and pay the price.

He put a hand on Charlie's leg. She was fast asleep. They had been on the go all afternoon – ever since Andy got to her school and pulled her out of her second-grade class with some half-remembered excuse . . . grandmother's very ill . . . called home . . . sorry to have to take her in the middle of the day. And beneath all that a great, swelling relief. How he had dreaded looking into Mrs Mishkin's room and seeing Charlie's seat empty, her books stacked neatly inside her desk: *No, Mr McGee . . . she went with your friends about two hours ago . . . they had a note from you . . . wasn't that all right?* Memories of Vicky coming back, the sudden terror of the empty house that day. His crazy chase after Charlie. Because they had had her once before, oh yes.

14

But Charlie had been there. How close had it been? Had he beaten them by half an hour? Fifteen minutes? Less? He didn't like to think about it. He had got them a late lunch at Nathan's and they had spent the rest of the afternoon just *going* – Andy could admit to himself now that he had been in a state of blind panic – riding subways, buses, but mostly just walking. And now she was worn out.

He spared her a long, loving look. Her hair was shoulder length, perfect blond, and in her sleep she had a calm beauty. She looked so much like Vicky that it hurt. He closed his own eyes.

In the front seat, the cab driver looked wonderingly at the five-hundred-dollar bill the guy had handed him. He tucked it away in the special belt pocket where he kept all of his tips. He didn't think it was strange that this fellow in the back had been walking around New York with a little girl and a five-hundred-dollar bill in his pocket. He didn't wonder how he was going to square this with his dispatcher. All he thought of was how excited his girlfriend, Glyn, was going to be. Glynis kept telling him that driving a taxi was a dismal, unexciting job. Well, wait until she saw his dismal, unexciting five-hundred-dollar bill.

In the back seat, Andy sat with his head back and his eyes closed. The headache was coming, coming, as inexorable as a riderless black horse in a funeral cortege. He could hear the hoofbeats of that horse in his temples: *thud . . . thud . . . thud.*

On the run. He and Charlie. He was thirty-four years old and until last year he had been an instructor of English at Harrison State College in Ohio. Harrison was a sleepy little college town. Good old Harrison, the very heart of mid-America. Good old Andrew McGee, fine, upstanding young man. Remember the riddle? Why is a farmer the pillar of his community? Because he's always outstanding in his field.

Thud, thud, thud, riderless black horse with red eyes coming down the halls of his mind, ironshod hooves digging up soft gray clods of brain tissue, leaving hoofprints to fill up with mystic crescents of blood.

The cabby had been a pushover. Sure. An outstanding cab driver.

He dozed and saw Charlie's face. And Charlie's face became Vicky's face.

Andy McGee and his wife, pretty Vicky. They had pulled her fingernails out, one by one. They had pulled out four of them and then she had talked. That, at least, was his deduction. Thumb, index, second, ring. Then: Stop. I'll talk. I'll tell you anything you want to know. Just stop the hurting. Please. So she had told. And then . . . perhaps it had been an accident . . . then his wife had died. Well, some things are bigger than both of us, and other things are bigger than all of us.

Things like the Shop, for instance.

Thud, thud, thud, riderless black horse coming on, coming on, and coming on: behold, a black horse.

Andy slept.

And remembered.

2

The man in charge of the experiment was Dr Wanless. He was fat and balding and had at least one rather bizarre habit.

'We're going to give each of you twelve young ladies and gentlemen an injection,' he said, shredding a cigarette into the ashtray in front of him. His small pink fingers plucked at the thin cigarette paper, spilling out neat little cones of golden-brown tobacco. 'Six of these injections will be water. Six of them will be water mixed with a tiny amount of a chemical compound which we call Lot Six. The exact nature of this compound is classified, but it is essentially an hypnotic and mild hallucinogenic. Thus you understand that the compound will be administered by the double-blind method . . . which is to say, neither you nor we will know who has gotten a clear dose and who has not until later. The dozen of you will be under close supervision for forty-eight hours following the injection. Questions?'

There were several, most having to do with the exact composition of Lot Six – that word *classified* was like putting bloodhounds on a convict's trail. Wanless slipped these questions quite adroitly. No one had asked the question twenty-two-year-old Andy McGee was most interested in. He considered raising his hand in the hiatus that fell upon the nearly deserted lecture hall in Harrison's combined Psychology/Sociology building and asking, Say, why are you ripping up perfectly good cigarettes like that? Better not to. Better to let the imagination run on a free rein while this boredom went on. He was trying to give up smoking. The oral retentive smokes them; the anal retentive shreds them. (This brought a slight grin to Andy's lips, which he covered with a hand.) Wanless's brother had died of lung cancer and the doctor was symbolically venting his aggressions on the cigarette industry. Or maybe it was just one of those flamboyant tics that college professors felt compelled to flaunt rather than suppress. Andy had one English teacher his sophomore year at Harrison (the man was now mercifully retired) who sniffed his tie constantly while lecturing on William Dean Howells and the rise of realism.

'If there are no more questions, I'll ask you to fill out these forms and will expect to see you promptly at nine next Tuesday.'

Two grad assistants passed out photocopies with twenty-five ridiculous questions to answer yes or no. *Have you ever undergone psychiatric counselling? – #8. Do you believe you have ever had an authentic psychic experience? – #14. Have you ever used hallucinogenic drugs? – #18.* After a slight pause, Andy checked 'no' to that one, thinking, *In this brave year 1969, who hasn't used them?*

He had been put on to this by Quincey Tremont, the fellow he had roomed with in college. Quincey knew that Andy's financial situation wasn't so hot. It was May of Andy's senior year; he was graduating fortieth in a class of five hundred and six, third in the English program. But that didn't buy no potatoes, as he had told Quincey, who was a psych major. Andy had a GA lined up for himself starting in the fall semester, along with a scholarship-loan package that would be just about enough to buy groceries and keep him in the Harrison grad program. But all of that was fall, and in the meantime there was the summer hiatus. The best he had been able to line up so far was a responsible, challenging position as an Arco gas jockey on the night shift.

'How would you feel about a quick two hundred?' Quincey had asked.

Andy brushed long, dark hair away from his green eyes and grinned. 'Which men's room do I set up my concession in?'

'No, it's a psych experiment,' Quincey said. 'Being run by the Mad Doctor, though. Be warned.'

'Who he?'

'Him Wanless, Tonto. Heap big medicine man in-um Psych Department.'

'Why do they call him the Mad Doctor?'

'Well,' Quincey said, 'he's a rat man and a Skinner man both. A behaviorist. The behaviorists are not exactly being overwhelmed with love these days.'

'Oh,' Andy said, mystified.

'Also, he wears very thick little rimless glasses, which makes him look quite a bit like the guy that shrank the people in *Dr Cyclops*. You ever see that show?'

Andy, who was a late-show addict, had seen it, and felt on safer ground. But he wasn't sure he wanted to participate in any experiments run by a prof who was classified as a.) a rat man and b.) a Mad Doctor.

'They're not trying to shrink people, are they?' he asked.

Quincey had laughed heartily. 'No, that's strictly for the special-effects people who work on the B horror pictures,' he said. 'The Psych Department has been testing a series of low-grade hallucinogens. They're working with the U.S. Intelligence Service.'

'CIA?' Andy asked.

'Not CIA, DIA, or NSA,' Quincey said. 'Lower profile than any of them. Have you ever heard of an outfit called the Shop?'

'Maybe in a Sunday supplement or something. I'm not sure.'

Quincey lit his pipe. 'These things work in about the same way all across the board,' he said. 'Psychology, chemistry, physics, biology . . . even the sociology boys get some of the folding green. Certain programs are subsidized by the government. Anything from the mating ritual of the tsetse fly to the possible disposal of used plutonium slugs. An outfit like the Shop has to spend all of its yearly budget to justify a like amount the following year.'

'That shit troubles me mightily,' Andy said.

'It troubles almost any thinking person,' Quincey said with a calm, untroubled smile. 'But the train just keeps rolling. What does our intelligence branch want with low-grade hallucinogens? Who knows? Not me. Not you. Probably they don't either. But the reports look good in closed committees come budget-renewal time. They have their pets in every department. At Harrison, Wanless is their pet in the Psych Department.'

'The administration doesn't mind?'

'Don't be naïve, my boy.' He had his pipe going to his satisfaction and was puffing great stinking clouds of smoke out into the ratty apartment living room. His voice accordingly became more rolling, more orotund, more Buckleyesque. 'What's good for Wanless is good for the Harrison Psychology Department, which next year will have its very own building – no more slumming with those sociology types. And what's good for Psych is good for Harrison State College. And for Ohio. And all that blah-blah.'

'Do you think it's safe?'

'They don't test it on student volunteers if it isn't safe,' Quincey said. 'If they have even the slightest question, they test it on rats and then on convicts. You can be sure that what they're putting into you has been put into roughly three hundred people before you, whose reactions have been carefully monitored.'

'I don't like this business about the CIA—'

'The Shop.'

'What's the difference?' Andy asked morosely. He looked at Quincey's poster of Richard Nixon standing in front of a crunched-up used car. Nixon was grinning, and a stubby V-for-victory poked up out of each clenched fist. Andy could still hardly believe the man had been elected president less than a year ago.

'Well, I thought maybe you could use the two hundred dollars, that's all.'

'Why are they paying so much?' Andy asked suspiciously.

Quincey threw up his hands. 'Andy, it is the government's treat! Can't you follow that? Two years ago the Shop paid something like three hundred thousand dollars for a feasibility study on a mass-produced exploding bicycle – and *that* was in the Sunday *Times*. Just another Vietnam thing, I guess, although probably nobody knows for sure. Like Fibber McGee used to say, "It seemed like a good idea at the time." ' Quincey knocked out his pipe with quick, jittery movements. 'To guys like that, every college campus in America is like one big Macy's. They buy a little here, do a little window-shopping there. Now if you don't want it—'

'Well, maybe I do. Are you going in on it?'

Quincey had smiled. His father ran a chain of extremely successful menswear stores in Ohio and Indiana. 'Don't need two hundred that bad,' he said. 'Besides, I hate needles.'

'Oh.'

'Look, I'm not trying to sell it, for Chrissakes; you just looked sort of hungry. The chances are fifty-fifty you'll be in the control group, anyway. Two hundred bucks for taking on water. Not even tapwater, mind you. *Distilled* water.'

'You can fix it?'

'I date one of Wanless's grad assistants,' Quincey said. 'They'll have maybe fifty applications, many of them brownnosers who want to make points with the Mad Doctor—'

'I wish you'd stop calling him that.'

'Wanless, then,' Quincey said, and laughed. 'He'll see that the apple polishers are weeded out personally. My girl will see that your application goes into his "in" basket. After that, dear man, you are on your own.'

So he had made out the application when the notice for volunteers went up on the Psych Department bulletin board. A week after turning it in, a young female GA (Quincey's girlfriend, for all Andy knew) had called on the phone to ask him some questions. He told her that his parents were dead; that his blood type was O; that he had never participated in a Psychology Department experiment before; that he was indeed currently enrolled in Harrison as an undergraduate, class of '69, in fact, and carrying more than the twelve credits needed to classify him as a full-time student. And yes, he was past the age of twenty-one and legally able to enter into any and all covenants, public and private.

A week later he had received a letter via campus mail telling him he had been accepted and asking for his signature on a release form. Please bring the signed form to Room 100, Jason Gearneigh Hall, on May the 6th.

And here he was, release form passed in, the cigarette-shredding Wanless departed (and he did indeed look a bit like the mad doctor in that Cyclops movie), answering questions about his religious experiences along with eleven other undergrads. Did he have epilepsy? No. His father had died suddenly of a heart attack when Andy was eleven. His mother had been killed in a car accident when Andy was seventeen – a nasty, traumatic thing. His only close family connection was his mother's sister, Aunt Cora, and she was getting well along in years.

He went down the column of questions, checking *no, no, no*. He checked only one YES question: *Have you ever suffered a fracture or serious sprain? If yes, specify.* In the space provided, he scribbled the fact that he had broken his left ankle sliding into second base during a Little League game twelve years ago.

He went back over his answers, trailing lightly upward with the tip of his Bic. That was when someone tapped him on the shoulder and a girl's voice, sweet and slightly husky, asked, 'Could I borrow that if you're done with it? Mine went dry.'

'Sure,' he said, turning to hand it to her. Pretty girl. Tall. Light-auburn hair, marvelously clear complexion.

Wearing a powder-blue sweater and a short skirt. Good legs. No stockings. Casual appraisal of the future wife.

He handed her his pen and she smiled her thanks. The overhead lights made copper glints in her hair, which had been casually tied back with a wide white ribbon, as she bent over her form again.

He took his form up to the GA at the front of the room. 'Thank you,' the GA said, as programmed as Robbie the Robot. 'Room Seventy, Saturday morning, nine A.M. Please be on time.'

'What's the countersign?' Andy whispered hoarsely.

The grad assistant laughed politely.

Andy left the lecture hall, started across the lobby toward the big double doors outside, the quad was green with approaching summer, students passing desultorily back and forth, and then remembered his pen. He almost let it go; it was only a nineteen-cent Bic, and he still had his final round of prelims to study for. But the girl had been pretty, maybe worth chatting up, as the British said. He had no illusions about his looks or his line, which were both pretty nondescript, or about the girl's probable status (pinned or engaged), but it was a nice day and he was feeling good. He decided to wait. At the very least, he would get another look at those legs.

She came out three or four minutes later, a few notebooks and a text under her arm. She was very pretty indeed, and Andy decided her legs had been worth waiting for. They were more than good; they were spectacular.

'Oh, there you are,' she said, smiling.

'Here I am,' said Andy McGee. 'What did you think of that?'

'I don't know,' she said. 'My friend said these experiments go on all the time – she was in one last semester with those J. B. Rhine ESP cards and got fifty dollars for it even though she missed almost all of them. So I just thought ·'

23

She finished the thought with a shrug and flipped her coppery hair neatly back over her shoulders.

'Yeah, me too,' he said, taking his pen back. 'Your friend in the Psych Department?'

'Yes,' she said, 'and my boyfriend, too. He's in one of Dr Wanless's classes, so he couldn't get in. Conflict of interest or something.'

Boyfriend. It stood to reason that a tall, auburn-haired beauty like this had one. That was the way the world turned.

'What about you?' she asked.

'Same story. Friend in the Psych Department. I'm Andy, by the way. Andy McGee.'

'I'm Vicky Tomlinson. And a little nervous about this, Andy McGee. What if I go on a bad trip or something?'

'This sounds like pretty mild stuff to me. And even if it is acid, well . . . lab acid is different from the stuff you can pick up on the street, or so I've heard. Very smooth, very mellow, and administered under very calm circumstances. They'll probably pipe in Cream or Jefferson Airplane.' Andy grinned.

'Do you know much about LSD?' she asked with a little cornerwise grin that he liked very much.

'Very little,' he admitted. 'I tried it twice – once two years ago, once last year. In some ways it made me feel better. It cleaned out my head . . . at least, that's what it felt like. Afterward, a lot of the old crud just seemed to be gone. But I wouldn't want to make a steady habit of it. I don't like feeling so out of control of myself. Can I buy you a Coke?'

'All right,' she agreed, and they walked over to the Union building together.

He ended up buying her two Cokes, and they spent the afternoon together. That evening they had a few beers at the local hangout. It turned out that she and the boyfriend

24

had come to a parting of the ways, and she wasn't sure exactly how to handle it. He was beginning to think they were married, she told Andy; had absolutely forbidden her to take part in the Wanless experiment. For that precise reason she had gone ahead and signed the release form and was now determined to go through with it even though she was a little scared.

'That Wanless really does look like a mad doctor,' she said, making rings on the table with her beer glass.

'How did you like that trick with the cigarettes?'

Vicky giggled. 'Weird way to quit smoking, huh?'

He asked her if he could pick her up on the morning of the experiment, and she had agreed gratefully.

'It would be good to go into this with a friend,' she said, and looked at him with her direct blue eyes. 'I really am a little scared, you know. George was so – I don't know, *adamant.*'

'Why? What did he say?'

'That's just it,' Vicky said. 'He wouldn't tell me anything, except that he didn't trust Wanless. He said hardly anyone in the department does, but a lot of them sign up for his tests because he's in charge of the graduate program. Besides, they know it's safe, because he just weeds them out again.'

He reached across the table and touched her hand. 'We'll both probably get the distilled water, anyway,' he said. 'Take it easy, kiddo. Everything's fine.'

But as it turned out, nothing was fine. Nothing.

3

albany
albany airport mister
hey mister, this is it we're here

Hand, shaking him. Making his head roll on his neck. Terrible headache – Jesus! Thudding, shooting pains.

'Hey mister, this is the airport.'

Andy opened his eyes, then shut them against the white light of an overhead sodium lamp. There was a terrible, shrieking whine, building up and up and up, and he winced against it. It felt as if steel darning needles were being jammed into his ears. Plane. Taking off. It began to come to him through the red fog of pain. Ah yes, Doc, it all comes back to me now.

'Mister?' The cabby sounded worried. 'Mister, you okay?'

'Headache.' His voice seemed to come from far away, buried in the jet-engine sound that was, mercifully, beginning to fade off. 'What time is it?'

'Nearly midnight. Slow haul getting up here. Don't tell me, I'll tell you. Buses won't be running, if that was your plan. Sure I can't take you home?'

Andy groped in his mind for the story he had told the cabby. It was important that he remember, monster headache or not. Because of the echo. If he contradicted the earlier story in any way, it could set up a ricochet effect in the cabby's mind. It might die out - in fact, probably would - but it might not. The cabby might seize on one point of it, develop a fixation on it; shortly it would be out of control, it would be all the cabby could think about; shortly after that, it would simply tear his mind apart. It had happened before.

'My car's in the lot,' he said. 'Everything is under control.'

'Oh.' The cabby smiled, relieved. 'Glyn isn't gonna believe this, you know. Hey! Don't tell me, I'll t–'

'Sure she'll believe it. You do, don't you?'

The driver grinned widely. 'I got the big bill to prove it, mister. Thanks.'

'Thank *you*,' Andy said. Struggle to be polite. Struggle to go on. For Charlie. If he had been alone, he would have

26

killed himself long ago. A man wasn't meant to bear pain like this.

'You sure you're okay, mister? You look awful white.'

'I'm fine, thanks.' He began to shake Charlie. 'Hey, kid.' He was careful not to use her name. It probably didn't matter, but the caution came as naturally as breathing. 'Wake up, we're here.'

Charlie muttered and tried to roll away from him.

'Come on, doll. Wake up, hon.'

Charlie's eyes fluttered open – the direct blue eyes she had got from her mother – and she sat up, rubbing her face. 'Daddy? Where are we?'

'Albany, hon. The airport.' And leaning closer, he muttered, 'Don't say anything yet.'

'Okay.' She smiled at the cab driver, and the cabby smiled back. She slipped out of the cab and Andy followed her, trying not to stagger.

'Thanks again, man,' the cabby said. 'Listen, hey. Great fare. Don't tell me, I'll tell you.'

Andy shook the outstretched hand. 'Take care.'

'I will. Glyn's just not gonna believe this action.'

The cabby got back in and pulled away from the yellow-painted curb. Another jet was taking off, the engine revving and revving until Andy felt as though his head would split in two pieces and fall to the pavement like a hollow gourd. He staggered a little, and Charlie put her hands on his arm.

'Oh, Daddy,' she said, and her voice was far away.

'Inside. I have to sit down.'

They went in, the little girl in the red pants and the green blouse, the big man with the shaggy black hair and the slumped shoulders. A skycap watched them go and thought it was a pure sin, a big man like that out after midnight, drunk as a lord by the look of him, with his little girl who should have been in bed hours ago leading him around like a Seeing Eye dog. Parents like that ought to be sterilized, the skycap thought.

Then they went in through the electric-eye-controlled doors and the skycap forgot all about them until some forty minutes later, when the green car pulled up to the curb and the two men got out to talk to him.

4

It was ten past midnight. The lobby of the terminal had been given over to the early-morning people: servicemen at the end of their leaves, harried-looking women riding herd on scratchy, up-too-late children, businessmen with pouches of weariness under their eyes, cruising kids in big boots and long hair, some of them with packs on their backs, a couple with cased tennis rackets. The loudspeaker system announced arrivals and departures and paged people like some omnipotent voice in a dream.

Andy and Charlie sat side by side at desks with TVs bolted to them. The TVs were scratched and dented and painted dead black. To Andy they looked like sinister, futuristic cobras. He plugged his last two quarters into them so they wouldn't be asked to leave the seats. Charlie's was showing a rerun of *The Rookies* and Johnny Carson was yucking it up with Sonny Bono and Buddy Hackett on Andy's.

'Daddy, do I have to?' Charlie asked for the second time. She was on the verge of tears.

'Honey, I'm used up,' he said. 'We have no money. We can't stay here.'

'Those bad men are coming?' she asked, and her voice dropped to a whisper.

'I don't know.' Thud, thud, thud in his brain. Not a riderless black horse anymore; now it was mailsacks filled

28

with sharp scraps of iron being dropped on him from a fifth-story window. 'We have to assume they are.'

'How could I get money?'

He hesitated and then said, 'You know.'

The tears began to come and trickled down her cheeks. 'It's not right. It's not right to steal.'

'I know it,' he said. 'But it's not right for them to keep coming at us, either. I explained it to you, Charlie. Or at least I tried.'

'About little bad and big bad?'

'Yes. Lesser and greater evil.'

'Does your head really hurt?'

'It's pretty bad,' Andy said. There was no use telling her that in an hour, or possibly two, it would be so bad he would no longer be able to think coherently. No use frightening her worse than she already was. No use telling her that he didn't think they were going to get away this time.

'I'll try,' she said, and got out of the chair. 'Poor Daddy,' she said, and kissed him.

He closed his eyes. The TV played on in front of him, a faraway babble of sound in the midst of the steadily growing ache in his head. When he opened his eyes again, she was just a distant figure, very small, dressed in red and green, like a Christmas ornament, bobbing away through the scattered people on the concourse.

Please God, let her be all right, he thought. *Don't let anyone mess with her, or scare her worse than she is already. Please and thank you, God. Okay?*

He closed his eyes again.

5

Little girl in red stretch pants and a green rayon blouse. Shoulder-length blond hair. Up too late, apparently by herself. She was in one of the few places where a little girl by herself could go unremarked after midnight. She passed people, but no one really saw her. If she had been crying, a security guard might have come over to ask her if she was lost, if she knew which airline her mommy and daddy were ticketed on, what their names were so they could be paged. But she wasn't crying, and she looked as if she knew where she was going.

She didn't exactly - but she had a pretty fair idea of what she was looking for. They needed money; that was what Daddy had said. The bad men were coming, and Daddy was hurt. When he got hurt like this, it got hard for him to think. He had to lie down and have as much quiet as he could. He had to sleep until the pain went away. And the bad men might be coming . . . the men from the Shop, the men who wanted to pick them apart and see what made them work - and to see if they could be used, made to do things.

She saw a paper shopping bag sticking out of the top of a trash basket and took it. A little way farther down the concourse she came to what she was looking for: a bank of pay phones.

Charlie stood looking at them, and she was afraid. She was afraid because Daddy had told her again and again that she shouldn't do it . . . since earliest childhood it had been the Bad Thing. She couldn't always control the Bad Thing. She might hurt herself, or someone else, or lots of people. The time

(oh mommy i'm sorry the hurt the bandages the screams she screamed i made my mommy scream and i never will again . . . never . . . because it is a Bad Thing)

in the kitchen when she was little . . . but it hurt too much to think of that. It was a Bad Thing because when you let it go, it went . . . everywhere. And that was scary.

There were other things. The push, for instance; that's what Daddy called it, the push. Only she could push a lot harder than Daddy, and she never got headaches afterward. But sometimes, afterward . . . there were fires.

The word for the Bad Thing clanged in her mind as she stood nervously looking at the telephone booths: *pyrokinesis.* 'Never mind that,' Daddy had told her when they were still in Port City and thinking like fools that they were safe. 'You're a firestarter, honey. Just one great big Zippo lighter.' And then it had seemed funny, she had giggled, but now it didn't seem funny at all.

The other reason she wasn't supposed to push was because *they* might find out. The bad men from the Shop. 'I don't know how much they know about you now,' Daddy had told her, 'but I don't want them to find out anymore. Your push isn't exactly like mine, honey. You can't make people . . . well, change their minds, can you?'

'No-ooo . . .'

'But you can make things move. And if they ever began to see a pattern, and connect that pattern to you, we'd be in even worse trouble than we are now.'

And it was stealing, and stealing was also a Bad Thing.

Never mind. Daddy's head was hurting him and they had to get to a quiet, warm place before it got too bad for him to think at all. Charlie moved forward.

There were about fifteen phonebooths in all, with circular sliding doors. When you were inside the booth, it was like being inside a great big Contac capsule with a phone inside it. Most of the booths were dark, Charlie saw as she drifted down past them. There was a fat lady in a pantsuit crammed into one of them, talking busily and smiling. And three booths from the end a young man in a service uniform was sitting on the little stool with the door open and his legs poking out. He was talking fast.

'Sally, look, I understand how you feel, but I can explain everything. Absolutely. I know . . . I know . . . but if you'll just let me—' He looked up, saw the little girl looking at him, and yanked his legs in and pulled the circular door closed, all in one motion, like a turtle pulling into its shell. Having a fight with his girlfriend, Charlie thought. Probably stood her up. I'd never let a guy stand me up.

Echoing loudspeaker. Rat of fear in the back of her mind, gnawing. All the faces were strange faces. She felt lonely and very small, grief-sick over her mother even now. This was stealing, but what did that matter? They had stolen her mother's life.

She slipped into the phonebooth on the end, shopping bag crackling. She took the phone off the hook and pretended she was talking – hello, Grampa, yes, Daddy and I just got in, we're fine – and looked out through the glass to see if anyone was being nosy. No one was. The only person nearby was a black woman getting flight insurance from a machine, and her back was to Charlie.

Charlie looked at the pay phone and suddenly *shoved* it.

A little grunt of effort escaped her, and she bit down on her lower lip, liking the way it squeezed under her teeth. No, there was no pain involved. It felt *good* to shove things, and that was another thing that scared her. Suppose she got to *like* this dangerous thing?

She shoved the pay phone again, very lightly, and suddenly a tide of silver poured out of the coin return. She tried to get her bag under it, but by the time she did, most of the quarters and nickels and dimes had spewed onto the floor. She bent over and swept as much as she could into the bag, glancing again and again out the window.

With the change picked up, she went on to the next

booth. The serviceman was still talking on the next phone up the line. He had opened the door again and was smoking. 'Sal, honest to Christ I did! Just ask your brother if you don't believe me! He'll—'

Charlie slipped the door shut, cutting off the slightly whining sound of his voice. She was only seven, but she knew a snowjob when she heard one. She looked at the phone, and a moment later it gave up its change. This time she had the bag positioned perfectly and the coins cascaded to the bottom with a musical little jingling sound.

The serviceman was gone when she came out, and Charlie went into his booth. The seat was still warm and the air smelled nastily of cigarette smoke in spite of the fan.

The money rattled into her bag and she went on.

6

Eddie Delgardo sat in a hard plastic contour chair, looking up at the ceiling and smoking. Bitch, he was thinking. She'll think twice about keeping her goddam legs closed next time. Eddie this and Eddie that and Eddie I never want to see you again and Eddie how could you be so *crew-ool*. But he had changed her mind about the old I-never-want-to-see-you-again bit. He was on thirty-day leave and now he was going to New York City, the Big Apple, to see the sights and tour the singles bars. And when he came back, Sally would be like a big ripe apple herself, ripe and ready to fall. None of that don't-you-have-any-respect-for-me stuff went down with Eddie Delgardo of Marathon, Florida. Sally Bradford was going to put out, and if she really believed that crap about him having had a vasectomy, it served her right. And then let her go running to her hick schoolteacher brother if she wanted to.

Eddie Delgardo would be driving an army supply truck in West Berlin. He would be—

Eddie's half-resentful, half-pleasant chain of daydreams was broken by a strange feeling of warmth coming from his feet; it was as if the floor had suddenly heated up ten degrees. And accompanying this was a strange but not completely unfamiliar smell . . . not something burning but . . . something *singeing*, maybe?

He opened his eyes and the first thing he saw was that little girl who had been cruising around by the phone-booths, little girl seven or eight years old, looking really ragged out. Now she was carrying a big paper bag, carrying it by the bottom as if it were full of groceries or something.

But his feet, that was the thing.

They were no longer warm. They were *hot*.

Eddie Delgardo looked down and screamed, '*Godamighty Jeesus!*'

His shoes were on fire.

Eddie leaped to his feet. Heads turned. Some woman saw what was happening and yelled in alarm. Two security guards who had been noodling with an Allegheny Airlines ticket clerk looked over to see what was going on.

None of which meant doodly-squat to Eddie Delgardo. Thoughts of Sally Bradford and his revenge of love upon her were the furthest things from his mind. His army-issue shoes were burning merrily. The cuffs of his dress greens were catching. He was sprinting across the concourse, trailing smoke, as if shot from a catapult. The women's room was closer, and Eddie, whose sense of self-preservation was exquisitely defined, hit the door straight-arm and ran inside without a moment's hesitation.

A young woman was coming out of one of the stalls, her skirt rucked up to her waist, adjusting her Underalls. She saw Eddie, the human torch, and let out a scream that the bathroom's tiled walls magnified enormously. There was a babble of 'What was that?' and 'What's going on?' from the few other occupied stalls. Eddie caught the pay-toilet door before it could swing back all the way and latch. He grabbed both sides of the stall at the top and hoisted himself feet first into the toilet. There was a hissing sound and a remarkable billow of steam.

The two security guards burst in.

'Hold it, you in there!' one of them cried. He had drawn his gun. 'Come out of there with your hands laced on top of your head!'

'You mind waiting until I put my feet out?' Eddie Delgardo snarled.

7

Charlie was back. And she was crying again.

'What happened, babe?'

'I got the money but . . . it got away from me again, Daddy . . . there was a man . . . a soldier . . . I couldn't help it . . .'

Andy felt the fear creep up on him. It was muted by the pain in his head and down the back of his neck, but it was there. 'Was . . . was there a fire, Charlie?'

She couldn't speak, but nodded. Tears coursed down her cheeks.

'Oh my God,' Andy whispered, and made himself get to his feet.

That broke Charlie completely. She put her face in her hands and sobbed helplessly, rocking back and forth.

A knot of people had gathered around the door of the women's room. It had been propped open, but Andy couldn't see . . . and then he could. The two security guards who had gone running down there were leading a tough-looking young man in an army uniform out of the bathroom and toward the security office. The young man was jawing at them loudly, and most of what he had to say was inventively profane. His uniform was mostly gone below the knees, and he was carrying two dripping, blackened things that might once have been shoes. Then they were gone into the office, the door slamming behind them. An excited babble of conversation swept the terminal.

Andy sat down again and put his arm around Charlie. It was very hard to think now; his thoughts were tiny silver fish swimming around in a great black sea of throbbing pain. But he had to do the best he could. He needed Charlie if they were going to get out of this.

'He's all right, Charlie. He's okay. They just took him down to the security office. Now, what happened?'

Through diminishing tears, Charlie told him. Overhearing the soldier on the phone. Having a few random thoughts about him, a feeling that he was trying to trick the girl he was talking to. 'And then, when I was coming back to you, I saw him . . . and before I could stop it . . . it happened. It just got away. I could have hurt him, Daddy. I could have hurt him bad. I set him on *fire!*'

'Keep your voice down,' he said. 'I want you to listen to me, Charlie. I think this is the most encouraging thing that's happened in some time.'

'Y-you do?' She looked at him in frank surprise.

'You say it got away from you,' Andy said, forcing the words. 'And it did. But not like before. It only got away a little bit. What happened was dangerous, honey, but . . . you might have set his hair on fire. Or his face.'

She winced away from that thought, horrified. Andy turned her face gently back to his.

'It's a subconscious thing, and it always goes out at someone you don't like,' he said. 'But . . . you didn't really hurt that guy, Charlie. You . . .' But the rest of it was gone

36

and only the pain was left. Was he still talking? For a moment he didn't even know.

Charlie could still feel that thing, that Bad Thing, racing around in her head, wanting to get away again, to do something else. It was like a small, vicious, and rather stupid animal. You had to let it out of its cage to do something like getting money from the phones . . . but it could do something else, something really bad

(like mommy in the kitchen oh mom i'm sorry)

before you could get it back in again. But now it didn't matter. She wouldn't think about it now, she wouldn't think about

(the bandages my mommy has to wear bandages because i hurt her)

any of it now. Her father was what mattered now. He was slumped over in his TV chair, his face stamped with pain. He was paper white. His eyes were bloodshot.

Oh, Daddy, she thought, *I'd trade even-Steven with you if I could. You've got something that hurts you but it never gets out of its cage. I've got something that doesn't hurt me at all but oh sometimes I get so scared—*

'I've got the money,' she said. 'I didn't go to all the telephones, because the bag was getting heavy and I was afraid it would break.' She looked at him anxiously. 'Where can we go, Daddy? You have to lie down.'

Andy reached into the bag and slowly began to transfer the change in handfuls to the pockets of his corduroy coat. He wondered if this night would ever end. He wanted to do nothing more than grab another cab and go into town and check them into the first hotel or motel in sight . . . but he was afraid. Cabs could be traced. And he had a strong feeling that the people from the green car were still close behind.

He tried to put together what he knew about the Albany airport. First of all, it was the Albany County Airport; it

37

really wasn't in Albany at all but in the town of Colonie. Shaker country – hadn't his grandfather told him once that this was Shaker country? Or had all of them died out now? What about highways? Turnpikes? The answer came slowly. There was a road . . . some sort of Way. Northway or Southway, he thought.

He opened his eyes and looked at Charlie. 'Can you walk aways, kiddo? Couple of miles, maybe?'

'Sure.' She had slept and felt relatively fresh. 'Can you?'

That was the question. He didn't know. 'I'm going to try,' he said. 'I think we ought to walk out to the main road and try to catch a ride, hon.'

'Hitchhike?' she asked.

He nodded. 'Tracing a hitchhiker is pretty hard, Charlie. If we're lucky, we'll get a ride with someone who'll be in Buffalo by morning.' And if we're not, we'll still be standing in the breakdown lane with our thumbs out when that green car comes rolling up.

'If you think it's okay,' Charlie said doubtfully.

'Come on,' he said, 'help me.'

Gigantic bolt of pain as he got to his feet. He swayed a little, closed his eyes, then opened them again. People looked surreal. Colors seemed too bright. A woman walked by on high heels, and every click on the airport tiles was the sound of a vault door being slammed.

'Daddy, are you sure you can?' Her voice was small and very scared.

Charlie. Only Charlie looked right.

'I think I can,' he said. 'Come on.'

They left by a different door from the one they had entered, and the skycap who had noticed them getting out of the cab was busy unloading suitcases from the trunk of a car. He didn't see them go out.

'Which way, Daddy?' Charlie asked.

He looked both ways and saw the Northway, curving

away below and to the right of the terminal building. How to get there, that was the question. There were roads everywhere – overpasses, underpasses, NO RIGHT TURN, STOP ON SIGNAL, KEEP LEFT, NO PARKING ANYTIME. Traffic signals flashing in the early-morning blackness like uneasy spirits.

'This way, I think,' he said, and they walked the length of the terminal beside the feeder road that was lined with LOADING AND UNLOADING ONLY signs. The sidewalk ended at the end of the terminal. A large silver Mercedes swept by them indifferently, and the reflected glow of the overhead sodium arcs on its surface made him wince.

Charlie was looking at him questioningly.

Andy nodded. 'Just keep as far over to the side as you can. Are you cold?'

'No, Daddy.'

'Thank goodness it's a warm night. Your mother would—'

His mouth snapped shut over that.

The two of them walked off into darkness, the big man with the broad shoulders and the little girl in the red pants and the green blouse, holding his hand, almost seeming to lead him.

8

The green car showed up about fifteen minutes later and parked at the yellow curb. Two men got out, the same two who had chased Andy and Charlie to the cab back in Manhattan. The driver sat behind the wheel.

An airport cop strolled up. 'You can't park here, sir,' he said. 'If you'll just pull up to—'

'Sure I can,' the driver said. He showed the cop his ID. The airport cop looked at it, looked at the driver, looked back at the picture on the ID.

'Oh,' he said. 'I'm sorry, sir. Is it something we should know about?'

'Nothing that affects airport security,' the driver said, 'but maybe you can help. Have you seen either of these two people tonight?' He handed the airport cop a picture of Andy, and then a fuzzy picture of Charlie. Her hair had been longer then. In the snap, it was braided into pigtails. Her mother had been alive then. 'The girl's a year or so older now,' the driver said. 'Her hair's a bit shorter. About to her shoulders.'

The cop examined the pictures carefully, shuffling them back and forth. 'You know, I believe I did see this little girl,' he said. 'Towhead, isn't she? Picture makes it a little hard to tell.'

'Towhead, right.'

'The man her father?'

'Ask me no questions, I'll tell you no lies.'

The airport cop felt a wave of dislike for the bland-faced young man behind the wheel of the nondescript green car. He had had peripheral doings with the FBI, the CIA, and the outfit they called the Shop before. Their agents were all the same, blankly arrogant and patronizing. They regarded anyone in a bluesuit as a kiddy cop. But when they'd had the hijacking here five years ago, it had been the kiddy cops who got the guy, loaded down with grenades, off the plane, and he had been in custody of the 'real' cops when he committed suicide by opening up his carotid artery with his own fingernails. Nice going, guys.

'Look . . . sir. I asked if the man was her father to try and find out if there's a family resemblance. Those pictures make it a little hard to tell.'

'They look a bit alike. Different hair colors.'

That much I can see for myself, you asshole, the airport cop thought. 'I saw them both,' the cop told the driver of the green car. 'He's a big guy, bigger than he looks in that picture. He looked sick or something.'

'Did he?' The driver seemed pleased.

'We've had a big night here, all told. Some fool also managed to light his own shoes on fire.'

The driver sat bolt upright behind the wheel. 'Say *what?*'

The airport cop nodded, happy to have got through the driver's bored façade. He would not have been so happy if the driver had told him he had just earned himself a debriefing in the Shop's Manhattan offices. And Eddie Delgardo probably would have beaten the crap out of him, because instead of touring the singles bars (and the massage parlors, and the Times Square porno shops) during the Big Apple segment of his leave, he was going to spend most of it in a drug-induced state of total recall, describing over and over again what had happened before and just after his shoes got hot.

9

The other two men from the green sedan were talking to airport personnel. One of them discovered the skycap who had noticed Andy and Charlie getting out of the cab and going into the terminal.

'Sure I saw them. I thought it was a pure-d shame, a man as drunk as that having a little girl out that late.'

'Maybe they took a plane,' one of the men suggested.

'Maybe so,' the skycap agreed. 'I wonder what that child's mother can be thinking of. I wonder if she knows what's going on.'

'I doubt if she does,' the man in the dark-blue Botany 500 suit said. He spoke with great sincerity. 'You didn't see them leave?'

'No, sir. Far as I know, they're still round here somewhere . . . unless their flight's been called, of course.'

10

The two men made a quick sweep through the main terminal and then through the boarding gates, holding their IDs up in their cupped hands for the security cops to see. They met near the United Airlines ticket desk.

'Dry,' the first said.

'Think they took a plane?' the second asked. He was the fellow in the nice blue Botany 500.

'I don't think that bastard had more than fifty bucks to his name . . . maybe a whole lot less than that.'

'We better check it.'

'Yeah. But quick.'

United Airlines. Allegheny. American. Braniff. The commuter airlines. No broad-shouldered man who looked sick had bought tickets. The baggage handler at Albany Airlines thought he had seen a little girl in red pants and a green shirt, though. Pretty blond hair, shoulder-length.

The two of them met again near the TV chairs where Andy and Charlie had been sitting not long ago. 'What do you think?' the first asked.

The agent in the Botany 500 looked excited. 'I think we ought to blanket the area,' he said. 'I think they're on foot.'

They headed back to the green car, almost trotting.

11

Andy and Charlie walked on through the dark along the soft shoulder of the airport feeder road. An occasional car swept by them. It was almost one o'clock. A mile behind them, in the terminal, the two men had rejoined their third partner at the green car. Andy and Charlie were now walking parallel to the Northway, which was to their right and below them, lit by the depthless glare of sodium lights. It might be possible to scramble down the embankment and try to thumb a ride in the breakdown lane, but if a cop came along, that would end whatever poor chance they still had to get away. Andy was wondering how far they would have to walk before they came to a ramp. Each time his foot came down, it generated a thud that resounded sickly in his head.

'Daddy? Are you still okay?'

'So far, so good,' he said, but he was not so very okay. He wasn't fooling himself, and he doubted if he was fooling Charlie.

'How much further is it?'

'Are you getting tired?'

'Not yet . . . but Daddy . . .'

He stopped and looked solemnly down at her. 'What is it, Charlie?'

'I feel like those bad men are around again,' she whispered.

'All right,' he said. 'I think we better just take a shortcut, honey. Can you get down that hill without falling?'

She looked at the grade, which was covered with dead October grass.

'I guess so,' she said doubtfully.

He stepped over the guardrail cables and then helped Charlie over. As it sometimes did in moments of extreme pain and stress, his mind attempted to flee into the past, to get away from the stress. There had been some good years, some good times, before the shadow began to steal gradually over their lives – first just over him and Vicky, then over all three, blotting out their happiness a little at a time, as inexorably as a lunar eclipse. It had been—

'*Daddy!*' Charlie called in sudden alarm. She had lost her footing. The dry grass was slippery, treacherous. Andy grabbed for her flailing arm, missed, and overbalanced himself. The thud as he hit the ground caused such pain in his head that he cried out loud. Then they were both

43

rolling and sliding down the embankment toward the Northway where the cars rushed past, much too fast to stop if one of them – he or Charlie – should tumble out onto the pavement.

12

The GA looped a piece of rubber flex around Andy's arm just above the elbow and said, 'Make a fist, please.' Andy did. The vein popped up obligingly. He looked away, feeling a little ill. Two hundred dollars or not, he had no urge to watch the IV set in place.

Vicky Tomlinson was on the next cot, dressed in a sleeveless white blouse and dove-gray slacks. She offered him a strained smile. He thought again what beautiful auburn hair she had, how well it went with her direct blue eyes . . . then the prick of pain, followed by dull heat, in his arm.

'There,' the grad assistant said comfortingly.

'There yourself,' Andy said. He was not comforted.

They were in Room 70 of Jason Gearneigh Hall, upstairs. A dozen cots had been trucked in, courtesy of the college infirmary, and the twelve volunteers were lying propped up on hypoallergenic foam pillows, earning their money. Dr Wanless started none of the IVs himself, but he was walking up and down between the cots with a word for everyone, and a little frosty smile. *We'll start to shrink anytime now,* Andy thought morbidly.

Wanless had made a brief speech when they were all assembled, and what he had said, when boiled down, amounted to: *Do not fear. You are wrapped snugly in the arms of Modern Science.* Andy had no great faith in Modern Science, which had given the world the H-bomb, napalm and the laser rifle, along with the Salk vaccine and Clearasil.

44

The grad assistant was doing something else now. Crimping the IV line.

The IV drip was five percent dextrose in water, Wanless had said . . . what he called a D_5W solution. Below the crimp, a small tip poked out of the IV line. If Andy got Lot Six, it would be administered by syringe through the tip. If he was in the control group, it would be normal saline. Heads or tails.

He glanced over at Vicky again. 'How you doin, kid?'

'Okay.'

Wanless had arrived. He stood between them, looking first at Vicky and then at Andy.

'You feel some slight pain, yes?' He had no accent of any kind, least of all a regional-American one, but he constructed his sentences in a way Andy associated with English learned as a second language.

'Pressure,' Vicky said. 'Slight pressure.'

'Yes? It will pass.' He smiled benevolently down at Andy. In his white lab coat he seemed very tall. His glasses seemed very small. The small and the tall.

Andy said, 'When do we start to shrink?'

Wanless continued to smile. 'Do you feel you will shrink?'

'Shhhhrrrrrink,' Andy said, and grinned foolishly. Something was happening to him. By God, he was getting high. He was getting off.

'Everything will be fine,' Wanless said, and smiled more widely. He passed on. Horseman, pass by, Andy thought bemusedly. He looked over at Vicky again. How bright her hair was! For some crazy reason it reminded him of the copper wire on the armature of a new motor . . . generator . . . alternator . . . flibbertigibbet . . .

He laughed aloud.

Smiling slightly, as if sharing the joke, the grad assistant crimped the line and injected a little more of the hypo's

45

contents into Andy's arm and strolled away again. Andy could look at the IV line now. It didn't bother him now. *I'm a pine tree*, he thought. *See my beautiful needles.* He laughed again.

Vicky was smiling at him. God, she was beautiful. He wanted to tell her how beautiful she was, how her hair was like copper set aflame.

'Thank you,' she said. 'What a nice compliment.' Had she said that? Or had he imagined it?

Grasping the last shreds of his mind, he said, 'I think I crapped out on the distilled water, Vicky.'

She said placidly, 'Me too.'

'Nice, isn't it?'

'Nice,' she agreed dreamily.

Somewhere someone was crying. Babbling hysterically. The sound rose and fell in interesting cycles. After what seemed like eons of contemplation, Andy turned his head to see what was going on. It was interesting. Everything had become interesting. Everything seemed to be in slow motion. Slomo, as the avant-garde campus film critic always put it in his columns. *In this film, as in others, Antonioni achieves some of his most spectacular effects with his use of slomo footage.* What an interesting, really clever word; it had the sound of a snake slipping out of a refrigerator: slomo.

Several of the grad assistants were running in slomo toward one of the cots that had been placed near Room 70's blackboard. The young fellow on the cot appeared to be doing something to his eyes. Yes, he was definitely doing something to his eyes, because his fingers were hooked into them and he seemed to be clawing his eyeballs out of his head. His hands were hooked into claws, and blood was gushing from his eyes. It was gushing in slomo. The needle flapped from his arm in slomo. Wanless was running in slomo. The eyes of the kid on the cot now looked like deflated poached eggs, Andy noted clinically. Yes indeed.

Then the white coats were all gathered around the cot, and you couldn't see the kid anymore. Directly behind him, a chart hung down. It showed the quadrants of the human brain. Andy looked at this with great interest for a while. *Verrry in-der-rresting*, as Arte Johnson said on *Laugh-In*.

A bloody hand rose out of the huddle of white coats, like the hand of a drowning man. The fingers were streaked with gore and shreds of tissue hung from them. The hand smacked the chart, leaving a bloodstain in the shape of a large comma. The chart rattled up on its roller with a smacking sound.

Then the cot was lifted (it was still impossible to see the boy who had clawed his eyes out) and carried briskly from the room.

A few minutes (hours? days? years?) later, one of the grad assistants came over to Andy's cot, examined his drip, and then injected some more Lot Six into Andy's mind.

'How you feeling, guy?' the GA asked, but of course he wasn't a GA, he wasn't a student, none of them were. For one thing, this guy looked about thirty-five, and that was a little long in the tooth for a graduate student. For another, this guy worked for the Shop. Andy suddenly knew it. It was absurd, but he knew it. And the man's name was . . .

Andy groped for it, and he got it. The man's name was Ralph Baxter.

He smiled. Ralph Baxter. Good deal.

'I feel okay,' he said. 'How's that other fella?'

'What other fella's that, Andy?'

'The one who clawed his eyes out,' Andy said serenely.

Ralph Baxter smiled and patted Andy's hand. 'Pretty visual stuff, huh, guy?'

'No, really,' Vicky said. 'I saw it, too.'

'You think you did,' the GA who was not a GA said. 'You just shared the same illusion. There was guy over there by the board who had a muscular reaction . . . something like a charley horse. No clawed eyes. No blood.'

He started away again.

Andy said, 'My man, it is impossible to share the same illusion without some prior consultation.' He felt immensely clever. The logic was impeccable, inarguable. He had old Ralph Baxter by the shorts.

Ralph smiled back, undaunted. 'With this drug, it's very possible,' he said. 'I'll be back in a bit, okay?'

'Okay, Ralph,' Andy said.

Ralph paused and came back toward where Andy lay on his cot. He came back in slomo. He looked thoughtfully down at Andy. Andy grinned back, a wide, foolish, drugged-out grin. Got you there, Ralph old son. Got you right by the proverbial shorts. Suddenly a wealth of information about Ralph Baxter flooded in on him, tons of stuff: he was thirty-five, he had been with the Shop for six years, before that he'd been with the FBI for two years, he had—

He had killed four people during his career, three men and one woman. And he had raped the woman after she was dead. She had been an AP stringer and she had known about—

That part wasn't clear. And it didn't matter. Suddenly Andy didn't want to know. The grin faded from his lips. Ralph Baxter was still looking down at him, and Andy was swept by a black paranoia that he remembered from his two previous LSD trips . . . but this was deeper and much more frightening. He had no idea how he could know such things about Ralph Baxter – or how he had known his name at all – but if he told Ralph that he knew, he was terribly afraid that he might disappear from Room 70 of Jason Gearneigh with the same swiftness as the boy who had clawed his eyes out. Or maybe all of that really had been a hallucination; it didn't seem real at all now.

Ralph was still looking at him. Little by little he began to smile. 'See?' he said softly. 'With Lot Six, all kinds of funky things happen.'

He left. Andy let out a slow sigh of relief. He looked over at Vicky and she was looking back at him, her eyes wide and frightened. *She's getting your emotions*, he thought. *Like a radio. Take it easy on her! Remember she's tripping, whatever else this weird shit is!*

He smiled at her, and after a moment, Vicky smiled uncertainly back. She asked him what was wrong. He told her he didn't know, probably nothing.

(but we're not talking – her mouth's not moving)

(it's not?)

(vicky? is that you)

(is it telepathy, andy? is it?)

He didn't know. It was something. He let his eyes slip closed.

Are those really grad assistants? she asked him, troubled. They don't look the same. Is it the drug, Andy? I don't know, he said, eyes still closed. I don't know who they are. What happened to that boy? The one they took away? He opened his eyes again and looked at her, but Vicky was shaking her head. She didn't remember. Andy was surprised and dismayed to find that he hardly remembered himself. It seemed to have happened years ago. Got a charley horse, hadn't he, that guy? A muscular twitch, that's all. He—

Clawed his eyes out.

But what did it matter, really?

Hand rising out of the huddle of white coats like the hand of a drowning man.

But it happened a long time ago. Like in the twelfth century.

Bloody hand. Striking the chart. The chart rattling up on its roller with a smacking sound.

Better to drift. Vicky was looking troubled again.

Suddenly music began to flood down from the speakers in the ceiling, and that was nice . . . much nicer than thinking about charley horses and leaking eyeballs. The music was soft and yet majestic. Much later, Andy decided (in consultation with Vicky) that it had been Rachmaninoff. And ever after when he heard Rachmaninoff, it brought back drifting, dreamy memories of that endless, timeless time in Room 70 of Jason Gearneigh Hall.

How much of it had been real, how much hallucination? Twelve years of off-and-on thought had not answered that question for Andy McGee. At one point, objects had seemed to fly through the room as if an invisible wind were blowing – paper cups, towels, a blood-pressure cuff, a deadly hail of pens and pencils. At another point, sometime later (or had it really been earlier? there was just no linear sequence), one of the test subjects had gone into a muscular seizure followed by cardiac arrest – or so it had seemed. There had been frantic efforts to restore him using mouth-to-mouth resuscitation, followed by a shot of something directly into the chest cavity, and finally a machine that made a high whine and had two black cups attached to thick wires. Andy seemed to remember one of the 'grad assistants' roaring, 'Zap him! Zap him! Oh, give them to me, you fuckhead!'

At another point he had slept, dozing in and out of a twilight consciousness. He spoke to Vicky and they told each other about themselves. Andy told her about the car accident that had taken his mother's life and how he had spent the next year with his aunt in a semi-nervous breakdown of grief. She told him that when she was seven, a teenage baby-sitter had assaulted her and now she was terribly afraid of sex, even more afraid that she might be

50

frigid, it was that more than anything else that had forced her and her boyfriend to the breakup. He kept . . . pressing her.

They told each other things that a man and a woman don't tell each other until they've known each other for years . . . things a man and a woman often never tell, not even in the dark marriage bed after decades of being together.

But did they *speak?*

That Andy never knew.

Time had stopped, but somehow it passed anyway.

13

He came out of the doze a little at a time. The Rachmaninoff was gone . . . if it had ever been there at all. Vicky was sleeping peacefully on the cot beside him, her hands folded between her breasts, the simple hands of a child who has fallen asleep while offering her bedtime prayers. Andy looked at her and was simply aware that at some point he had fallen in love with her. It was a deep and complete feeling, above (and below) question.

After a while he looked around. Several of the cots were empty. There were maybe five test subjects left in the room. Some were sleeping. One was sitting up on his cot and a grad assistant – a perfectly normal grad assistant of perhaps twenty-five – was questioning him and writing notes on a clipboard. The test subject apparently said something funny, because both of them laughed – in the low, considerate way you do when others around you are sleeping.

Andy sat up and took inventory of himself. He felt fine. He tried a smile and found that it fit perfectly. His muscles lay peacefully against one another. He felt eager and fresh, every perception sharply honed and somehow innocent. He could remember feeling this way as a kid, waking up on Saturday morning, knowing his bike was heeled over on its kickstand in the garage, and feeling that the whole weekend stretched ahead of him like a carnival of dreams where every ride was free.

One of the grad assistants came over and said, 'How you feeling, Andy?'

Andy looked at him. This was the same guy that had injected him – when? A year ago? He rubbed a palm over his cheek and heard the rasp of beard stubble. 'I feel like Rip van Winkle,' he said.

The GA smiled. 'It's only been forty-eight hours, not twenty years. How do you feel, really?'

'Fine.'

'Normal?'

'Whatever that word means, yes. Normal. Where's Ralph?'

'Ralph?' The GA raised his eyebrows.

'Yes, Ralph Baxter. About thirty-five. Big guy. Sandy hair.'

The grad assistant smiled. 'You dreamed him up,' he said.

Andy looked at the GA uncertainly. 'I did what?'

'Dreamed him up. Hallucinated him. The only Ralph I know who's involved in all the Lot Six tests in any way is a Dartan Pharmaceutical rep named Ralph Steinham. And he's fifty-five or so.'

Andy looked at the GA for a long time without saying anything. Ralph an illusion? Well, maybe so. It had all the paranoid elements of a dope dream, certainly; Andy seemed to remember thinking Ralph was some sort of secret agent who had wasted all sorts of people. He smiled a little. The GA smiled back . . . a little too readily, Andy thought. Or was that paranoia, too? Surely it was.

The guy who had been sitting up and talking when Andy

woke up was now being escorted from the room, drinking from a paper cup of orange juice.

Cautiously, Andy said: 'No one got hurt, did they?'

'Hurt?'

'Well – no one had a convulsion, did they? Or–'

The grad assistant leaned forward, looking concerned. 'Say, Andy, I hope you won't go spreading anything like that around campus. It would play bloody hell with Dr Wanless's research program. We have Lots Seven and Eight coming up next semester, and–'

'Was there anything?'

'There was one boy who had a muscular reaction, minor but quite painful,' the GA said. 'It passed in less than fifteen minutes with no harm done. But there's a witch-hunt atmosphere around here now. End the draft, ban ROTC, ban Dow Chemical job recruiters because they make napalm . . . Things get out of proportion, and I happen to think this is pretty important research.'

'Who was the guy?'

'Now you know I can't tell you that. All I am saying is please remember you were under the influence of a mild hallucinogenic. Don't go mixing up your drug-induced fantasies with reality and then start spreading the combination around.'

'Would I be allowed to do that?' Andy asked.

The GA looked puzzled. 'I don't see how we could stop you. Any college experimental program is pretty much at the mercy of its volunteers. For a lousy two hundred bucks we can hardly expect you to sign an oath of allegiance, can we?'

Andy felt relief. If this guy was lying, he was doing a really superlative job of it. It had all been a series of hallucinations. And on the cot beside his, Vicky was beginning to stir.

'Now what about it?' the GA asked, smiling. 'I think I'm supposed to be asking the questions.'

And he did ask questions. By the time Andy finished answering them, Vicky was fully awake, looking rested and calm and radiant, and smiling at him. The questions were detailed. Many of them were the questions Andy himself would have asked.

So why did he have the feeling they were all window dressing?

14

Sitting on a couch in one of the smaller Union lounges that evening, Andy and Vicky compared hallucinations.

She had no memory of the thing that troubled him the most: that bloody hand waving limply above the knot of white tunics, striking the chart, and then disappearing. Andy had no recollection of the thing that was most vivid to her: a man with long blond hair had set up a folding table by her cot, so that it was just at her eye level. He had put a row of great big dominoes on the table and said, 'Knock them down, Vicky. Knock them all down.' And she had raised her hands to push them over, wanting to oblige, and the man had gently but firmly pressed her hands back down on her chest. 'You don't need your hands, Vicky,' he had said. 'Just knock them down.' So she had looked at the dominoes and they had all fallen over, one after the other. A dozen or so in all.

'It made me feel very tired,' she told Andy, smiling that small, slantwise smile of hers. 'And I had gotten this idea somehow that we were discussing Vietnam, you know. So I said something like, "Yes, that proves it, if South Vietnam goes, they all go." And he smiled and patted my hands and said, "Why don't you sleep for a while, Vicky? You must be tired." So I did.' She shook her head. 'But now it doesn't seem real at all. I think I must have made it up entirely or built a hallucination around some perfectly normal test. You don't remember seeing him, do you? Tall guy with shoulder-length blond hair and a little scar on his chin?'

Andy shook his head.

'But I still don't understand how we could share *any* of the same fantasies,' Andy said, 'unless they've developed a drug over there that's telepathic as well as an hallucinogenic. I know there's been some talk about that in the last few years . . . the idea seems to be that if hallucinogens can heighten perception . . .' He shrugged, then grinned. 'Carlos Castaneda, where are you when we need you?'

'Isn't it more likely that we just discussed the same fantasy and then forgot we did?' Vicky asked.

He agreed it was a strong possibility, but he still felt disquieted by the whole experience. It had been, as they say, a bummer.

Taking his courage in his hands, he said, 'The only thing I really am sure of is that I seem to be falling in love with you, Vicky.'

She smiled nervously and kissed the corner of his mouth. 'That's sweet, Andy, but—'

'But you're a little afraid of me. Of men in general, maybe.'

'Maybe I am,' she said.

'All I'm asking for is a chance.'

'You'll have your chance,' she said. 'I like you, Andy. A lot. But please remember that I get scared. Sometimes I just . . . get scared.' She tried to shrug lightly, but it turned into something like a shudder.

'I'll remember,' he said, and drew her into his arms and kissed her. There was a moment's hesitation, and then she kissed back, holding his hands firmly in hers.

15

'*Daddy!*' Charlie screamed.

The world revolved sickly in front of Andy's eyes. The sodium arc lamps lining the Northway were below him, the ground was above him and shaking him loose. Then he was on his butt, sliding down the lower half of the embankment like a kid on a slide. Charlie was below him rolling helplessly over and over.

Oh no, she's going to shoot right out into the traffic—

'Charlie!' he yelled hoarsely, hurting his throat, his head. 'Watch it!'

Then she was down, squatting in the breakdown lane, washed by the harsh lights of a passing car, sobbing. A moment later he landed beside her with a solid *whap!* that rocketed all the way up his spine to his head. Things doubled in front of his eyes, tripled, and then gradually settled down.

Charlie was sitting on her haunches, her head cradled in her arms.

'Charlie,' he said, touching her arm. 'It's all right, honey.'

'I wish I did go in front of the cars!' she cried out, her voice bright and vicious with a self-loathing that made Andy's heart ache in his chest. 'I deserve to for setting that man on fire!'

'Shhh,' he said. 'Charlie, you don't have to think of that anymore.'

He held her. The cars swashed by them. Any one of them could be a cop, and that would end it. At this point it would almost be a relief.

Her sobs faded off little by little. Part of it, he realized, was simple tiredness. The same thing that was aggravating his headache past the screaming point and bringing this unwelcome flood of memories. If they could only get somewhere and lie down. . . .

'Can you get up, Charlie?'

She got to her feet slowly, brushing the last of the tears away. Her face was a pallid moonlet in the dark. Looking at her, he felt a sharp lance of guilt. She should be snugly tucked into a bed somewhere in a house with a shrinking mortgage, a teddy bear crooked under one arm, ready to go back to school the next morning and do battle for God, country, and the second grade. Instead, she was standing in the breakdown lane of a turnpike spur in upstate New York at one-fifteen in the morning, on the run, consumed with guilt because she had inherited something from her mother and father – something she herself had had no more part in determining than the direct blue of her eyes. How do you explain to a seven-year-old girl that Daddy and Mommy had once needed two hundred dollars and the people they had talked to said it was all right, but they had lied?

'We're going to hook us a ride,' Andy said, and he couldn't tell if he had slung his arm around her shoulders to comfort her or to support himself. 'We'll get to a hotel or a motel and we'll sleep. Then we'll think about what to do next. That sound all right?'

Charlie nodded listlessly.

'Okay,' he said, and cocked this thumb. The cars rushed by it, unheeding, and less than two miles away the green car was on its way again. Andy knew nothing of this; his harried mind had turned back to that night with Vicky in the Union. She was staying at one of the dorms and he had dropped her off there, relishing her lips again on the step just outside the big double doors, and she had put her arms hesitantly around his neck, this girl who had still been a virgin. They had been young, Jesus they had been young.

57

The cars rushed by, Charlie's hair lifted and dropped in each backwash of air, and he remembered the rest of what had happened that night twelve years ago.

16

Andy started across campus after seeing Vicky into her dorm, headed for the highway where he would hitch a ride into town. Although he could feel it only faintly against his face, the May wind beat strongly through the elms lining the mall, as if an invisible river ran through the air just above him, a river from which he could detect only the faintest, farthest ripples.

Jason Gearneigh Hall was on his way and he stopped in front of its dark bulk. Around it, the trees with their new foliage danced sinuously in the unseen current of that river of wind. A cool chill wormed its way down his spine and then settled in his stomach, freezing him lightly. He shivered even though the evening was warm. A big silver-dollar moon rode between the growing rafts of clouds – gilded keelboats running before the wind, running on that dark river of air. The moonlight reflected on the building's windows, making them glare like blankly unpleasant eyes.

Something happened in there, he thought. *Something more than what we were told or led to expect. What was it?*

In his mind's eye he saw that drowning, bloody hand again – only this time he saw it striking the chart, leaving a bloodstain in the shape of a comma . . . and then the chart rolling up with a rattling, smacking sound.

He walked toward the building. Crazy. They're not going to let you into a lecture hall at past ten o'clock. And—

And I'm scared.

Yes. That was it. Too many disquieting half-memories. Too easy to persuade himself they had only been fantasies;

Vicky was already on her way to accomplishing that. A test subject clawing his eyes out. Someone screaming that she wished she were dead, that being dead would be better than this, even if it meant going to hell and burning there for eternity. Someone else going into cardiac arrest and then being bundled out of sight with chilling professionalism. Because, let's face it, Andy old kid, thinking about telepathy doesn't scare you. What scares you is the thought that one of those things might have happened.

Heels clicking, he walked up to the big double doors and tried them. Locked. Behind them he could see the empty lobby. Andy knocked, and when he saw someone coming out of the shadows, he almost ran. He almost ran because the face that was going to appear out of those swimming shadows would be the face of Ralph Baxter, or of a tall man with shoulder-length blond hair and a scar on his chin.

But it was neither; the man who came over to the lobby doors and unlocked them and stuck his querulous face out was a typical college security guard: about sixty-two, lined cheeks and forehead, wary blue eyes that were rheumy from too much bottle time. A big time clock was clipped to his belt.

'Building's closed!' he said.

'I know,' Andy said, 'but I was part of an experiment in Room Seventy that finished up this morning and—'

'That don't matter! Building closes at nine on weeknights! Come back tomorrow!'

'—and I think I left my watch in there,' Andy said. He didn't own a watch. 'Hey, what do you say? Just one quick look around.'

'I can't do that,' the night man said, but all at once he sounded strangely unsure.

With no thought at all about it one way or another, Andy said in a low voice: 'Sure you can. I'll just take a look and

59

then I'll be out of your way. You won't even remember I was here, right?'

A sudden weird feeling in his head: it was as if he had reached out and *pushed* this elderly night security man, only with his head instead of his hands. And the guard did take two or three uncertain steps backward, letting go of the door.

Andy stepped in, a little concerned. There was a sudden sharp pain in his head, but it subsided to a low throb that was gone half an hour later.

'Say, are you all right?' he asked the security man.

'Huh? Sure, I'm okay.' The security man's suspicion was gone; he gave Andy a smile that was entirely friendly. 'Go on up and look for your watch, if you want to. Take your time. I probably won't even remember that you're here.'

And he strolled off.

Andy looked after him disbelievingly and then rubbed his forehead absently, as if to soothe the mild ache there. What in God's name had he done to that old duck? *Something*, that was for sure.

He turned, went to the stairs, and began climbing them. The upper hall was deeply shadowed and narrow; a nagging feeling of claustrophobia slipped around him and seemed to tighten his breathing, like an invisible dogcollar. Up here, the building had poked into that river of wind, and the air went skating under the eaves, screaming thinly. Room 70 had two double doors, the top halves two squares of frosted, pebbled glass. Andy stood outside them, listening to the wind move through the old gutters and downspouts, rattling the rusty leaves of dead years. His heart was thudding heavily in his chest.

He almost walked away from it then; it seemed suddenly easier not to know, just to forget it. Then he reached out and grasped one of the doorknobs, telling himself there was nothing to worry about anyway because the damn room would be locked and good riddance to it.

Except that it wasn't. The knob turned freely. The door opened.

The room was empty, lit only by stuttering moonlight through the moving branches of the old elms outside. There was enough light for him to see that the cots had been removed. The blackboard had been erased and washed. The chart was rolled up like a windowshade, only the pull ring dangling. Andy stepped toward it, and after a moment he reached up with a hand that trembled slightly and pulled it down.

Quadrants of the brain; the human mind served up and marked like a butcher's diagram. Just seeing it made him get that trippy feeling again, like an acid flash. Nothing fun about it; it was sickening, and a moan escaped his throat, as delicate as a silver strand of spiderweb.

The bloodstain was there, comma-black in the moon's uneasy light. A printed legend that had undoubtedly read *CORPUS CALLOSUM* before this weekend's experiment now read *COR   OSUM*, the comma-shaped stain intervening.

Such a small thing.

Such a huge thing.

He stood in the dark, looking at it, starting to shake for real. How much of it did this make true? Some? Most? All? None of the above?

From behind him he heard a sound, or thought he did: the stealthy squeak of a shoe.

His hands jerked and one of them struck the chart with that same awful smacking sound. It rattled back up on its roller, the sound dreadfully loud in this black pit of a room.

A sudden knocking on the moonlight-dusted far window; a branch, or perhaps dead fingers streaked with gore and

61

tissue: *let me in I left my eyes in there oh let me in let me in—*

He whirled in a slow-motion dream, a *slomo* dream, sinkingly sure that it would be that boy, a spirit in a white robe, dripping black holes where his eyes had been. His heart was a live thing in his throat.

No one there.

No *thing* there.

But his nerve was broken and then the branch began its implacable knocking again, he fled, not bothering to close the classroom door behind him. He sprinted down the narrow corridor and suddenly footfalls *were* pursuing him, echoes of his own running feet. He went down the stairs two at a time and so came back into the lobby, breathing hard, the blood hammering at his temples. The air in his throat prickled like cut hay.

He didn't see the security man anywhere about. He left, shutting one of the big glass lobby doors behind him and slinking down the walk to the quad like the fugitive he would later become.

17

Five days later, and much against her will, Andy dragged Vicky Tomlinson down to Jason Gearneigh Hall. She had already decided she never wanted to think about the experiment again. She had drawn her two-hundred-dollar check from the Psychology Department, banked it, and wanted to forget where it had come from.

He persuaded her to come, using eloquence he hadn't been aware he possessed. They went at the two-fifty change of classes; the bells of Harrison Chapel played a carillon in the dozing May air. 'Nothing can happen to us in broad daylight,' he said, uneasily refusing to clarify, even in his own mind, exactly what he might be afraid of. 'Not with dozens of people all around.'

'I just don't want to go, Andy,' she had said, but she had gone.

There were two or three kids leaving the lecture room with books under their arms. Sunshine painted the windows a prosier hue than the diamond-dust of moonlight Andy remembered. As Andy and Vicky entered, a few others trickled in for their three-o'clock biology seminar. One of them began to talk softly and earnestly to a pair of the others about an end-ROTC march that was coming off that weekend. No one took the slightest notion of Andy and Vicky.

'All right,' Andy said, and his voice was thick and nervous. 'See what you think.'

He pulled the chart down by the dangling ring. They were looking at a naked man with his skin flayed away and his organs labeled. His muscles looked like interwoven skeins of red yarn. Some wit had labeled him Oscar the Grouch.

'Jesus!' Andy said.

She gripped his arm and her hand was warm with nervous perspiration. 'Andy,' she said. 'Please, let's go. Before someone recognizes us.'

Yes, he was ready to go. The fact that the chart had been changed somehow scared him more than anything else. He jerked the pull ring down sharply and let it go. It made that same smacking sound as it went up.

Different chart. Same sound. Twelve years later he could still hear the sound it made – when his aching head would let him. He never stepped into Room 70 of Jason Gearneigh Hall after that day, but he was acquainted with that sound.

He heard it frequently in his dreams . . . and saw that questing, drowning, bloodstained hand.

18

The green car whispered along the airport feeder road toward the Northway entrance ramp. Behind the wheel, Norville Bates sat with his hands firmly at ten and two o'clock. Classical music came from the FM receiver in a muted, smooth flow. His hair was now short and combed back, but the small, semicircular scar on his chin hadn't changed – the place where he had cut himself on a jagged piece of Coke bottle as a kid. Vicky, had she still been alive, would have recognized him.

'We have one unit on the way,' the man in the Botany 500 suit said. His name was John Mayo. 'The guy's a stringer. He works for DIA as well as us.'

'Just an ordinary whore,' the third man said, and all three of them laughed in a nervous, keyed-up way. They knew they were close; they could almost smell blood. The name of the third man was Orville Jamieson, but he preferred to be called OJ, or even better, The Juice. He signed all his office memos OJ. He had signed one The Juice and that bastard Cap had given him a reprimand. Not just an oral one; a written one that had gone in his record.

'You think it's the Northway, huh?' OJ asked.

Norville Bates shrugged. 'Either the Northway or they headed into Albany,' he said. 'I gave the local yokel the hotels in town because it's his town, right?'

'Right,' John Mayo said. He and Norville got along well together. They went back a long way. All the way back to Room 70 of Jason Gearneigh Hall, and *that*, my friend, should anyone ever ask you had been *hairy*. John never wanted to go through anything that hairy again. He had been the man who zapped the kid who went into cardiac arrest. He had been a medic during the early days in Nam and he knew what to do with the defibrillator – in theory, at least. In practice, it hadn't gone so well, and the kid had got away from them. Twelve kids got Lot Six that day. Two of them had died – the kid who had gone into cardiac arrest and a girl who died six days later in her dorm, apparently of a sudden brain embolism. Two others had gone hopelessly insane – one of them the boy who had blinded himself, the other a girl who later developed a total paralysis from the neck down. Wanless had said that was psychological, but who the fuck knew? It had been a nice day's work, all right.

'The local yokel is taking his wife along,' Norville was saying. 'She's looking for her granddaughter. Her son ran away with the little girl. Nasty divorce case, all of that. She doesn't want to notify the police unless she has to, but she's afraid the son might be going mental. If she plays it right, there isn't a night clerk in town that won't tell her if the two of them have checked in.'

'If she plays it right,' OJ said. 'With these stringers you can never tell.'

John said, 'We're going to the closest on-ramp, right?'

'Right,' Norville said. 'Just three, four minutes now.'

'Have they had enough time to get down there?'

'They have if they were busting ass. Maybe we'll be able to pick them up trying to thumb a ride right there on the ramp. Or maybe they took a shortcut and went over the side into the breakdown lane. Either way, all we have to do is cruise along until we come to them.'

'Where you headed, buddy, hop in,' The Juice said, and laughed. There was a .357 Magnum in a shoulder holster under his left arm. He called it The Windsucker.

'If they already hooked them a ride, we're shit out of luck, Norv,' John said.

Norville shrugged. 'Percentage play. It's quarter past one in the morning. With the rationing, traffic's thinner than ever. What's Mr Businessman going to think if he sees a big guy and a little girl trying to hitch a ride?'

'He's gonna think it's bad news,' John said.

'That's a big ten-four.'

The Juice laughed again. Up ahead the stop-and-go light that marked the Northway ramp gleamed in the dark. OJ put his hand on the walnut stock of The Windsucker. Just in case.

19

The van passed them by, backwashing cool air . . . and then its brakelights flashed brighter and it swerved over into the breakdown lane about fifty yards farther up.

'Thank God,' Andy said softly. 'You let me do the talking, Charlie.'

'All right, Daddy.' She sounded apathetic. The dark circles were back under her eyes. The van was backing up as they walked toward it. Andy's head felt like a slowly swelling lead balloon.

There was a vision from the Thousand and One Nights painted on the side – caliphs, maidens hiding under gauzy masks, a carpet floating mystically in the air. The carpet was undoubtedly meant to be red, but in the light of the turnpike sodiums it was the dark maroon of drying blood.

Andy opened the passenger door and boosted Charlie up and in. He followed her. 'Thanks, mister,' he said. 'Saved our lives.'

'My pleasure,' the driver said. 'Hi, little stranger.'

'Hi,' Charlie said in a small voice.

The driver checked the outside mirror, drove down the breakdown lane at a steadily increasing pace, and then crossed into the travel lane. Glancing past Charlie's slightly bowed head, Andy felt a touch of guilt: the driver was exactly the sort of young man Andy himself always passed by when he saw him standing on the shoulder with his thumb out. Big but lean, he wore a heavy black beard that curled down to his chest and a big felt hat that looked like a prop in a movie about feudin Kentucky hillbillies. A cigarette that looked home-rolled was cocked in the corner of his mouth, curling up smoke. Just a cigarette, by the smell; no sweet odor of cannabis.

'Where you headed, my man?' the driver asked.

'Two towns up the line,' Andy said.

'Hastings Glen?'

'That's right.'

The driver nodded. 'On the run from someone, I guess.'

Charlie tensed and Andy put a soothing hand on her back and rubbed gently until she loosened up again. He had detected no menace in the driver's voice.

'There was a process server at the airport,' he said.

The driver grinned – it was almost hidden beneath his fierce beard – plucked the cigarette from his mouth, and offered it delicately to the wind sucking just outside his half-open vent window. The slipstream gulped it down.

'Something to do with the little stranger here is my guess,' he said.

'Not far wrong,' Andy said.

The driver fell silent. Andy settled back and tried to cope with his headache. It seemed to have leveled off at a final screaming pitch. Had it ever been this bad before? Impossible to tell. Each time he overdid it, it seemed like the worst ever. It would be a month before he dared use the push again. He knew that two towns up the line was not nearly far enough, but it was all he could manage tonight. He was tipped over. Hastings Glen would have to do.

'Who do you pick, man?' the driver asked him.

'Huh?'

67

'The Series. The San Diego Padres in the World Series – how do you figure that?'

'Pretty far out,' Andy agreed. His voice came from far away, a tolling undersea bell.

'You okay, man? You look pale.'

'Headache,' Andy said. 'Migraine.'

'Too much pressure,' the driver said. 'I can dig it. You staying at a hotel? You need some cash? I could let you have five. Wish it was more, but I'm on my way to California, and I got to watch it careful. Just like the Joads in *The Grapes of Wrath*.'

Andy smiled gratefully. 'I think we're okay.'

'Fine.' He glanced at Charlie, who had dozed off. 'Pretty little girl, my man. Are you watching out for her?'

'As best I can,' Andy said.

'All right,' the driver said. 'That's the name of that tune.'

20

Hastings Glen was little more than a wide place in the road; at this hour all the traffic lights in town had turned to blinkers. The bearded driver in the hillbilly hat took them up the exit ramp, through the sleeping town, and down Route 40 to the Slumberland Motel, a redwood place with the skeletal remains of a harvested cornfield in back and a pinkish-red neon sign out front that stuttered the nonword VA A CY into the dark. As her sleep deepened, Charlie had tilted farther and farther to the left, until her head was resting on the driver's blue-jeaned thigh. Andy had offered to shift her, and the driver shook his head.

'She's fine, man. Let her sleep.'

'Would you mind dropping us off a little bit past?' Andy asked. It was hard to think, but this caution came almost intuitively.

Don't want the night man to know you don't have a car?' The driver smiled. 'Sure, man. But a place like that, they wouldn't give a squirt if you pedaled in on a unicycle.' The van's tires crunched the gravel shoulder. 'You positive you couldn't use five?'

'I guess I could,' Andy said reluctantly. 'Would you write down your address for me? I'll mail it back to you.'

The driver's grin reappeared. 'My address is "in transit," ' he said, getting out his wallet. 'But you may see my happy smiling face again, right? Who knows. Grab onto Abe, man.' He handed the five to Andy and suddenly Andy was crying – not a lot, but crying.

'No, man,' the driver said kindly. He touched the back of Andy's neck lightly. 'Life is short and pain is long and we were all put on this earth to help each other. The comic-book philosophy of Jim Paulson in a nutshell. Take good care of the little stranger.'

'Sure,' Andy said, brushing his eyes. He put the five-dollar bill in the pocket of his corduroy coat. 'Charlie? Hon? Wake up. Just a little bit longer now.'

21

Three minutes later Charlie was leaning sleepily against him while he watched Jim Paulson go up the road to a closed restaurant, turn around, and then head back past them toward the Interstate. Andy raised his hand. Paulson raised his in return. Old Ford van with the Arabian Nights on the side, jinns and grand viziers and a mystic, floating carpet. Hope California's good to you, guy, Andy thought, and then the two of them walked back toward the Slumberland Motel.

'I want you to wait for me outside and out of sight,' Andy said. 'Okay?'

'Okay, Daddy.' Very sleepy.

He left her by an evergreen shrub and walked over to the office and rang the night bell. After about two minutes, a middle-aged man in a bathrobe appeared, polishing his glasses. He opened the door and let Andy in without a word.

'I wonder if I could have the unit down on the end of the left wing,' Andy said. 'I parked there.'

'This time of year, you could have *all* of the west wing if you wanted it,' the night man said, and smiled around a mouthful of yellow dentures. He gave Andy a printed index card and a pen advertising business supplies. A car passed by outside, silent headlights that waxed and waned.

Andy signed the card Bruce Rozelle. Bruce was driving a 1978 Vega, New York license LMS 240. He looked at the blank marked ORGANIZATION/COMPANY for a moment, and then, in a flash of inspiration (as much as his aching head would allow), he wrote United Vending Company of America. And checked CASH under form of payment.

Another car went by out front.

The clerk initialed the card and tucked it away. 'That's seventeen dollars and fifty cents.'

'Do you mind change?' Andy asked. 'I never did get a chance to cash up, and I'm dragging around twenty pounds of silver. I hate these country milk runs.'

'Spends just as easy. I don't mind.'

'Thanks.' Andy reached into his coat pocket, pushed aside the five-dollar bill with his fingers, and brought out a fistful of quarters, nickels, and dimes. He counted out fourteen dollars, brought out some more change, and made up the rest. The clerk had been separating the coins into neat piles and now he swept them into the correct compartments of the cash drawer.

'You know,' he said, closing the drawer and looking at Andy hopefully. 'I'd knock five bucks off your room bill if you could fix my cigarette machine. It's been out of order for a week.'

Andy walked over to the machine, which stood in the corner, pretended to look at it, and then walked back. 'Not our brand,' he said.

'Oh. Shit. Okay. Goodnight, buddy. You'll find an extra blanket on the closet shelf if you should want it.'

'Fine.'

He went out. The gravel crunched beneath his feet, hideously amplified in his ears, sounding like stone cereal. He walked over to the evergreen shrub where he had left Charlie and Charlie wasn't there.

'Charlie?'

No answer. He switched the room key on its long green plastic tab from one hand to the other. Both hands were suddenly sweaty.

'Charlie?'

Still no answer. He thought back and now it seemed to him that the car that had gone past when he had been filling out the registration card had been slowing down. Maybe it had been a green car.

His heartbeat began to pick up, sending jolts of pain up to his skull. He tried to think what he should do if Charlie was gone, but he couldn't think. His head hurt too badly. He—

There was a low, snorting, snoring sound from deeper back in the bushes. A sound he knew very well. He leaped toward it, gravel spurting out from under his shoes. Stiff evergreen branches scraped his legs and raked back the tails of his corduroy jacket.

Charlie was lying on her side on the verge of the motel lawn, knees drawn up nearly to her chin, hands between them. Fast asleep. Andy stood with his eyes closed for a moment and then shook her awake for what he hoped would be the last time that night. That long, long night.

71

Her eyelids fluttered, and then she was looking up at him. 'Daddy?' she asked, her voice was blurred, still half in her dreams. 'I got out of sight like you said.'

'I know, honey,' he said. 'I know you did. Come on. We're going to bed.'

22

Twenty minutes later they were both in the double bed of Unit 16, Charlie fast asleep and breathing evenly, Andy still awake but drifting toward sleep, only the steady thump in his head still holding him up. And the questions.

They had been on the run for about a year. It was almost impossible to believe, maybe because it hadn't *seemed* so much like running, not when they had been in Port City, Pennsylvania, running the Weight-Off program. Charlie had gone to school in Port City, and how could you be on the run if you were holding a job and your daughter was going to first grade? They had almost been caught in Port City, not because they had been particularly good (although they were terribly dogged, and that frightened Andy a lot) but because Andy had made that crucial lapse – he had allowed himself temporarily to forget they were fugitives.

No chance of that now.

How close were they? Still back in New York? If only he could believe that – they hadn't got the cabby's number; they were still tracking him down. More likely they were in Albany, crawling over the airport like maggots over a pile of meat scraps. Hastings Glen? Maybe by morning. But maybe not. Hastings Glen was fifteen miles from the airport. No need to let paranoia sweep away good sense.

I deserve it! I deserve to go in front of the cars for setting that man on fire!

His own voice replying: *It could have been worse. It could have been his face.*

72

Voices in a haunted room.

Something else came to him. He was supposed to be driving a Vega. When morning came and the night man didn't see a Vega parked in front of Unit 16, would he just assume his United Vending Company man had pushed on? Or would he investigate? Nothing he could do about it now. He was totally wasted.

I thought there was something funny about him. He looked pale, sick. And he paid with change. He said he worked for a vending-machine company, but he couldn't fix the cigarette machine in the lobby.

Voices in a haunted room.

He shifted onto his side, listening to Charlie's slow, even breathing. He thought they had taken her, but she'd only gone farther back in the bushes. Out of sight. Charlene Norma McGee, Charlie since . . . well, since forever. *If they took you, Charlie, I don't know what I'd do.*

23

One last voice, his roommate Quincey's voice, from six years ago.

Charlie had been a year old then, and of course they knew she wasn't normal. They had known that since she was a week old and Vicky had brought her into their bed with them because when she was left in the little crib, the pillow began to . . . well, began to smolder. The night they had put the crib away forever, not speaking in their fright, a fright too big and too strange to be articulated, it had got hot enough to blister her cheek and she had screamed most of the night, in spite of the Solarcaine Andy had found in the medicine chest. What a crazyhouse that first year had been, no sleep, endless fear. Fires in the wastebaskets when her bottles were late; once the curtains had burst into flame, and if Vicky hadn't been in the room—

It was her fall down the stairs that had finally prompted him to call Quincey. She had been crawling then, and was quite good at going up the stairs on her hands and knees and then backing down again the same way. Andy had been sitting with her that day; Vicky was out at Senter's with one of her friends, shopping. She had been hesitant about going, and Andy nearly had to throw her out the door. She was looking too used lately, too tired. There was something starey in her eyes that made him think about those combat-fatigue stories you heard during wartime.

He had been reading in the living room, near the foot of the stairs. Charlie was going up and down. Sitting on the stairs was a teddy bear. He should have moved it, of course, but each time she went up, Charlie went around it, and he had become lulled – much as he had become lulled by what appeared to be their normal life in Port City.

As she came down the third time, her feet got tangled around the bear and she came all the way to the bottom, thump, bump, and tumble, wailing with rage and fear. The stairs were carpeted and she didn't even have a bruise – God watches over drunks and small children, that had been Quincey's saying, and that was his first conscious thought of Quincey that day – but Andy rushed to her, picked her up, held her, cooed a lot of nonsense to her while he gave her the quick once-over, looking for blood, or a limb hanging wrong, signs of concussion. And—

And he *felt* it pass him – the invisible, incredible bolt of death from his daughter's mind. It felt like the backwash of warm air from a highballing subway train, when it's summertime and you're standing maybe a little too close on the platform. A soft, soundless passage of warm air . . . and then the teddy bear was on fire. Teddy had hurt Charlie; Charlie would hurt Teddy. The flames roared up, and for a moment, as it charred, Andy was looking at its black shoebutton eyes through a sheet of flame, and the

74

flames were spreading to the carpeting on the stair where the bear had tumbled.

Andy put his daughter down and ran for the fire extinguisher on the wall near the TV. He and Vicky didn't talk about the thing their daughter could do – there were times when Andy wanted to, but Vicky wouldn't hear of it; she avoided the subject with hysterical stubbornness, saying there was nothing wrong with Charlie, *nothing wrong* – but fire extinguishers had appeared silently, undiscussed, with almost the same stealth as dandelions appear during that period when spring and summer overlap. They didn't talk about what Charlie could do, but there were fire extinguishers all over the house.

He grabbed this one, smelling the heavy aroma of frying carpet, and dashed for the stairs . . . and still there was time to think about that story, the one he had read as a kid, 'It's a *Good* Life,' by some guy named Jerome Bixby, and that had been about a little kid who had enslaved his parents with psychic terror, a nightmare of a thousand possible deaths, and you never knew . . . you never knew when the little kid was going to get mad . . .

Charlie was wailing, sitting on her butt at the foot of the stairs.

Andy twisted the knob on the fire extinguisher savagely and sprayed foam on the spreading fire, dousing it. He picked up Teddy, his fur stippled with dots and puffs and dollops of foam, and carried him back downstairs.

Hating himself, yet knowing in some primitive way that it had to be done, the line had to be drawn, the lesson learned, he jammed the bear almost into Charlie's screaming, frightened, tear-streaked face. *Oh you dirty bastard*, he had thought desperately, *why don't you just go out to the kitchen and get a paring knife and cut a line up each cheek? Mark her that way?* And his mind had seized on that. Scars.

Yes. That's what he had to do. Scar his child. Burn a scar on her soul.

'Do you like the way Teddy looks?' he roared. The bear was scalded, the bear was blackened, and in his hand it was still as warm as a cooling lump of charcoal. 'Do you like Teddy to be all burned so you can't play with him anymore, Charlie?'

Charlie was crying in great, braying whoops, her skin all red fever and pale death, her eyes swimming with tears. *'Daaaaa! Ted! Ted!'*

'Yes, Teddy,' he said grimly. 'Teddy's all burned, Charlie. You burned Teddy. And if you burn Teddy, you might burn Mommy. Daddy. Now . . . *don't you do it anymore!'* He leaned closer to her, not picking her up yet, not touching her. 'Don't you do it anymore because *it is a Bad Thing!'*

'Daaaaaaaaaaa—'

And that was all the heartbreak he could stand to inflict, all the horror, all the fear. He picked her up, held her, walked her back and forth until – a very long time later – her sobs tapered off to irregular hitchings of her chest, and sniffles. When he looked at her, she was asleep with her cheek on his shoulder.

He put her on the couch and went to the phone in the kitchen and called Quincey.

Quincey didn't want to talk. He was working for a large aircraft corporation in that year of 1975, and in the notes that accompanied each of his yearly Christmas cards to the McGees he described his job as Vice-President in Charge of Stroking. When the men who made the airplanes had problems, they were supposed to go see Quincey. Quincey would help them with their problems – feelings of alienation, identity crises, maybe just a feeling that their jobs were dehumanizing them – and they wouldn't go back to the line and put the widget where the wadget was supposed to go and therefore the planes wouldn't crash and the world would continue to be safe for democracy. For this Quincey made thirty-two thousand dollars a year, seventeen thousand more than Andy made. 'And I don't feel a bit guilty,' he had written. 'I consider it a small salary to extract for keeping America afloat almost single-handed.'

That was Quincey, as sardonically funny as ever. Except he hadn't been sardonic and he hadn't been funny that day when Andy called from Ohio with his daughter sleeping on the couch and the smell of burned bear and singed carpeting in his nostrils.

'I've heard things,' Quincey said finally, when he saw that Andy wasn't going to let him off without *something*. 'But sometimes people listen in on phones, old buddy. It's the era of Watergate.'

'I'm scared,' Andy said. 'Vicky's scared. And Charlie's scared too. What have you heard, Quincey?'

'Once upon a time there was an experiment in which twelve people participated,' Quincey said. 'About six years ago. Do you remember that?'

'I remember it,' Andy said grimly.

'There aren't many of those twelve people left. There were four, the last I heard. And two of them married each other.'

'Yes,' Andy said, but inside he felt growing horror. Only four left? What was Quincey talking about?

'I understand one of them can bend keys and shut doors without even touching them.' Quincey's voice, thin, coming across two thousand miles of telephone cable, coming through switching stations, through the open-relay points, through junction boxes in Nevada, Idaho, Colorado, Iowa. A million places to tap into Quincey's voice.

'Yes?' he said, straining to keep his voice level. And he thought of Vicky, who could sometimes turn on the radio or turn off the TV without going anywhere near it – and

Vicky was apparently not even aware she was doing those things.

'Oh yes, he's for real,' Quincey was saying. 'He's – what would you say? – a documented case. It hurts his head if he does those things too often, but he can do them. They keep him in a little room with a door he can't open and a lock he can't bend. They do tests on him. He bends keys. He shuts doors. And I understand he's nearly crazy.'

'Oh . . . my . . . God,' Andy said faintly.

'He's part of the peace effort, so it's all right if he goes crazy,' Quincey went on. 'He's going crazy so two hundred and twenty million Americans can stay safe and free. Do you understand?'

'Yes,' Andy had whispered.

'What about the two people who got married? Nothing. So far as they know. They live quietly, in some quiet middle-American state like Ohio. There's maybe a yearly check on them. Just to see if they're doing anything like bending keys or closing doors without touching them or doing funny little mentalist routines at the local Backyard Carnival for Muscular Dystrophy. Good thing those people can't do anything like that, isn't it, Andy?'

Andy closed his eyes and smelled burned cloth. Sometimes Charlie would pull open the fridge door, look in, and then crawl off again. And if Vicky was ironing, she would glance at the fridge door and it would swing shut again – all without her being aware that she was doing anything strange. That was sometimes. At other times it didn't seem to work, and she would leave her ironing and close the refrigerator door herself (or turn off the radio, or turn on the TV). Vicky couldn't bend keys or read thoughts or fly or start fires or predict the future. She could sometimes shut a door from across the room and that was about the extent of it. Sometimes, after she had done several of these things, Andy had noticed that she would complain of a

78

headache or an upset stomach, and whether that was a physical reaction or some sort of muttered warning from her subconscious, Andy didn't know. Her ability to do these things got maybe a little stronger around the time of her period. Such small things, and so infrequently, that Andy had come to think of them as normal. As for himself . . . well he could push people. There was no real name for it; perhaps autohypnosis came closest. And he couldn't do it often, because it gave him headaches. Most days he could forget completely that he wasn't utterly normal and never really had been since that day in Room 70 of Jason Gearneigh.

He closed his eyes and on the dark field inside his eyelids he saw that comma-shaped bloodstain and the nonwords COR OSUM.

'Yes, it's a good thing,' Quincey went on, as if Andy had agreed. 'Or they might put them in two little rooms where they could work full-time to keep two hundred and twenty million Americans safe and free.'

'A good thing,' Andy agreed.

'Those twelve people,' Quincey said, 'maybe they gave those twelve people a drug they didn't fully understand. It might have been that someone – a certain Mad Doctor – might have deliberately misled them. Or maybe he thought he was misleading them and they were deliberately leading him on. It doesn't matter.'

'No.'

'So this drug was given to them and maybe it changed their chromosomes a little bit. Or a lot. Or who knows. And maybe two of them got married and decided to have a baby and maybe the baby got something more than her eyes and his mouth. Wouldn't they be interested in that child?'

'I bet they would,' Andy said, now so frightened he was

79

having trouble talking at all. He had already decided that he would not tell Vicky about calling Quincey.

'It's like you got lemon, and that's nice, and you got meringue, and *that's* nice, too, but when you put them together, you've got . . . a whole new taste treat. I bet they'd want to see just what that child could do. They might just want to take it and put it in a little room and see if it could help make the world safe for democracy. And I think that's all I want to say, old buddy, except . . . keep your head down.'

24

Voices in a haunted room.

Keep your head down.

He turned his head on the motel pillow and looked at Charlie, who was sleeping deeply. *Charlie kid, what are we going to do? Where can we go and be left alone? How is this going to end?*

No answer to any of these questions.

And at last he slept, while not so far away a green car cruised through the dark, still hoping to come upon a big man with broad shoulders in a corduroy jacket and a little girl with blond hair in red pants and a green blouse.

Longmont, Virginia:
The Shop

1

Two handsome Southern plantation homes faced each other across a long and rolling grass lawn that was crisscrossed by a few gracefully looping bike paths and a two-lane crushed-gravel drive that came over the hill from the main road. Off to one side of one of these houses was a large barn, painted a bright red and trimmed a spotless white. Near the other was a long stable, done in the same handsome red with white trim. Some of the best horseflesh in the South was quartered here. Between the barn and the stable was a wide, shallow duckpond, calmly reflecting the sky.

In the 1860s, the original owners of these two homes had gone off and got themselves killed in the war, and all survivors of both families were dead now. The two estates had been consolidated into one piece of government property in 1954. It was Shop headquarters.

At ten minutes past nine on a sunny October day – the day after Andy and Charlie left New York for Albany in a taxicab – an elderly man with kindly, sparkling eyes and wearing a woolen British driving cap on his head biked toward one of the houses. Behind him, over the second knoll, was the checkpoint he had come through after a computer ID system had okayed his thumbprint. The checkpoint was inside a double run of barbed wire. The outer run, seven feet high, was marked every sixty feet by

signs that read CAUTION! GOVERNMENT PROPERTY   LOW
ELECTRIC CHARGE RUNS THROUGH THIS FENCE! During the
day, the charge was indeed low. At night, the on-property
generator boosted it to a lethal voltage, and each morning
a squad of five groundskeepers circled it in little electric
golf carts, picking up the bodies of crisped rabbits, moles,
birds, groundhogs, an occasional skunk lying in a pool of
smell, sometimes a deer. And twice, human beings, equally
cooked. The space between the outer and inner runs of
barbed wire was ten feet. Day and night, guard dogs
circled the installation in this run. The guard dogs were
Dobermans, and they had been trained to stay away from
the electrified wire. At each corner of the installation there
were guard towers, also built of spanking-red barnboard
and trimmed in white. They were manned by personnel
who were expert in the use of various items of death-
dealing hardware. The whole place was monitored by TV
cameras, and the views these various cameras presented
were constantly scanned by computer. The Longmont
facility was secure.

The elderly man biked on, with a smile for the people he
passed. An old, baldheaded man in a baseball cap was
walking a thin-ankled filly. He raised his hand and called,
'Hi, Cap! Ain't this some kind of a day!'

'Knock your eye out,' the man on the bike agreed. 'Have
a good one, Henry.'

He reached the front of the northernmost of the two
homes, dismounted his bike, and put down its kickstand.
He breathed deeply of the mild morning air, then trotted
sprily up the wide porch steps and between the broad
Doric columns.

He opened the door and stepped into the wide receiving
hall. A young woman with red hair sat behind a desk, a
statistics-analysis book open in front of her. One hand was

holding her place in the book. The other was in her desk drawer, lightly touching a .38 Smith & Wesson.

'Good morning, Josie,' the elderly gent said.

'Hi, Cap. You're running a little behind, aren't you?' Pretty girls could get away with this; if it had been Duane's day on the front desk, he could not have done. Cap was not a supporter of women's liberation.

'My top gear's sticking, darlin.' He put his thumb in the proper slot. Something in the console thudded heavily, and a green light fluttered and then remained steady on Josie's board. 'You be good, now.'

'Well, I'll be careful,' she said archly, and crossed her legs.

Cap roared laughter and walked down the hall. She watched him go, wondering for a moment if she should have told him that that creepy old man Wanless had come in some twenty minutes ago. He'd know soon enough, she supposed, and sighed. What a way to screw up the start of a perfectly fine day, having to talk to an old spook like that. But she supposed that a person like Cap, who held a position of great responsibility, had to take the sour with the sweet.

2

Cap's office was at the back of the house. A large bay window gave a magnificent view of the back lawn, the barn, and the duckpond, which was partially screened with alders. Rich McKeon was halfway down the lawn, sitting astride a miniature tractor-lawnmower. Cap stood looking at him with his arms crossed behind his back for a moment and then went over to the Mr Coffee in the corner. He poured some coffee in his U.S.N. cup, added Cremora and then sat down and thumbed the intercom.

'Hi, Rachel,' he said.

'Hello, Cap. Dr Wanless is—'

'I knew it,' Cap said. 'I *knew* it. I could smell that old whore the minute I came in.'

'Shall I tell him you're just too busy today?'

'Don't tell him any such thing,' Cap said stoutly. 'Just let him sit out there in the yellow parlor the whole frigging morning. If he doesn't decide to go home, I suppose I can see him before lunch.'

'All right, sir.' Problem solved – for Rachel, anyway, Cap thought with a touch of resentment. Wanless wasn't really her problem at all. And the fact was, Wanless was getting to be an embarrassment. He had outlived both his usefulness and his influence. Well, there was always the Maui compound. And then there was Rainbird.

Cap felt a little inward shudder at that . . . and he wasn't a man who shuddered easily.

He held down the intercom toggle again. 'I'll want the entire McGee file again, Rachel. And at ten-thirty I want to see Al Steinowitz. If Wanless is still here when I finish with Al, you can send him in.'

'Very good, Cap.'

Cap sat back, steepled his fingers, and looked across the room at the picture of George Patton on the wall. Patton was standing astride the top hatch of a tank as if he thought he were Duke Wayne or someone. 'It's a hard life if you don't weaken,' he told Patton's image, and sipped his coffee.

3

Rachel brought the file in on a whisper-wheeled library cart ten minutes later. There were six boxes of papers and reports, four boxes of photographs. There were telephone transcripts as well. The McGee phone had been bugged since 1978.

'Thanks, Rachel.'

'You're welcome. Mr Steinowitz will be here at ten-thirty.'

'Of course he will. Has Wanless died yet?'

'I'm afraid not,' she said, smiling. 'He's just sitting out there and watching Henry walk the horses.'

'Shredding his goddam cigarettes?'

Rachel covered her mouth like a schoolgirl, giggled, and nodded. 'He's gone through half a pack already.'

Cap grunted. Rachel left and he turned to the files. He had been through them how many times in the last eleven months? A dozen? Two dozen? He had the extracta nearly by heart. And if Al was right, he would have the two remaining McGees under detection by the end of the week. The thought caused a hot little trickle of excitement in his belly.

He began leafing through the McGee file at random, pulling a sheet here, reading a snatch there. It was his way of plugging back into the situation. His conscious mind was in neutral, his subconscious in high gear. What he wanted now was not detail but to put his hand to the whole thing. As baseball players say, he needed to find the handle.

Here was a memo from Wanless himself, a younger Wanless (ah, but they had all been younger then), dated September 12, 1968. Half a paragraph caught Cap's eye:

. . . of an enormous importance in the continuing study of controllable psychic phenomena. Further testing on animals would be counterproductive (see overleaf 1) and, as I emphasized at the group meeting this summer, testing on convicts or any deviant personality might lead to very real problems if Lot Six is even fractionally as powerful as we suspect (see overleaf 2). I therefore continue to recommend . . .

You continue to recommend that we feed it to controlled groups of college students under all outstanding contingency plans for failure, Cap thought. There had been no waffling on Wanless's part in those days. No indeed. His motto in those days had been full speed ahead and devil take the hindmost. Twelve people had been tested. Two of them had died, one during the test, one shortly afterward. Two had gone hopelessly insane, and both of them were maimed – one blind, one suffering from psychotic paralysis, both of them confined at the Maui compound, where they would remain until their miserable lives ended. So then there were eight. One of them had died in a car accident in 1972, a car accident that was almost certainly no accident at all but suicide. Another had leaped from the roof of the Cleveland Post Office in 1973, and there was no question at all about that one; he had left a note saying he 'couldn't stand the pictures in his head any longer.' The Cleveland police had diagnosed it as suicidal depression and paranoia. Cap and the Shop had diagnosed it as lethal Lot Six hangover. And that had left six.

Three others had committed suicide between 1974 and 1977, for a known total of four suicides and a probable total of five. Almost half the class, you might say. All four of the definite suicides had seemed perfectly normal right up to the time they had used the gun, or the rope, or jumped from the high place. But who knew what they might have been going through? Who really knew?

So then there were three. Since 1977, when the long-dormant Lot Six project had suddenly got red hot again, a fellow named James Richardson, who now lived in Los Angeles, had been under constant covert surveillance. In 1969 he had taken part in the Lot Six experiment, and during the course of the drug's influence, he had demonstrated the same startling range of talents as the rest of them: telekinesis, thought transference, and maybe the most interesting manifestation of all, at least from the Shop's specialized point of view: mental domination.

But as had happened with the others, James Richardson's drug-induced powers seemed to have disappeared completely with the wearing off of the drug. Follow-up interviews in 1971, 1973, and 1975 had shown nothing. Even Wanless had had to admit that, and he was a fanatic on the subject of Lot Six. Steady computer readouts on a random basis (and they were a lot less random since the McGee thing had started to happen) had shown no indication at all that Richardson was using any sort of psi power, either consciously or unconsciously. He had graduated in 1971, drifted west through a series of lower-echelon managerial jobs – no mental domination there – and now worked for the Telemyne Corporation.

Also, he was a fucking faggot.

Cap sighed.

They were continuing to keep an eye on Richardson, but Cap had been personally convinced that the man was a washout. And that left two, Andy McGee and his wife. The serendipity of their marriage had not been lost on the Shop, or on Wanless, who had begun to bombard the office with memos, suggesting that any offspring of that marriage would bear close watching – counting his chickens before they had hatched, you could say – and on more than one occasion Cap had toyed with the idea of telling Wanless they had learned Andy McGee had had a vasectomy. That would have shut the old bastard up. By then Wanless had had his stroke and was effectively useless, really nothing but a nuisance.

There had been only the one Lot Six experiment. The results had been so disastrous that the coverup had been massive and complete . . . and expensive. The order came down from on high to impose an indefinite moratorium on further testing. Wanless had plenty to scream about that day, Cap thought . . . and scream he had. But there had been no sign at all that the Russians or any other world power was interested in drug-induced psionics, and the top brass had concluded that in spite of some positive results, Lot Six was a blind alley. Looking at the long-term results, one of the scientists who had worked on the project compared it to dropping a jet engine into an old Ford. It went like hell, all right . . . until it hit the first obstacle. 'Give us another ten thousand years of evolution,' this fellow had said, 'and we'll try it again.'

Part of the problem had been that when the drug-induced psi powers were at their height, the test subjects had also been tripping out of their skulls. No control was possible. And coming out the other side, the top brass had been nearly shitting their pants. Covering up the death of an agent, or even of a bystander to an operation – that was one thing. Covering up the death of a student who had suffered a heart attack, the disappearance of two others, and lingering traces of hysteria and paranoia in yet others – that was a different matter altogether. All of them had friends and associates, even if one of the requirements by which the test subjects had been picked was a scarcity of close relatives. The costs and the risks had been enormous. They had involved nearly seven hundred thousand dollars in hush money and the sanction of at least one person – the godfather of the fellow who had clawed his eyes out. The godfather just would not quit. He was going to get to the root of the matter. As it turned out, the only place the godfather had got was to the bottom of the Baltimore Trench, where he presumably still was, with two cement blocks tied around whatever remained of his legs.

And still, a great deal of it – too damn much – had just been luck.

So the Lot Six project had been shelved with a continuing yearly budget allotment. The money was used to continue random surveillance on the survivors in case something turned up – some pattern.

Eventually, one had.

Cap hunted through a folder of photographs and came up with an eight-by-ten glossy black-and-white of the girl. It had been taken three years ago, when she was four and attending the Free Children's Nursery School in Harrison. The picture had been taken with a telephoto lens from the back of a bakery van and later blown up and cropped to turn a picture of a lot of boys and girls at playtime into a portrait of a smiling little girl with her pigtails flying and the pistol grip of a jumprope in each hand.

Cap looked at this picture sentimentally for some time. Wanless, in the aftermath of his stroke, had discovered fear. Wanless now thought the little girl would have to be sanctioned. And although Wanless was among the outs these days, there were those who concurred with his opinion – those who were among the ins. Cap hoped like hell that it wouldn't come to that. He had three grandchildren himself, two of them just about Charlene McGee's age.

Of course they would have to separate the girl from her father. Probably permanently. And he would almost certainly have to be sanctioned . . . after he had served his purpose, of course.

It was quarter past ten. He buzzed Rachel. 'Is Albert Steinowitz here yet?'

'Just this minute arrived, sir.'

'Very good. Send him in, please.'

4

'I want you to take personal charge of the endgame, Al.'

'Very good, Cap.'

Albert Steinowitz was a small man with a yellow-pale

89

complexion and very black hair; in earlier years he had sometimes been mistaken for the actor Victor Jory. Cap had worked with Steinowitz off and on for nearly eight years – in fact they had come over from the navy together – and to him Al had always looked like a man about to enter the hospital for a terminal stay. He smoked constantly, except in here, where it wasn't allowed. He walked with a slow, stately stride that invested him with a strange kind of dignity, and impenetrable dignity is a rare attribute in any man. Cap, who saw all the medical records of Section One agents, knew that Albert's dignified walk was bogus; he suffered badly from hemorrhoids and had been operated on for them twice. He had refused a third operation because it might mean a colostomy bag on his leg for the rest of his life. His dignified walk always made Cap think of the fairy tale about the mermaid who wanted to be a woman and the price she paid for legs and feet. Cap imagined that her walk had been rather dignified, too.

'How soon can you be in Albany?' he asked Al now.

'An hour after I leave here.'

'Good. I won't keep you long. What's the status up there?'

Albert folded his small, slightly yellow hands in his lap. 'The state police are cooperating nicely. All highways leading out of Albany have been roadblocked. The blocks are set up in concentric circles with Albany County Airport at their center. Radius of thirty-five miles.'

'You're assuming they didn't hitch a ride.'

'We have to,' Albert said. 'If they hooked a ride with someone who took them two hundred miles or so, of course we'll have to start all over again. But I'm betting they're inside that circle.'

'Oh? Why is that, Albert?' Cap leaned forward. Albert Steinowitz was, without a doubt, the best agent, except maybe for Rainbird, in the Shop's employ. He was bright, intuitive – and ruthless when the job demanded that.

'Partly hunch,' Albert said. 'Partly the stuff we got back from the computer when we fed in everything we knew about the last three years of Andrew McGee's life. We asked it to pull out any and all patterns that might apply to this ability he's supposed to have.'

'He does have it, Al,' Cap said gently. 'That's what makes this operation so damned delicate.'

'All right, he has it,' Al said. 'But the computer readouts suggest that his ability to use it is extremely limited. If he overuses it, it makes him sick.'

'Right. We're counting on that.'

'He was running a storefront operation in New York, a Dale Carnegie kind of thing.'

Cap nodded. Confidence Associates, an operation aimed mainly at timid executives. Enough to keep him and the girl in bread, milk, and meat, but not much more.

'We've debriefed his last group,' Albert Steinowitz said. 'There were sixteen of them, and each of them paid a split tuition fee – one hundred dollars at enrollment, a hundred more halfway through the course, if they felt the course was helping them. Of course they all did.'

Cap nodded. McGee's talent was admirably suited for investing people with confidence He literally *pushed* them into it.

'We fed their answers to several key questions into the computer. The questions were, did you feel better about yourself and the Confidence Associates course at specific times? Can you remember days at work following your Confidence Associates meetings when you felt like a tiger? Have you—'

'Felt like a tiger?' Cap asked. 'Jesus, you asked them if they felt like *tigers?*'

'The computer suggests the wording.'

'Okay, go on.'

'The third key question was, have you had any specific, measurable success at your job since taking the Confidence Associates course? That was the question they could all respond to with the most objectivity and reliability, because people tend to remember the day they got the raise or the pat on the back from the boss. They were eager to talk. I found it a little spooky, Cap. He sure did what he promised. Of the sixteen, eleven of them have had promotions – *eleven*. Of the other five, three are in jobs where promotions are made only at certain set times.'

'No one is arguing McGee's capability,' Cap said. 'Not anymore.'

'Okay. I'm getting back around to the point here. It was a six-week course. Using the answers to the key questions, the computer came up with four spike dates . . . that is, days when McGee probably supplemented all the usual hip-hip-hooray-you-can-do-it-if-you-try stuff with a good hard push. The dates we have are August seventeenth, September first, September nineteenth . . . and October fourth.'

'Proving?'

'Well, he pushed that cab driver last night. Pushed him hard. That dude is still rocking and reeling. We figure Andy McGee is tipped over. Sick. Maybe immobilized.' Albert looked at Cap steadily. 'Computer gave us a twenty-six-percent probability that he's dead.'

'*What?*'

'Well, he's overdone it before and wound up in bed. He's doing something to his brain . . . God knows what. Giving himself pinprick hemorrhages, maybe. It could be a progressive thing. The computer figures there's slightly better than a one-in-four chance he's dead, either of a heart attack or, more probably, a stroke.'

'He had to use it before he was recharged,' Cap said.

Albert nodded and took something out of his pocket. It was encased in limp plastic. He passed it to Cap, who looked at it and then passed it back.

'What's that supposed to mean?' he asked.

'Not that much,' Al said, looking at the bill in its plastic envelope meditatively. 'Just what McGee paid his cab fare with.'

'He went to Albany from New York City on a one-dollar bill, huh?' Cap took it back and looked at it with renewed interest. 'Cab fares sure must be . . . what the hell!' He dropped the plastic-encased bill on his desk as if it were hot and sat back, blinking.

'You too, huh?' Al said. 'Did you see it?'

'Christ, I don't know what I saw,' Cap said, and reached for the ceramic box where he kept his acid neutralizers. 'For just a second it didn't look like a one-dollar bill at all.'

'But now it does?'

Cap peered at the bill. 'It sure does. That's George, all – *Christ!*' He sat back so violently this time that he almost rapped the back of his head on the dark wood paneling behind his desk. He looked at Al. 'The face . . . seemed to change for a second there. Grew glasses, or something. Is it a trick?'

'Oh, it's a hell of a good trick,' Al said, taking the bill back. 'I saw it as well, although I don't anymore. I think I've adjusted to it now . . . although I'll be damned if I know how. It's not there, of course. It's just some kind of crazy hallucination. But I even made the face. It's Ben Franklin.'

'You got this from the cab driver?' Cap asked, looking at the bill, fascinated, waiting for the change again. But it was only George Washington.

Al laughed. 'Yeah,' he said. 'We took the bill and gave him a check for five hundred dollars. He's better off, really.'

'Why?'

'Ben Franklin isn't on the five hundred, he's on the hundred. Apparently McGee didn't know.'

'Let me see that again.'

Al handed the one-dollar bill back to Cap, and Cap stared fixedly at it for almost a full two minutes. Just as he was about to hand it back, it flickered again – unsettling. But at least this time he felt that the flicker was definitely in his mind, and not in the bill, or on it, or whatever.

'I'll tell you something else,' Cap said. 'I'm not sure, but I don't think Franklin's wearing glasses on his currency portrait, either. Otherwise, it's . . .' He trailed off, not sure how to complete the thought. Goddam *weird* came to mind, and he dismissed it.

'Yeah,' Al said. 'Whatever it is, the effect is dissipating. This morning I showed it to maybe six people. A couple of them thought they saw something, but not like that cab driver and the girl he lives with.'

'So you're figuring he pushed too hard?'

'Yes. I doubt if he could keep going. They may have slept in the woods, or in an outlying motel. They may have broken into a summer cabin in the area. But I think they're around and we'll be able to put the arm on them without too much trouble.'

'How many men do you need to do the job?'

'We've got what we need,' Al said. 'Counting the state police, there are better than seven hundred people in on this little houseparty. Priority A-one-A. They're going door to door and house to house. We've checked every hotel and motel in the immediate Albany area already – better than forty of them. We're spreading into the neighboring towns now. A man and a little girl . . . they stick out like a sore thumb. We'll get them. Or the girl, if he's dead.' Albert stood up. 'And I think I ought to get on it. I'd like to be there when it goes down.'

'Of course you would. Bring them to me, Al.'

'I will,' Albert said, and walked toward the door.

'Albert?'

He turned back, a small man with an unhealthy yellow complexion. 'Who *is* on the five hundred? Did you check that out?'

Albert Steinowitz smiled. 'McKinley,' he said. 'He was assassinated.'

He went out, closing the door gently behind him, leaving Cap to consider.

5

Ten minutes later, Cap thumbed the intercom again. 'Is Rainbird back from Venice yet, Rachel?'

'As of yesterday,' Rachel said, and Cap fancied he could hear the distaste even in Rachel's carefully cultivated Boss Secretary tones.

'Is he here or at Sanibel?' The Shop maintained an R-and-R facility on Sanibel Island, Florida.

There was a pause as Rachel checked with the computer.

'Longmont, Cap. As of eighteen hundred yesterday. Sleeping off the jet lag, perhaps.'

'Have someone wake him up,' Cap said. 'I'd like to see him when Wanless leaves . . . always assuming Wanless is still here?'

'As of fifteen minutes ago he was.'

'All right . . . let's say Rainbird at noon.'

'Yes, sir.'

'You're a good girl, Rachel.'

'Thank you, sir.' She sounded touched. Cap liked her, liked her very much.

'Send in Dr Wanless please, Rachel.'

He settled back, joined his hands in front of him, and thought, *For my sins*.

6

Dr Joseph Wanless had suffered his stroke on the same day Richard Nixon announced his resignation of the presidency – August 8, 1974. It had been a cerebral accident of moderate severity, and he had never come all the way back physically. Nor mentally, in Cap's opinion. It was only following the stroke that Wanless's interest in the Lot Six experiment and follow-up had become constant and obsessive.

He came into the room leaning over a cane, the light from the bay window catching his round, rimless glasses and making them glare blankly. His left hand was a drawn-up claw. The left side of his mouth drifted in a constant glacial sneer.

Rachel looked at Cap sympathetically over Wanless's shoulder and Cap nodded that she could go. She did, closing the door quietly.

'The good doctor,' Cap said humorlessly.

'How does it progress?' Wanless asked, sitting down with a grunt.

'Classified,' Cap said. 'You know that, Joe. What can I do for you today?'

'I have seen the activity around this place,' Wanless said, ignoring Cap's question. 'What else had I to do while I cooled my heels all morning?'

'If you come without an appointment—'

'You think you nearly have them again,' Wanless said. 'Why else that hatchet man Steinowitz? Well, maybe you do. Maybe so. But you have thought so before, haven't you?'

'What do you want, Joe?' Cap didn't like to be reminded of past failures. They had actually had the girl for a while. The men who had been involved in that were still not operational and maybe never would be.

'What do I always want?' Wanless asked, hunched over his cane. Oh Christ, Cap thought, the old fuck's going to wax rhetorical. 'Why do I stay alive? To persuade you to sanction them both. To sanction that James Richardson as well. To sanction the ones on Maui. Extreme sanction, Captain Hollister. Expunge them. Wipe them off the face of the earth.'

Cap sighed.

Wanless gestured toward the library cart with his claw-hand and said, 'You've been through the files again, I see.'

'I have them almost by heart,' Cap said, and then smiled a little. He had been eating and drinking Lot Six for the last year; it had been a constant item on the agenda at every meeting during the two years before that. So maybe Wanless wasn't the only obsessive character around here, at that.

The difference is, I get paid for it. With Wanless it's a hobby. A dangerous hobby.

'You read them but you don't learn,' Wanless said. 'Let me try once more to convert you to the way of truth, Captain Hollister.'

Cap began to protest, and then the thought of Rainbird and his noon appointment came to mind, and his face smoothed out. It became calm, even sympathetic. 'All right,' he said. 'Fire when ready, Gridley.'

'You still think I'm crazy, don't you? A lunatic.'

'You said that, not I.'

'It would be well for you to remember that I was the first one to suggest a testing program with di-lysergic triune acid.'

'I have days when I wish you hadn't,' Cap said. If he closed his eyes, he could still see Wanless's first report, a two-hundred-page prospectus on the drug that had first been known as DLT, then, among the technicians involved, as 'booster-acid,' and finally as Lot Six. Cap's predecessor

97

had okayed the original project; that gentleman had been buried in Arlington with full military honors six years ago.

'All I am saying is that my opinion should carry some weight,' Wanless said. He sounded tired this morning; his words were slow and furry. The twisted sneer on the left side of his mouth did not move as he spoke.

'I'm listening,' Cap said.

'So far as I am able to tell, I am the only psychologist or medical man who still has your ear at all. Your people have become blinded by one thing and one thing only: what this man and this girl can mean to the security of America . . . and possibly to the future balance of power. From what we've been able to tell by following this McGee's backtrail, he is a kind of benign Rasputin. He can make . . .'

Wanless droned on, but Cap lost him temporarily. *Benign Rasputin*, he thought. Purple as the phrase was, he rather liked it. He wondered what Wanless would say if told the computer had issued one-in-four odds that McGee had sanctioned himself getting out of New York City. Probably would have been overjoyed. And if he had showed Wanless that strange bill? Probably have another stroke, Cap thought, and covered his mouth to hide a smile.

'It is the girl I am primarily worried about,' Wanless told him for the twentieth? thirtieth? fiftieth? time. 'McGee and Tomlinson marrying . . . a thousand-to-one chance. It should have been prevented at all costs. Yet who could have foreseen—'

'You were all in favor of it at the time,' Cap said, and then added dryly, 'I do believe you would have given the bride away if they'd asked you.'

'None of us realized,' Wanless muttered. 'It took a stroke to make me see. Lot Six was nothing but a synthetic copy of a pituitary extract, after all . . . an incredibly powerful painkiller-hallucinogen that we did not understand then and that we don't understand now. We know – or at least we are ninety-nine-percent sure – that the natural counterpart of this substance is responsible in some way for the occasional flashes of psi ability that nearly all human beings demonstrate from time to time. A surprisingly wide range of phenomena: precognition, telekinesis, mental domination, bursts of superhuman strength, temporary control over the sympathetic nervous system. Did you know that the pituitary gland becomes suddenly overactive in nearly all biofeedback experiments?'

Cap did. Wanless had told him this and all the rest times without number. But there was no need to answer; Wanless's rhetoric was in full fine flower this morning, the sermon well-launched. And Cap was disposed to listen . . . this one last time. Let the old man have his turn at bat. For Wanless, it was the bottom of the ninth.

'Yes, this is true,' Wanless answered himself. 'It's active in biofeedback, it's active in REM sleep, and people with damaged pituitaries rarely dream normally. People with damaged pituitaries have a tremendously high incidence of brain tumours and leukemia. The pituitary gland, Captain Hollister. It is, speaking in terms of evolution, the oldest endocrine gland in the human body. During early adolescence it dumps many times its own weight in glandular secretions into the bloodstream. It's a terribly important gland, a terribly mysterious gland. If I believed in the human soul, Captain Hollister, I would say it resides within the pituitary gland.'

Cap grunted.

'We know these things,' Wanless said, 'and we know that Lot Six somehow changed the physical composition of the pituitary glands of those who participated in the experiment. Even that of your so-called "quiet one," James Richardson. Most importantly, we can deduce from the girl that it also changes the chromosome structure in some

99

way . . . and that the change in the pituitary gland may be a genuine mutation.'

'The X factor was passed on.'

'No,' Wanless said. 'That is one of the many things you fail to grasp, Captain Hollister. Andrew McGee became an X factor in his postexperiment life. Victoria Tomlinson became a Y factor – also affected, but not in the same way as her husband. The woman retained a low-threshold telekinetic power. The man retained a mid-level mental-dominance ability. The little girl, though . . . the little girl, Captain Hollister . . . what is she? We don't really know. She is the Z factor.'

'We intend to find out,' Cap said softly.

Now both sides of Wanless's mouth sneered. 'You intend to find out,' he echoed. 'Yes, if you persist, you certainly may . . . you blind, obsessive fools.' He closed his eyes for a moment and put one hand over them. Cap watched him calmly.

Wanless said: 'One thing you know already. She lights fires.'

'Yes.'

'You assume that she has inherited her mother's telekinetic ability. In fact, you strongly suspect it.'

'Yes.'

'As a very small child, she was totally unable to control these . . . these talents, for want of a better word . . .'

'A small child is unable to control its bowels,' Cap said, using one of the examples set forth in the extracta. 'But as the child grows older––'

'Yes, yes, I am familiar with the analogy. But an older child may still have accidents.'

Smiling, Cap answered, 'We're going to keep her in a fireproof room.'

'A cell.'

Still smiling, Cap said, 'If you prefer.

'I offer you this deduction,' Wanless said. 'She does not like to use this ability she has. She has been frightened of it, and this fright has been instilled in her quite deliberately. I will give you a parallel example. My brother's child. There were matches in the house. Freddy wanted to play with them. Light them and then shake them out. "Pretty, pretty," he would say. And so my brother set out to make a complex. To frighten him so badly he would never play with the matches again. He told Freddy that the heads of the matches were sulfur and that they would make his teeth rot and fall out. That looking at struck matches would eventually blind him. And finally, he held Freddy's hand momentarily over a lit match and singed him with it.'

'Your brother,' Cap murmured, 'sounds like a true prince among men.'

'Better a small red place on the boy's hand than a child in the burn unit, wetpacked, with third-degree burns over sixty percent of his body,' Wanless said grimly.

'Better still to put the matches out of the child's reach.'

'Can you put Charlene McGee's matches out of her reach?' Wanless asked.

Cap nodded slowly. 'You have a point of a sort, but—'

'Ask yourself this, Captain Hollister: how must it have been for Andrew and Victoria McGee when this child was an infant? After they begin to make the necessary connection? The bottle is late. The baby cries. At the same time, one of the stuffed animals *right there in the crib with her* bursts into smoky flame. There is a mess in the diaper. The baby cries. A moment later the dirty clothes in the hamper begin to burn spontaneously. You have the records, Captain Hollister; you know how it was in that house. A fire extinguisher and a smoke detector in every single room. And once it was her *hair*, Captain Hollister; they came into her room and found her standing in her crib and screaming and her *hair* was on fire.'

'Yes,' Cap said, 'it must have made them goddam nervous.'

'So,' Wanless said, 'they toilet-trained her . . . and they fire-trained her.'

'Fire-training,' Cap mused.

'Which is only to say that, like my brother and his boy Freddy, they made a complex. You have quoted me that analogy, Captain Hollister, so let us examine it for a moment. What is toilet-training? It is making a complex, pure and simple.' And suddenly astonishingly, the old man's voice climbed to a high, wavering treble, the voice of a woman scolding a baby. Cap looked on with disgusted astonishment.

'You bad baby!' Wanless cried. 'Look what you've done! It's nasty, baby, see how nasty it is? It's nasty to do it in your pants! Do grown-ups do it in their pants? Do it on the pot, baby, on the *pot*.'

'Please,' Cap said, pained.

'It is the making of a complex,' Wanless said. 'Toilet-training is accomplished by focusing the child's attention on his own eliminatory processes in a way we would consider unhealthy if the object of fixation were something different. How strong is the complex inculcated in the child, you might ask? Richard Damon of the University of Washington asked himself this question and made an experiment to find out. He advertised for fifty student volunteers. He filled them up with water and soda and milk until they all badly needed to urinate. After a certain set time had passed, he told them they could go . . . if they went in their pants.'

'That's disgusting!' Cap said loudly. He was shocked and sickened. That wasn't an experiment; it was an exercise in degeneracy.

'See how well the complex has set in your own psyche,' Wanless said quietly 'You did not think it was so disgusting when you were twenty months old. Then, when you had to go, you went. You would have gone sitting on the pope's lap if someone had set you there and you had to go. The point of the Damon experiment, Captain Hollister, is this: most of them *couldn't*. They understood that the ordinary rules of behavior had been set aside, at least for the course of the experiment; they were each alone in quarters at least as private as the ordinary bathroom . . . but fully eighty-eight percent of them just *couldn't*. No matter how strong the physical need was, the complex instilled by their parents was stronger.'

'This is nothing but pointless wandering,' Cap said curtly.

'No, it isn't. I want you to consider the parallels between toilet-training and fire-training . . . and the one significant difference, which is the quantum leap between the *urgency* of accomplishing the former and the latter. If the child toilet-trains slowly, what are the consequences? Minor unpleasantness. His room smells if not constantly aired. The mamma is chained to her washing machine. The cleaners may have to be called in to shampoo the carpet after the job is finally done. At the very worst, the baby may have a constant diaper rash, and that will only happen if the baby's skin is very sensitive or if the mamma is a sloven about keeping him clean. But the consequences to a child who can make *fire* . . .'

His eyes glittered. The left side of his mouth sneered.

'My estimation of the McGees as parents is very high,' Wanless said. 'Somehow they got her through it. I would imagine they began the job long before parents usually begin the toilet-training process; perhaps even before she was able to crawl. "Baby mustn't! Baby hurt herself! No, no, no! Bad girl! Bad girl! *Ba-ad* girl!"'

'But your own computer suggests by its readouts that she is overcoming her complex, Captain Hollister. She is in an enviable position to do it. She is young, and the complex has not had a chance to set in a bed of years until it becomes like cement. And she has her father with her! Do you realize the significance of that simple fact? No, you do not. The father is the authority figure. He holds the psychic reins of every fixation in the female child. Oral, anal, genital; behind each, like a shadowy figure standing behind a curtain, is the father-authority figure. To the girl-child he is Moses; the laws are his laws, handed down she knows not how, but his to enforce. He is perhaps the only person on earth who can remove this block. Our complexes, Captain Hollister, always give us the most agony and psychic distress when those who have inculcated them die and pass beyond argument . . . and mercy.'

Cap glanced at his watch and saw that Wanless had been in here almost forty minutes. It felt like hours. 'Are you almost done? I have another appointment—'

'When complexes go, they go like dams bursting after torrential rains,' Wanless said softly. 'We have a promiscuous girl who is nineteen years old. Already she has had three hundred lovers. Her body is as hot with sexual infection as that of a forty-year-old prostitute. But until she was seventeen she was a virgin. Her father was a minister who told her again and again as a little girl that sex inside marriage was a necessary evil, that sex outside marriage was hell and damnation, that sex was the apple of original sin. When a complex like that goes, it goes like a breaking dam. First there is a crack or two, little trickling rills of water so small as to escape notice. And according to your computer's information, that is where we are now with this little girl. Suggestions that she has used her ability to help her father, at her father's urging. And then it all goes at once, spewing out millions of gallons of water, destroying everything in its path, drowning everyone caught in its way, changing the landscape forever!'

Wanless's croaking voice had risen from its original soft pitch to a broken-voiced old man's shout – but it was more peevish than magnificent.

'Listen,' he said to Cap. 'For once, listen to me. Drop the blinders from your eyes. The man is not dangerous in and of himself. He has a little power, a toy, a plaything. He understands that. He has not been able to use it to make a million dollars. He does not rule men and nations. He has used his power to help fat women lose weight. He has used it to help timid executives gain confidence. He is unable to use the power often or well . . . some inner physiological factor limits him. But the girl is incredibly dangerous. She is on the run with her daddy, faced with a survival situation. She is badly frightened. And he is frightened as well, which is what makes him dangerous. Not in and of himself, but because you are forcing him to reeducate the little girl. You are forcing him to change her conceptions about the power inside her. You are forcing him to force her to *use* it.'

Wanless was breathing hard.

Playing out the scenario – the end was now in sight – Cap said calmly, 'What do you suggest?'

'The man must be killed. Quickly. Before he can do anymore pick-and-shovel work on the complex he and his wife built into the little girl. And the girl must also be killed, I believe. In case the damage has already been done.'

'She's only a little girl, Wanless, after all. She can light fires, yes. Pyrokinesis, we call it. But you're making it sound like armageddon.'

'Perhaps it will be,' Wanless said. 'You mustn't let her age and size fool you into forgetting the Z factor . . . which is exactly what you are doing, of course. Suppose lighting fires is only the tip of this iceberg? Suppose the talent grows? She is seven. When John Milton was seven, he was perhaps a small boy grasping a stick of charcoal and laboring to write his own name in letters his mamma and daddy could understand. He was a baby. John Milton grew up to write *Paradise Lost*.'

'I don't know what the hell you're talking about,' Cap said flatly.

'I am talking about the potential for destruction. I am talking about a talent which is linked to the pituitary gland, a gland which is nearly dormant in a child Charlene McGee's age. What happens when she becomes an adolescent and that gland awakes from its sleep and becomes for twenty months the most powerful force in the human body, ordering everything from the sudden maturation of the primary and secondary sex characteristics to an increased production of visual purple in the eye? Suppose you have a child capable of eventually creating a nuclear explosion *simply by the force of her will?*'

'That's the most insane thing I've ever heard.'

'Is it? Then let me progress from insanity to utter lunacy, Captain Hollister. Suppose there is a little girl out there someplace this morning who has within her, lying dormant only for the time being, the power to someday crack the very planet in two like a china plate in a shooting gallery?'

They looked at each other in silence. And suddenly the intercom buzzed.

After a moment, Cap leaned over and thumbed it. 'Yes, Rachel?' Goddamned if the old man hadn't had him there, for just a moment. He was like some awful gore-crow, and that was another reason Cap didn't like him. He was a go-getter himself, and if there was one thing he couldn't stand, it was a pessimist.

'You have a call on the scrambler,' Rachel said. 'From the service area.'

'All right, dear. Thanks. Hold it for a couple of minutes, okay?'

'Yes, sir.'

He sat back in his chair. 'I have to terminate this interview, Dr Wanless. You may be sure that I'll consider everything you've said very carefully.'

'Will you?' Wanless asked. The frozen side of his mouth seemed to sneer cynically.

'Yes.'

Wanless said: 'The girl . . . McGee . . . and this fellow Richardson . . . they are the last three marks of a dead equation, Captain Hollister. Erase them. Start over. The girl is very dangerous.'

'I'll consider everything you've said,' Cap repeated.

'Do so.' And Wanless finally began to struggle to his feet, propping himself on his cane. It took him a long time. At last he was up.

'Winter is coming,' he said to Cap. 'These old bones dread it.'

'Are you staying in Longmont tonight?'

'No, Washington.'

Cap hesitated and then said, 'Stay at the Mayflower. I may want to get in touch with you.'

Something in the old man's eyes – gratitude? Yes, almost certainly that. 'Very good, Captain Hollister,' he said, and worked his way back to the door on his cane – an old man who had once opened Pandora's box and now wanted to shoot all of the things that had flown out instead of putting them to work.

When the door had snicked closed behind him, Cap breathed a sigh of relief and picked up the scrambler phone.

'Who am I talking to?'

'Orv Jamieson, sir.'

'Have you got them, Jamieson?'

'Not yet, sir, but we found something interesting at the airport.'

'What's that?'

'All the pay phones are empty. We found a few quarters and dimes on the floors of some of them.'

'Jimmied?'

'No, sir. That's why I called you. They haven't been jimmied, they're just empty. Phone company's going crazy.'

'All right, Jamieson.'

'It speeds things up. We've been figuring that maybe the guy hid the girl outside and only checked himself in. But either way, we figure now that we're looking for a guy who paid with a lot of change.'

'If they are at a motel and not shacked up at a summer camp somewhere.'

'Yes, sir.'

'Carry on, OJ.'

'Yes, sir. Thank you.' He sounded absurdly pleased that his nickname had been remembered.

Cap hung up. He sat with his eyes half closed for five minutes, thinking. The mellow autumn light fell through the bay window and lit the office, warmed it. Then he leaned forward and got Rachel again.

'Is John Rainbird there?'

'Yes he is, Cap.'

'Give me another five minutes and then send him in. I want to talk to Norville Bates out in the service area. He's the head honcho until Al gets there.'

'Yes, sir,' Rachel said, a little doubtfully. 'It will have to be an open line. Walkie-talkie link-up. Not very—'

'Yes, that's fine,' he said impatiently.

It took two minutes. Bates's voice was thin and crackling. He was a good man – not very imaginative, but a plugger. The kind of man Cap wanted to have holding the fort until Albert Steinowitz could get there. At last Norville came on the line and told Cap they were beginning to spread out into the surrounding towns – Oakville, Tremont, Messalonsett, Hastings Glen, Looton.

'All right, Norville, that's good,' Cap said. He thought of Wanless saying *You are forcing him to reeducate the little girl.* He thought of Jamieson telling him all the phones were empty. McGee hadn't done that. The girl had done it. And then, because she was still up, she had burned that soldier's shoes off, probably by accident. Wanless would be pleased to know that Cap was going to take fifty percent of his advice after all – the old turd had been amazingly eloquent this morning.

'Things have changed,' Cap said. 'We've got to have the big boy sanctioned. Extreme sanction. You follow?'

'Extreme sanction,' Norville said flatly. 'Yes, sir.'

'Very good, Norville,' Cap said softly. He put the phone down and waited for John Rainbird to come in.

The door opened a moment later and there he stood, as big as life and twice as ugly. He was so naturally quiet, this half Cherokee, that if you had been looking down at your desk, reading or answering correspondence, you wouldn't have been aware that anyone was in the room with you at all. Cap knew how rare that was. Most people could sense another person in the room: Wanless had once called that ability not a sixth sense but a bottom-of-the-barrel sense, a knowledge born of infinitesimal input from the five normal senses. But with Rainbird, you didn't know. Not one of the whisker-thin sensory tripwires so much as vibrated. Al Steinowitz had said a strange thing about Rainbird once over glasses of port in Cap's living room: 'He's the one human being I ever met who doesn't push air in front of him when he walks.' And Cap was glad Rainbird was on their side, because he was the only human *he* had ever met who completely terrified him.

Rainbird was a troll, an orc, a balrog of a man. He stood two inches shy of seven feet tall, and he wore his glossy black hair drawn back and tied in a curt ponytail. Ten years before, a Claymore had blown up in his face during his second tour of Vietnam, and now his countenance was a horrorshow of scar tissue and runneled flesh. His left eye was gone. There was nothing where it had been but a ravine. He would not have plastic surgery or an artificial eye because, he said, when he got to the happy hunting ground beyond, he would be asked to show his battlescars. When he said such things, you did not know whether to believe him or not; you did not know if he was serious or leading you on for reasons of his own.

Over the years, Rainbird had been a surprisingly good agent – partially because the last thing on earth he looked like was an agent, mostly because there was an apt, ferociously bright mind behind that mask of flesh. He spoke four languages fluently and had an understanding of three others. He was taking a sleep course in Russian. When he spoke, his voice was low, musical, and civilized.

'Good afternoon, Cap.'

'Is it afternoon?' Cap asked, surprised.

Rainbird smiled, showing a big set of perfectly white teeth – shark's teeth, Cap thought. 'By fourteen minutes,' he said. 'I picked up a Seiko digital watch on the black market in Venice. It is fascinating. Little black numbers that change constantly. A feat of technology. I often think, Cap, that we fought the war in Vietnam not to win but to perform feats of technology. We fought it in order to create the cheap digital wristwatch, the home Ping-Pong game that hooks up to one's TV, the pocket calculator. I look at my new wristwatch in the dark of night. It tells me I am closer to my death, second by second. That is good news.'

'Sit down, old friend,' Cap said. As always when he talked to Rainbird, his mouth was dry and he had to restrain his hands, which wanted to twine and knot together on the polished surface of his desk. All of that, and he believed that Rainbird *liked* him – if Rainbird could be said to like anyone.

Rainbird sat down. He was wearing old bluejeans and a faded chambray shirt.

'How was Venice?' Cap asked.

'Sinking,' Rainbird said.

'I have a job for you, if you want it. It is a small one, but it may lead to an assignment you'll find considerably more interesting.'

'Tell me.'

'Strictly volunteer,' Cap persisted. 'You're still on R and R.'

'Tell me,' Rainbird repeated gently, and Cap told him. He was with Rainbird for only fifteen minutes, but it seemed an hour. When the big Indian left, Cap breathed a long sigh. Both Wanless and Rainbird in one morning – that would take the snap out of anyone's day. But the morning was over now, a lot had been accomplished, and who knew what might lie ahead this afternoon? He buzzed Rachel.

'Yes, Cap?'

'I'll be eating in, darling. Would you get me something from the cafeteria? It doesn't matter what. Anything. Thank you, Rachel.'

Alone at last. The scrambler phone lay silent on its thick base, filled with microcircuits and memory chips and God alone knew what else. When it buzzed again, it would probably be Albert or Norville to tell him that it was over in New York – the girl taken, her father dead. That would be good news.

Cap closed his eyes again. Thoughts and phrases floated through his mind like large, lazy kites. Mental domination. Their think-tank boys said the possibilities were enormous. Imagine someone like McGee close to Castro, or the Ayatollah Khomeini. Imagine him getting close enough to that pinko Ted Kennedy to suggest in a low voice of utter conviction that suicide was the best answer. Imagine a man like that sicced on the leaders of the various communist guerrilla groups. It was a shame they had to lose him. But . . . what could be made to happen once could be made to happen again.

The little girl. Wanless saying *The power to someday crack the very planet in two like a china plate in a shooting gallery* . . . ridiculous, of course. Wanless had gone as crazy as the little boy in the D. H. Lawrence story, the one who could pick the winners at the racetrack. Lot Six had turned into battery acid for Wanless; it had eaten a number of large, gaping holes in the man's good sense. She was a little *girl*, not a doomsday weapon. And they had to hang onto her at least long enough to document what she was and to chart what she could be. That alone would be enough to reactivate the Lot Six testing program. If she could be persuaded to use her powers for the good of the country, so much the better.

So much the better, Cap thought.

The scrambler phone suddenly uttered its long, hoarse cry.

His pulse suddenly leaping, Cap grabbed it.

The Incident at the
Manders Farm

1

While Cap discussed her future with Al Steinowitz in Longmont, Charlie McGee was sitting on the edge of the motel bed in Unit Sixteen of the Slumberland, yawning and stretching. Bright morning sunlight fell aslant through the window, out of a sky that was a deep and blameless autumn blue. Things seemed so much better in the good daylight.

She looked at her daddy, who was nothing but a motionless hump under the blankets. A fluff of black hair stuck out — that was all. She smiled. He always did his best. If he was hungry and she was hungry and there was only an apple, he would take one bite and make her eat the rest. When he was awake, he always did his best.

But when he was sleeping, he stole all the blankets.

She went into the bathroom, shucked off her underpants, and turned on the shower. She used the toilet while the water got warm and then stepped into the shower stall. The hot water hit her and she closed her eyes, smiling. Nothing in the world was any nicer than the first minute or two in a hot shower.

(you were bad last night)

A frown creased her brow.

(No. Daddy said not.)

(lit that man's shoes on fire, bad girl, very bad, do you like teddy all black?)

The frown deepened. Unease was now tinctured with fear and shame. The idea of her teddy bear never even fully surfaced; it was an underthought, and as so often happened, her guilt seemed to be summed up in a smell — a burned, charred smell. Smoldering cloth and stuffing. And this smell summoned hazy pictures of her mother and father leaning over her, and they were *big* people, giants; and they were scared; they were angry, their voices were big and crackling, like boulders jumping and thudding down a mountainside in a movie.

(*'bad girl! very bad! you mustn't, Charlie! never! never! never!'*)

How old had she been then? Three? Two? How far back could a person remember? She had asked Daddy that once and Daddy said he didn't know. He said he remembered getting a bee sting and his mother had told him that happened when he was only fifteen months old.

This was her earliest memory: the giant faces leaning over her; the big voices like boulders rolling downhill; and a smell like a burned waffle. That smell had been her hair. She had lit her own hair on fire and had burned nearly all of it off. It was after that that Daddy mentioned 'help' and Mommy got all funny, first laughing, then crying, then laughing again so high and strange that Daddy had slapped her face. She remembered that because it was the only time that she knew of that her daddy had done something like that to her mommy. Maybe we ought to think about getting 'help' for her, Daddy had said. They were in the bathroom and her head was wet because Daddy had put her in the shower. Oh, yes, her mommy had said, let's go see Dr Wanless, he'll give us plenty of 'help,' just like he did before . . . then the laughing, the crying, more laughter, and the slap.

(*you were so BAD last night*)

'No.' she murmured in the drumming shower. 'Daddy

114

said not. Daddy said it could have . . . been . . . his . . . face.'

(YOU WERE VERY BAD LAST NIGHT)

But they had needed the change from the telephones. Daddy had said so.

VERY BAD!

And then she began to think about Mommy again, about the time when she had been five, going on six. She didn't like to think about this but the memory was here now and she couldn't put it aside. It had happened just before the bad men had come and hurt Mommy

(killed her, you mean, they killed her)

yes, all right, before they *killed* her, and took Charlie away. Daddy had taken her on his lap for storytime, only he hadn't had the usual storybooks about Pooh and Tigger and Mr Toad and Willy Wonka's Great Glass Elevator. Instead he had a number of thick books with no pictures. She had wrinkled her nose in distaste and asked for Pooh instead.

'No, Charlie,' he had said. 'I want to read you some other stories, and I need you to listen. You're old enough now, I think, and your mother thinks so, too. The stories may scare you a little bit, but they're important. They're true stories.'

She remembered the names of the books Daddy had read the stories from, because the stories *had* scared her. There was a book called *Lo!* by a man named Charles Fort. A book called *Stanger Than Science* by a man named Frank Edwards. A book called *Night's Truth*. And there had been another book called *Pyrokinesis: A Case Book*, but Mommy would not let Daddy read anything from that one. 'Later,' Mommy had said, 'when she's much older, Andy.' And then that book had gone away. Charlie had been glad.

The stories were scary, all right. One was about a man who had burned to death in a park. One was about a lady

115

who had burned up in the living room of her trailer home, and nothing in the whole room had been burned but the lady and a little bit of the chair she had been sitting in while she watched TV. Parts of it had been too complicated for her to understand, but she remembered one thing: a policeman saying: 'We have no explanation for this fatality. There was nothing left of the victim but teeth and a few charred pieces of bone. It would have taken a blowtorch to do that to a person, and nothing around her was even charred. We can't explain why the whole place didn't go up like a rocket.'

The third story had been about a big boy – he was eleven or twelve – who had burned up while he was at the beach. His daddy had put him in the water, burning himself badly in the process, but the boy had still gone on burning until he was all burned up. And a story about a teenage girl who had burned up while explaining all her sins to the priest in the confession room. Charlie knew all about the Catholic confession room because her friend Deenie had told her. Deenie said you had to tell the priest all the bad stuff you had done all week long. Deenie didn't go yet because she hadn't had first holy communion, but her brother Carl did. Carl was in the fourth grade, and he had to tell everything, even the time he sneaked into his mother's room and took some of her birthday chocolates. Because if you didn't tell the priest, you couldn't be washed in THE BLOOD OF CHRIST and you would go to THE HOT PLACE.

The point of all these stories had not been lost on Charlie. She had been so frightened after the one about the girl in the confession room that she burst into tears. 'Am I going to burn myself up?' She wept. 'Like when I was little and caught my hair on fire? Am I going to burn to pieces?'

And Daddy and Mommy had looked upset. Mommy was pale and kept chewing at her lips, but Daddy had put an arm around her and said, 'No, honey. Not if you always remember to be careful and not think about that   . thing. That thing you do sometimes when you're upset and scared.'

'What is it?' Charlie had cried. 'What is it, tell me what is it, I don't even know, I'll never do it, I *promise!*'

Mommy had said, 'As far as we can tell, honey, it's called pyrokinesis. It means being able to light fires sometimes just by thinking about fires. It usually happens when people are upset. Some people apparently have that . that power all their lives and never even know it. And some people . . . well, the power gets hold of them for a minute and they . . .' She couldn't finish.

'They burn themselves up,' Daddy had said. 'Like when you were little and caught your hair on fire, yes. But you can get control of that, Charlie. You *have* to. And God knows it isn't your fault.' His eyes and Mommy's had met for a moment when he said that, and something had seemed to pass between them.

Hugging her around the shoulders, he had said, 'Sometimes you can't help it, I know. It's an accident, like when you were smaller and you forget to go to the bathroom because you were playing and you wet your pants. We used to call that having an accident do you remember?'

'I never do that anymore.'

'No, of course you don't. And in a little while, you'll have control of this other thing in just the same way. But for now, Charlie, you've got to promise us that you'll *never never never* get upset that way if you can help it In that way that makes you start fires. And if you do, if you can't help it, push it *away* from yourself. At a wastebasket or an ashtray. Try to get outside. Try to push it at water, if there's any around.'

'But never at a person, Mommy had said, and her face was still and pale and grave That would be very danger ous, Charlie. That would be a very bad girl. Because you could' – she struggled, forced the words up and out – 'you could kill a person.'

And then Charlie had wept hysterically, tears of terror and remorse, because both of Mommy's hands were bandaged, and she knew why Daddy had read her all the scary stories. Because the day before, when Mommy told her she couldn't go over to Deenie's house because she hadn't picked up her room, Charlie had got *very* angry, and suddenly the firething had been there, popping out of nowhere as it always did, like some evil jack-in-the-box, nodding and grinning, and she had been so angry she had shoved it out of herself and at her mommy and then Mommy's hands had been on fire. And it hadn't been *too* bad

(could have been worse could have been her face)

because the sink had been full of soapy water for the dishes, it hadn't been *too* bad, but it had been *VERY BAD*, and she had promised them both that she would *never never never —*

The warm water drummed on her face, her chest, her shoulders, encasing her in a warm envelope, a cocoon, easing away memories and care. Daddy had *told* her it was all right. And if Daddy said a thing was so, it was. He was the smartest man in the world.

Her mind turned from the past to the present, and she thought about the men who were chasing them. They were from the government, Daddy said, but not a good part of the government. They worked for a part of the government called the Shop. The men chased them and chased them. Everywhere they went, after a little while, those Shop men showed up.

I wonder how they'd like it if I set them on fire? a part of her asked coolly, and she squeezed her eyes shut in guilty horror. It was nasty to think that way. It was bad.

Charlie reached out, grasped the HOT shower faucet, and shut it off with a sudden hard twist of her wrist. For the next two minutes she stood shivering and clutching her slight body under the ice-cold, needling spray, wanting to get out, not allowing herself to.

When you had bad thoughts, you had to pay for them. Deenie had told her so.

2

Andy woke up a little at a time, vaguely aware of the drumming sound of the shower. At first it had been part of a dream: he was on Tashmore Pond with his grandfather and he was eight years old again, trying to get a squirming nightcrawler onto his hook without sticking the hook into his thumb. The dream had been incredibly vivid. He could see the splintery wicker creel in the bow of the boat, he could see the red tire patches on Granther McGee's old green boots, he could see his own old and wrinkled first baseman's mitt, and looking at it made him remember that he had Little League practice tomorrow at Roosevelt Field. But this was tonight, the last light and the drawing dark balanced perfectly on the cusp of twilight, the pond so still that you could see the small clouds of midges and noseeums skimming over its surface, which was the color of chrome. Heat lightning flashed intermittently . . . or maybe it was real lightning, because it was raining. The first drops darkened the wood of Granther's dory, weatherbeaten white, in penny-sized drops. Then you could hear it on the lake, a low and mysterious hissing sound, like—

—like the sound of a—

—*shower, Charlie must be in the shower.*

He opened his eyes and looked at an unfamiliar beamed ceiling. *Where are we?*

It fell back into place a piece at a time, but there was an

instant of frightened free-fall that came of having been in too many places over the last year, of having too many close shaves and being under too much pressure. He thought longingly of his dream and wished he could be back in it with Granther McGee, who had been dead for twenty years now.

Hastings Glen. He was in Hastings Glen. *They* were in Hastings Glen.

He wondered about his head. It hurt, but not like last night, when that bearded guy had let them off. The pain was down to a steady low throb. If this one followed previous history, the throb would be just a faint ache by this evening, and entirely gone by tomorrow.

The shower was turned off.

He sat up in bed and looked at his watch. It was quarter to eleven.

'Charlie?'

She came back into the bedroom, rubbing herself vigorously with a towel.

'Good morning, Daddy.'

'Good morning. How are you?'

'Hungry,' she said. She went over to the chair where she had put her clothes and picked up the green blouse. Sniffed it. Grimaced. 'I need to change my clothes.'

'You'll have to make do with those for a while, babe. We'll get you something later on today.'

'I hope we don't have to wait that long to eat.'

'We'll hitch a ride,' he said, 'and stop at the first café we come to.'

'Daddy, when I started school, you told me never to ride with strangers.' She was into her underpants and green blouse, and was looking at him curiously.

Andy got out of bed, walked over to her, and put his hands on her shoulders. 'The devil you don't know is

120

sometimes better than the one you do,' he said. 'Do you know what that means, keed?'

She thought about it carefully. The devil they knew was those men from the Shop, she guessed. The men that had chased them down the street in New York the day before. The devil they didn't know—

'I guess it means that most people driving cars don't work for that Shop,' she said.

He smiled back. 'You got it. And what I said before still holds, Charlie: when you get into a bad fix, you sometimes have to do things you'd never do if things were going good.'

Charlie's smile faded. Her face became serious, watchful. 'Like getting the money to come out of the phones?'

'Yes,' he said.

'And it wasn't bad?'

'No. Under the circumstances, it wasn't bad.'

'Because when you get into a bad fix, you do what you have to do to get out of it.'

'With some exceptions, yes.'

'What are exceptions, Daddy?'

He ruffled her hair. 'Never mind now, Charlie. Lighten up.'

But she wouldn't. 'And I didn't mean to set that man's shoes on fire. I didn't do it on purpose.'

'No, of course you didn't.'

Then she did lighten up; her smile, so much like Vicky's, came out radiantly. 'How does your head feel this morning, Daddy?'

'Much better, thanks.'

'Good.' She looked at him closely. 'Your eye looks funny.'

'Which eye?'

She pointed at his left. 'That one.'

'Yeah?' He went into the bathroom and wiped a clear place on the steamed mirror.

He looked at his eye for a long time, his good humor fading. His right eye looked just as it always had, a gray green – the color of the ocean on an overcast spring day. His left eye was also gray green, but the white was badly bloodshot, and the pupil looked smaller than the right pupil. And the eyelid had a peculiar droop that he had never noticed before.

Vicky's voice suddenly rang into his mind. It was so clear that she might have been standing beside him. *The headaches, they scare me, Andy. You're doing something to yourself as well as to other people when you use that push or whatever you want to call it.*

The thought was followed by the image of a balloon being blown up . . . and up . . . and up . . . and finally exploding with a loud bang.

He began to go over the left side of his face carefully, touching it everywhere with the tips of his right fingers. He looked like a man in a TV commercial marveling over the closeness of his shave. He found three spots one below his left eye, one on his left cheekbone, and one just below the left temple – where there was no feeling at all. Fright drifted through the hollow places of his body like quiet early-evening mist. The fright was not so much for himself as it was for Charlie, for what would happen to her if she got left on her own.

As if he had called her, he could see her beyond him in the mirror.

'Daddy?' She sounded a little scared. 'You okay?'

'Fine,' he said. His voice sounded good. There was no tremor in it; nor was it too confident, falsely booming. 'Just thinking how much I need a shave.'

She put a hand over her mouth and giggled. 'Scratchy like a Brillo pad. Yuck. Gross.'

He chased her into the bedroom and rubbed his scratchy cheek against her smooth one. Charlie giggled and kicked.

3

As Andy was tickling his daughter with his stubbly beard, Orville Jamieson, aka OJ, aka The Juice, and another Shop agent named Bruce Cook were getting out of a light-blue Chevy outside the Hastings Diner.

OJ paused for a moment, looking down Main Street with its slant parking, its appliance store, its grocery store, its two gas stations, its one drugstore, its wooden municipal building with a plaque out front commemorating some historical event no one gave a shit about. Main Street was also Route 40, and the McGees were not four miles from where OJ and Bruce Cook now stood.

'Look at this burg,' OJ said, disgusted. 'I grew up close to here. Town called Lowville. You ever hear of Lowville, New York?'

Bruce Cook shook his head.

'It's near Utica, too. Where they make Utica Club beer. I was never so happy in my life as I was the day I got out of Lowville.' OJ reached under his jacket and readjusted The Windsucker in its holster.

'There's Tom and Steve,' Bruce said. Across the street, a light-brown Pacer had pulled into a parking slot just vacated by a farm truck. Two men in dark suits were getting out of the Pacer. They looked like bankers. Farther down the street, at the blinker light, two more Shop people were talking to the old cunt that crossed the school kids at lunchtime. They were showing her the picture and she was shaking her head. There were ten Shop agents here in Hastings Glen, all of them coordinating with Norville Bates, who was back in Albany waiting for Cap's personal ramrod, Al Steinowitz.

'Yeah, Lowville,' OJ sighed. 'I hope we get those two suckers by noon. And I hope my next assignment's Karachi. Or Iceland. Any place, as long as it's not upstate New York. This is too close to Lowville. Too close for comfort.'

'You think we will have them by noon?' Bruce asked.

OJ shrugged. 'We'll have them by the time the sun goes down. You can count on that.'

They went into the diner, sat at the counter, and ordered coffee. A young waitress with a fine figure brought it to them.

'How long you been on, sis?' OJ asked her.

'If you got a sis, I pity her,' the waitress said. 'If there's any fambly resemblance, that is.'

'Don't be that way, sis,' OJ said, and showed her his ID. She looked at it a long time. Behind her, an aging juvenile delinquent in a motorcycle jacket was pushing buttons on a Seeberg.

'I been on since seven,' she said. 'Same as any other morning. Prolly you want to talk to Mike. He's the owner.' She started to turn away and OJ caught her wrist in a tight grip. He didn't like women who made fun of his looks. Most women were sluts anyway, his mother had been right about that even if she hadn't been right about much else. And his mother surely would have known what to think about a high-tit bitch like this one.

'Did I say I wanted to talk to the owner, sis?'

She was starting to be frightened now, and that was okay with OJ. 'N-no.'

'That's right. Because I want to talk to you, not to some guy that's been out in the kitchen scrambling eggs and making Alpoburgers all morning.' He took the picture of Andy and Charlie out of his pocket and handed it to her, not letting go of her wrist. 'You recognize them, sis? Serve them their breakfast this morning, maybe?'

'Let go. You're *hurting* me.' All the color had gone out of her face except for the whore's rouge she had tricked herself up with. Probably she had been a cheerleader in high school. The kind of girl who laughed at Orville Jamieson when he asked them out because he had been president of the Chess Club instead of quarterback on the football team. Bunch of cheap Lowville whores. God, he hated New York. Even New York City was too fucking close.

'You tell me if you waited on them or if you didn't. Then I'll let go. *Sis.*'

She looked briefly at the picture. 'No! I didn't. Now let—'

'You didn't look long enough, *sis.* You better look again.'

She looked again. 'No! No!' she said loudly. 'I've never seen them! Let me go, can't you?'

The elderly jd in the cut-rate Mammoth Mart leather jacket sauntered over, zippers jingling, thumbs hooked in his pants pockets.

'You're bothering the lady,' he said.

Bruce Cook gazed at him with open, wide-eyed contempt. 'Be careful we don't decide to bother you next, pizza-face,' he said.

'Oh,' the old kid in the leather jacket said, and his voice was suddenly very small. He moved away quickly, apparently remembering that he had pressing business on the street.

Two old ladies in a booth were nervously watching the little scene at the counter. A big man in reasonably clean cook's whites – Mike, the owner, presumably – was standing in the kitchen doorway, also watching. He held a butcher knife in one hand, but he held it with no great authority.

'What do you guys want?' he asked.

'They're feds,' the waitress said nervously. 'They—'

'Didn't serve them? You're sure?' OJ asked. '*Sis?*'

'I'm sure,' she said. She was nearly crying now.

'You better be. A mistake can get you five years in jail, *sis.*'

'I'm sure,' she whispered. A tear spilled over the bottom curve of one eye and slipped down her cheek. 'Please let go. Don't hurt me anymore.'

OJ squeezed tighter for one brief moment, liking the feel of the small bones moving under his hand, liking the knowledge that he could squeeze harder yet and snap them . . . and then he let go. The diner was silent except for the voice of Stevie Wonder coming from the Seeberg, assuring the frightened patrons of the Hastings Diner that they could feel it all over. Then the two old ladies got up and left in a hurry.

OJ picked up his coffee cup, leaned over the counter, poured the coffee on the floor, and then dropped the cup, which shattered. Thick china shrapnel sprayed in a dozen different directions. The waitress was crying openly now.

'Shitty brew,' OJ said.

The owner made a halfhearted gesture with the knife, and OJ's face seemed to light up.

'Come on, man,' he said, half-laughing. 'Come on. Let's see you try.'

Mike put the knife down beside the toaster and suddenly cried out in shame and outrage: 'I fought in Vietnam! My brother fought in Vietnam! I'm gonna write my congressman about this! You wait and see if I don't!'

OJ looked at him. After a while Mike lowered his eyes, scared.

The two of them went out.

The waitress scooched and began to pick up broken pieces of coffee cup, sobbing.

Outside, Bruce said, 'How many motels?'

'Three motels, six sets of tourist cabins,' OJ said, looking

126

down toward the blinker. It fascinated him. In the Lowville of his youth there had been a diner with a plaque over the double Silex hotplate and that plaque had read IF YOU DON'T LIKE OUR TOWN, LOOK FOR A TIMETABLE. How many times had he longed to pull that plaque off the wall and stuff it down someone's throat?

'There are people checking them out,' he said as they walked back toward their light-blue Chevrolet, part of a government motor pool paid for and maintained by tax dollars. 'We'll know soon now.'

4

John Mayo was with an agent named Ray Knowles. They were on their way out along Route 40 to the Slumberland Motel. They were driving a late-model tan Ford, and as they rode up the last hill separating them from an actual view of the motel, a tire blew.

'Shit-*fire*,' John said as the car began to pogo up and down and drag to the right. 'That's fucking government issue for you. Fucking retreads.' He pulled over onto the soft shoulder and put on the Ford's four-way flashers. 'You go on,' he said. 'I'll change the goddam tire.'

'I'll help,' Ray said. 'It won't take us five minutes.'

'No, go on. It's right over this hill, should be.'

'You sure?'

'Yeah. I'll pick you up. Unless the spare's flat, too. It wouldn't surprise me.'

A rattling farm truck passed them. It was the one OJ and Bruce Cook had seen leaving town as they stood outside the Hastings Diner.

Ray grinned. 'It better not be. You'd have to put in a requisition in quadruplicate for a new one.'

John didn't grin back. 'Don't I know it,' he said glumly.

They went around to the trunk and Ray unlocked it. The spare was in good shape.

'Okay,' John said. 'Go on.'

'It really wouldn't take but five minutes to change that sucker.'

'Sure, and those two aren't at that motel. But let's play it as if it were real. After all, they have to be somewhere.'

'Yeah, okay.'

John took the jack and spare out of the trunk. Ray Knowles watched him for a moment and then started walking along the shoulder toward the Slumberland Motel.

5

Just beyond the motel, Andy and Charlie McGee were standing on the soft shoulder of Highway 40. Andy's worries that someone might notice he didn't have a car had proved groundless; the woman in the office was interested in nothing but the small Hitachi TV on the counter. A miniature Phil Donahue had been captured inside, and the woman was watching him avidly. She swept the key Andy offered into the mail slot without even looking away from the picture.

'Hope y'enjoyed y'stay,' she said. She was working on a box of chocolate coconut doughnuts and had got to the halfway mark.

'Sure did,' Andy said, and left.

Charlie was waiting for him outside. The woman had given him a carbon copy of his bill, which he stuffed into the side pocket of his cord jacket as he went down the steps. Change from the Albany pay phones jingled mutedly.

'Okay, Daddy?' Charlie asked as they moved away toward the road.

'Lookin good,' he said, and put an arm around her

shoulders. To their right and back over the hill, Ray Knowles and John Mayo had just had their flat tire.

'Where are we going, Daddy?' Charlie asked.

'I don't know,' he said.

'I don't like it. I feel nervous.'

'I think we're well ahead of them,' he said. 'Don't worry. They're probably still looking for the cab driver who took us to Albany.'

But he was whistling past the graveyard; he knew it and probably Charlie did, too. Just standing here beside the road made him feel exposed, like a cartoon jailbird in a striped suit. Quit it, he told himself. Next thing you'll be thinking they're everywhere – one behind every tree and a bunch of them right over the next hill. Hadn't somebody said that perfect paranoia and perfect awareness were the same thing?

'Charlie–' he began.

'Let's go to Granther's,' she said.

He looked at her, startled. His dream rushed back at him, the dream of fishing in the rain, the rain that had turned into the sound of Charlie's shower. 'What made you think of that?' he asked. Granther had died long before Charlie was born. He had lived his whole life in Tashmore, Vermont, a town just west of the New Hampshire border. When Granther died, the place on the lake went to Andy's mother, and when she died, it came to Andy. The town would have taken it for back taxes long since, except that Granther had left a small sum in trust to cover them.

Andy and Vicky had gone up there once a year during the summer vacation until Charlie was born. It was twenty miles off the nearest two-lane road, in wooded, unpopulated country. In the summer there were all sorts of people on Tashmore Pond, which was really a lake with the small town of Bradford, New Hampshire, on the far side. But by this time of year all the summer camps would be empty. Andy doubted if the road in was even plowed in the winter.

'I don't know,' Charlie said. 'It just . . . came into my mind. This minute.' On the other side of the hill, John Mayo was opening the trunk of the Ford and making his inspection of the spare tire.

'I dreamed about Granther this morning,' Andy said slowly. 'First time I'd thought about him in a year or more, I guess. So I suppose you could say he just came into my head, too.'

'Was it a good dream, Daddy?'

'Yes,' he said, and smiled a little. 'Yes, it was.'

'Well, what do you think?'

'I think it's a great idea,' Andy said. 'We can go there and stay for a while and think about what we should do. How we should handle this. I was thinking if we could get to a newspaper and tell our story so that a lot of people knew about it, they'd have to lay off.'

An old farm truck was rattling toward them, and Andy stuck out his thumb. On the other side of the hill, Ray Knowles was walking up the soft shoulder of the road.

The farm truck pulled over, and a guy wearing biballs and a New York Mets baseball cap looked out.

'Well there's a purty little miss,' he said, smiling. 'What's your name, missy?'

'Roberta,' Charlie said promptly. Roberta was her middle name.

'Well, Bobbi, where you headed this morning?' the driver asked.

'We're on our way to Vermont,' Andy said. 'St Johnsbury. My wife was visiting her sister and she ran into a little problem.'

'Did she now,' the farmer said, and said no more, but gazed at Andy shrewdly from the corners of his eyes.

'Labor,' Andy said, and manufactured a wide smile. 'This one's got a new brother. One-forty-one this morning.'

'His name is Andy,' Charlie said. 'Isn't that a nice name?'

'I think it's a corker,' the farmer said. 'You hop on in here and I'll get you ten miles closer to St Johnsbury, anyhow.'

They got in and the farm truck rattled and rumbled back onto the road, headed into the bright morning sunlight. At the same time, Ray Knowles was breasting the hill. He saw an empty highway leading down to the Slumberland Motel. Beyond the Motel, he saw the farm truck that had passed their car a few minutes ago just disappearing from view.

He saw no need to hurry.

6

The farmer's name was Manders – Irv Manders. He had just taken a load of pumpkins into town, where he had a deal with the fellow who ran the A&P. He told them that he used to deal with the First National, but the fellow over there just had no understanding about pumpkins. A jumped-up meat cutter and no more, was the opinion of Irv Manders. The A&P manager, on the other hand, was a corker. He told them that his wife ran a touristy sort of shop in the summertime, and he kept a roadside produce stand, and between the two of them they got along right smart.

'You won't like me minding your beeswax,' Irv Manders told Andy, 'but you and your button here shouldn't be thumbin. Lord, no. Not with the sort of people you find ramming the roads these days. There's a Greyhound terminal in the drugstore back in Hastings Glen. That's what you want.'

'Well—' Andy said. He was nonplussed, but Charlie stepped neatly into the breach.

'Daddy's out of work,' she said brightly. 'That's why my mommy had to go and stay with Auntie Em to have the baby. Auntie Em doesn't like Daddy. So we stayed at home. But now we're going to see Mommy. Right, Daddy?'

'That's sort of private stuff, Bobbi,' Andy said, sounding uncomfortable. He *felt* uncomfortable. There were a thousand holes in Charlie's story.

'Don't you say another word,' Irv said. 'I know about trouble in families. It can get pretty bitter at times. And I know about being hard-up. It ain't no shame.'

Andy cleared his throat but said nothing. He could think of nothing to say. They rode in silence for a while.

'Say, why don't you two come home and take lunch with me and the wife?' Irv asked suddenly.

'Oh no, we couldn't do—'

'We'd be happy to,' Charlie said. 'Wouldn't we, Daddy?'

He knew that Charlie's intuitions were usually good ones, and he was too mentally and physically worn down to go against her now. She was a self-possessed and aggressive little girl, and more than once Andy had wondered to himself just who was running this show.

'If you're sure there's enough—' he said.

'Always enough,' Irv Manders said, finally shifting the farm truck into third gear. They were rattling between autumn-bright trees: maples, elms, poplars. 'Glad to have you.'

'Thank you very much,' Charlie said.

'My pleasure, button,' Irv said. 'Be my wife's, too, when she gets a look at you.'

Charlie smiled.

Andy rubbed his temples. Beneath the fingers of his left hand was one of those patches of skin where the nerves seemed to have died. He didn't feel good about this, somehow. That feeling that they were closing in was still very much with him.

7

The woman who had checked Andy out of the Slumberland Motel not twenty minutes ago was getting nervous. She had forgotten all about Phil Donahue.

'You're sure this was the man,' Ray Knowles was saying for the third time. She didn't like this small, trim, somehow tight man. Maybe he worked for the government, but that was no comfort to Lena Cunningham. She didn't like his narrow face, she didn't like the lines around his cool blue eyes, and most of all she didn't like the way he kept shoving that picture under her nose.

'Yes, that was him,' she said again. 'But there was no little girl with him. Honest, mister. My husband'll tell you the same. He works nights. It's got so we hardly ever see each other, except at supper. He'll tell—'

The other man came back in, and with ever-mounting alarm, Lena saw that he had a walkie-talkie in one hand and a great big pistol in the other.

'It was them,' John Mayo said. He was almost hysterical with anger and disappointment. 'Two people slept in that bed. Blond hairs on one pillow, black on the other. Goddam that flat tire! Goddam it all to hell! Damp towels hanging on the rod in the bathroom! Fucking shower's still dripping! We missed them by maybe five minutes, Ray!'

He jammed the pistol back into its shoulder holster.

'I'll get my husband,' Lena said faintly.

'Never mind,' Ray said. He took John's arm and led him outside. John was still swearing about the flat. 'Forget the tire, John. Did you talk to OJ back in town?'

'I talked to him and he talked to Norville. Norville's on

133

his way from Albany, and he's got Al Steinowitz with him. He landed not ten minutes ago.'

'Well, that's good. Listen, think a minute, Johnny. They must have been hitching.'

'Yeah, I guess so. Unless they boosted a car.'

'The guy's an English instructor. He wouldn't know how to boost a candy bar out of a concession stand in a home for the blind. They were hitching, all right. They hitched from Albany last night. They hitched this morning. I'd bet you this year's salary that they were standing there by the side of the road with their thumbs out while I was walking up that hill.'

'If it hadn't been for that flat—' John's eyes were miserable behind his wire-framed glasses. He saw a promotion flapping away on slow, lazy wings.

'Fuck the flat!' Ray said. 'What passed us? After we got the flat, what passed us?'

John thought about it as he hooked the walkie-talkie back on his belt. 'Farm truck,' he said.

'That's what I remember, too,' Ray said. He glanced around and saw Lena Cunningham's large moon face peering out the motel office window at them. She saw him seeing her and the curtain fell back into place.

'Pretty rickety truck,' Ray said. 'If they don't turn off the main road, we ought to be able to catch up to them.'

'Let's go, then,' John said. 'We can keep in touch with Al and Norville by way of OJ on the walkie-talkie.'

They trotted back to the car and got in. A moment later the tan Ford roared out of the parking lot, spewing white crushed gravel out from beneath its rear tires. Lena Cunningham watched them go with relief. Running a motel was not what it once had been.

She went back to wake up her husband.

8

As the Ford with Ray Knowles behind the wheel and John Mayo riding shotgun was roaring down Route 40 at better than seventy miles an hour (and as a caravan of ten or eleven similar nondescript late-model cars were heading toward Hastings Glen from the surrounding areas of search), Irv Manders hand-signaled left and turned off the highway onto an unmarked stretch of tar-and-patch that headed roughly northeast. The truck rattled and banged along. At his urging, Charlie had sung most of her nine-song repertoire, including such golden hits as 'Happy Birthday to You,' 'This Old Man,' 'Jesus Loves Me,' and 'Camptown Races.' Irv and Andy both sang along with that one.

The road twisted and wound its way over a series of increasingly wooded ridges and then began to descend toward flatter country that had been cultivated and harvested. Once a partridge burst from a cover of goldenrod and old hay at the left side of the road and Irv shouted, 'Get im, Bobbi!' and Charlie pointed her finger and chanted '*Bam-ba-DAM!*' and then giggled wildly.

A few minutes later Irv turned off on a dirt road, and a mile farther along they came to a battered red, white, and blue mailbox with MANDERS stenciled on the side. Irv turned into a rutted driveway that was nearly half a mile long.

'Must cost you an arm and a leg to keep it plowed in the winter,' Andy said.

'Do it m'self,' Irv said.

They came to a big white frame farmhouse, three stories tall and set off with mint-green trim. To Andy it looked like the sort of house that might have started off fairly ordinary and then grown eccentric as the years passed. Two sheds were attached to the rear, one of them zigging thisaway, the other zagging thataway. On the south side, a greenhouse wing had been added, and a big screened-in porch stood out from the north side like a stiff skirt.

Behind the house was a red barn that had seen better days, and between the house and the barn was what New Englanders call a dooryard – a flat dirt stretch of ground where a couple of dozen chickens clucked and strutted. When the truck rattled toward them they fled, squawking and fluttering their useless wings, past a chopping block with an ax buried in it.

Irv drove the truck into the barn, which had a sweet hay smell Andy remembered from his summers in Vermont. When Irv switched the truck off, they all heard a low, musical mooing from somewhere deeper in the barn's shadowy interior.

'You got a *cow*,' Charlie said, and something like rapture came over her face. 'I can *hear* it.'

'We've got three,' Irv said. 'That's Bossy you hear – a very original name, wouldn't you say, button? She thinks she's got to be milked three times a day. You can see her later, if your daddy says you can.'

'Can I, Daddy?'

'I guess so,' Andy said, mentally surrendering. Somehow they had gone out beside the road to thumb a ride and had got shanghaied instead.

'Come on in and meet the wife.'

They strolled across the dooryard, pausing for Charlie to examine as many of the chickens as she could get close to. The back door opened and a woman of about forty-five came out onto the back steps. She shaded her eyes and called, 'You there, Irv! Who you brought home?'

Irv smiled. 'Well, the button here is Roberta. This fellow is her daddy. I didn't catch his name yet, so I dunno if we're related.'

Andy stepped forward and said, 'I'm Frank Burton,

ma'am. Your husband invited Bobbi and me home for lunch, if that's all right. We're pleased to know you.'

'Me too,' Charlie said, still more interested in the chickens than in the woman – at least for the moment.

'I'm Norma Manders,' she said. 'Come in. You're welcome.' But Andy saw the puzzled look she threw at her husband.

They all went inside, through an entryway where stovelengths were stacked head high and into a huge kitchen that was dominated by a woodstove and a long table covered with red and white checked oilcloth. There was an elusive smell of fruit and paraffin in the air. The smell of canning, Andy thought.

'Frank here and his button are on their way to Vermont,' Irv said. 'I thought it wouldn't hurt em to get outside of a little hot food on their way.'

'Of course not,' she agreed. 'Where is your car, Mr Burton?'

'Well—' Andy began. He glanced at Charlie, but she was going to be no help; she was walking around the kitchen in small steps, looking at everything with a child's frank curiosity.

'Frank's had a little trouble,' Irv said, looking directly at his wife. 'But we don't have to talk about that. At least, not right now.'

'All right,' Norma said. She had a sweet and direct face – a handsome woman who was used to working hard. Her hands were red and chapped. 'I've got chicken and I could put together a nice salad. And there's lots of milk. Do you like milk, Roberta?'

Charlie didn't look around. She's lapsed on the name, Andy thought. Oh, Jesus, this just gets better and better.

'Bobbi!' he said loudly.

She looked around then, and smiled a little too widely. 'Oh, sure,' she said. 'I love milk.'

Andy saw a warning glance pass from Irv to his wife: *No questions, not now.* He felt a sinking despair. Whatever had been left of their story had just gone swirling away. But there was nothing to do except sit down to lunch and wait to see what Irv Manders had on his mind.

9

'How far from the motel are we?' John Mayo asked.

Ray glanced down at the odometer. 'Seventeen miles,' he said, and pulled over. 'That's far enough.'

'But maybe—'

'No, if we were going to catch them, we would have by now. We'll go on back and rendezvous with the others.'

John struck the heel of his hand against the dashboard. 'They turned off somewhere,' he said. 'That goddam flat shoe! This job's been bad luck from the start, Ray. An egghead and a little girl. And we keep missing them.'

'No, I think we've got them,' Ray said, and took out his walkie-talkie. He pulled the antenna and tipped it out the window. 'We'll have a cordon around the whole area in half an hour. And I bet we don't hit a dozen houses before someone around here recognizes that truck. Late-sixties dark-green International Harvester, snowplow attachment on the front, wooden stakes around the truck bed to hold on a high load. I still think we'll have them by dark.'

A moment later he was talking to Al Steinowitz, who was nearing the Slumberland Motel. Al briefed his agents in turn. Bruce Cook remembered the farm truck from town. OJ did, too. It had been parked in front of the A&P.

Al sent them back to town, and half an hour later they all knew that the truck that had almost certainly stopped to give the two fugitives a lift belonged to Irving Manders, RFD #5, Baillings Road, Hastings Glen, New York.

It was just past twelve-thirty P.M.

138

10

The lunch was very nice. Charlie ate like a horse – three helpings of chicken with gravy, two of Norma Manders's hot biscuits, a side dish of salad, and three of her home-canned dill pickles. They finished off with slices of apple pie garnished with wedges of cheddar – Irv offering his opinion that 'Apple pie without a piece of cheese is like a smooch without a squeeze.' This earned him an affectionate elbow in the side from his wife. Irv rolled his eyes, and Charlie laughed. Andy's appetite surprised him. Charlie belched and then covered her mouth guiltily.

Irv smiled at her. 'More room out than there is in, button.'

'If I eat any more, I think I'll split,' Charlie answered. 'That's what my mother always used to . . . I mean, that's what she always says.'

Andy smiled tiredly.

'Norma,' Irv said, getting up, 'why don't you and Bobbi go on out and feed those chickens?'

'Well, lunch is still spread over half an acre,' Norma said.

'I'll pick up lunch,' Irv said. 'Want to have a little talk with Frank, here.'

'Would you like to feed the chickens, honey?' Norma asked Charlie.

'I sure would.' Her eyes were sparkling.

'Well, come on then. Do you have a jacket? It's turned a bit chilly.'

'Uh . . .' Charlie looked at Andy.

'You can borrow a sweater of mine,' Norma said. That look passed between her and Irv again. 'Roll the sleeves up a little bit and it will be fine.'

'Okay.'

Norma got an old and faded warmup jacket from the

entryway and a frayed white sweater that Charlie floated in, even with the cuffs turned up three or four times.

'Do they peck?' Charlie asked a little nervously.

'Only their food, honey.'

They went out and the door closed behind them. Charlie was still chattering. Andy looked at Irv Manders, and Irv looked back calmly.

'You want a beer, Frank?'

'It isn't Frank,' Andy said. 'I guess you know that.'

'I guess I do. What is your handle?'

Andy said, 'The less you know, the better off you are.'

'Well, then,' Irv said, 'I'll just call you Frank.'

Faintly, they heard Charlie squeal with delight from outside. Norma said something, and Charlie agreed.

'I guess I could use a beer,' Andy said.

'Okay.'

Irv got two Utica Clubs from the refrigerator, opened them, set Andy's on the table and his on the counter. He got an apron from a hook by the sink and put it on. The apron was red and yellow and the hem was flounced, but somehow he managed to avoid looking silly.

'Can I help you?' Andy asked.

'No, I know where everything goes,' Irv said. 'Most everything, anyhow. She changes things from week to week. No woman wants a man to feel right at home in her kitchen. They like help, sure, but they feel better if you have to ask them where to put the casserole dish or where they put the Brillo.'

Andy, remembering his own days as Vicky's kitchen apprentice, smiled and nodded.

'Meddling around in other folk's business isn't my strong point,' Irv said, drawing water in the kitchen sink and adding detergent. 'I'm a farmer, and like I told you, my wife runs a little curio shop down where Baillings Road crosses the Albany Highway. We've been here almost twenty years.'

He glanced back at Andy.

'But I knew there was somethin wrong from the minute I saw you two standing by the road back there. A grown man and a little girl just aren't the kind of pair you usually see hitching the roads. Know what I mean?'

Andy nodded and sipped his beer.

'Furthermore, it looked to me like you'd just come out of the Slumberland, but you had no traveling gear, not so much as an overnight case. So I just about decided to pass you by. Then I stopped. Because . . . well, there's a difference between not meddling in other folks' business and seeing something that looks damn bad and turning a blind eye to it.'

'Is that how we look to you? Damn bad?'

'Then,' Irv said, 'not now.' He was washing the old mismatched dishes carefully, stacking them in the drainer. 'Now I don't know just what to make of you two. My first thought was it must be you two the cops are looking for.' He saw the change come over Andy's face and the sudden way Andy set his beer can down. 'I guess it is you,' he said softly. 'I was hopin it wasn't.'

'What cops?' Andy asked harshly.

'They've got all the main roads blocked off coming in and out of Albany,' Irv said. 'If we'd gone another six miles up Route Forty, we would have run on one of those blocks right where Forty crosses Route Nine.'

'Well, why didn't you just go ahead?' Andy asked. 'That would have been the end of it for you. You would have been out of it.'

Irv was starting on the pots now, pausing to hunt through the cupboards over the sink. 'See what I was saying? I can't find the gloriosky Brillo   Wait, here it is   Why didn't I just take you up the road to the cops? Let's say I wanted to satisfy my own natural curiosity.'

'You have some questions, huh?'

'All kinds of them,' Irv said. 'A grown man and a little girl hitching rides, the little girl hasn't got any overnight case, and the cops are after them. So I have an idea. It isn't so farfetched. I think that maybe here's a daddy who wanted custody of his button and couldn't get it. So he snatched her.'

'It sounds pretty farfetched to me.'

'Happens all the time, Frank. And I think to myself, the mommy didn't like that so well and swore out a warrant on the daddy. That would explain all the roadblocks. You only get coverage like that for a big robbery . . . or a kidnapping.'

'She's my daughter, but her mother didn't put the police on us,' Andy said. 'Her mother has been dead for a year.'

'Well, I'd already kind of shitcanned the idea,' Irv said. 'It don't take a private eye to see the two of you are pretty close. Whatever else may be going on, it doesn't appear you've got her against her will.'

Andy said nothing.

'So here we are at my problem,' Irv said. 'I picked the two of you up because I thought the little girl might need help. Now I don't know where I'm at. You don't strike me as the desperado type. But all the same, you and your little girl are going under false names, you're telling a story that's just as thin as a piece of tissue paper, and you look sick, Frank. You look just about as sick as a man can get and still stay on his feet. So those are my questions. Any you could answer, it might be a good thing.'

'We came to Albany from New York and hitched a ride to Hastings Glen early this morning,' Andy said. 'It's bad to know they're here, but I think I knew it. I think Charlie knew it, too.' He had mentioned Charlie's name, and that was a mistake, but at this point it didn't seem to matter.

'What do they want you for, Frank?'

Andy thought for a long time, and then he met Irv's frank gray eyes. He said: 'You came from town, didn't you? See any strange people there? City types? Wearing these neat, off-the-rack suits that you forget almost as soon as the guys wearing them are out of sight? Driving late-model cars that sort of just fade into the scenery?'

It was Irv's turn to think. 'There were two guys like that in the A&P,' he said. 'Talking to Helga. She's one of the checkers. Looked like they were showing her something.'

'Probably our picture,' Andy said. 'They're government agents. They're working with the police, Irv. A more accurate way of putting it would be that the police are working for them. The cops don't know why we're wanted.'

'What sort of government agency we talking about? FBI?'

'No. The Shop.'

'What? That CIA outfit?' Irv looked frankly disbelieving.

'They don't have anything at all to do with the CIA,' Andy said. 'The Shop is really the DSI – Department of Scientific Intelligence. I read in an article about three years ago that some wiseacre nicknamed it the Shop in the early sixties, after a science-fiction story called "The Weapon Shops of Ishtar." By a guy named van Vogt, I think, but that doesn't matter. What they're supposed to be involved in are domestic scientific projects which may have present or future application to matters bearing on national security. That definition is from their charter, and the thing they're most associated with in the public mind is the energy research they're funding and supervising – electro-magnetic stuff and fusion power. They're actually involved in a lot more. Charlie and I are part of an experiment that happened a long time ago. It happened before Charlie was even born. Her mother was also involved. She was murdered. The Shop was responsible.'

Irv was silent for a while. He let the dishwater out of the sink, dried his hands, and then came over and began to wipe the oilcloth that covered the table. Andy picked up his beer can.

'I won't say flat out that I don't believe you,' Irv said finally. 'Not with some of the things that have gone on under cover in this country and then come out. CIA guys giving people drinks spiked with LSD and some FBI agent accused of killing people during the Civil Rights marches and money in brown bags and all of that. So I can't say right out that I don't believe you. Let's just say you haven't convinced me yet.'

'I don't think it's even me that they really want anymore,' Andy said. 'Maybe it was, once. But they've shifted targets. It's Charlie they're after now.'

'You mean the national government is after a first- or second-grader for reasons of national security?'

'Charlie's no ordinary second-grader,' Andy said. 'Her mother and I were injected with a drug which was coded Lot Six. To this day I don't know exactly what it was. Some sort of synthetic glandular secretion would be my best guess. It changed the chromosomes of myself and of the lady I later married. We passed those chromosomes on to Charlie, and they mixed in some entirely new way. If she could pass them on to her children, I guess she'd be called a mutant. If for some reason she can't, or if the change has caused her to be sterile, I guess she'd be called a sport or a mule. Either way, they want her. They ·vant to study her, see if they can figure out what makes her able to do what she can do. And even more, I think they want her as an exhibit. They want to use her to reactivate the Lot Six program.'

'What is it she can do?' Irv asked.

Through the kitchen window they could see Norma and Charlie coming out of the barn. The white sweater flopped and swung around Charlie's body, the hem coming down to her calves. There was high color in her cheeks, and she was talking to Norma, who was smiling and nodding.

Andy said softly, 'She can light fires.'

'Well, so can I,' Irv said. He sat down again and was looking at Andy in a peculiar, cautious way. The way you look at people you suspect of madness.

'She can do it simply by thinking about it,' Andy said. 'The technical name for it is pyrokinesis. It's a psi talent, like telepathy, telekinesis, or precognition – Charlie has a dash of some of those as well, by the way – but pyrokinesis is much rarer . . . and much more dangerous. She's very much afraid of it, and she's right to be. She can't always control it. She could burn up your house, your barn, or your front yard if she set her mind to it. Or she could light your pipe.' Andy smiled wanly. 'Except that while she was lighting your pipe, she might also burn up your house, your barn, and your front yard.'

Irv finished his beer and said, 'I think you ought to call the police and turn yourself in, Frank. You need help.'

'I guess it sounds pretty nutty, doesn't it?'

'Yes,' Irv said gravely. 'It sounds nutty as anything I ever heard.' He was sitting lightly, slightly tense on his chair, and Andy thought, *He's expecting me to do something loony the first chance I get.*

'I suppose it doesn't matter much anyway,' Andy said. 'They'll be here soon enough. I think the police would actually be better. At least you don't turn into an unperson as soon as the police get their hands on you.'

Irv started to reply, and then the door opened. Norma and Charlie came in. Charlie's face was bright, her eyes sparkling. 'Daddy!' she said. 'Daddy, I fed the—'

She broke off. Some of the color left her cheeks, and she looked narrowly from Irv Manders to her father and back to Irv again. Pleasure faded from her face and was replaced with a look of harried misery. *The way she looked last night*, Andy thought. *The way she looked yesterday when I grabbed her out of school. It goes on and on, and where's the happy ending for her?*

'You told,' she said. 'Oh Daddy, why did you tell?'

Norma stepped forward and put a protective arm around Charlie's shoulders. 'Irv, what's going on here?'

'I don't know,' Irv said. 'What do you mean he told, Bobbi?'

'That's not my name,' she said. Tears had appeared in her eyes. 'You know that's not my name.'

'Charlie,' Andy said. 'Mr Manders knew something was wrong. I told him, but he didn't believe me. When you think about it, you'll understand why.'

'I don't understand anyth—' Charlie began, her voice rising stridently. Then she was quiet. Her head cocked sideways in a peculiar listening gesture, although as far as any of the others could tell there was nothing to listen to. As they watched, Charlie's face simply drained of color; it was like watching some rich liquid poured out of a pitcher.

'What's the matter, honey?' Norma asked, and cast a worried glance at Irv.

'They're coming, Daddy,' Charlie whispered. Her eyes were wide circles of fear. 'They're coming for us.'

11

They had rendezvoused at the corner of Highway 40 and the unnumbered blacktop road Irv had turned down – on the Hastings Glen town maps it was marked as the Old Baillings Road. Al Steinowitz had finally caught up with the rest of his men and had taken over quickly and decisively. There were sixteen of them in five cars. Heading up the road toward Irv Manders's place, they looked like a fast-moving funeral procession.

Norville Bates had handed over the reins – and the responsibility – of the operation to Al with genuine relief and with a question about the local and state police who had been rung in on the operation.

'We're keeping this one dark for now,' Al said. 'If we get them, we'll tell them they can fold their roadblocks. If we don't, we'll tell them to start moving in toward the center of the circle. But between you and me, if we can't handle them with sixteen men, we can't handle them, Norv.'

Norv sensed the mild rebuke and said no more. He knew it would be best to take the two of them with no outside interference, because Andrew McGee was going to have an unfortunate accident as soon as they got him. A fatal accident. With no bluesuits hanging around, it could happen that much sooner.

Ahead of him and Al, the brakelights of OJ's car flashed briefly, and then the car turned onto a dirt road. The others followed.

12

'I don't understand any of this,' Norma said. 'Bobbi . . . Charlie . . . can't you calm down?'

'You don't understand,' Charlie said. Her voice was high and strangled. Looking at her made Irv jumpy. Her face was like that of a rabbit caught in a snare. She pulled free of Norma's arm and ran to her father, who put his hands on her shoulders.

'I think they're going to kill you, Daddy,' she said.

'What?'

'Kill you,' she repeated. Her eyes were staring and

glazed with panic. Her mouth worked frantically. 'We have to run. We have to—'

Hot. Too hot in here.

He glanced to his left. Mounted on the wall between the stove and the sink was an indoor thermometer, the kind that can be purchased from any mail-order catalogue. At the bottom of this one, a plastic red devil with a pitchfork was grinning and mopping his brow. The motto beneath his cloven hooves read: HOT ENOUGH FOR YA?

The mercury in the thermometer was slowly rising, an accusing red finger.

'Yes, that's what they want to do,' she said. 'Kill you, kill you like they did Mommy, take me away, I won't, I won't let it happen, *I won't let it—*'

Her voice was rising. Rising like the column of mercury.

'*Charlie!* Watch what you're doing!'

Her eyes cleared a little. Irv and his wife had drawn together.

'Irv . . . what—?'

But Irv had seen Andy's glance at the thermometer, and suddenly he believed. It was hot in here now. Hot enough to sweat. The mercury in the thermometer stood just above ninety degrees.

'Holy Jesus Christ,' he said hoarsely. 'Did she do that, Frank?'

Andy ignored him. His hands were still on Charlie's shoulders. He looked into her eyes. 'Charlie – do you think it's too late? How does it feel to you?'

'Yes,' she said. All the color was gone from her face. 'They're coming up the dirt road now. Oh Daddy, I'm scared.'

'You can stop them, Charlie,' he said quietly.

She looked at him.

'Yes,' he said.

'But – Daddy – it's bad. I know it is. I could kill them.'

148

'Yes,' he said. 'Maybe now it's kill or be killed. Maybe it's come down to that.'

'It's not bad?' Her voice was almost inaudible.

'Yes,' Andy said. 'It is. Never kid yourself that it isn't. And don't do it if you can't handle it, Charlie. Not even for me.'

They looked at each other, eye to eye, Andy's eyes tired and bloodshot and frightened, Charlie's eyes wide, nearly hypnotized.

She said: 'If I do . . . something . . . will you still love me?'

The question hung between them, lazily revolving.

'Charlie,' he said, 'I'll always love you. No matter what.'

Irv had been at the window and now he crossed the room to them. 'I think I got some tall apologizing to do,' he said. 'There's a whole line of cars coming up the road. I'll stand with you, if you want. I got my deer gun.' But he looked suddenly frightened, almost sick.

Charlie said: 'You don't need your gun.'

She slipped out from under her father's hands and walked across to the screen door, in Norma Manders's knitted white sweater looking even smaller than she was. She let herself out.

After a moment, Andy found his feet and went after her. His stomach felt frozen, as if he'd just gobbled a huge Dairy Queen cone in three bites. The Manderses stayed behind. Andy caught one last look at the man's baffled, frightened face, and a random thought – *that'll teach you to pick up hitchhikers* – darted across his consciousness.

Then he and Charlie were on the porch, watching the first of the cars turn up the long driveway. The hens squawked and fluttered. In the barn, Bossy mooed again for someone to come and milk her. And thin October sunshine lay over the wooded ridges and autumn-brown fields of this small upstate–New York town. It had been

149

almost a year of running, and Andy was surprised to find an odd sense of relief mixed in with his sharp terror. He had heard that in its extremity, even a rabbit will sometimes turn and face the dogs, driven back to some earlier, less meek nature at the instant before it must be torn apart.

At any rate, it was good not to be running. He stood with Charlie, the sunshine mellow on her blond hair.

'Oh Daddy,' she moaned. 'I can't hardly stand up.'

He put his arm around her shoulders and pulled her more tightly against his side.

The first car stopped at the head of the dooryard and two men got out.

13

'Hi, Andy,' Al Steinowitz said, and smiled. 'Hi, Charlie.' His hands were empty, but his coat was open. Behind him the other man stood alertly by the car, hands at his sides. The second car stopped behind the first and four more men spilled out. All the cars were stopping, all the men getting out. Andy counted a dozen and then stopped counting.

'Go away,' Charlie said. Her voice was thin and high in the cool early afternoon.

'You've led us a merry chase,' Al said to Andy. He looked at Charlie. 'Honey, you don't have to—'

'*Go away!*' she screamed.

Al shrugged and smiled disarmingly. 'Fraid I can't do that, honey. I have my orders. No one wants to hurt you or your daddy.'

'*You liar! You're s'posed to kill him! I know it!*'

Andy spoke and was a little surprised to find that his voice was completely steady. 'I advise you to do as my daughter says. You've surely been briefed enough to know

150

why she's wanted. You know about the soldier at the airport.'

OJ and Norville Bates exchanged a sudden uneasy look.

'If you'll just get in the car, we can discuss all of this,' Al said. 'Honest to gosh, there's nothing going on here except—'

'We know what's going on,' Andy said.

The men who had been in the last two or three cars were beginning to fan out and stroll, almost casually toward the porch.

'Please,' Charlie said to the man with the strangely yellow face. 'Don't make me do anything.'

'It's no good, Charlie,' Andy said.

Irv Manders came out onto the porch. 'You men are trespassing,' he said. 'I want you to get the hell off my property.'

Three of the Shop men had come up the front steps of the porch and were now standing less than ten yards away from Andy and Charlie, to their left. Charlie threw them a warning, desperate glance and they stopped – for the moment.

'We're government agents, sir,' Al Steinowitz said to Irv in a low, courteous voice. 'These two folks are wanted for questioning. Nothing more.'

'I don't care if they're wanted for assassinating the President,' Irv said. His voice was high, cracking. 'Show me your warrant or get the Christ off my property.'

'We don't need a warrant,' Al said. His voice was edged with steel now.

'You do unless I woke up in Russia this morning,' Irv said. 'I'm telling you to get off, and you better get high-steppin, mister. That's my last word on it.'

'Irv, come inside!' Norma cried.

Andy could feel something building in the air, building up around Charlie like an electric charge. The hair on his arms suddenly began to stir and move, like kelp in an invisible tide. He looked down at her and saw her face, so small, now so strange.

It's coming, he thought helplessly. *It's coming, oh my God it really is.*

'Get out!' he shouted at Al. 'Don't you understand what she's going to do? Can't you feel it? Don't be a fool, man!'

'Please,' Al said. He looked at the three men standing at the far end of the porch and nodded to them imperceptibly. He looked back at Andy. 'If we can only discuss this—'

'Watch it, Frank!' Irv Manders screamed.

The three men at the end of the porch suddenly charged at them, pulling their guns as they came. 'Hold it, hold it!' one of them yelled. 'Just stand still! Hands over your—'

Charlie turned toward them. As she did so, half a dozen other men, John Mayo and Ray Knowles among them, broke for the porch's back steps with their guns drawn.

Charlie's eyes widened a little, and Andy felt something hot pass by him in a warm puff of air.

The three men at the front end of the porch had got halfway toward them when their hair caught on fire.

A gun boomed, deafeningly loud, and a splinter of wood perhaps eight inches long jumped from one of the porch's supporting posts. Norma Manders screamed, and Andy flinched. But Charlie seemed not to notice. Her face was dreamy and thoughtful. A small Mona Lisa smile had touched the corners of her mouth.

She's enjoying this, Andy thought with something like horror. *Is that why she's so afraid of it? Because she likes it?*

Charlie was turning back toward Al Steinowitz again. The three men he had sent running down toward Andy and Charlie from the front end of the porch had forgotten their duty to God, country, and the Shop. They were beating at the flames on their heads and yelling. The pungent smell of fried hair suddenly filled the afternoon.

Another gun went off. A window shattered.

'Not the girl!' Al shouted. *'Not the girl!'*

Andy was seized roughly. The porch swirled with a confusion of men. He was dragged toward the railing through the chaos. Then someone tried to pull him a different way. He felt like a tug-of-war rope.

'Let him go!' Irv Manders shouted, bull-throated. 'Let him—'

Another gun went off and suddenly Norma was screaming again, screaming her husband's name over and over.

Charlie was looking down at Al Steinowitz, and suddenly the cold, confident look was gone from Al's face and he was in terror. His yellow complexion grew positively cheesy.

'No, don't,' he said in an almost conversational tone of voice. 'Don't—'

It was impossible to tell where the flames began. Suddenly his pants and his sportcoat were blazing. His hair was a burning bush. He backed up, screaming, bounced off the side of his car, and half-turned to Norville Bates, his arms stretched out.

Andy felt that soft rush of heat again, a displacement of air, as if a hot slug thrown at rocket-speed had just passed his nose.

Al Steinowitz's face caught on fire.

For a moment he was all there, screaming silently under a transparent caul of flame, and then his features were blending, merging, running like tallow. Norville shrank away from him. Al Steinowitz was a flaming scarecrow. He staggered blindly down the driveway, waving his arms, and then collapsed facedown beside the third car. He didn't look like a man at all; he looked like a burning bundle of rags.

The people on the porch had frozen, staring dumbly at this unexpected blazing development. The three men whose hair Charlie had fired had all managed to put themselves out. They were all going to look decidedly strange in the future (however short that might be); their hair, short by regulation, now looked like blackened, tangled clots of ash on top of their heads.

'Get out,' Andy said hoarsely. 'Get out quickly. She's never done anything like this before *and I don't know if she can stop.*'

'I'm all right, Daddy,' Charlie said. Her voice was calm, collected, and strangely indifferent. 'Everything's okay.'

And that was when the cars began to explode.

They all went up from the rear; later, when Andy replayed the incident at the Manders farm in his mind, he was quite sure of that. They all went up from the rear, where the gas tanks were.

Al's light-green Plymouth went first, exploding with a muffled *whrrr-rump!* sound. A ball of flame rose from the back of the Plymouth, too bright to look at. The rear window blew in. The Ford John and Ray had come in went next, barely two seconds later. Hooks of metal whickered through the air and pattered on the roof.

'Charlie!' Andy shouted. *'Charlie, stop it!'*

She said in that same calm voice: 'I can't.'

The third car went up.

Someone ran. Someone else followed him. The men on the porch began to back away. Andy was tugged again, he resisted, and suddenly no one at all was holding him. And suddenly they were all running, their faces white, eyes stare-blind with panic. One of the men with the charred hair tried to vault over the railing, caught his foot, and fell headfirst into a small side garden where Norma had grown beans earlier in the year. The stakes for the beans to climb on were still there, and one of them rammed through this fellow's throat and came out the other side with a wet punching sound that Andy never forgot. He twitched in

154

the garden like a landed trout, the bean-pole protruding from his neck like the shaft of an arrow, blood gushing down the front of his shirt as he made weak gargling sounds.

The rest of the cars went up then like an ear-shattering string of firecrackers. Two of the fleeing men were tossed aside like ragdolls by the concussion, one of them on fire from the waist down, the other peppered with bits of safety glass.

Dark, oily smoke rose in the air. Beyond the driveway, the far hills and fields twisted and writhed through the heat-shimmer as if recoiling in horror. Chickens ran madly everywhere, clucking crazily. Suddenly three of them exploded into flame and went rushing off, balls of fire with feet, to collapse on the far side of the dooryard.

'Charlie, stop it right now! Stop it!'

A trench of fire raced across the dooryard on a diagonal, the very dirt blazing in a single straight line, as if a train of gunpowder had been laid. The flame reached the chopping block with Irv's ax buried in it, made a fairy-ring around it, and suddenly collapsed inward. The chopping block whooshed into flame.

'CHARLIE FOR CHRIST'S SAKE!'

Some Shop agent's pistol was lying on the verge of grass between the porch and the blazing line of cars in the driveway. Suddenly the cartridges in it began to go off in a series of sharp, clapping explosions. The gun jigged and flipped bizarrely in the grass.

Andy slapped her as hard as he could.

Her head rocked back, her eyes blue and vacant. Then she was looking at him, surprised and hurt and dazed, and he suddenly felt enclosed in a capsule of swiftly building heat. He took in a breath of air that felt like heavy glass. The hairs in his nose felt as if they were crisping.

Spontaneous combustion, he thought. *I'm going up in a burst of spontaneous combustion—*

Then it was gone.

Charlie staggered on her feet and put her hands up to her face. And then, through her hands, came a shrill, building scream of such horror and dismay that Andy feared her mind had cracked.

'*DAAAAADEEEEEEEEE—*'

He swept her into his arms, hugged her.

'Shhh,' he said. 'Oh Charlie, honey, shhhh.'

The scream stopped, and she went limp in his arms. Charlie had fainted.

14

Andy picked her up in his arms and her head rolled limply against his chest. The air was hot and rich with the smell of burning gasoline. Flames had already crawled across the lawn to the ivy trellis; fingers of fire began to climb the ivy with the agility of a boy on midnight business. The house was going to go up.

Irv Manders was leaning against the kitchen screen door, his legs splayed. Norma knelt beside him. He had been shot above the elbow, and the sleeve of his blue workshirt was a bright red. Norma had torn a long strip of her dress off at the hem and was trying to get his shirtsleeve up so she could bind the wound. Irv's eyes were open. His face was an ashy gray, his lips were faintly blue, and he was breathing fast.

Andy took a step toward them and Norma Manders flinched backward, at the same time placing her body over her husband's. She looked up at Andy with shiny, hard eyes.

'Get away,' she hissed. 'Take your monster and get away.'

15

OJ ran.

The Windsucker bounced up and down under his arm as he ran. He ignored the road as he ran. He ran in the field. He fell down and got up and ran on. He twisted his ankle in what might have been a chuckhole and fell down again, a scream jerking out of his mouth as he sprawled. Then he got up and ran on. At times it seemed that he was running alone, and at times it seemed that someone was running with him. It didn't matter. All that mattered was getting away, away from that blazing bundle of rags that had been Al Steinowitz ten minutes before, away from that burning train of cars, away from Bruce Cook who lay in a small garden patch with a stake in his throat. Away, away, away. The Windsucker fell out of its holster, struck his knee painfully, and fell in a tangle of weeds, forgotten. Then OJ was in a patch of woods. He stumbled over a fallen tree and sprawled full length. He lay there, breathing raggedly, one hand pressed to his side, where a painful stitch had formed. He lay weeping tears of shock and fear. He thought: *No more assignments in New York. Never. That's it. Everybody out of the pool. I'm never setting foot in New York again even if I live to be two hundred.*

After a little while OJ got up and began to limp toward the road.

16

'Let's get him off the porch,' Andy said. He had laid Charlie on the grass beyond the dooryard. The side of the house was burning now, and sparks were drifting down on the porch like big, slow-moving fireflies.

'Get away,' she said harshly. 'Don't touch him.'

'The house is burning,' Andy said. 'Let me help you.

'Get away! You've done enough!'

'Stop it, Norma.' Irv looked at her. 'None of what happened was this man's fault. So shut your mouth.'

She looked at him as if she had a great many things to say, and then shut her mouth with a snap.

'Get me up,' Irv said. 'Legs feel all rubber. Think maybe I pissed myself. Shouldn't be surprised. One of those bastards shot me. Don't know which one. Lend a hand, Frank.'

'It's Andy,' he said, and got an arm around Irv's back. Little by little Irv came up. 'I don't blame your missus. You should have passed us by this morning.'

'If I had it to do over again, I'd do it just the same way,' Irv said. 'Gosh-damn people coming on my land with guns. Gosh-damn bastards and fucking bunch of government whoremasters and . . . ooooww-oooh, *Christ!*'

'Irv?' Norma cried.

'Hush, woman. I got it nocked now. Come on, Frank, or Andy, or whatever your name is. It's gettin hot.'

It was. A puff of wind blew a coil of sparks onto the porch as Andy half dragged Irv down the steps and into the dooryard. The chopping block was a blackened stump. There was nothing left of the chickens Charlie had set on fire but a few charred bones and a peculiar, dense ash that might have been feathers. They had not been roasted; they had been cremated.

'Set me down by the barn,' Irv gasped. 'I want to talk to you.'

'You need a doctor,' Andy said.

'Yeah, I'll get my doctor. What about your girl?'

'Fainted.' He set Irv down with his back against the barn door. Irv was looking up at him. A little color had come into his face, and that bluish cast was leaving his lips. He was sweating. Behind them, the big white farmhouse that had stood here on the Baillings Road since 1868 was going up in flames.

'There's no human being should be able to do what she can,' Irv said.

'That may well be,' Andy said, and then he looked from Irv and directly into Norma Manders's stony, unforgiving face. 'But then, no human being should have to have cerebral palsy or muscular dystrophy or leukemia. But it happens. And it happens to children.'

'She didn't get no say.' Irv nodded. 'All right.'

Still looking at Norma, Andy said, 'She's no more a monster than a kid in an iron lung or in a home for retarded children.'

'I'm sorry I said that,' Norma replied, and her glance wavered and fell from Andy's. 'I was out feeding the chickens with her. Watching her pet the cow. But mister, my house is burning down, and people are dead.'

'I'm sorry.'

'The house is insured, Norma,' Irv said, taking her hand with his good one.

'That doesn't do anything about my mother's dishes that her mother gave to her,' Norma said. 'Or my nice secretary, or the pictures we got at the Schenectady art show last July.' A tear slipped out of one eye and she wiped it away with her sleeve. 'And all the letters you wrote to me when you were in the army.'

'Is your button going to be all right?' Irv asked.

'I don't know.'

'Well, listen. Here's what you can do if you want to. There's an old Willys Jeep out behind the barn—'

'Irv, no! Don't get into this any deeper!'

He turned to look at her, his face gray and lined and sweaty. Behind them, their home burned. The sound of popping shingles was like that of horse chestnuts in a Christmas fire.

'Those men came with no warrants nor blueback paper of any kind and tried to take them off our land,' he said. 'People I'd invited in like it's done in a civilized country with decent laws. One of them shot me, and one of them tried to shoot Andy here. Missed his head by no more than a quarter of an inch.' Andy remembered the first deafening report and the splinter of wood that had jumped from the porch support post. He shivered. 'They came and did those things. What do you want me to do, Norma? Sit here and turn them over to the secret police if they get their peckers up enough to come back? Be a good German?'

'No,' she said huskily. 'No, I guess not.'

'You don't have to—' Andy began.

'I feel I do,' Irv said. 'And when they come back . . . they will be back, won't they, Andy?'

'Oh yes. They'll be back. You just bought stock in a growth industry, Irv.'

Irv laughed, a whistling, breathless sound. 'That's pretty good, all right. Well, when they show up here, all I know is that you took my Willys. I don't know more than that. And to wish you well.'

'Thank you,' Andy said quietly.

'We got to be quick,' Irv said. 'It's a long way back to town, but they'll have seen the smoke by now. Fire trucks'll be coming. You said you and the button were going to Vermont. Was that much the truth?'

'Yes,' Andy said.

There was a moaning sound to their left. 'Daddy—'

Charlie was sitting up. The red pants and green blouse were smeared with dirt. Her face was pale, her eyes were terribly confused. 'Daddy, what's burning? I smell something burning. Am I doing it? *What's burning?*'

Andy went to her and gathered her up. 'Everything is all right,' he said, and wondered why you had to say that to children even when they knew perfectly well, as you did, that it wasn't true. 'Everything's fine. How do you feel, hon?'

Charlie was looking over his shoulder at the burning line of cars, the convulsed body in the garden, and the Manders house, which was crowned with fire. The porch was also wrapped in flames. The wind was carrying the smoke and heat away from them, but the smell of gas and hot shingles was strong.

'I did that,' Charlie said, almost too low to hear. Her face began to twist and crumple again.

'Button!' Irv said sternly.

She glanced over at him, through him. 'Me,' she moaned.

'Set her down,' Irv said. 'I want to talk to her.'

Andy carried Charlie over to where Irv sat propped up against the barn door and set her down.

'You listen to me, button,' Irv said. 'Those men meant to kill your daddy. You knew it before I did, maybe before he did, although I'll be damned if I know how. Am I right?'

'Yes,' Charlie said. Her eyes were still deep and miserable. 'But you don't get it. It was like the soldier, but worse. I couldn't . . . couldn't hold onto it anymore. It was going everyplace. I burned up some of your chickens . . . and I almost burned up my father.' The miserable eyes spilled over and she began to cry helplessly.

'Your daddy's fine,' Irv said. Andy said nothing. He remembered that sudden strangling sensation, being enclosed in that heat capsule.

'I'm never going to do it again,' she said. '*Never*.'

'All right,' Andy said, and put a hand on her shoulder. 'All right, Charlie.'

'*Never*,' she repeated with quiet emphasis.

'You don't want to say that, button,' Irv said, looking up at her. 'You don't want to block yourself off like that. You'll do what you have to do. You'll do the best you can.

And that's all you can do. I believe the one thing the God of this world likes best is to give the business to people who say "never." You understand me?'

'No,' Charlie whispered.

'But you will, I think,' Irv said, and looked at Charlie with such deep compassion that Andy felt his throat fill with sorrow and fear. Then Irv glanced at his wife. 'Bring me that there stick by your foot, Norma.'

Norma brought the stick and put it into his hand and told him again that he was overdoing it, that he had to rest. And so it was only Andy that heard Charlie say 'Never' again, almost inaudibly, under her breath, like a vow taken in secrecy.

17

'Look here, Andy,' Irv said, and drew a straight line in the dust. 'This is the dirt road we came up. The Baillings Road. If you go a quarter of a mile north, you'll come to a woods road on your right. A car can't make it up that road, but the Willys should do it if you keep her wound up and use an educated foot on the clutch. A couple of times it's gonna look like that road just up and died, but you keep going and you'll pick it up again. It's not on any map, you understand? Not on any map.'

Andy nodded, watching the stick draw the woods road.

'It'll take you twelve miles east, and if you don't get stuck or lost, you'll come out on Route One-fifty-two near Hoag Corners. You turn left -- north -- and about a mile up One-fifty-two you'll come to another woods road. It's low ground, swampy, mushy. The Willys might do it, might not. I ain't been on that road in five years, I guess. It's the only one I know that goes east toward Vermont and won't be road-blocked off. That second road is gonna bring you out on Highway Twenty-two, north of Cherry Plain and south of the Vermont border. By then you should be out of the worst of it – although I s'pose they'll have your name and pictures on the wire. But we wish you the best. Don't we, Norma?'

'Yes,' Norma said, and the word was almost a sigh. She looked at Charlie. 'You saved your dad's life, little girl. That's the thing to remember.'

'Is it?' Charlie said, and her voice was so perfectly toneless that Norma Manders looked bewildered and a little afraid. Then Charlie tried a hesitant smile and Norma smiled back, relieved.

'Keys are in the Willys, and–' He cocked his head to one side. 'Hark!'

It was the sound of sirens, rising and falling in cycles, still faint but drawing closer.

'It's the FD,' Irv said. 'You better go, if you're goin.'

'Come on, Charlie,' Andy said. She came to him, her eyes red from her tears. The small smile had disappeared like hesitant sunlight behind the clouds, but Andy felt greatly encouraged that it had been there at all. The face she wore was a survivor's face, shocked and wounded. In that moment, Andy wished he had her power; he would use it, and he knew whom he would use it on.

He said, 'Thank you, Irv.'

'I'm sorry,' Charlie said in a small voice. 'About your house and your chickens and . . . and everything else.'

'It sure wasn't your fault, button,' Irv said. 'They brought it on themselves. You watch out for your daddy.'

'All right,' she said.

Andy took her hand and led her around the barn to where the Willys was parked under a shakepole leanto.

The fire sirens were very close by the time he had got it started and driven it across the lawn to the road. The house was an inferno now. Charlie would not look at it. The last Andy saw of the Manderses was in the rearview mirror of the canvas-topped Jeep: Irv leaning against the barn, the piece of white skirting knotted around his wounded arm stained red, Norma sitting beside him. His good arm was around her. Andy waved, and Irv gestured a bit in return with his bad arm. Norma didn't wave, thinking, perhaps, of her mother's china, her secretary, the love letters – all the things of which insurance money is ignorant and always has been.

18

They found the first woods road just where Irv Manders had said they would. Andy put the Jeep in four-wheel drive and turned onto it.

'Hold on, Charlie,' he said. 'We're gonna bounce.'

Charlie held on. Her face was white and listless, and looking at her made Andy nervous. *The cottage*, he thought. *Granther McGee's cottage on Tashmore Pond. If we can only get there and rest. She'll get herself back together and then we'll think about what we should do.*

We'll think about it tomorrow. Like Scarlett said, it's another day.

The Willys roared and pitched its way up the road, which was no more than a two-wheel track with bushes and even a few stunted pines growing along the crown. This land had been logged over maybe ten years ago, and Andy doubted if it had been used since then, except by an occasional hunter. Six miles up it did seem to 'up and die,' and Andy had to stop twice to move trees that had blown down. The second time he looked up from his exertions, heart and head pounding almost sickeningly, and saw a large doe looking at him thoughtfully. She held a moment longer and then was gone into the deeper woods with a flip of her white tail. Andy looked back at Charlie and saw she was watching the deer's progress with something like wonder . . . and he felt encouraged again. A little farther on they found the wheel-ruts again, and around three o'clock they came out on the stretch of two-lane blacktop that was Route 152.

19

Orville Jamieson, scratched and muddy and barely able to walk on his bad ankle, sat by the side of the Baillings Road about a half a mile from the Manders farm and spoke into his walkie-talkie. His message was relayed back to a temporary command post in a van parked in the main street of Hastings Glen. The van had radio equipment with a built-in scrambler and a powerful transmitter. OJ's report was scrambled, boosted, and sent to New York City, where a relay station caught it and sent it on to Longmont, Virginia, where Cap sat in his office, listening.

Cap's face was no longer bright and jaunty, as it had been when he biked to work that morning. OJ's report was nearly unbelievable: they had known the girl had *something*, but this story of sudden carnage and reversal was (at least to Cap) like a bolt of lightning from a clear blue sky. Four to six men dead, the others driven helter-skelter into the woods, half a dozen cars in flames, a house burning to the ground, a civilian wounded and about to blab to anyone and everyone who cared to listen that a bunch of neo-Nazis had turned up on his doorstep with no warrant and had attempted to kidnap a man and a little girl whom he had invited home to lunch.

When OJ finished his report (and he never really did; he only began to repeat himself in a kind of semihysteria), Cap hung up and sat in his deep swivel chair and tried to think. He did not think a covert operation had gone so spectacularly wrong since the Bay of Pigs – and this was on American soil.

165

The office was gloomy and filled with thick shadows now that the sun had got around to the other side of the building, but he didn't turn on the lights. Rachel had buzzed him on the intercom and he had told her curtly he didn't want to talk to anyone, anyone at all.

He felt old.

He heard Wanless saying: *I am talking about the potential for destruction.* Well, it wasn't just a question of potential any longer, was it? *But we're going to have her*, he thought, looking blankly across the room. *Oh yes, we're going to have her.*

He thumbed for Rachel.

'I want to talk to Orville Jamieson as soon as he can be flown here,' he said. 'And I want to talk to General Brackman in Washington, A-one-A priority. We've got a potentially embarrassing situation in New York State, and I want you to tell him that right out.'

'Yes, sir,' Rachel said respectfully.

'I want a meeting with all six subdirectors at nineteen hundred hours. Also A-one-A. And I want to talk to the chief of state police up there in New York.' They had been part of the search sweep, and Cap wanted to point that out to them. If mud was going to be thrown, he would be sure to save back a good, big bucket of it for them. But he also wanted to point out that behind a united front, they might still all be able to come out of this looking fairly decent.

He hesitated and then said, 'And when John Rainbird calls in, tell him I want to talk to him. I have another job for him.'

'Yes, sir.'

Cap let go of the intercom toggle. He sat back in his chair and studied the shadows.

'Nothing has happened that can't be fixed,' he said to the shadows. That had been his motto all his life   not printed in crewel and hung up, not embossed on a copper desk plaque, but it was printed on his heart as truth.

Nothing that can't be fixed. Until tonight, until OJ's report, he had believed that. It was a philosophy that had brought a poor Pennsylvania miner's kid a long way. And he believed it still, although in a momentarily shaken manner. Between Manders and his wife, they probably had relatives scattered from New England to California, and each one was a potential lever. There were enough top-secret files right here in Longmont to ensure that any congressional hearing on Shop methods would be . . . well, a little hard of hearing. The cars and even the agents were only hardware, although it would be a long time before he would really be able to get used to the idea that Al Steinowitz was gone. Who could there possibly be to replace Al? That little kid and her old man were going to pay for what they had done to Al, if for nothing else. He would see to it.

But the girl. Could the girl be fixed?

There were ways. There were methods of containment.

The McGee files were still on the library cart. He got up, went to them, and began thumbing through them rest-lessly. He wondered where John Rainbird was at this moment.

Washington, D.C.

1

At the moment Cap Hollister had his passing thought about him, John Rainbird was sitting in his room at the Mayflower Hotel watching a television game called *The Crosswits*. He was naked. He sat in the chair with his bare feet neatly together and watched the program. He was waiting for it to get dark. After it got dark, he would begin waiting for it to get late. When it was late, he would begin waiting for it to get early. When it got early and the pulse of the hotel was at its slowest, he would stop waiting and go upstairs to Room 1217 and kill Dr Wanless. Then he would come down here and think about whatever Wanless would have told him before he died, and sometime after the sun came up, he would sleep briefly.

John Rainbird was a man at peace. He was at peace with almost everything – Cap, the Shop, the United States. He was at peace with God, Satan, and the universe. If he was not yet at complete peace with himself, that was only because his pilgrimage was not yet over. He had many coups, many honorable scars. It did not matter that people turned away from him in fear and loathing. It did not matter that he had lost one eye in Vietnam. What they paid him did not matter. He took it and most of it went to buy shoes. He had a great love of shoes. He owned a home in Flagstaff, and although he rarely went there himself, he had all his shoes sent there. When he did get a chance to go to his house, he admired the shoes – Gucci, Bally, Bass, Adidas, Van Donen. Shoes. His house was a strange forest;

shoe trees grew in every room and he would go from room to room admiring the shoefruit that grew on them. But when he was alone, he went barefoot. His father, a full-blooded Cherokee, had been buried barefoot. Someone had stolen his burial moccasins.

Other than shoes, John Rainbird was interested in only two things. One of them was death. His own death, of course; he had been preparing for this inevitability for twenty years or more. Dealing death had always been his business and was the only trade he had ever excelled at. He became more and more interested in it as he grew older, as an artist will become more interested in the qualities and levels of light, as writers will feel for character and nuance like blindmen reading braille. What interested him most was the actual *leaving* . . . the actual exhalation of the soul . . . the exit from the body and what human beings knew as life and the passing into something else. What must it be like to feel yourself slipping away? Did you think it was a dream from which you would awake? Was the Christian devil there with his fork, ready to jam it through your shrieking soul and carry it down to hell like a piece of meat on a shish kebab? Was there joy? Did you know you were going? What is it that the eyes of the dying see?

Rainbird hoped he would have the opportunity to find out for himself. In his business, death was often quick and unexpected, something that happened in the flick of an eye. He hoped that when his own death came, he would have time to prepare and feel everything. More and more lately he had watched the faces of the people he killed, trying to see the secret in the eyes.

Death interested him.

What also interested him was the little girl they were all so concerned with. This Charlene McGee. As far as Cap knew, John Rainbird had only the vaguest knowledge of the McGees and none at all of Lot Six. Actually, Rainbird knew almost as much as Cap himself – something that surely would have marked him for extreme sanction if Cap had known. They suspected that the girl had some great or potentially great power – maybe a whole batch of them. He would like to meet this girl and see what her powers were. He also knew that Andy McGee was what Cap called 'a potential mental dominant,' but that did not concern John Rainbird. He had not yet met a man who could dominate him.

The Crosswits ended. The news came on. None of it was good. John Rainbird sat, not eating, not drinking, not smoking, clean and empty and husked out, and waited for the killing time to come around.

2

Earlier that day Cap had thought uneasily of how silent Rainbird was. Dr Wanless never heard him. He awoke from a sound sleep. He awoke because a finger was tickling him just below the nose. He awoke and saw what appeared to be a monster from a nightmare hulking over his bed. One eye glinted softly in the light from the bathroom, the light he always left on when he was in a strange place. Where the other eye should have been there was only an empty crater.

Wanless opened his mouth to scream, and John Rainbird pinched his nostrils shut with the fingers of one hand and covered his mouth with the other. Wanless began to thrash.

'Shhh,' Rainbird said. He spoke with the pleased indulgence of a mother to her baby at fresh-diaper time.

Wanless struggled harder.

'If you want to live, be still and be quiet,' Rainbird said.

Wanless looked up at him, heaved once, and then lay still.

'Will you be quiet?' Rainbird asked.

Wanless nodded. His face was growing very red.

Rainbird removed his hands and Wanless began to gasp hoarsely. A small rivulet of blood trickled from one nostril.

'Who . . . are you . . . Cap . . . send you?'

'Rainbird,' he said gravely. 'Cap sent me, yes.'

Wanless's eyes were huge in the dark. His tongue snaked out and licked his lips. Lying in his bed with the sheets kicked down around his knuckly ankles, he looked like the world's oldest child.

'I have money,' he whispered very fast. 'Swiss bank account. Lots of money. All yours. Never open my mouth again. Swear before God.'

'It's not your money that I want, Dr Wanless,' Rainbird said.

Wanless gazed up at him, the left side of his mouth sneering madly, his left eyelid drooping and quivering.

'If you would like to be alive when the sun comes up,' Rainbird said, 'you will talk to me, Dr Wanless. You will lecture me. I will be a seminar of one. I will be attentive; a good pupil. And I will reward you with your life, which you will live far away from the view of Cap and the Shop. Do you understand?'

'Yes,' Wanless said hoarsely.

'Do you agree?'

'Yes . . . but what—?'

Rainbird held two fingers to his lips and Dr Wanless hushed immediately. His scrawny chest rose and fell rapidly.

'I am going to say two words,' Rainbird said, 'and then your lecture will begin. It will include everything that you know, everything you suspect, everything you theorize. Are you ready for those two words, Dr Wanless?'

'Yes,' Dr Wanless said.

'Charlene McGee,' Rainbird said, and Dr Wanless began

to speak. His words came slowly at first, and then he began to speed up. He talked. He gave Rainbird the complete history of the Lot Six tests and the climactic experiment. Much of what he said Rainbird already knew, but Wanless also filled in a number of blank spots. The professor went through the entire sermon he had given Cap that morning, and here it did not fall on deaf ears. Rainbird listened carefully, frowning sometimes, clapping softly and chuckling at Wanless's toilet-training metaphor. This encouraged Wanless to speak even faster, and when he began to repeat himself, as old men will, Rainbird reached down again, pinched Wanless's nose shut with one hand again, and covered his mouth with the other again.

'Sorry,' Rainbird said.

Wanless bucked and sunfished under Rainbird's weight. Rainbird applied more pressure, and when Wanless's struggles began to lessen, Rainbird abruptly removed the hand he had been using to pinch Wanless's nose shut. The sound of the good doctor's hissing breath was like air escaping from a tire with a big nail in it. His eyes were rolling wildly in their sockets, rolling like the eyes of a fear-maddened horse . . . but they were still too hard to see.

Rainbird seized the collar of Dr Wanless's pajama jacket and yanked him sideways on the bed so that the cold white light from the bathroom shone directly across his face.

Then he pinched the doctor's nostrils closed again.

A man can sometimes survive for upward of nine minutes without permanent brain damage if his air is cut off and he remains completely quiet; a woman, with slightly greater lung capacity and a slightly more efficient carbon-dioxide-disposal system, may last ten or twelve. Of course, struggling and terror cuts that survival time a great deal.

Dr Wanless struggled briskly for forty seconds, and then his efforts to save himself began to flag. His hands beat lightly at the twisted granite that was John Rainbird's face. His heels drummed a muffled retreat tattoo on the carpeting. He began to drool against Rainbird's callused palm.

This was the moment.

Rainbird leaned forward and studied Wanless's eyes with a childlike eagerness.

But it was the same, always the same. The eyes seemed to lose their fear and fill instead with a great puzzlement. Not wonder, not dawning comprehension or realization or awe, just puzzlement. For a moment those two puzzled eyes fixed on John Rainbird's one, and Rainbird knew he was being seen. Fuzzily, perhaps, fading back and back as the doctor went out and out, but he was being *seen*. Then there was nothing but glaze. Dr Joseph Wanless was no longer staying at the Mayflower Hotel; Rainbird was sitting on this bed with a life-size doll.

He sat still, one hand still over the doll's mouth, the other pinching the doll's nostrils tightly together. It was best to be sure. He would remain so for another ten minutes.

He thought about what Wanless had told him concerning Charlene McGee. Was it possible that a small child could have such a power? He supposed it might be. In Calcutta he had seen a man put knives into his body – his legs, his belly, his chest, his neck – and then pull them out, leaving no wounds. It might be possible. And it was certainly . . . interesting.

He thought about these things, and then found himself wondering what it would be like to kill a child. He had never knowingly done such a thing (although once he had placed a bomb on an airliner and the bomb had exploded, killing all sixty-seven aboard, and perhaps one or more of them had been children, but that was not the same thing; it was impersonal). It was not a business in which the death of children was often required. They were not, after all, some terrorist organization like the IRA or the PLO, no matter how much some people – some of the yellowbellies in the Congress, for instance – would like to believe they were.

They were, after all, a scientific organization.

Perhaps with a child the result would be different. There might be another expression in the eyes at the end, something besides the puzzlement that made him feel so empty and so – yes, it was true – so sad.

He might discover part of what he needed to know in the death of a child.

A child like this Charlene McGee.

'My life is like the straight roads in the desert,' John Rainbird said softly. He looked absorbedly into the dull blue marbles that had been the eyes of Dr Wanless. 'But your life is no road at all, my friend . . . my good friend.'

He kissed Wanless first on one cheek and then on the other. Then he pulled him back onto the bed and threw a sheet over him. It came down softly, like a parachute, and outlined Wanless's jutting and now tideless nose in white lawn.

Rainbird left the room.

That night he thought about the girl who could supposedly light fires. He thought about her a great deal. He wondered where she was, what she was thinking, what she was dreaming. He felt very tender about her, very protective.

By the time he drifted off to sleep, at just past six A.M., he was sure: the girl would be his.

Tashmore, Vermont

1

Andy and Charlie McGee arrived at the cottage on Tashmore Pond two days after the burning at the Manders farm. The Willys hadn't been in great shape to start with, and the muddy plunge over the woods roads that Irv had directed them onto had done little to improve it.

When dusk came on the endless day that had begun in Hastings Glen, they had been less then twenty yards from the end of the second – and worse – of the two woods roads. Below them, but screened off by a heavy growth of bushes, was Route 22. Although they couldn't see the road, they could hear the occasional swish and whine of passing cars and trucks. They slept that night in the Willys, bundled up for warmth. They set out again the next morning – yesterday morning – at just past five A.M., with daylight nothing but a faint white tone in the east.

Charlie looked pallid and listless and used up. She hadn't asked him what would happen to them if the roadblocks had been shifted east. It was just as well, because if the roadblocks had been shifted, they would be caught, and that was simply all there was to it. There was no question of ditching the Willys, either; Charlie was in no shape to walk, and for that matter, neither was he.

So Andy had pulled out onto the highway and all that day in October they had jigged and jogged along secondary roads under a white sky that promised rain but never quite delivered it. Charlie slept a great deal, and Andy worried about her – worried that she was using the sleep in an unhealthy way, using it to flee what had happened instead of trying to come to terms with it.

He stopped twice at roadside diners and picked up burgers and fries. The second time he used the five-dollar bill that the van driver, Jim Paulson, had laid on him. Most of the remaining phone change was gone. He must have lost some of it out of his pockets during that crazy time at the Manders place, but he didn't recall it. Something else was gone as well; those frightening numb places on his face had faded away sometime during the night. Those he didn't mind losing.

Most of Charlie's share of the burgers and fries went uneaten.

Last night they had driven into a highway rest area about an hour after dark. The rest area was deserted. It was autumn, and the season of the Winnebagos had passed for another year. A rustic woodburned sign read: NO CAMPING   NO FIRES   LEASH YOUR DOG $500 FINE FOR LITTERING.

'They're real sports around here,' Andy muttered, and drove the Willys down the slope beyond the far edge of the gravel parking lot and into a copse beside a small, chuckling stream. He and Charlie got out and went wordlessly down to the water. The overcast held, but it was mild; there were no stars visible and the night seemed extraordinarily dark. They sat down for a while and listened to the brook tell its tale. He took Charlie's hand and that was when she began to cry – great, tearing sobs that seemed to be trying to rip her apart.

He took her in his arms and rocked her. 'Charlie,' he murmured. 'Charlie, Charlie, don't. Don't cry.'

'Please don't make me do it again, Daddy,' she wept. 'Because if you said to I'd do it and then I guess I'd kill myself, so please . . . please . . . never . . .'

'I love you,' he said. 'Be quiet and stop talking about killing yourself. That's crazy-talk.'

'No,' she said. 'It isn't. Promise, Daddy.'

He thought for a long time and then said slowly: 'I don't know if I can, Charlie. But I promise to try. Will that be good enough?'

Her troubled silence was answer enough.

'I get scared, too,' he said softly. 'Daddies get scared, too. You better believe it.'

They spent that night, too, in the cab of the Willys. They were back on the road by six o'clock in the morning. The clouds had broken up, and by ten o'clock it had become a flawless, Indian-summery day. Not long after they crossed the Vermont state line they saw men riding ladders like masts in tossing apple trees and trucks in the orchards filled with bushel baskets of Macs.

At eleven-thirty they turned off Route 34 and onto a narrow, rutted dirt road marked PRIVATE PROPERTY, and something in Andy's chest loosened. They had made it to Granther McGee's place. They were here.

They drove slowly down toward the pond, a distance of perhaps a mile and a half. October leaves, red and gold, swirled across the road in front of the Jeep's blunt nose. Just as glints of water began to show through the trees, the road branched in two. A heavy steel chain hung across the smaller branch, and from the chain a rust-flecked yellow sign: NO TRESPASSING BY ORDER OF COUNTY SHERIFF. Most of the rust flecks had formed around six or eight dimples in the metal, and Andy guessed that some summer kid had spent a few minutes working off his boredom by plinking at the sign with his .22. But that had been years ago.

He got out of the Willys and took his keyring out of his pocket. There was a leather tab on the ring with his initials. A.McG., almost obliterated. Vicky had given him that piece of leather for Christmas one year -- a Christmas before Charlie had been born.

He stood by the chain for a moment, looking at the leather tab, then at the keys themselves. There were almost two dozen of them. Keys were funny things; you could index a life by the keys that had a way of collecting on your keyring. He supposed that some people, undoubtedly people who had realized a higher degree of organization than he had, simply threw their old keys away, just as those same organizational types made a habit of cleaning their wallets out every six months or so. Andy had never done either.

Here was the key that opened the east-wing door of Prince Hall back in Harrison, where his office had been. His key to the office itself. To the English Department office. Here was the key to the house in Harrison that he had seen for the last time on the day the Shop killed his wife and kidnapped his daughter. Two or three more he couldn't even identify. Keys were funny things, all right.

His vision blurred. Suddenly he missed Vicky, and needed her as he hadn't needed her since those first black weeks on the road with Charlie. He was so tired, so scared, and so full of anger. In that moment, if he'd had every employee of the Shop lined up in front of him along Granther's road, and if someone had handed him a Thompson submachine gun . . .

'Daddy?' It was Charlie's voice, anxious. 'Can't you find the key?'

'Yes, I've got it,' he said. It was among the rest, a small Yale key on which he had scratched T.P. for Tashmore Pond with his jackknife. The last time they had been here was the year Charlie was born, and now Andy had to wiggle the key a little before the stiff tumblers would turn. Then the lock popped open and he laid the chain down on the carpet of fall leaves.

He drove the Willys through and then repadlocked the chain.

The road was in bad shape, Andy was glad to see. When they came up regularly every summer, they would stay three or four weeks and he would always find a couple of days to work on the road – get a load of gravel from Sam Moore's gravel pit and put it down in the worst of the ruts, cut back the brush, and get Sam himself to come down with his old dragger and even it out. The camp road's other, broader fork led down to almost two dozen camp homes and cottages strung along the shorefront, and those folks had their Road Association, annual dues. August business meeing and all (although the business meeting was really only an excuse to get really loaded before Labor Day came and put an end to another summer), but Granther's place was the only one down this way, because Granther himself had bought all the land for a song back in the depths of the Depression.

In the old days they'd had a family car, a Ford wagon. He doubted if the old wagon would have made it down here now, and even the Willys, with its high axles, bottomed out once or twice. Andy didn't mind at all. It meant that no one had been down here.

'Will there be electricity, Daddy?' Charlie asked.

'No,' he said, 'and no phone, either. We don't dare get the electricity turned on, kiddo. It'd be like holding up a sign saying HERE WE ARE. But there are kerosene lamps and two range-oil drums. If the stuff hasn't been ripped off, that is.' That worried him a little. Since the last time they'd been down here, the price of range oil had gone up enough to make the theft worthwhile, he supposed.

'Will there be—' Charlie began.

'Holy shit,' Andy said. He jammed on the brakes. A tree had fallen across the road up ahead, a big old birch pushed down by some winter storm. 'I guess we walk from here.

It's only a mile or so anyway. We'll hike it.' Later he would have to come back with Granther's one-handed buck and cut the tree up. He didn't want to leave Irv's Willys parked here. It was too open.

He ruffled her hair. 'Come on.'

They got out of the Willys, and Charlie scooted effortlessly under the birch while Andy clambered carefully over, trying not to skewer himself anywhere important. The leaves crunched agreeably under their feet as they walked on, and the woods were aromatic with fall. A squirrel looked down at them from a tree, watching their progress closely. And now they began to see bright slashes of blue again through the trees.

'What did you start to say back there when we came to the tree?' Andy asked her.

'If there would be enough oil for a long time. In case we stay the winter.'

'No, but there's enough to start with. And I'm going to cut a lot of wood. You'll haul plenty of it, too.'

'Ten minutes later the road widened into a clearing on the shore of Tashmore Pond and they were there. They both stood quietly for a moment. Andy didn't know what Charlie was feeling, but for him there was a rush of remembrance too total to be called anything so mild as nostalgia. Mixed up in the memories was his dream of three mornings ago – the boat, the squirming nightcrawler, even the tire patches on Granther's boots.

The cottage was five rooms, wood over fieldstone base. A deck jutted out toward the lake, and a stone pier poked out into the water itself. Except for the drifts of leaves and the blowdowns of three winters, the place hadn't changed a bit. He almost expected Granther himself to come strolling out, wearing one of those green and black checked shirts, waving and bellowing for him to come on up, asking him if he'd got his fishing license yet, because the brown trout were still biting good around dusk.

It had been a good place, a safe place. Far across Tashmore Pond, the pines glimmered gray-green in the sunshine. *Stupid trees*, Granther had said once, *don't even know the difference between summer and winter*. The only sign of civilization on the far side was still the Bradford Town Landing. No one had put up a shopping center or an amusement park. The wind still talked in the trees here. The green shingles still had a mossy, woodsy look, and pine needles still drifted in the roof angles and in the cup of the wooden gutter. He had been a boy here, and Granther had shown him how to bait a hook. He had had his own bedroom here, paneled in good maple, and he had dreamed a boy's dreams in a narrow bed and had awakened to the sound of water lapping the pier. He had been a man here as well, making love to his wife in the double bed that had once belonged to Granther and his wife -- that silent and somehow baleful woman who was a member of the American Society of Atheists and would explain to you, should you ask, the Thirty Greatest Inconsistencies in the King James Bible, or, should you prefer, the Laughable Fallacy of the Clockspring Theory of the Universe, all with the thudding, irrevocable logic of a dedicated preacher.

'You miss Mom, don't you?' Charlie said in a forlorn voice.

'Yeah,' he said. 'Yeah, I do.'

'Me too,' Charlie said. 'You had fun here, didn't you?'

'We did,' he agreed. 'Come on, Charlie.'

She held back, looking at him.

'Daddy, will things ever be all right for us again? Will I be able to go to school and things?'

He considered a lie, but a lie was a poor answer. 'I don't know,' he said. He tried to smile, but it wouldn't come; he found he could not even stretch his lips convincingly. 'I don't know, Charlie.'

2

Granther's tools were all still neatly racked in the toolshed portion of the boathouse, and Andy found a bonus he had hoped for but had told himself not to hope for too much: nearly two cords of wood, neatly split and time-seasoned in the bay beneath the boathouse. Most of it he had split himself, and it was still under the sheet of ragged, dirty canvas he had thrown over it. Two cords wouldn't take them through the winter, but by the time he finished carving up the blowdowns around the camp and the birch back on the road, they would be well set.

He took the bucksaw back up to the fallen tree and cut it up enough to get the Willys through. By then it was nearly dark, and he was tired and hungry. No one had bothered to rip off the well-stocked pantry, either; if there had been vandals or thieves on snowmobiles over the last six winters, they had stuck to the more populous southern end of the lake. There were five shelves packed with Campbell's soups and Wyman's sardines and Dinty Moore beef stew and all sorts of canned vegetables. There was also still half a case of Rival dog food on the floor – a legacy of Granther's good old dog Bimbo – but Andy didn't think it would come to that.

While Charlie looked at the books on the shelves in the big living room, Andy went into the small root cellar that was three steps down from the pantry, scratched a wooden match on one of the beams, stuck his finger into the knothole in one of the boards that lined the sides of the little dirt-floored room, and pulled. The board came out and Andy looked inside. After a moment he grinned. Inside the cobweb-festooned little bolt-hole were four

184

mason jars filled with a clear, slightly oily-looking liquid that was one-hundred-percent-pure white lightning – what Granther called 'father's mule-kick.'

The match burned Andy's fingers. He shook it out and lit a second. Like the dour New England preachers of old (from whom she had been a direct descendant), Hulda McGee had no liking, understanding, or tolerance for the simple and slightly stupid male pleasures. She had been a Puritan atheist, and this had been Granther's little secret, which he had shared with Andy the year before he died.

Besides the white lightning, there was a caddy for poker chips. Andy pulled it out and felt in the slot at the top. There was a crackling sound, and he pulled out a thin sheaf of bills – a few tens and fives and some ones. Maybe eighty dollars all told. Granther's weakness had been seven-card stud, and this was what he called his 'struttin money.'

The second match burned his fingers, and Andy shook it out. Working in the dark, he put the poker chips back, money and all. It was good to know it was there. He replaced the board and went back through the pantry.

'Tomato soup do you?' he asked Charlie. Wonder of wonders, she had found all the Pooh books on one of the shelves and was currently somewhere in the Hundred Acre Wood with Pooh and Eeyore.

'Sure,' she said, not looking up.

He made a big pot of tomato soup and opened them each a tin of sardines. He lit one of the kerosene lamps after carefully drawing the drapes and put it in the middle of the dining table. They sat down and ate, neither of them talking much. Afterward he smoked a cigarette, lighting it over the chimney of the lamp. Charlie discovered the card drawer in Grandma's Welsh dresser; there were eight or nine decks in there, each of them missing a jack or a deuce or something, and she spent the rest of the evening sorting them and playing with them while Andy prowled through the camp.

Later, tucking her into bed, he asked her how she felt.

'Safe,' she said with no hesitation at all. 'Goodnight, Daddy.'

If it was good enough for Charlie, it was good enough for him. He sat with her awhile, but she dropped off to sleep quickly and with no trouble, and he left after propping her door open so he would hear her if she became restless in the night.

3

Before turning in, Andy went back down to the root cellar, got one of the jars of white lightning, poured himself a small knock in a juice glass, and went out through the sliding door and onto the deck. He sat in one of the canvas director's chairs (mildewy smell; he wondered briefly if something could be done about that) and looked out at the dark, moving bulk of the lake. It was a trifle chilly, but a couple of small sips at Granther's mule-kick took care of the chill quite nicely. For the first time since that terrible chase up Third Avenue, he too felt safe and at rest.

He smoked and looked out across Tashmore Pond.

Safe and at rest, but not for the first time since New York City. For the first time since the Shop had come back into their lives on that terrible August day fourteen months ago. Since then they had either been running or hunkering down, and either way there was no rest.

He remembered talking to Quincey on the telephone with the smell of burned carpeting in his nostrils. He in Ohio, Quincey out there in California, which in his few letters he always called the Magic Earthquake Kingdom. *Yes, it's a good thing*, Quincey had said. *Or they might put them in two little rooms where they could work full-time to keep*

two hundred and twenty million Americans safe and free. . . .
I bet they'd just want to take that child and put it in a little
room and see if it could help make the world safe for democracy.
And I think that's all I want to say, old buddy, except . . .
keep your head down.

He thought he had been scared then. He hadn't known
what scared was. Scared was coming home and finding
your wife dead with her fingernails pulled out. They had
pulled out her nails to find out where Charlie was. Charlie
had been spending two days and two nights at her friend
Terri Dugan's house. A month or so later they had been
planning to have Terri over to their house for a similar
length of time. Vicky had called it the Great Swap of 1980.

Now, sitting on the deck and smoking, Andy could
reconstruct what had happened, although then he had
existed in nothing but a blur of grief and panic and rage:
it had been the blindest good luck (or perhaps a little more
than luck) that had enabled him to catch up with them at
all.

They had been under surveillance, the whole family.
Must have been for some time. And when Charlie hadn't
come home from summer daycamp that Wednesday afternoon, and didn't show up on Thursday or Thursday
evening either, they must have decided that Andy and
Vicky had tumbled to the surveillance. Instead of discov-
ering that Charlie was doing no more than staying at a
friend's house not two miles away, they must have decided
that they had taken their daughter and gone underground.

It was a crazy, stupid mistake, but it hadn't been the
first such on the Shop's part — according to an article Andy
had read in *Rolling Stone*, the Shop had been involved and
heavily influential in precipitating a bloodbath over an
airplane hijacking by Red Army terrorists (the hijack had
been aborted — at the cost of sixty lives), in selling heroin
to the Organization in return for information on mostly

187

harmless Cuban-American groups in Miami, and in the communist takeover of a Caribbean island that had once been known for its multimillion-dollar beachfront hotels and its voodoo-practicing population.

With such a series of colossal gaffes under the Shop's belt, it became less difficult to understand how the agents employed to keep watch on the McGee family could mistake a child's two nights at a friend's house as a run for the tall timber. As Quincey would have said (and maybe he had), if the most efficient of the Shop's thousand or more employees had to go to work in the private sector, they would have been drawing unemployment benefits before their probationary periods were up.

But there had been crazy mistakes on both sides, Andy reflected – and if the bitterness in that thought had become slightly vague and diffuse with the passage of time, it had once been sharp enough to draw blood, a many-tined bitterness, with each sharp point tipped with the curare of guilt. He had been scared by the things Quincey implied on the phone that day Charlie tripped and fell down the stairs, but apparently he hadn't been scared enough. If he had been, perhaps they *would* have gone underground.

He had discovered too late that the human mind can become hypnotized when a life, or the life of a family, begins to drift out of the normal range of things and into a fervid fantasy-land that you are usually asked to accept only in sixty-minute bursts on TV or maybe for one-hundred-ten-minute sittings in the local Cinema I.

In the wake of his conversation with Quincey, a peculiar feeling had gradually crept over him: it began to seem that he was constantly stoned. A tap on his phone? People watching them? A possibility that they might all be scooped up and dropped into the basement rooms of some government complex? There was such a tendency to smile a silly smile and just watch these things loom up, such a tendency to do the civilized thing and pooh-pooh your own instincts. . . .

Out on Tashmore Pond there was a sudden dark flurry and a number of ducks took off into the night, headed west. A half-moon was rising, casting a dull silver glow across their wings as they went. Andy lit another cigarette. He was smoking too much, but he would get a chance to go cold turkey soon enough; he had only four or five left.

Yes, he had suspected there was a tap on the phone. Sometimes there would be an odd double click after you picked it up and said hello. Once or twice, when he had been talking to a student who had called to ask about an assignment or to one of his colleagues, the connection had been mysteriously broken. He had suspected that there might be bugs in the house, but he had never torn the place apart looking for them (had he suspected he might find them? . And several times he had suspected – no, had been almost sure – that they were being watched.

They had lived in the Lakeland district of Harrison, and Lakeland was the sublime archetype of suburbia. On a drunk night you could circle six or eight blocks for hours, just looking for your own house. The people who were their neighbors worked for the IBM plant outside town, Ohio Semi-Conductor in town, or taught at the college. You could have drawn two ruler-straight lines across an average-family-income sheet, the lower line at eighteen and a half thousand and the upper one at maybe thirty thousand, and almost everyone in Lakeland would have fallen in the area between.

You got to know people. You nodded on the street to Mrs Bacon, who had lost her husband and had since been remarried to vodka – and she looked it; the honeymoon with that particular gentleman was playing hell with her face and figure. You tipped a V at the two girls with the white Jag who were renting the house on the corner of

Jasmine Street and Lakeland Avenue – and wondered what spending the night with the two of them would be like. You talked baseball with Mr Hammond on Laurel Lane as he everlastingly trimmed his hedges. Mr Hammond was with IBM ('Which stands for I've Been Moved,' he would tell you endlessly as the electric clippers hummed and buzzed), originally from Atlanta and a rabid Atlanta Braves fan. He loathed Cincinnati's Big Red Machine, which did not exactly endear him to the neighborhood. Not that Hammond gave a shit. He was just waiting for IBM to hand him a fresh set of walking papers.

But Mr Hammond was not the point. Mrs Bacon wasn't the point, nor were those two luscious peaches in their white Jag with the dull red primer paint around the headlights. The point was that after a while your brain formed its own subconscious subset: people who belong in Lakeland.

But in the months before Vicky was killed and Charlie snatched from the Dugans' house, there had been people around who didn't belong to that subset. Andy had dismissed them, telling himself it would be foolish to alarm Vicky just because talking to Quincey had made him paranoid.

The people in the light-gray van. The man with the red hair that he had seen slouched behind the wheel of an AMC Matador one night and then behind the wheel of a Plymouth Arrow one night about two weeks later and then in the shotgun seat of the gray van about ten days after that. Too many salesmen came to call. There had been evenings when they had come home from a day out or from taking Charlie to see the latest Disney epic when he had got the feeling that someone had been in the house, that things had been moved around the tiniest bit.

That feeling of being watched.

But he hadn't believed it would go any further than

watching. That had been *his* crazy mistake. He was still not entirely convinced that it had been a case of panic on their part. They might have been planning to snatch Charlie and himself, killing Vicky because she was relatively useless – who really needed a low-grade psychic whose big trick for the week was closing the refrigerator door from across the room?

Nevertheless, the job had a reckless, hurry-up quality to it that made him think that Charlie's surprise disappearance had made them move more quickly than they had intended. They might have waited if it had been Andy who dropped out of sight, but it hadn't been. It had been Charlie, and she was the one they were really interested in. Andy was sure of that now.

He got up and stretched, listening to the bones in his spine crackle. Time he went to bed, time he stopped hashing over these old, hurtful memories. He was not going to spend the rest of his life blaming himself for Vicky's death. He had only been an accessory before the fact, after all. And the rest of his life might not be that long, either. The action on Irv Manders's porch hadn't been lost on Andy McGee. They had meant to waste him. It was only Charlie they wanted now.

He went to bed, and after a while he slept. His dreams were not easy ones. Over and over he saw that trench of fire running across the beaten dirt of the dooryard, saw it divide to make a fairy-ring around the chopping block, saw the chickens going up like living incendiaries. In the dream, he felt the heat capsule around him, building and building.

She said she wasn't going to make fires anymore.

And maybe that was best.

Outside, the cold October moon shone down on Tash-more Pond on Bradford, New Hampshire, across the water, and on the rest of New England. To the south, it shone down on Longmont, Virginia.

4

Sometimes Andy McGee had feelings – hunches of extraordinary vividness. Ever since the experiment in Jason Gearneigh Hall. He didn't know if the hunches were a low-grade sort of precognition or not, but he had learned to trust them when he got them.

Around noon on that August day in 1980, he got a bad one.

It began during lunch in the Buckeye Room, the faculty lounge on the top floor of the Union building. He could even pinpoint the exact moment. He had been having creamed chicken on rice with Ev O'Brian, Bill Wallace, and Don Grabowski, all in the English Department. Good friends, all of them. And as usual, someone had brought along a Polish joke for Don, who collected them. It had been Ev's joke, something about being able to tell a Polish ladder from a regular one because the Polish ladder had the word STOP lettered on the top rung. All of them were laughing when a small, very calm voice spoke up in Andy's mind.

(something's wrong at home)

That was all. That was enough. It began to build up almost the same way that his headaches built up when he overused the push and tipped himself over. Only this wasn't a head thing; all his emotions seemed to be tangling themselves up, almost lazily, as if they were yarn and some bad-tempered cat had been let loose along the runs of his nervous system to play with them and snarl them up.

He stopped feeling good. The creamed chicken lost whatever marginal appeal it had had to begin with. His stomach began to flutter, and his heart was beating rapidly, as if he had just had a bad scare. And then the fingers of his right hand began abruptly to throb, as if he had got them jammed in a door.

Abruptly he stood up. Cold sweat was breaking on his forehead.

'Look, I don't feel so good,' he said. 'Can you take my one o'clock, Bill?'

'Those aspiring poets? Sure. No problem. What's wrong?'

'I don't know. Something I ate, maybe.'

'You look sort of pale,' Don Grabowski said. 'You ought to cruise over to the infirmary, Andy.'

'I may do that,' Andy said.

He left, but with no intention whatever of going to the infirmary. It was quarter past twelve, the late-summer campus drowsing through the last week of the final summer session. He raised a hand to Ev, Bill, and Don as he hurried out. He had not seen any of them since that day.

He stopped on the Union's lower level, let himself into a telephone booth, and called home. There was no answer. No real reason why there should have been; with Charlie at the Dugans, Vicky could have been out shopping, having her hair done, she could have been over at Tammy Upmore's house or even having lunch with Eileen Bacon. Nevertheless, his nerves cranked up another notch. They were nearly screaming now.

He left the Union building and half walked, half ran to the station wagon, which was in the Prince Hall parking lot. He drove across town to Lakeland. His driving was jerky and poor. He jumped lights, tailgated, and came close to knocking a hippie off his ten-speed Olympia. The hippie gave him the finger. Andy barely noticed. His heart was triphammering now. He felt as if he had taken a hit of speed.

They lived on Conifer Place – in Lakeland, as in so many

suburban developments built in the fifties, most of the streets seemed named for trees or shrubs. In the midday August heat, the street seemed queerly deserted. It only added to his feeling that something bad had happened. The street looked wider with so few cars parked along the curbs. Even the few kids playing here and there could not dispel that strange feeling of desertion; most of them were eating lunch or over at the playground. Mrs Flynn from Laurel Lane walked past with a bag of groceries in a wheeled caddy, her paunch as round and tight as a soccer ball under her avocado-colored stretch pants. All up and down the street, lawn sprinklers twirled lazily, fanning water onto the grass and rainbows into the air.

Andy drove the offside wheels of the wagon up over the curb and then slammed on the brakes hard enough to lock his seatbelt momentarily and to make the wagon's nose dip toward the pavement. He turned off the engine with the gearshift still in Drive, something he never did, and went up the cracked cement walk that he kept meaning to patch and somehow never seemed to get around to. His heels clacked meaninglessly. He noticed that the venetian blind over the big living-room picture window *mural window*, the realtor who had sold them the house called it, *here ya gotcha basic mural window* was drawn, giving the house a closed, secretive aspect he didn't like. Did she usually pull the blind? To keep as much of the summer heat out as possible, maybe? He didn't know. He realized there were a great many things he didn't know about her life when he was away.

He reached for the doorknob, but it didn't turn; it only slipped through his fingers. Did she lock the door when he was gone? He didn't believe it. That wasn't Vicky. His worry – no, it was terror now – increased. And yet there was one moment (which he would never admit to himself later), one small moment when he felt nothing but an urge to turn away from that locked door. Just hightail it. Never mind Vicky, or Charlie, or the weak justifications that would come later.

Just run.

Instead, he groped in his pocket for his keys.

In his nervousness he dropped them and had to bend to pick them up – car keys, the key to the east wing of Prince Hall, the blackish key that unlocked the chain he put across Granther's road at the end of each summer visit. Keys had a funny way of accumulating.

He plucked his housekey from the bunch and unlocked the door. He went in and shut it behind him. The light in the living room was a low, sick yellow. It was hot. And still. Oh God it was so still.

'Vicky?'

No answer. And all that no answer meant was that she wasn't here. She had put on her boogie shoes, as she liked to say, and had gone marketing or visiting. Except that she wasn't doing either of those things. He felt sure of it. And his hand, his right hand . . . why were the fingers throbbing so?

'Vicky!'

He went into the kitchen. There was a small Formica table out there with three chairs. He and Vicky and Charlie usually ate their breakfast in the kitchen. One of the chairs now lay on its side like a dead dog. The salt shaker had overturned and salt was spilled across the table's surface. Without thinking about what he was doing, Andy pinched some of it between the thumb and first finger of his left hand and tossed it back over his shoulder, muttering under his breath, as both his father and his Granther had done before him, 'Salt salt malt malt bad luck stay away.'

There was a pot of soup on the Hotpoint. It was cold. The empty soup can stood on the counter. Lunch for one. But where was she?

'Vicky!' he hollered down the stairs. Dark down there. The laundry room and the family room, which ran the length of the house.

No answer.

He looked around the kitchen again. Neat and tidy. Two of Charlie's drawings, made at the Vacation Bible School she had attended in July, held on the refrigerator with small plastic vegetables that had magnetic bases. An electric bill and a phone bill stuck on the spike with the motto PAY THESE LAST written across the base. Everything in its place and a place for everything.

Except the chair was overturned. Except the salt was spilled.

There was no spit in his mouth, none at all. His mouth was as dry and slick as chrome on a summer day.

Andy went upstairs, looked through Charlie's room, their room, the guest room. Nothing. He went back through the kitchen, flicked on the stairway light, and went downstairs. Their Maytag washer gaped open. The dryer fixed him with one glassy porthole eye. Between them, on the wall, hung a sampler Vicky had bought somewhere; it read HONEY, WE'RE ALL WASHED UP. He went into the family room and fumbled for the light switch, fingers brushing at the wall, crazily sure that at any moment unknown cold fingers would close over his and guide them to the switch. Then he found the plate at last, and the fluorescent bars set into the Armstrong ceiling glowed alive.

This was a good room. He had spent a lot of time down here, fixing things up, smiling at himself all the time because, in the end, he had become all those things that as undergraduates they had sworn they would not become. All three of them had spent a lot of time down here. There was a TV built into the wall, a Ping-Pong table, an oversized backgammon board. More board games were cased against one wall, there were some coffee-table-sized books ranged along a low table that Vicky had made from barnboard. One wall had been dressed in paperbacks. Hung on the walls were several framed and matted afghan squares that Vicky had knitted; she joked that she was great at individual squares but simply didn't have the stamina to knit a whole damn blanket. There were Charlie's books in a special kid-sized bookcase, all of them carefully arranged in alphabetical order, which Andy had taught her one boring snowy night two winters before and which still fascinated her.

A good room.

An empty room.

He tried to feel relief. The premonition, hunch, whatever you wanted to call it, had been wrong. She just wasn't here. He snapped off the light and went back into the laundry room.

The washing machine, a front-loader they had picked up at a yard sale for sixty bucks, still gaped open. He shut it without thinking, much as he had tossed a pinch of the spilled salt over his shoulder. There was blood on the washer's glass window. Not much. Only three or four drops. But it was blood.

Andy stood staring at it. It was cooler down here, too cool, it was like a morgue down here. He looked at the floor. There was more blood on the floor. It wasn't even dry. A little sound, a soft, squealing whisper, came from his throat.

He began to walk around the laundry room, which was nothing but a small alcove with white plaster walls. He opened the clothes hamper. It was empty but for one sock. He looked in the cubbyhole under the sink. Nothing but Lestoil and Tide and Biz and Spic 'n Span. He looked under the stairs. Nothing there but cobwebs and the plastic leg of one of Charlie's older dolls – that dismembered limb lying patiently down here and waiting for rediscovery for God knew how long.

He opened the door between the washer and the dryer and the ironing board whistled down with a ratchet and a crash and there beneath it, her legs tied up so that her knees were just below her chin, her eyes open and glazed and dead, was Vicky Tomlinson McGee with a cleaning rag stuffed in her mouth. There was a thick and sickening smell of Pledge furniture polish in the air.

He made a low gagging noise and stumbled backward. His hands flailed, as if to drive this terrible vision away, and one of them struck the control panel of the dryer and it whirred into life. Clothes began to tumble and click inside. Andy screamed. And then he ran. He ran up the stairs and stumbled going around the corner into the kitchen and sprawled flat and bumped his forehead on the linoleum. He sat up, breathing hard.

It came back. It came back in slow motion, like a football instant replay where you see the quarterback sacked or the winning pass caught. It haunted his dreams in the days that came later. The door swinging open, the ironing board falling down to the horizontal with a ratcheting sound, reminding him somehow of a guillotine, his wife crammed into the space beneath and in her mouth a rag that had been used to polish the furniture. It came back in a kind of total recall and he knew he was going to scream again and so he slammed his forearm into his mouth and he bit it and the sound that came out was a fuzzy, blocked howl. He did that twice, and something came out of him and he was calm. It was the false calm of shock, but it could be used. The amorphous fear and the unfocused terror fell away. The throbbing in his right hand was gone. And the thought that stole into his mind now was as cold as the calmness that had settled over him, as cold as the shock, and that thought was *CHARLIE*.

He got up, started for the telephone, and then turned back to the stairs. He stood at the top for a moment, biting at his lips, steeling himself, and then he went back down. The dryer turned and turned. There was nothing in there but a pair of his jeans, and it was the big brass button at the waist that made that clicking, clinking sound as they turned and fell, turned and fell. Andy shut the dryer off and looked into the ironing-board closet.

'Vicky,' he said softly.

She stared at him with her dead eyes, his wife. He had walked with her, held her hand, entered her body in the dark of night. He found himself remembering the night she had drunk too much at a faculty party and he had held her head while she threw up. And that memory became the day he had been washing the station wagon and he had gone into the garage for a moment to get the can of Turtle Wax and she had picked up the hose and had run up behind him and stuffed the hose down the back of his pants. He remembered getting married and kissing her in front of everyone, relishing that kiss, her mouth, her ripe, soft mouth.

'Vicky,' he said again, and uttered a long, trembling sigh.

He pulled her out and worked the rag from her mouth. Her head lolled limp on her shoulders. He saw that the blood had come from her right hand, where some of her fingernails had been pulled. There was a small trickle of blood from one of her nostrils, but none anywhere else. Her neck had been broken by a single hard blow.

'Vicky,' he whispered.

Charlie, his mind whispered back.

In the still calm that now filled his head, he understood that Charlie had become the important thing, the only important thing. Recriminations were for the future.

He went back into the family room, not bothering to

turn on the light this time. Across the room, by the Ping-Pong table, was a couch with a drop cloth over it. He took the drop cloth and went back into the laundry room and covered Vicky with it. Somehow, the immobile shape of her under the sofa's drop cloth was worse. It held him nearly hypnotized. Would she never move again? Could that be?

He uncovered her face and kissed her lips. They were cold.

They pulled her nails, his mind marveled. *Jesus Christ, they pulled her nails.*

And he knew why. They wanted to know where Charlie was. Somehow they had lost track of her when she went to Terri Dugan's house instead of coming home after day-camp. They had panicked, and now the watching phase was over. Vicky was dead – either on purpose or because some Shop operative had got overzealous. He knelt beside Vicky and thought it was possible that, prodded by her fear, she had done something rather more spectacular than shutting the fridge door from across the room. She might have shoved one of them away or knocked the feet out from beneath one of them. Too bad she hadn't had enough to throw them into the wall at about fifty miles an hour, he thought.

It could have been that they knew just enough to make them nervous, he supposed. Maybe they had even been given specific orders: *The woman may be extremely dangerous. If she does something – anything – to jeopardize the operation, get rid of her. Quick.*

Or maybe they just didn't like leaving witnesses. Something more than their share of the taxpayer's dollar was at stake, after all.

But the blood. He should be thinking about the blood, which hadn't even been dry when he discovered it, only tacky. They hadn't been gone long when he arrived.

More insistently his mind said: *Charlie!*

He kissed his wife again and said, 'Vicky, I'll be back.'

But he had never seen Vicky again, either.

He had gone upstairs to the telephone and looked up the Dugans' number in Vicky's Phone-Mate. He dialed the number and Joan Dugan answered.

'Hi, Joan,' he said, and now the shock was aiding him: his voice was perfectly calm, an everyday voice. 'Could I speak to Charlie for a second?'

'Charlie?' Mrs Dugan sounded doubtful. 'Well, she went with those two friends of yours. Those teachers. Is . . . wasn't that all right?'

Something inside of him went skyrocketing up and then came plunging down. His heart, maybe. But it would do no good to panic this nice woman whom he had only met socially four or five times. It wouldn't help him, and it wouldn't help Charlie.

'Damn,' he said. 'I was hoping to catch her still there. When did they go?'

Mrs Dugan's voice faded a little. 'Terri, when did Charlie go?'

A child's voice piped something. He couldn't tell what. There was sweat between his knuckles.

'She says about fifteen minutes ago.' She was apologetic. 'I was doing the laundry and I don't have a watch. One of them came down and spoke to me. It *was* all right, wasn't it, Mr McGee? He looked all right . . .'

A lunatic impulse came to him, to just laugh lightly and say *Doing the laundry, were you? So was my wife. I found her crammed in under the ironing board. You got off lucky today, Joan.*

He said, 'That's fine. Were they coming right here, I wonder?'

The question was relayed to Terri, who said she didn't

know. Wonderful, Andy thought. My daughter's life is in the hands of another six-year-old girl.

He grasped at a straw.

'I have to go down to the market on the corner,' he said to Mrs Dugan. 'Will you ask Terri if they had the car or the van? In case I see them.'

This time he heard Terri. 'It was the van. They went away in a gray van, like the one David Pasioco's father has.'

'Thanks,' he said. Mrs Dugan said not to mention it. The impulse came again, this time just to scream *My wife is dead!* down the line at her. *My wife is dead and why were you doing your laundry while my daughter was getting into a gray van with a couple of strange men?*

Instead of screaming that or anything, he hung up and went outside. The heat whacked him over the head and he staggered a little. Had it been this hot when he came? It seemed much hotter now. The mailman had come. There was a Woolco advertising circular sticking out of the mailbox that hadn't been there before. The mailman had come while he was downstairs cradling his dead wife in his arms. His poor dead Vicky: they had pulled out her nails, and it was funny – much funnier than the way the keys had of accumulating, really – how the fact of death kept coming at you from different sides and different angles. You tried to jig and jog, you tried to protect yourself on one side, and the truth of it bored right in on another side. Death is a football player, he thought, one big mother. Death is Franco Harris or Sam Cunningham or Mean Joe Green. And it keeps throwing you down on your ass right there at the line of scrimmage.

Get your feet moving, he thought. Fifteen minutes' lead time – that's not so much. It's not a cold trail yet. Not unless Terri Dugan doesn't know fifteen minutes from half an hour to two hours. Never mind that, anyway. Get going.

He got going. He went back to the station wagon, which was parked half on and half off the sidewalk. He opened the driver's-side door and then spared a glance back at his neat suburban house on which the mortgage was half paid. The bank let you take a 'payment vacation' two months a year if you needed it. Andy had never needed it. He looked at the house dozing in the sun, and again his shocked eyes were caught by the red flare of the Woolco circular sticking out of the mailbox, and *whap!* death hit him again, making his eyes blur and his teeth clamp down.

He got in the car and drove away toward Terri Dugan's street, not going on any real, logical belief that he could pick up their trail but only on blind hope. He had not seen his house on Conifer Place in Lakeland since then.

His driving was better now. Now that he knew the worst, his driving was a lot better. He turned on the radio and there was Bob Seger singing 'Still the Same.'

He drove across Lakeland, moving as fast as he dared. For one terrible moment he came up blank on the name of the street, and then it came to him. The Dugans lived on Blassmore Place. He and Vicky had joked about that: Blassmore Place, with houses designed by Bill Blass. He started to smile a little at the memory, and *whap!* the fact of her death hit him again, rocking him.

He was there in ten minutes. Blassmore Place was a short dead end. No way out for a gray van at the far end, just a cyclone fence that marked the edge of the John Glenn Junior High School.

Andy parked the wagon at the intersection of Blassmore Place and Ridge Street. There was a green-over-white house on the corner. A lawn sprinkler twirled. Out front were two kids, a girl and a boy of about ten. They were taking turns on a skateboard. The girl was wearing shorts, and she had a good set of scabs on each knee.

He got out of the wagon and walked toward them. They looked him up and down carefully.

'Hi,' he said. 'I'm looking for my daughter. She passed by here about half an hour ago in a gray van. She was with . . . well, some friends of mine. Did you see a gray van go by?'

The boy shrugged vaguely.

The girl said, 'You worried about her, mister?'

'You saw the van, didn't you?' Andy asked pleasantly, and gave her a very slight push. Too much would be counterproductive. She would see the van going in any direction he wanted, including skyward.

'Yeah, I saw a van,' she said. She got on the skateboard and glided toward the hydrant on the corner and then jumped off. 'It went right up there.' She pointed farther up Blassmore Place. Two or three intersections up was Carlisle Avenue, one of Harrison's main thoroughfares. Andy had surmised that would be the way they would go, but it was good to be sure.

'Thanks,' he said, and got back into the wagon.

'You worried about her?' the girl repeated.

'Yes, I am, a little,' Andy said.

He turned the wagon around and drove three blocks up Blassmore Place to the junction with Carlisle Avenue. This was hopeless, utterly hopeless. He felt a touch of panic, just a small hot spot, but it would spread. He made it go away, made himself concentrate on getting as far down their trail as possible. If he had to use the push, he would. He could give a lot of small helping pushes without making himself feel ill. He thanked God that he hadn't used the talent – or the curse, if you wanted to look at it that way – all summer long. He was up and fully charged, for whatever that was worth.

Carlisle Avenue was four lanes wide and regulated here by a stop-and-go light. There was a car wash on his right and an abandoned diner on his left. Across the street was an Exxon station and Mike's Camera Store. If they had turned left, they had headed downtown. Right, and they would be headed out toward the airport and Interstate 80.

Andy turned into the car wash. A young guy with an incredible shock of wiry red hair spilling over the collar of his dull green coverall jived over. He was eating a Popsicle.

'No can do, man,' he said before Andy could even open his mouth. 'The rinse attachment busted about an hour ago. We're closed.'

'I don't want a wash,' Andy said. 'I'm looking for a gray van that went through the intersection maybe half an hour ago. My daughter was in it, and I'm a little worried about her.'

'You think somebody might have snatched her?' He went right on eating his Popsicle.

'No, nothing like that,' Andy said. 'Did you see the van?'

'Gray van? Hey, goodbuddy, you have any idea how many cars go by here in just one hour? Or half an hour? Busy street, man. Carlisle is a very busy street.'

Andy cocked his thumb over his shoulder. 'It came from Blassmore Place. That's not so busy.' He got ready to add a little push, but he didn't have to. The young guy's eyes suddenly brightened. He broke his Popsicle in two like a wishbone and sucked all the purple ice off one of the sticks in a single improbable slurp.

'Yeah, okay, right,' he said. 'I did see it. I'll tell you why I noticed. It cut across our tarmac to beat the light. I don't care myself, but it irritates the *shit* out of the boss when they do that. Not that it matters today with the rinser on the fritz. He's got something else to be irritated about.'

'So the van headed toward the airport.'

The guy nodded, flipped one of the Popsicle sticks back over his shoulder, and started on the remaining chunk. 'Hope you find your girl, goodbuddy. If you don't mind a little, like, gray-tuitous advice, you ought to call the cops if you're really worried.'

'I don't think that would do much good,' Andy said. 'Under the circumstances.'

He got back in the wagon again, crossed the tarmac himself, and turned onto Carlisle Avenue. He was now headed west. The area was cluttered with gas stations, car washes, fast-food franchises, used-car lots. A drive-in advertised a double bill consisting of THE CORPSE GRINDERS and BLOODY MERCHANTS OF DEATH. He looked at the marquee and heard the ironing board ratcheting out of its closet like a guillotine. His stomach rolled over.

He passed under a sign announcing that you could get on I-80 a mile and a half farther west, if that was your pleasure. Beyond that was a smaller sign with an airplane on it. Okay, he had got this far. Now what?

Suddenly he pulled into the parking lot of a Shakey's Pizza. It was no good stopping and asking along here. As the car-wash guy had said, Carlisle was a busy street. He could push people until his brains were leaking out his ears and only succeed in confusing himself. It was the turnpike or the airport, anyway. He was sure of it. The lady or the tiger.

He had never in his life *tried* to make one of the hunches come. He simply took them as gifts when they did come, and usually acted on them. Now he slouched farther down in the driver's seat of the wagon, touching his temples lightly with the tips of his fingers, and tried to make something come. The motor was idling, the radio was still on. The Rolling Stones. Dance, little sister, dance.

Charlie, he thought. She had gone off to Terri's with her clothes stuffed in the knapsack she wore just about everywhere. That had probably helped to fool them. The last time he had seen her, she was wearing jeans and a salmon-colored shell top. Her hair was in pigtails, as it almost always was. A nonchalant good-bye, Daddy, and a kiss and holy Jesus, Charlie, where are you now?

Nothing came.

Never mind. Sit a little longer. Listen to the Stones. Shakey's Pizza. You get your choice, thin crust or crunchy. You pays your money and you takes your choice, as Granther McGee used to say. The Stones exhorting little sister to dance, dance, dance. Quincey saying they'd probably put her in a room so two hundred and twenty million Americans could be safe and free. Vicky. He and Vicky had had a hard time with the sex part of it at first. She had been scared to death. Just call me the Ice Maiden, she had said through her tears after that first miserable botched time. No sex, please, we're British. But somehow the Lot Six experiment had helped with that – the totality they had shared was, in its own way, like mating. Still it had been difficult. A little at·a time. Gentleness. Tears. Vicky beginning to respond, then stiffening, crying out *Don't, it'll hurt, don't, Andy, stop it!* And somehow it was the Lot Six experiment, that common experience, that had enabled him to go on trying, like a safecracker who knows that there is a way, always a way. And there had come a night when they got through it. Later there came a night when it was all right. Then, suddenly, a night when it was glorious. Dance, little sister, dance. He had been with her when Charlie was born. A quick, easy delivery. Quick to fix, easy to please. . . .

Nothing was coming. The trail was getting colder and he had nothing. The airport or the turnpike? The lady or the tiger?

The Stones finished. The Doobie Brothers came on, wanting to know without love, where would you be right now. Andy didn't know. The sun beat down. The lines in the Shakey's parking lot had been freshly painted. They were very white and firm against the black-top. The lot was more than three quarters full. It was lunchtime. Had Charlie got her lunch? Would they feed her? Maybe

(maybe they'll stop make a service stop you know at one of those HoJos along the pike – after all they can't drive can't drive can't drive)

Where? Can't drive where?

(can't drive all the way to Virginia without making a rest stop can they? I mean a little girl has got to stop and take a tinkle sometime, doesn't she?)

He straightened up, feeling an immense but numb feeling of gratitude. It had come, just like that. Not the airport, which would have been his first guess, if he had only been guessing. Not the airport but the turnpike. He wasn't completely sure the hunch was bona fide, but he was pretty sure. And it was better than not having any idea at all.

He rolled the station wagon over the freshly painted arrow pointing the way out and turned right on Carlisle again. Ten minutes later he was on the turnpike, headed east with a toll ticket tucked into the battered, annotated copy of *Paradise Lost* on the seat beside him. Ten minutes after that, Harrison, Ohio, was behind him. He had started on the trip east that would bring him to Tashmore, Vermont, fourteen months later.

The calm held. He played the radio loud and that helped. Song followed song and he only recognized the older ones because he had pretty much stopped listening to pop music three or four years ago. No particular reason; it had just happened. They still had the jump on him, but the calm insisted with its own cold logic that it wasn't a very good jump – and that he would be asking for trouble if he just started roaring along the passing lane at seventy.

He pegged the speedometer at just over sixty, reasoning that the men who had taken Charlie would not want to exceed the fifty-five speed limit. They could flash their credentials at any Smokey who pulled them down for speeding, that was true, but they might have a certain amount of difficulty explaining a screaming six-year-old child just the same. It might slow them down, and it would surely get them in dutch with whoever was pulling the strings on this show.

They could have drugged her and hidden her, his mind whispered. *Then if they got stopped for busting along at seventy, even eighty, they'd only have to show their paper and keep right on going. Is an Ohio state cop going to toss a van that belongs to the Shop?*

Andy struggled with that as eastern Ohio flowed by. First, they might be scared to drug Charlie. Sedating a child can be a tricky business unless you're an expert . . . and they might not be sure what sedation would do to the powers they were supposed to be investigating. Second, a state cop might just go ahead and toss the van anyway, or at least hold them in the breakdown lane while he checked the validity of their ID. Third, why should they be busting their asses? They had no idea anyone was onto them. It was still not one o'clock. Andy was supposed to be at the college until two o'clock. The Shop people would not expect him to arrive back home until two-twenty or so at the earliest and probably felt they could count on anywhere from twenty minutes to two hours after that before the alarm was raised. Why shouldn't they just be loafing along?

Andy went a little faster.

Forty minutes passed, then fifty. It seemed longer. He was beginning to sweat a little; worry was nibbling through the artificial ice of calm and shock. Was the van really someplace up ahead, or had the whole thing been so much wishful thinking?

The traffic patterns formed and re-formed. He saw two gray vans. Neither of them looked like the one he had seen cruising around Lakeland. One was driven by an elderly man with flying white hair. The other was full of freaks smoking dope. The driver saw Andy's close scrutiny and waved a roach clip at him. The girl beside him popped up her middle finger, kissed it gently, and tipped it Andy's way. Then they were behind him.

His head was beginning to ache. The traffic was heavy, the sun was bright. Each car was loaded with chrome, and each piece of chrome had its own arrow of sun to flick into his eyes. He passed a sign that said REST AREA I MILE AHEAD.

He had been in the passing lane. Now he signaled right and slipped into the travel lane again. He let his speed drop to forty-five, then to forty. A small sports car passed him and the driver blipped his horn at Andy in irritated fashion as he went by.

REST AREA, the sign announced. It wasn't a service stop, simply a turn-out with slant parking, a water fountain, and bathrooms. There were four or five cars parked in there and one gray van. *The* gray van. He was almost sure of it. His heart began to slam against the walls of his chest. He turned in with a quick twist of the station wagon's wheel, and the tires made a low wailing sound.

He drove slowly down the entranceway toward the van, looking around, trying to take in everything at once. There were two picnic tables with a family at each one. One group was just clearing up and getting ready to go, the mother putting leftovers into a bright orange carrier bag, the father and the two kids policing up the junk and taking it over to the trash barrel. At the other table a young man and woman were eating sandwiches and potato salad. There was a sleeping baby in a carrier seat between them. The baby was wearing a corduroy jumper with a lot of dancing elephants on it. On the grass, between two big and beautiful old elms, were two girls of about twenty, also having lunch. There was no sign of Charlie or of any men who looked both young enough and tough enough to belong to the Shop.

Andy killed the station wagon's engine. He could feel his heartbeat in his eyeballs now. The van looked empty. He got out.

An old woman using a cane came out of the ladies' comfort station and walked slowly toward an old burgundy Biscayne. A gent of about her age got out from behind the wheel, walked around the hood, opened her door, and handed her in. He went back, started up the Biscayne, a big jet of oily blue smoke coming from the exhaust pipe, and backed out.

The men's-room door opened and Charlie came out. Flanking her on the left and right were men of about thirty in sport coats, open-throated shirts, and dark double-knit pants. Charlie's face looked blank and shocked. She looked from one of the men to the other and then back at the first. Andy's guts began to roll helplessly. She was wearing her packsack. They were walking toward the van. Charlie said something to one of them and he shook his head. She turned to the other. He shrugged, then said something to his partner over Charlie's head. The other one nodded. They turned around and walked toward the drinking fountain.

Andy's heart was beating faster than ever. Adrenaline spilled into his body in a sour, jittery flood. He was scared, scared plenty, but something else was pumping up inside him and it was anger, it was total fury. The fury was even better than the calm. It felt almost sweet. Those were the two men out there that had killed his wife and stolen his daughter, and if they weren't right with Jesus, he pitied them.

As they went to the drinking fountain with Charlie; their backs were to him. Andy got out of the wagon and stepped behind the van.

The family of four who had just finished their lunch walked over to a new midsized Ford, got in, and backed out. The mother glanced over at Andy with no curiosity at all, the way people look at each other when they are on long trips, moving slowly through the digestive tract of the U.S. turnpike system. They drove off, showing a Michigan plate. There were now three cars and the gray van and Andy's station wagon parked in the rest area. One of the cars belonged to the girls. Two more people were strolling across the grounds, and there was one man inside the little information booth, looking at the I-80 map, his hands tucked into the back pockets of his jeans.

Andy had no idea of exactly what he was going to do.

Charlie finished her drink. One of the two men bent over and took a sip. Then they started back toward their van. Andy was looking at them from around the van's back-left corner. Charlie looked scared, really scared. She had been crying. Andy tried the back door of the van, not knowing why, but it was no good anyway; it was locked.

Abruptly he stepped out into full view.

They were very quick. Andy saw the recognition come into their eyes immediately, even before the gladness flooded Charlie's face, driving away that look of blank, frightened shock.

'*Daddy!*' she cried shrilly, causing the young couple with the baby to look around. One of the girls under the elms shaded her eyes to see what was happening.

Charlie tried to run to him and one of the men grabbed her by the shoulder and hauled her back against him, half-twisting her packsack from her shoulders. An instant later there was a gun in his hand. He had produced it from somewhere under his sport coat like a magician doing an evil trick. He put the barrel against Charlie's temple.

The other man began to stroll unhurriedly away from Charlie and his partner, then began to move in on Andy. His hand was in his coat, but his conjuring was not as good as his partner's had been; he was having a little trouble producing his gun.

'Move away from the van if you don't want anything to happen to your daughter,' the one with the gun said.

'*Daddy!*' Charlie cried again.

Andy moved slowly away from the van. The other fellow, who was prematurely bald, had his gun out now. He pointed it at Andy. He was less than five feet away. 'I advise you very sincerely not to move,' he said in a low voice. 'This is a Colt forty-five and it makes a *giant* hole.'

The young guy with his wife and baby at the picnic table got up. He was wearing rimless glasses and he looked severe. 'What exactly is going on here?' he asked in the carrying, enunciated tones of a college instructor.

The man with Charlie turned toward him. The muzzle of his gun floated slightly away from her so that the young man could see it. 'Government business,' he said. 'Stay right where you are; everything is fine.'

The young man's wife grabbed his arm and pulled him down.

Andy looked at the balding agent and said in a low, pleasant voice, 'That gun is much too hot to hold.'

Baldy looked at him, puzzled. Then, suddenly, he screamed and dropped his revolver. It struck the pavement and went off. One of the girls under the elms let out a puzzled, surprised shout. Baldy was holding his hand and dancing around. Fresh white blisters appeared on his palm, rising like bread dough.

The man with Charlie stared at his partner, and for a

moment the gun was totally distracted from her small head.

'You're blind,' Andy told him, and pushed just as hard as he could. A sickening wrench of pain twisted through his head.

The man screamed suddenly. He let go of Charlie and his hands went to his eyes.

'Charlie,' Andy said in a low voice, and his daughter ran to him and clutched his legs in a trembling bear hug. The man inside the information booth ran out to see what was going on.

Baldy, still clutching his burned hand, ran toward Andy and Charlie. His face worked horribly.

'Go to sleep,' Andy said curtly, and pushed again. Baldy dropped sprawling as if pole-axed. His forehead bonked on the pavement. The young wife of the stern young man moaned.

Andy's head hurt badly now, and he was remotely glad that it was summer and that he hadn't used the push, even to prod a student who was letting his grades slip for no good reason, since perhaps May. He was charged up – but charged up or not, God knew he was going to pay for what he was doing this hot summer afternoon.

The blind man was staggering around on the grass, holding his hands up to his face and screaming. He walked into a green barrel with PUT LITTER IN ITS PLACE stenciled on its side and fell down in an overturned jumble of sandwich bags, beer cans, cigarette butts, and empty soda bottles.

'Oh Daddy, jeez I was so scared,' Charlie said, and began to cry.

'The wagon's right over there. See it?' Andy heard himself say. 'Get in and I'll be with you in a minute.'

'Is Mommy here?'

'No. Just get in, Charlie.' He couldn't deal with that now. Now, somehow, he had to deal with these witnesses.

'What the hell is this?' the man from the information booth asked, bewildered.

'My eyes,' the man who had had his gun up to Charlie's head screamed 'My *eyes*, my *eyes*. What did you do to my eyes, you son of a bitch?' He got up. There was a sandwich bag sticking to one of his hands. He began to totter off toward the information booth, and the man in the bluejeans darted back inside.

'Go, Charlie.'

'Will you come, Daddy?'

'Yes, in just a second. Now go.'

Charlie went, blond pigtails bouncing. Her packsack was still hanging askew.

Andy walked past the sleeping Shop agent, thought about his gun, and decided he didn't want it. He walked over to the young people at the picnic table. Keep it small, he told himself. Easy. Little taps. Don't go starting any echoes. The object is not to hurt these people.

The young woman grabbed her baby from its carrier seat rudely, waking it. It began to cry. 'Don't you come near me, you crazy person!' she said.

Andy looked at the man and his wife.

'None of this is very important,' he said, and pushed. Fresh pain settled over the back of his head like a spider . . . and sank in.

The young man looked relieved. 'Well, thank God.'

His wife offered a tentative smile. The push hadn't taken so well with her; her maternity had been aroused.

'Lovely baby you have there,' Andy said. 'Little boy, isn't it?'

The blind man stepped off the curbing, pitched forward, and struck his head on the doorpost of the red Pinto that probably belonged to the two girls. He howled. Blood flowed from his temple. *'I'm blind!'* he screamed again.

The young woman's tentative smile became radiant. 'Yes, a boy,' she said. 'His name is Michael.'

'Hi, Mike,' Andy said. He ruffled the baby's mostly bald head.

'I can't think why he's crying,' the young woman said. 'He was sleeping so well until just now. He must be hungry.'

'Sure, that's it,' her husband said.

'Excuse me.' Andy walked toward the information booth. There was no time to lose now. Someone else could turn into this roadside bedlam at any time.

'What is it, man?' the fellow in the bluejeans asked. 'Is it a bust?'

'Nah, nothing happened,' Andy said, and gave another light push. It was starting to make him feel sick now. His head thudded and pounded.

'Oh,' the fellow said. 'Well, I was just trying to figure out how to get to Chagrin Falls from here. Excuse me.' And he sauntered back inside the information booth.

The two girls had retreated to the security fence that separated the turn-out from the private farmland beyond it. They stared at him with wide eyes. The blind man was now shuffling around on the pavement in a circle with his arms held stiffly out in front of him. He was cursing and weeping.

Andy advanced slowly toward the girls, holding his hands out to show them there was nothing in them. He spoke to them. One of them asked him a question and he spoke again. Shortly they both began to smile relieved smiles and to nod. Andy waved to them and they both waved in return. Then he walked rapidly across the grass toward the station wagon. His forehead was beaded with cold sweat and his stomach was rolling greasily. He could only pray that no one would drive in before he and Charlie got away, because there was nothing left. He was completely tipped over. He slid in behind the wheel and keyed the engine.

'Daddy,' Charlie said, and threw herself at him, buried her face against his chest. He hugged her briefly and then backed out of the parking slot. Turning his head was agony. The black horse. In the aftermath, that was the thought that always came to him. He had let the black horse out of its stall somewhere in the dark barn of his subconscious and now it would again batter its way up and down through his brain. He would have to get them someplace and lay up. Quick. He wasn't going to be capable of driving for long.

'The black horse,' he said thickly. It was coming. No . . . no. It wasn't coming; it was here. *Thud . . . thud . . . thud.* Yes, it was here. It was free.

'*Daddy, look out!*' Charlie screamed.

The blind man had staggered directly across their path. Andy braked. The blind man began to pound on the hood of the wagon and scream for help. To their right, the young mother had begun to breast-feed her baby. Her husband was reading a paperback. The man from the information booth had gone over to talk to the two girls from the red Pinto – perhaps hoping for some quickie experience kinky enough to write up for the Penthouse *Forum*. Sprawled out on the pavement, Baldy slept on.

The other operative pounded on the hood of the wagon again and again. 'Help me!' he screamed. 'I'm blind! Dirty bastard did something to my eyes! *I'm blind!*'

'Daddy,' Charlie moaned.

For a crazy instant, he almost floored the accelerator. Inside his aching head he could hear the sound the tires would make, could feel the dull thudding of the wheels as they passed over the body. He had kidnapped Charlie and held a gun to her head. Perhaps he had been the one who had stuffed the rag into Vicky's mouth so she wouldn't scream when they pulled out her fingernails. It would be so very good to kill him . . . except then what would separate him from them?

He laid on the horn instead. It sent another bright spear of agony through his head. The blind man leaped away from the car as if stung. Andy hauled the wheel around and drove past him. The last thing he saw in the rearview mirror as he drove down the reentry lane was the blind man sitting on the pavement, his face twisted in anger and terror . . . and the young woman placidly raising baby Michael to her shoulder to burp him.

He entered the flow of turnpike traffic without looking. A horn blared; tires squalled. A big Lincoln swerved around the wagon and the driver shook his fist at them.

'Daddy, are you okay?'

'I will be,' he said. His voice seemed to come from far away. 'Charlie, look at the toll ticket and see what the next exit is.'

The traffic blurred in front of his eyes. It doubled, trebled, came back together, then drifted into prismatic fragments again. Sun reflecting off bright chrome everywhere.

'And fasten your seatbelt, Charlie.'

The next exit was Hammersmith, twenty miles farther up. Somehow he made it. He thought later that it was only the consciousness of Charlie sitting next to him, depending on him, that kept him on the road. Just as Charlie had got him through all the things that came after – the knowledge of Charlie, needing him. Charlie McGee, whose parents had once needed two hundred dollars.

There was a Best Western at the foot of the Hammersmith ramp, and Andy managed to get them checked in, specifying a room away from the turnpike. He used a bogus name.

'They'll be after us, Charlie,' he said. 'I need to sleep. But only until dark, that's all the time we can take . . . all we dare to take. Wake me up when it's dark.'

She said something else, but then he was falling on the bed. The world was blurring down to a gray point, and then even the point was gone and everything was darkness, where the pain couldn't reach. There was no pain and there were no dreams. When Charlie shook him awake again on that hot August evening at quarter past seven, the room was stifling hot and his clothes were soaked with sweat. She had tried to make the air conditioner work but hadn't been able to figure out the controls.

'It's okay,' he said. He swung his feet onto the floor and put his hands on his temples, squeezing his head so it wouldn't blow up.

'Is it any better, Daddy?' she asked anxiously.

'A little,' he said. And it was . . . but only a little. 'We'll stop in a little while and get some chow. That'll help some more.'

'Where are we going?'

He shook his head slowly back and forth. He had only the money he had left the house with that morning – about seventeen dollars. He had his Master Charge and his Visa, but he had paid for their room with the two twenties he always kept in the back of his wallet (*my run-out money, he sometimes told Vicky, joking, but how hellishly true* that had turned out to be) rather than use either one of them. Using either of those cards would be like painting a sign: THIS WAY TO THE FUGITIVE COLLEGE INSTRUCTOR AND HIS DAUGHTER. The seventeen dollars would buy them some burgers and top off the wagon's gas tank once. Then they would be stone broke.

'I don't know, Charlie,' he said. 'Just away.'

'When are we going to get Mommy?'

Andy looked up at her and his headache started to get worse again. He thought of the drops of blood on the floor and on the washing-machine porthole. He thought of the smell of Pledge.

'Charlie—' he said, and could say no more. There was no need, anyway.

She looked at him with slowly widening eyes. Her hand drifted up to her trembling mouth.

'Oh no, Daddy . . . please say it's no.'

'Charlie—'

She screamed, *'Oh please say it's no!'*

'Charlie, those people who—'

'Please say she's all *right*, say she's all *right*, say she's all *right!*'

The room, the room was so hot, the air conditioning was off, that was all it was, but it was so *hot*, his head aching, the sweat rolling down his face, not cold sweat now but hot, like oil, *hot*—

'No,' Charlie was saying, 'No, no, no, no, no.' She shook her head. Her pigtails flew back and forth, making him think absurdly of the first time he and Vicky had taken her to the amusement park, the carousel—

It wasn't the lack of air conditioning.

'Charlie!' He yelled. 'Charlie, the bathtub! *The water!*'

She screamed. She turned her head toward the open bathroom door and there was a sudden blue flash in there like a lightbulb burning out. The showerhead fell off the wall and clattered into the tub, twisted and black. Several of the blue tiles shattered to fragments.

He barely caught her when she fell, sobbing.

'Daddy, I'm sorry, I'm sorry—'

'It's all right,' he said shakily, and enfolded her. From the bathroom, thin smoke drifted out of the fused tub. All the porcelain surfaces had crack-glazed instantly. It was as

220

if the entire bathroom had been run through some powerful but defective firing kiln. The towels were smoldering.

'It's all right,' he said, holding her, rocking her. 'Charlie, it's all right, it's gonna be all right, somehow it'll come right, I promise.'

'I want Mommy,' she sobbed.

He nodded. He wanted her, too. He held Charlie tightly to him and smelled ozone and porcelain and cooked Best Western towels. She had almost flash-fried them both.

'It's gonna be all right,' he told her, and rocked her, not really believing it, but it was the litany, it was the Psalter, the voice of the adult calling down the black well of years into the miserable pit of terrorized childhood; it was what you said when things went wrong; it was the nightlight that could not banish the monster from the closet but perhaps only keep it at bay for a little while; it was the voice without power that must speak nevertheless.

'It's gonna be all right,' he told her, not really believing it, knowing as every adult knows in his secret heart that nothing is really all right, ever. 'It's gonna be all right.'

He was crying. He couldn't help it now. His tears came in a flood and he held her to his chest as tightly as he could.

'Charlie, I swear to you, somehow, it's gonna be all right.'

5

The one thing they had not been able to hang around his neck – as much as they might have liked to – was the murder of Vicky. Instead, they had elected to simply erase what had happened in the laundry room. Less trouble for them. Sometimes – not often – Andy wondered what their neighbors back in Lakeland might have speculated. Bill collectors? Marital problems? Maybe a drug habit or an incident of child abuse? They hadn't known anyone on Conifer Place well enough for it to have been any more than idle dinnertable chat, a nine days' wonder soon forgotten when the bank that held the mortgage released their house.

Sitting on the deck now and looking out into darkness, Andy thought he might have had more luck that day than he had known (or been able to appreciate). He had arrived too late to save Vicky, but he had left before the Removal People arrived.

There had never been a thing about it in the paper, not even a squib about how – funny thing! – an English instructor named Andrew McGee and his family had just up and disappeared. Perhaps the Shop had got that quashed, too. Surely he had been reported missing; one or all of the guys he had been eating lunch with that day would have done that much. But it hadn't made the papers, and of course, bill collectors don't advertise.

They would have hung it on me if they could,' he said, unaware that he had spoken aloud.

But they couldn't have. The medical examiner could have fixed the time of death, and Andy, who had been in plain sight of some disinterested third party (and in the case of Eh-116, Style and the Short Story, from ten to eleven-thirty, twenty-five disinterested third parties) all that day, could not have been set up to take the fall. Even if he'd been unable to provide substantiation for his movements during the critical time, there was no motive.

So the two of them had killed Vicky and then gone haring off after Charlie – but not without notifying what Andy thought of as the Removal People (and in his mind's eye he even saw them that way, smooth-faced young men dressed in white coveralls). And sometime after *he* had gone haring off after Charlie, maybe as short a time as five minutes, but almost surely no longer than an hour, the

Removal People would have rolled up to his door. While Conifer Place dozed the afternoon away, Vicky had been Removed.

They might even have reasoned – correctly – that a missing wife would have been more of a problem for Andy than a provably dead one. No body, no estimated time of death. No estimated time of death, no alibi. He would be watched, cosseted, politely tied down. Of course they would have put Charlie's description out on the wire – Vicky's too, for that matter – but Andy would not have been free to simply go tearing off on his own. So she had been Removed, and now he didn't even know where she was buried. Or maybe she had been cremated. Or—

Oh shit why are you doing this to yourself?

He stood up abruptly and poured the remainder of Granther's mule-kick over the deck railing. It was all in the past; none of it could be changed; it was time to stop thinking about it.

A neat trick if you could do it.

He looked up at the dark shapes of the trees and squeezed the glass tightly in his right hand, and the thought crossed his mind again.

Charlie I swear to you, somehow it's gonna be all right.

6

That winter in Tashmore, so long after his miserable awakening in that Ohio motel, it seemed his desperate prediction had finally come true.

It was not an idyllic winter for them. Not long after Christmas, Charlie caught a cold and snuffled and coughed her way through to early April, when it finally cleared up for good. For a while she ran a fever. Andy fed her aspirin halves and told himself that if the fever did not go down in three days' time, he would have to take her to the doctor

223

across the lake in Bradford, no matter what the consequences. But her fever did go down, and for the rest of the winter Charlie's cold was only a constant annoyance to her. Andy managed to get himself a minor case of frostbite on one memorable occasion in March and nearly managed to burn them both up one screaming, subzero night in February by overloading the woodstove. Ironically, it was Charlie who woke up in the middle of the night and discovered the cottage was much too hot.

On December 14 they celebrated his birthday and on March 24 they celebrated Charlie's. She was eight, and sometimes Andy looked at her with a kind of wonder, as if catching sight of her for the first time. She was not a little girl anymore; she stood to past his elbow. Her hair had got long again, and she had taken to braiding it to keep it out of her eyes. She was going to be beautiful. She already was, red nose and all.

They were without a car. Irv Manders's Willys had frozen solid in January, and Andy thought the block was cracked. He had started it every day, more from a sense of responsibility than anything else, because not even four-wheel drive would have pulled them out of Granther's camp after the New Year. The snow, undisturbed except for the tracks of squirrels, chipmunks, a few deer, and a persistent raccoon that came around to sniff hopefully at the garbage hold, was almost two feet deep by then.

There were old-fashioned cross-country skis in the small shed behind the cottage – three pairs of them, but none that would fit Charlie. It was just as well. Andy kept her indoors as much as possible. They could live with her cold, but he did not want to risk a return of the fever.

He found an old pair of Granther's ski boots, dusty and cracked with age, tucked away in a cardboard toilet-tissue box under the table where the old man had once planed shutters and made doors. Andy oiled them, flexed them, and then found he still could not fill Granther's shoes without stuffing the toes full of newspaper. There was something funny about that, but he also found it a touch ominous. He thought about Granther a lot that long winter and wondered what he would have made of their predicament.

Half a dozen times that winter he hooked up the cross-country skis (no modern snap-bindings here, only a confusing and irritating tangle of straps, buckles, and rings) and worked his way across the wide, frozen expanse of Tashmore Pond to the Bradford Town Landing. From there, a small, winding road led into the village, tucked neatly away in the hills two miles east of the lake.

He always left before first light, with Granther's knapsack on his back, and never arrived back before three in the afternoon. On one occasion he barely beat a howling snowstorm that would have left him blinded and directionless and wandering on the ice. Charlie cried with relief when he came in -- and then went into a long, alarming coughing fit.

The trips to Bradford were for supplies and clothes for him and Charlie. He had Granther's struttin money, and later on, he broke into three of the larger camps at the far end of Tashmore Pond and stole money. He was not proud of this, but it seemed to him a matter of survival. The camps he chose might have sold on the real-estate market for eighty thousand dollars apiece, and he supposed the owners could afford to lose their thirty or forty dollars' worth of cookie-jar money – which was exactly where most of them kept it. The only other thing he touched that winter was the large range-oil drum behind the large, modern cottage quaintly named CAMP CONFUSION. From this drum he took about forty gallons of oil.

He didn't like going to Bradford. He didn't like the certain knowledge that the oldsters who sat around the big potbellied stove down by the cash register were talking about the stranger who was staying across the lake in one of the camps. Stories had a way of getting around, and sometimes they got into the wrong ears. It wouldn't take much – only a whisper – for the Shop to make an inevitable connection between Andy, his grandfather, and his grandfather's cottage in Tashmore, Vermont. But he simply didn't know what else to do. They had to eat, and they couldn't spend the entire winter living on canned sardines. He wanted fresh fruit for Charlie, and vitamin pills, and clothes. Charlie had arrived with nothing to her name but a dirty blouse, a pair of red pants, and a single pair of underdrawers. There was no cough medicine that he trusted, there were no fresh vegetables, and, crazily enough, hardly any matches. Every camp he broke into had a fireplace, but he found only a single box of Diamond wooden matches.

He could have gone farther afield – there were other camps and cottages – but many of the other areas were plowed out and patrolled by the Tashmore constabulary. And on many of the roads there were at least one or two year-round residents.

In the Bradford general store he was able to buy all the things he needed, including three pairs of heavy pants and three woolen shirts that were approximately Charlie's size. There was no girls' underwear, and she had to make do with size-eight Jockey shorts. This disgusted and amused Charlie by turns.

Making the six-mile round trip across to Bradford on Granther's skis was both a burden and a pleasure to Andy. He didn't like leaving Charlie alone, not because he didn't trust her but because he always lived with the fear of coming back and finding her gone . . . or dead. The old boots gave him blisters no matter how many pairs of socks he put on. If he tried to move too fast, he gave himself headaches, and then he would remember the small numb places on his face and envision his brain as an old bald tire, a tire that had been used so long and hard that it was down to the canvas in places. If he had a stroke in the middle of this damned lake and froze to death, what would happen to Charlie then?

But he did his best thinking on these trips. The silence had a way of clearing the head. Tashmore Pond itself was not wide – Andy's path across it from the west bank to the east was less than a mile – but it was very long. With the snow lying four feet deep over the ice by February, he sometimes paused halfway across and looked slowly to his right and left. The lake then appeared to be a long corridor floored with dazzling white tile – clean, unbroken, stretching out of sight in either direction. Sugar-dusted pines bordered it all around. Above was the hard, dazzling, and merciless blue sky of winter, or the low and featureless white of coming snow. There might be the far-off call of a crow, or the low, rippling thud of the ice stretching, but that was all. The exercise toned up his body. He grew a warm singlet of sweat between his skin and his clothes, and it felt good to work up a sweat and then wipe it off your brow. He had somehow forgotten that feeling while teaching Yeats and Williams and correcting bluebooks.

In this silence, and through the exertion of working his body hard, his thoughts came clear and he worked the problem over in his mind. Something had to be done – should have been done long since, but that was in the past. They had come to Granther's place for the winter, but they were still running. The uneasy way he felt about the old-timers sitting around the stove with their pipes and their inquisitive eyes was enough to ram that fact home. He and Charlie were in a corner, and there had to be some way out of it.

And he was still angry, because *it wasn't right*. They *had* no right. His family were American citizens, living in a supposedly open society, and his wife had been murdered, his daughter kidnapped, the two of them hunted like rabbits in a hedgerow.

He thought again that if he could get the story across to someone – or to several someones – the whole thing could be blown out of the water. He hadn't done it before because that odd hypnosis – the same sort of hypnosis that had resulted in Vicky's death – had continued, at least to some degree. He hadn't wanted his daughter growing up like a freak in a sideshow. He hadn't wanted her institutionalized – not for the good of the country and not for her own good. And worst of all, he had continued to lie to himself. Even after he had seen his wife crammed into the ironing closet in the laundry with that rag in her mouth, he had continued to lie to himself and tell himself that sooner or later they would be left alone. *Just playing for funzies*, they had said as kids. *Everybody has to give back the money at the end.*

Except they weren't kids, they weren't playing for funzies, and nobody was going to give him and Charlie anything back when the game was over. This game was for keeps.

In silence he began to understand certain hard truths. In a way, Charlie *was* a freak, not much different from the thalidomide babies of the sixties or those girl children of mothers who had taken DES; the doctors just hadn't known that those girl children were going to develop vaginal tumors in abnormal numbers fourteen or sixteen years down the road. It was not Charlie's fault, but that did not change the fact. Her strangeness, her freakishness, was simply on the inside. What she had done at the Manders farm had been terrifying, totally terrifying, and since then Andy had found himself wondering just how far her ability reached, how far it *could* reach. He had read a lot of the literature of parapsychology during their year on the dodge,

228

enough to know that both pyrokinesis and telekinesis were suspected to be tied in with certain poorly understood ductless glands. His reading had also told him that the two talents were closely related, and that most documented cases centered around girls not a whole lot older than Charlie was right now.

She had been able to initiate that destruction at the Manders farm at the age of seven. Now she was nearly eight. What might happen when she turned twelve and entered adolescence? Maybe nothing. Maybe a great deal. She said she wasn't going to use the power anymore, but if she was forced to use it? What if it began to come out spontaneously? What if she began to light fires in her sleep as a part of her own strange puberty, a fiery counterpart of the nocturnal seminal emissions most teenage boys experienced? What if the Shop finally decided to call off its dogs. . . and Charlie was kidnapped by some foreign power?

Questions, questions.

On his trips across the pond, Andy tried to grapple with them and came reluctantly to believe that Charlie might have to submit to some sort of custody for the rest of her life, if only for her own protection. It might be as necessary for her as the cruel leg braces were for the victims of muscular dystrophy or the strange prosthetics for the thalidomide babies.

And then there was the question of his own future. He remembered the numb places, the bloodshot eye. No man wants to believe that his own death-warrant has been signed and dated, and Andy did not completely believe that, but he was aware that two or three more hard pushes might kill him, and he realized that his normal life expectancy might already have been considerably shortened. Some provision had to be made for Charlie in case that happened.

But not the Shop's way.

Not the small room. He would not allow that to happen.

So he thought it over, and at last he came to a painful decision.

7

Andy wrote six letters. They were almost identical. Two were to Ohio's United States senators. One was to the woman who represented the district of which Harrison was a part in the U.S. House of Representatives. One was to the New York *Times*. One was to the Chicago *Tribune*. And one was to the Toledo *Blade*. All six letters told the story of what had happened, beginning with the experiment in Jason Gearneigh Hall and ending with his and Charlie's enforced isolation on Tashmore Pond.

When he had finished, he gave one of the letters to Charlie to read. She went through it slowly and carefully, taking almost an hour. It was the first time she had got the entire story, from beginning to end.

'You're going to mail these?' she asked when she finished.

'Yes,' he said. 'Tomorrow. I think tomorrow will be the last time I dare go across the pond.' It had at last begun to warm up a little. The ice was still solid, but it creaked constantly now, and he didn't know how much longer it would be safe.

'What will happen, Daddy?'

He shook his head. 'I don't know for sure. All I can do is hope that once the story is out, those people who have been chasing us will have to give it up.'

Charlie nodded soberly. 'You should have done it before.'

'Yes,' he said, knowing that she was thinking of the near cataclysm at the Manders farm last October. 'Maybe I should have. But I never had a chance to think much,

Charlie. Keeping us going was all I had time to think about. And what thinking you do get a chance to do when you're on the run . . . well, mostly it's stupid thinking. I kept hoping they'd give up and leave us alone. That was a terrible mistake.'

'They won't make me go away, will they?' Charlie asked. 'From you, I mean. We can stay together, can't we, Daddy?'

'Yes,' he said, not wanting to tell her that his conception of what might happen after the letters were mailed and received was probably as vague as hers. It was just 'after.'

'Then that's all I care about. And I'm not going to make anymore fires.'

'All right,' he said, and touched her hair. His throat was suddenly thick with a premonitory dread, and something that had happened near here suddenly occurred to him, something that he hadn't thought of for years. He had been out with his father and Granther, and Granther had given Andy his .22, which he called his varmint rifle, when Andy clamored for it. Andy had seen a squirrel and wanted to shoot it. His dad had started to protest, and Granther had hushed him with an odd little smile.

Andy had aimed the way Granther taught him; he squeezed the trigger rather than just jerking back on it (as Granther had also taught him), and he shot the squirrel. It tumbled off its limb like a stuffed toy, and Andy ran excitedly for it after handing the gun back to Granther. Up close, he had been struck dumb by what he saw. Up close, the squirrel was no stuffed toy. It wasn't dead. He had got it in the hindquarters and it lay there dying in its own bright dapples of blood, its black eyes awake and alive and full of a horrible suffering. Its fleas, knowing the truth already, were trundling off the body in three busy little lines.

His throat had closed with a snap, and at the age of nine,

231

Andy tasted for the first time that bright, painty flavor of self-loathing. He stared numbly at his messy kill, aware that his father and grandfather were standing behind him, their shadows lying over him – three generations of McGees standing over a murdered squirrel in the Vermont woods. And behind him, Granther said softly, *Well, you done it, Andy. How do you like it?* And the tears had come suddenly, overwhelming him, the hot tears of horror and realization – the realization that once it's done, it's done. He swore suddenly that he would never kill anything with a gun again. He swore it before God.

I'm not going to make anymore fires, Charlie had said, and in his mind Andy heard Granther's reply to him on the day he had shot the squirrel, the day he had sworn to God he would never do anything like that again. *Never say that, Andy. God loves to make a man break a vow. It keeps him properly humble about his place in the world and his sense of self-control.* About what Irv Manders had said to Charlie.

Charlie had found a complete set of Bomba the Jungle Boy books in the attic and was working her way slowly but surely through them. Now Andy looked at her, sitting in a dusty shaft of sunlight in the old black rocker, sitting just where his grandmother had always sat, usually with a basket of mending between her feet, and he struggled with an urge to tell her to take it back, to take it back while she still could, to tell her that she didn't understand the terrible temptation: if the gun was left there long enough, sooner or later you would pick it up again.

God loves to make a man break a vow.

8

No one saw Andy mail his letters except Charles Payson, the fellow who had moved into Bradford in November and had since been trying to make a go of the old Bradford

Notions 'n' Novelties shop. Payson was a small, sad-faced man who had tried to buy Andy a drink on one of his visits to town. In the town itself, the expectation was that if Payson didn't make it work during the coming summer, Notions 'n' Novelties would have a FOR SALE OR LEASE sign back in the window by September 15. He was a nice enough fellow, but he was having a hard scrabble. Bradford wasn't the town it used to be.

Andy walked up the street – he had left his skis stuck in the snow at the head of the road leading down to the Bradford Town Landing – and approached the general store. Inside, the oldsters watched him with mild interest. There had been a fair amount of talk about Andy that winter. The consensus about yonder man there was that he was on the run from something – a bankruptcy, maybe, or a divorce settlement. Maybe an angry wife who had been cheated out of custody of the kid: the small clothes Andy had bought hadn't been lost on them. The consensus was also that he and the kid had maybe broken into one of the camps across the Pond and were spending the winter there. Nobody brought this possibility up to Bradford's constable, a johnny-come-lately who had lived in town for only twelve years and thought he owned the place. Yonder man came from across the lake, from Tashmore, from Vermont. None of the old-timers who sat around Jake Rowley's stove in the Bradford general store had much liking for Vermont ways, them with their income tax and their snooty bottle law and that fucking Russian laid up in his house like a Czar, writing books no one could understand. Let Vermonters handle their own problems, was the unanimous, if unstated, view.

'He won't be crossin the pond much longer,' one of them said. He took another bite from his Milky Way bar and began to gum it.

'Not less he's got him a pair of water wings,' another answered, and they all chuckled.

'We won't be seein him much longer,' Jake said complacently as Andy approached the store. Andy was wearing Granther's old coat and had a blue wool band pulled over his ears, and some memory – perhaps a family resemblance going back to Granther himself – danced fleetingly in Jake's mind and then blew away. 'When the ice starts to go out, he'll just dry up and blow away. Him and whoever he's keepin over there.'

Andy stopped outside, unslung his pack, and took out several letters. Then he came inside. The men forgathered there examined their nails, their watches, the old Pearl Kineo stove itself. One of them took out a gigantic blue railroad bandanna and hawked mightily into it.

Andy glanced around. 'Morning, gentlemen.'

'Mawnin to you,' Jake Rowley said. 'Get you anything?'

'You sell stamps, don't you?'

'Oh yes, Gov'ment trusts me that far.'

'I'd like six fifteens, please.'

Jake produced them, tearing them carefully from one of the sheets in his old black postage book. 'Something else for you today.'

Andy thought, then smiled. It was the tenth of March. Without answering Jake, he went to the card rack beside the coffe grinder and picked out a large, ornate birthday card. TO YOU, DAUGHTER, ON YOUR SPECIAL DAY, it said. He brought it back and paid for it.

'Thanks,' Jake said, and rang it up.

'Very welcome,' Andy replied, and went out. They watched him adjust his headband, then stamp his letters one by one. The breath smoked out of his nostrils. They watched him go around the building to where the postbox stood, but none of them sitting around the stove could have testified in court as to whether or not he mailed those letters. He came back into view shouldering into his pack.

'Off he goes,' one of the old-timers remarked.

'Civil enough fella,' Jake said, and that closed the subject. Talk turned to other matters.

Charles Payson stood in the doorway of his store, which hadn't done three hundred dollars' worth of custom all winter long, and watched Andy go. Payson could have testified that the letters had been mailed; he had stood right here and watched him drop them into the slot in a bunch.

When Andy disappeared from sight, Payson went back inside and through the doorway behind the counter where he sold penny candy and Bang caps and bubble gum and into the living quarters behind. His telephone had a scrambler device attached to it. Payson called Virginia for instructions.

9

There was and is no post office in Bradford, New Hampshire (or in Tashmore, Vermont, for that matter); both towns were too small. The nearest post office to Bradford was in Teller, New Hampshire. At one-fifteen P.M. on that March 10, the small postal truck from Teller pulled up in front of the general store and the postman emptied the mail from the standing box around to the side where Jake had pumped Jenny gas until 1970. The deposited mail consisted of Andy's six letters and a postcard from Miss Shirley Devine, a fifty-year-old maiden lady, to her sister in Tampa, Florida. Across the lake, Andy McGee was taking a nap and Charlie McGee was building a snowman.

The postman, Robert Everett, put the mail in a bag, swung the bag into the back of his blue and white truck, and then drove on to Williams, another small New Hampshire town in Teller's zip-code area. Then he U-turned in the middle of what the Williams residents laughingly called Main Street and started back to Teller, where all the mail would be sorted and sent on at about three o'clock that afternoon. Five miles outside of town, a beige Chevrolet Caprice was parked across the road, blocking both of the narrow lanes. Everett parked by the snowbank and got out of his truck to see if he could help.

Two men approached him from the car. They showed him their credentials and explained what they wanted.

'No!' Everett said. He tried on a laugh and it came out sounding incredulous, as if someone had just told him they were going to open Tashmore Beach for swimming this very afternoon.

'If you doubt we are who we say we are—' one of them began. This was Orville Jamieson, sometimes known as OJ, sometimes known as The Juice. He didn't mind dealing with this hick postman; he didn't mind anything as long as his orders didn't take him any closer than three miles to that hellish little girl.

'No, it ain't that; it ain't that at all,' Robert Everett said. He was scared, as scared as any man is when suddenly confronted with the force of the government, when gray enforcement bureaucracy suddenly takes on a real face, like something grim and solid swimming up out of a crystal ball. He was determined nonetheless. 'But what I got here is the mail. The *U.S.* mail. You guys must understand that.'

'This is a matter of national security,' OJ said. After the fiasco in Hastings Glen, a protective cordon had been thrown around the Manders place. The grounds and the remains of the house had got the fine-tooth-comb treatment. As a result, OJ had recovered The Windsucker, which now rested comfortably against the left side of his chest.

'You say so, but that ain't good enough,' Everett said.

OJ unbuttoned his Carroll Reed parka so that Robert Everett could see The Windsucker. Everett's eyes widened, and OJ smiled a little. 'Now, you don't want me to pull this, do you?'

Everett couldn't believe this was happening. He tried one last time. 'Do you guys know the penalty for robbing the U.S. mail? They put you in Leavenworth, Kansas, for that.'

'You can clear it with your postmaster when you get back to Teller,' the other man said, speaking for the first time. 'Now let's quit this fucking around, okay? Give us the bag of out-of-town mail.'

Everett gave him the small sack of mail from Bradford and Williams. They opened it right there on the road and sorted through it impersonally. Robert Everett felt anger and a kind of sick shame. What they were doing wasn't right, not even if it was the secrets of the nuclear bomb in there. Opening the U.S. mail by the side of the road wasn't right. Ludicrously, he found himself feeling about the same way he would have felt if a strange man had come barging into his house and pulled off his wife's clothes.

'You guys are going to hear about this,' he said in a choked, scared voice. 'You'll see.'

'Here they are,' the other fellow said to OJ. He handed him six letters, all addressed in the same careful hand. Robert Everett recognized them well enough. They had come from the box at the Bradford general store. OJ put the letters in his pocket and the two of them walked back to their Caprice, leaving the opened bag of mail on the road.

'You guys are going to hear about this!' Everett cried in a shaking voice.

Without looking back, OJ said, 'Speak to your postmaster before you speak to anyone else. If you want to keep your Postal Service pension, that is.'

They drove away. Everett watched them go, raging, scared, sick to his stomach. At last he picked up the mailbag and tossed it back into the truck.

'Robbed,' he said, surprised to find he was near tears. 'Robbed, I been robbed, oh goddammit, I been robbed.'

He drove back to Teller as fast as the slushy roads would allow. He spoke to his postmaster, as the men had suggested. The Teller postmaster was Bill Cobham, and Everett was in Cobham's office for better than an hour. At times their voices came through the office door, loud and angry.

Cobham was fifty-six. He had been with the Postal Service for thirty-five years, and he was badly scared. At last he succeeded in communicating his fright to Robert Everett as well. And Everett never said a word, not even to his wife, about the day he had been robbed on the Teller Road between Bradford and Williams. But he never forgot it, and he never completely lost that sense of anger and shame . . . and disillusion.

10

By two-thirty Charlie had finished her snowman, and Andy, a little rested from his nap, had got up. Orville Jamieson and his new partner, George Sedaka, were on an airplane. Four hours later, as Andy and Charlie were sitting down to a game of five hundred rummy, the supper dishes washed and drying in the drainer, the letters were on Cap Hollister's desk.

238

Cap and Rainbird

1

On March 24, Charlie McGee's birthday, Cap Hollister sat behind his desk filled with a great and ill-defined unease. The *reason* for the unease was not ill-defined; he expected John Rainbird in not quite an hour, and that was too much like expecting the devil to turn up on the dime. So to speak. And at least the devil stuck to a bargain once it was struck, if you believed his press releases, but Cap had always felt there was something in John Rainbird's personality that was fundamentally ungovernable. When all was said and done, he was nothing more than a hit man, and hit men always self-destruct sooner or later. Cap felt that when Rainbird went, it would be with a spectacular bang. Exactly how much did he know about the McGee operation? No more than he had to, surely, but . . . it nagged at him. Not for the first time he wondered if after this McGee affair was over it might not be wise to arrange an accident for the big Indian. In the memorable words of Cap's father, Rainbird was as crazy as a man eating rat-turds and calling it caviar.

He sighed. Outside, a cold rain flew against the windows, driven by a strong wind. His study, so bright and pleasant in summer, was now filled with shifting gray shadows. They were not kind to him as he sat here with the McGee file on its library trolley at his left hand. The winter had aged him; he was not the same jaunty man who had biked up to the front door on that day in October when the McGees had escaped again, leaving a firestorm behind.

Lines on his face that had been barely noticeable then had now deepened into fissures. He had been forced into the humiliation of bifocals – old man's glasses, he thought them – and adjusting to them had left him feeling nauseated for the first six weeks he wore them. These were the small things, the outward symbols of the way things had gone so crazily, maddeningly wrong. These were the things he bitched about to himself because all of his training and upbringing had schooled him against bitching about the grave matters that lay so closely below the surface.

As if that damned little girl were a personal jinx, the only two women he had cared deeply about since the death of his mother had both died of cancer this winter – his wife, Georgia, three days after Christmas, and his personal secretary, Rachel, only a little over a month ago.

He had known Georgia was gravely ill, of course; a mastectomy fourteen months before her death had slowed but not stopped the progress of the disease. Rachel's death had been a cruel surprise. Near the end he could remember (how unforgivable we sometimes seem in retrospect) joking that she needed fattening up, and Rachel throwing the jokes right back at him.

Now all he had left was the Shop – and he might not have that much longer. An insidious sort of cancer had invaded Cap himself. What would you call it? Cancer of the confidence? Something like that. And in the upper echelons, that sort of disease was nearly always fatal. Nixon, Lance, Helms . . . all victims of cancer of the credibility.

He opened the McGee file and took out the latest additions – the six letters Andy had mailed less than two weeks ago. He shuffled through them without reading them. They were all essentially the same letter and he had the contents almost by heart. Below them were glossy photographs, some taken by Charles Payson, some taken by other agents on the Tashmore side of the Pond. There were photos showing Andy walking up Bradford's main street. Photos of Andy shopping in the general store and paying for his purchases. Photos of Andy and Charlie standing by the boathouse at the camp, Irv Manders's Willys a snow-covered hump in the background. A photo showing Charlie sliding down a hard and sparkling incline of snow-crust on a flattened cardboard box, her hair flying out from beneath a knitted cap that was too large for her. In this photo her father was standing behind her, mittened hands on hips, head thrown back, bellowing laughter. Cap had looked at this photo often and long and soberly and was sometimes surprised by a trembling in his hands when he put it aside. He wanted them that badly.

He got up and went to the window for a moment. No Rich McKeon cutting grass today. The alders were bare and skeletal, the duckpond between the two houses a slatelike, bare expanse. There were dozens of important items on the Shop's plate this early spring, a veritable smorgasbord, but for Cap there was really only one, and that was the matter of Andy McGee and his daughter Charlene.

The Manders fiasco had done a lot of damage. The Shop had ridden that out, and so had he, but it had begun a critical groundswell that would break soon enough. The critical center of that groundswell was the way the McGees had been handled from the day Victoria McGee had been killed and the daughter lifted – lifted however briefly. A lot of the criticism had to do with the fact that a college instructor who had never even been in the army had been able to take his daughter away from two trained Shop agents, leaving one of them mad and one in a coma that had lasted for six months. The latter agent was never going to be any good for anything again; if anyone spoke the word 'sleep' within his earshot, he keeled over bonelessly and might stay out from four hours to an entire day. In a bizarre sort of way it was funny.

The other major criticism had to do with the fact that the McGees had managed to stay one step ahead for so long. It made the Shop look bad. It made them all look dumb.

But most of the criticism was reserved for the incident at the Manders farm itself, because that had damned near blown the entire agency out of the water. Cap knew that the whispering had begun. The whispering, the memos, maybe even the testimony at the ultrasecret congressional hearings. *We don't want him hanging on like Hoover. This Cuban business went entirely by the boards because he couldn't get his head out of that damned McGee file. Wife died very recently, you know. Great shame. Hit him hard. Whole McGee business nothing but a catalogue of ineptitude. Perhaps a younger man . . .*

But none of them understood what they were up against. They thought they did, but they didn't. Again and again he had seen the rejection of the simple fact that the little girl was a pyrokinetic – a firestarter. Literally dozens of reports suggested that the fire at the Manders farm had been started by a gasoline spill, by the woman's breaking a kerosene lamp, by spontaneous-fucking-combustion, and God only knew what other nonsense. Some of those reports came from people who had been there.

Standing at the window, Cap found himself perversely wishing that Wanless were here. Wanless had understood. He could have talked to Wanless about this . . . this dangerous blindness.

He went back to the desk. There was no sense kidding himself; once the undermining process began, there was no way to stop it. It really was like a cancer. You could retard its growth by calling in favors (and Cap had called in ten years' worth just to keep himself in the saddle this last winter); you might even be able to force it into remission. But sooner or later, you were gone. He felt he had from now until July if he played the game by the rules, from now until maybe November if he decided to really dig in and get tough. That, however, might mean ripping the agency apart at the seams, and he did not want to do that. He had no wish to destroy something he had invested half his life in. But he would if he had to: he was going to see this through to the end.

The major factor that had allowed him to stay in control was the speed with which they had located the McGees again. Cap was glad to take credit for that since it helped to prop up his position, but all it had really taken was computer time.

They had been living with this business long enough to have time to plow the McGee field both wide and deep. Filed away in the computer were facts on more than two hundred relatives and four hundred friends all the way around the McGee-Tomlinson family tree. These friendships stretched all the way back to Vicky's best friend in the first grade, a girl named Kathy Smith, who was now Mrs Frank Worthy, of Cabral, California, and who had probably not spared a thought for Vicky Tomlinson in twenty years or more.

The computer was given the 'last-seen' data and promptly spit out a list of probabilities. Heading the list was the name of Andy's deceased grandfather, who had owned a camp on Tashmore Pond in Vermont; ownership had since passed to Andy. The McGees had vacationed there, and it was within reasonable striking distance of the Manders farm by way of the back roads. The computer felt that if Andy and Charlie were to make for any 'known place,' it would be this place.

Less than a week after they had moved into Granther's, Cap knew they were there. A loose cordon of agents was

243

set up around the camp. Arrangements had been made for the purchase of Notions 'n' Novelties in Bradford on the probability that whatever shopping they needed to do would be done in Bradford.

Passive surveillance, nothing more. All the photographs had been taken with telephoto lenses under optimum conditions for concealment. Cap had no intention of risking another firestorm.

They could have take Andy quietly on any of his trips across the lake. They could have shot them both as easily as they had got the picture of Charlie sledding on the cardboard carton. But Cap wanted the girl, and he had now come to believe that if they were going to have any real control over her, they would need her father as well.

After locating them again, the most important objective had been to make sure they kept quiet. Cap didn't need a computer to tell him that as Andy grew more frightened, the chances that he would seek outside help went up and up. Before the Manders affair, a press leak could have been handled or lived with. Afterward, press interference became a different ballgame altogether. Cap had nightmares just thinking about what would happen if the New York *Times* got hold of such a thing.

For a brief period, during the confusion that had followed the firestorm, Andy could have got his letters out. But apparently the McGees had been living with their own confusion. Their golden chance to mail the letters or make some phone calls had passed unused . . . and very well mightn't have come to anything, anyway. The woods were full of crackpots these days, and newspeople were as cynical as anyone else. Theirs had become a glamour occupation. They were more interested in what Margaux and Bo and Suzanne and Cheryl were doing. It was safer.

Now the two of them were in a box. Cap had had the entire winter to consider options. Even at his wife's funeral he had been running through his options. Gradually he had settled upon a plan of action and now he was prepared to tip that plan into motion. Payson, their man in Bradford, said that the ice was getting ready to go out on Tashmore Pond. And McGee had finally mailed his letters. Already he would be getting impatient for a response – and perhaps beginning to suspect his letters had never arrived at their intended sources. They might be getting ready to move, and Cap liked them right where they were.

Beneath the photos was a thick typed report – better than three hundred pages – bound in a blue TOP SECRET cover. Eleven doctors and psychologists had put the combination report and prospectus together under the overall direction of Dr Patrick Hockstetter, a clinical psychologist and psychotherapist. He was, in Cap's opinion, one of the ten or twelve most astute minds at the Shop's disposal. At the eight hundred thousand dollars it had cost the taxpayer to put the report together, he ought to have been. Thumbing through the report now, Cap wondered what Wanless, that old doomsayer, would have made of it.

His own intuition that they needed Andy alive was confirmed in here. The postulate Hockstetter's crew had based their own chain of logic on was the idea that all the powers they were interested in were exercised voluntarily, having their first cause in the willingness of the possessor to use them . . . and the key word was *will*.

The girl's powers, of which pyrokinesis was only the cornerstone, had a way of getting out of control, of jumping nimbly over the barriers of her will, but this study, which incorporated all the available information, indicated that it was the girl herself who elected whether or not to set things in motion – as she had done at the Manders farm when she realized that the Shop agents were trying to kill her father.

He rifled through the recap of the original Lot Six

experiment. All the graphs and computer readouts boiled down to the same thing: will as the first cause.

Using will as the basis for everything. Hockstetter and his colleagues had gone through an amazing catalogue of drugs before deciding on Thorazine for Andy and a new drug called Orasin for the girl. Seventy pages of gobbledygook in the report came down to the fact that the drugs would make them feel high, dreamy, floaty. Neither of them would be able to exercise enough will to choose between chocolate milk and white, let alone enough to start fires or convince people they were blind, or whatever.

They could keep Andy McGee drugged constantly. They had no real use for him; both the report and Cap's own intuition suggested that he was a dead end, a burned-out case. It was the girl who interested them. Give me six months, Cap thought, and we'll have enough. Just long enough to map the terrain inside that amazing little head. No House or Senate subcommittee would be able to resist the promise of chemically induced psi powers and the enormous implications it would have on the arms race if that little girl was even half of what Wanless suspected.

And there were other possibilities. They were not in the blue-backed report, because they were too explosive for even a TOP SECRET heading. Hockstetter, who had become progressively more excited as the picture took shape before him and his committee of experts, had mentioned one of these possibilities to Cap only a week ago.

'This Z factor,' Hockstetter said. 'Have you considered any of the ramifications if it turns out that the child isn't a mule but a genuine mutation?'

Cap had, although he did not tell Hockstetter that. It raised the interesting question of eugenics . . . the potentially explosive question of eugenics, with its lingering connotations of Nazism and superraces – all the things Americans had fought World War II to put an end to. But it was one thing to sink a philosophical well and produce a gusher of bullshit about usurping the power of God and quite another to produce laboratory evidence that the offspring of Lot Six parents might be human torches, levitators, tele- or telempaths, or God only knew what else. Ideals were cheap things to hold as long as there were no solid arguments for their overthrow. If there were, what then? Human breeding farms? As crazy as it sounded, Cap could visualize it. It could be the key to everything. World peace, or world domination, and when you got rid of the trick mirrors of rhetoric and bombast, weren't they really the same thing?

It was a whole can of worms. The possibilities stretched a dozen years into the future. Cap knew the best he himself could realistically hope for was six months, but it might be enough to set policy – to survey the land on which the tracks would be laid and the railroad would run. It would be his legacy to the country and to the world. Measured against this, the lives of a runaway college instructor and his ragamuffin daughter were less than dust in the wind.

The girl could not be tested and observed with any degree of validity if she was constantly drugged, but her father would be their hostage to fortune. And on the few occasions they wanted to run tests on him, the reverse would hold. It was a simple system of levers. And as Archimedes had observed, a lever long enough would move the world.

The intercom buzzed.

'John Rainbird is here,' the new girl said. Her usual bland receptionist's tone was threadbare enough to show the fear beneath.

On that one I don't blame you, babe, Cap thought.

'Send him in, please.'

Same old Rainbird.

He came in slowly, dressed in a brown and balding leather jacket over a faded plaid shirt. Old and scuffed Dingos peeked out from beneath the cuffs of his faded straight-leg jeans. The top of his huge head seemed almost to brush the ceiling. The gored ruin of his empty eye-socket made Cap shudder inwardly.

'Cap,' he said, and sat down. 'I have been in the desert too long.'

'I've heard about your Flagstaff house,' Cap said. 'And your shoe collection.'

John Rainbird only stared at him unblinkingly with his good eye.

'How come I never see you in anything but those old shitkickers?' Cap asked.

Rainbird smiled thinly and said nothing. The old unease filled Cap and he found himself wondering again how much Rainbird knew, and why it bothered him so much.

'I have a job for you,' he said.

'Good. Is it the one I want?'

Cap looked at him, surprised, considering, and then said, 'I think it is.'

'Then tell me, Cap.'

Cap outlined the plan that would bring Andy and Charlie McGee to Longmont. It didn't take long.

'Can you use the gun?' he asked when he was finished.

'I can use any gun. And your plan is a good one. It will succeed.'

'How nice of you to give it your stamp of approval,' Cap said. He tried for light irony and only succeeded in sounding petulant. God damn the man anyway.

'And I will fire the gun,' Rainbird said. 'On one condition.'

Cap stood up, planted his hands on his desk, which was littered with components from the McGee file, and leaned toward Rainbird.

'No,' he said. 'You don't make conditions with me.'

'I do this time,' Rainbird said. 'But you will find it an easy one to fulfill, I think.'

'No,' Cap repeated. Suddenly his heart was hammering in his chest, although with fear or anger he was not sure. 'You misunderstand. I am in charge of this agency and this facility. I am your superior. I believe you spent enough time in the army to understand the concept of a superior officer.'

'Yes,' Rainbird said, smiling, 'I scragged one or two in my time. Once directly on Shop orders. *Your* orders, Cap.'

'Is that a threat?' Cap cried. Some part of him was aware that he was overreacting, but he seemed unable to help himself. 'God damn you, is that a threat? If it is, I think you've lost your senses completely! If I decide I don't want you to leave this building, all I have to do is press a button! There are thirty men who can fire that rifle—'

'But none can fire it with such assurance as this one-eyed red nigger,' Rainbird said. His gentle tone had not changed. 'You think you have them now, Cap, but they are will-o'-the-wisps. Whatever gods there are may not want you to have them. They may not want you to set them down in your rooms of deviltry and emptiness. You have thought you had them before.' He pointed to the file material heaped on the library trolley and then to the blue-backed folder. 'I've read the material. And I've read your Dr Hockstetter's report.'

'The devil you have!' Cap exclaimed, but he could see the truth in Rainbird's face. He had. Somehow he had. Who gave it to him? he raged. Who?

'Oh yes,' Rainbird said. 'I have what I want, when I want it. People give it to me. I think . . . it must be my 'pretty face.' His smile widened and became suddenly, horribly predatory. His good eye rolled in its socket.

'What are you saying to me?' Cap asked. He wanted a glass of water.

'Just that I have had a long time in Arizona to walk and smell the winds that blow . . . and for you, Cap, it smells bitter, like the wind off an alkali flat. I had time to do a lot of reading and a lot of thinking. And what I think is that I may be the only man in all the world who can surely bring those two here. And it may be that I am the only man in all the world who can do something with the little girl once she's here. Your fat report, your Thorazine and your Orasin – there may be more here than drugs can cope with. More dangers than you can understand.'

Hearing Rainbird was like hearing the ghost of Wanless, and Cap was now in the grip of such fear and such fury that he couldn't speak.

'I will do all this,' Rainbird said kindly. 'I will bring them here and you will do all your tests.' He was like a father giving a child permission to play with some new toy. 'On the condition that you give the girl to me for disposal when you are finished with her.'

'You're mad,' Cap whispered.

'How right you are,' Rainbird said, and laughed. 'So are you. Mad as a hatter. You sit here and make your plans for controlling a force beyond your comprehension. A force that belongs only to the gods themselves . . . and to this one little girl.'

'And what's to stop me from having you erased? Right here and now?'

'My word,' Rainbird said, 'that if I disappear, such a shockwave of revulsion and indignation will run through this country within the month that Watergate will look like the filching of penny candy in comparison. My word that if I disappear, the Shop will cease to exist within six weeks,

250

and that within six months you will stand before a judge for sentencing on crimes serious enough to keep you behind bars for the rest of your life.' He smiled again, showing crooked tombstone teeth. 'Do not doubt me, Cap. My days in this reeking, putrescent vineyard have been long, and the vintage would be a bitter one indeed.'

Cap tried to laugh. What came out was a choked snarl.

'For over ten years I have been putting my nuts and forage by,' Rainbird said serenely, 'like any animal that has known winter and remembers it. I have such a potpourri, Cap – photos, tapes, Xerox copies of documents that would make the blood of our good friend John Q. Public run cold.'

'None of that is possible,' Cap said, but he knew Rainbird was not bluffing, and he felt as if a cold, invisible hand were pressing down on his chest.

'Oh, very possible,' Rainbird said. 'For the last three years I've been in a state of information passing-gear, because for the last three years I've been able to tap into your computer whenever I liked. On a time-sharing basis, of course, which makes it expensive, but I have been able to pay. My wages have been very fine, and with investment they have grown. I stand before you, Cap – or sit, which is the truth, but less poetic – as a triumphant example of American free enterprise in action.'

'No,' Cap said.

'Yes,' Rainbird replied. 'I am John Rainbird, but I am also the U.S. Bureau for Geological Understudies. Check, if you like. My computer code is AXON. Check the time-sharing codes in your main terminal. Take the elevator. I'll wait.' Rainbird crossed his legs and the cuff of his right pantsleg pulled up, revealing a rip and a bulge in a seam of one of his boots. He looked like a man who could wait out the age, if that were necessary.

Cap's mind was whirling. 'Access to the computer on a

time-sharing basis, perhaps. That still doesn't tap you into—'

'Go see Dr Noftzieger,' Rainbird said kindly. 'Ask him how many ways there are to tap into a computer once you have access on a time-sharing basis. Two years ago, a bright twelve-year-old tapped into the USC computer. And by the way, I know *your* access code, Cap. It's BROW this year. Last year it was RASP. I thought that was much more appropriate.'

Cap sat and looked at Rainbird. His mind had divided, it seemed, had become a three-ring circus. Part of it was marveling that he had never heard John Rainbird say so much at one time. Part of it was trying to grapple with the idea that this maniac knew all of the Shop's business. A third part was remembering a Chinese curse, a curse that sounded deceptively pleasant until you sat down and really thought about it. *May you live in interesting times.* For the last year and a half he had lived in extremely interesting times. He felt that just one more interesting thing would drive him totally insane.

And then he thought of Wanless again – with dragging, dawning, horror. He felt almost as if . . . as if . . . he were turning into Wanless. Beset with demons on every side but helpless to fight them off or even to enlist help.

'What do you want, Rainbird?'

'I've told you already, Cap. I want nothing but your word that my involvement with this girl Charlene McGee will not end with the rifle but begin there. I want to' – Rainbird's eye darkened and became thoughtful, moody, introspective – 'I want to know her intimately.'

Cap looked at him, horror-struck.

Rainbird understood suddenly, and he shook his head at Cap contemptuously. 'Not *that* intimately. Not in the biblical sense But I'll know her. She and I are going to be friends, Cap. If she is as powerful as all things indicate, she and I are going to be great friends.'

Cap made a sound of humor: not a laugh, exactly; more of a shrill giggle.

The expression of contempt on Rainbird's face did not change. 'No, of course you don't think that is possible. You look at my face and you see a monster. You look at my hands and see them covered with the blood you ordered me to spill. But I tell you, Cap, it will happen. The girl has had no friend for going on two years. She has had her father and that is all. You see her as you see me, Cap. It is your great failing. You look, you see a monster. Only in the girl's case, you see a useful monster. Perhaps this is because you are a white man. White men see monsters everywhere. White men look at their own pricks and see monsters.' Rainbird laughed again.

Cap had at last begun to calm down and to think reasonably. 'Why should I allow it, even if all you say is true? Your days are numbered and we both know it. You've been hunting your own death for twenty years. Anything else has been incidental, only a hobby. You'll find it soon enough. And then it ends for all of us. So why should I give you the pleasure of having what you want?'

'Perhaps it's as you say. Perhaps I have been hunting my own death – a more colorful phrase than I would have expected from you, Cap. Maybe you should have the fear of God put into you more often.'

'You're not my idea of God,' Cap said.

Rainbird grinned. 'More like the Christian devil, sure. But I tell you this – if I had really been hunting my own death, I believe I would have found it long before this. Perhaps I've been stalking it for play. But I have no desire to bring you down, Cap, or the Shop, or U.S. domestic intelligence. I am no idealist. I only want this little girl. And you may find you need me. You may find that I am able to accomplish things that all the drugs in Dr Hockstetter's cabinet will not.'

'And in return?'

'When the affair of the McGees ends, the U.S. Bureau for Geological Understudies will cease to exist. Your computer chief, Noftzieger, can change all his codings. And you, Cap, will fly to Arizona with me on a public airline. We will enjoy a good dinner at my favorite Flagstaff restaurant and then we will go back to my house, and behind it, in the desert, we will start a fire of our own and barbecue a great many papers and tapes and films. I will even show you my shoe collection, if you like.'

Cap thought it over. Rainbird gave him time, sitting calmly.

At last Cap said, 'Hockstetter and his colleagues suggest it may take two years to open the girl up completely. It depends on how deeply her protective inhibitions go.'

'And you will be gone in four to six months.'

Cap shrugged.

Rainbird touched the side of his nose with one index finger and cocked his head – a grotesque fairy-tale gesture. 'I think we can keep you in the saddle much longer than that, Cap. Between the two of us, we know where hundreds of bodies are buried – literally as well as figuratively. And I doubt if it will take years. We'll both get what we want, in the end. What do you say?'

Cap thought about it. He felt old and tired and at a complete loss. 'I guess,' he said, 'that you have made yourself a deal.'

'Fine,' Rainbird said briskly. 'I will be the girl's orderly, I think. No one at all in the established scheme of things. That will be important to her. And of course she will never know I was the one who fired the rifle. That would be dangerous knowledge, wouldn't it? Very dangerous.'

'Why?' Cap said finally. 'Why have you gone to these insane lengths?'

'Do they seem insane?' Rainbird asked lightly. He got up and took one of the pictures from Cap's desk. It was the photo of Charlie sliding down the slope of crusted snow on her flattened cardboard box, laughing. 'We all put our nuts and forage by for winter in this business, Cap. Hoover did it. So did CIA directors beyond counting. So have you, or you would be drawing a pension right now. When I began, Charlene McGee wasn't even born, and I was only covering my own ass.'

'But why the girl?'

Rainbird didn't answer for a long time. He was looking at the photograph carefully, almost tenderly. He touched it.

'She is very beautiful,' he said. 'And very young. Yet inside her is your Z factor. The power of the gods. She and I will be close.' His eye grew dreamy. 'Yes, we will be very close.'

In the Box

1

On March 27, Andy McGee decided abruptly that they could stay in Tashmore no longer. It had been more than two weeks since he had mailed his letters, and if anything was going to come of them, it already would have. The very fact of the continuing silence around Granther's camp made him uneasy. He supposed he could simply have been dismissed out of hand as a crackpot in every case, but . . . he didn't believe it.

What he believed, what his deepest intuition whispered, was that his letters had been somehow diverted.

And that would mean they knew where he and Charlie were.

'We're going,' he told Charlie. 'Let's get our stuff together.'

She only looked at him with her careful eyes, a little scared, and said nothing. She didn't ask him where they were going or what they were going to do, and that made him nervous, too. In one of the closets he had found two old suitcases, plastered with ancient vacation decals – Grand Rapids, Niagara Falls, Miami Beach – and the two of them began to sort what they would take and what they would leave.

Blinding bright sunlight streamed in through the windows on the east side of the cottage. Water dripped and gurgled in the downspouts. The night before, he had got little sleep; the ice had gone out and he had lain awake listening to it – the high, ethereal, and somehow uncanny sound of the old yellow ice splitting and moving slowly down toward the neck of the pond, where the Great Hancock River spilled eastward across New Hampshire and all of Maine, growing progressively more smelly and polluted until it vomited, noisome and dead, into the Atlantic. The sound was like a prolonged crystal note or perhaps that of a bow drawn endlessly across a high violin string – a constant, fluted *zzziiiiiinnnggg* that settled over the nerve endings and seemed to make them vibrate in sympathy. He had never been here at ice-out before and was not sure he would ever want to be again. There was something terrible and otherworldly about that sound as it vibrated between the silent evergreen walls of this low and eroded bowl of hills.

He felt that they were very near again, like the barely seen monster in a recurring nightmare. The day after Charlie's birthday, he had been on one of his tramps, the cross-country skis buckled uncomfortably onto his feet, and he had come across a line of snowshoe tracks leading up to a tall spruce tree. There were indents in the crust like periods where the snowshoes had been taken off and jammed into the snow on their tails. There was a flurried confusion where the wearer had later refastened his snow-shoes ('slushboats,' Granther had always called them, holding them in contempt for some obscure reason of his own). At the base of the tree, Andy had found six Vantage cigarette butts and a crumpled yellow package that had once contained Kodak Tri-X film. More uneasy than ever, he had taken off the skis and climbed up into the tree. Halfway up he had found himself on a direct line-of-sight with Granther's cottage a mile away. It was small and apparently empty. But with a telephoto lens . . .

He hadn't mentioned his find to Charlie.

The suitcases were packed. Her continued silence forced

him into nervous speech, as if by not talking she was accusing him.

'We're going to hitch a ride into Berlin,' he said, 'and then we'll get a Greyhound back to New York City. We're going to the offices of the New York *Times*—'

'But, Daddy, you sent them a letter.'

'Honey, they might not have gotten it.'

She looked at him in silence for a moment and then said, 'Do you think *they* took it?'

'Of course n—' He shook his head and started again. 'Charlie, I just don't know.'

Charlie didn't reply. She knelt, closed one of the suitcases, and began fumbling ineffectually with the clasps.

'Let me help you, hon.'

'*I can do it!*' She screamed at him, and then began to cry.

'Charlie, don't,' he said. 'Please, hon. It's almost over.'

'No, it's not,' she said, crying harder. 'It's never going to be over.'

2

There were an even dozen agents around Granther McGee's cabin. They had taken up their positions the night before. They all wore mottled white and green clothing. None of them had been at the Manders farm, and none of them was armed except for John Rainbird, who had the rifle, and Don Jules, who carried a .22 pistol.

'I am taking no chances of having someone panic because of what happened back in New York,' Rainbird had told Cap. 'That Jamieson still looks as if his balls are hanging around his knees.'

Similarly, he would not hear of the agents going armed. Things had a way of happening, and he didn't want to come out of the operation with two corpses. He had handpicked all of the agents, and the one he had chosen to take Andy McGee was Don Jules. Jules was small, thirty-ish, silent, morose. He was good at his job. Rainbird knew, because Jules was the only man he had chosen to work with more than once. He was quick and practical. He did not get in the way at critical moments.

'McGee will be out at some point during the day,' Rainbird had told them at the briefing. 'The girl usually comes out, but McGee always does. If the man comes out alone, I'll take him and Jules will get him out of sight quickly and quietly. If the girl should come out alone, same thing. If they come out together, I'll take the girl and Jules will take McGee. The rest of you are just spear carriers – do you understand that?' Rainbird's eye glared over them. 'You're there in case something goes drastically wrong, and that is all. Of course, if something *does* go drastically wrong, most of you will be running for the lake with your pants on fire. You're along in case that one chance in a hundred turns up where you can do something. Of course, it's understood that you're also along as observers and witnesses in case I fuck up.'

This had earned a thin and nervous chuckle.

Rainbird raised one finger. 'If any one of you miscues and puts their wind up somehow, I'll personally see that you end up in the lousiest jungle valley of South America I can find – with a cored asshole. Believe that, gentlemen. You are spear carriers in my show. Remember it.'

Later, at their 'staging area' – an abandoned motel in St Johnsbury – Rainbird had taken Don Jules aside.

'You have read the file on this man,' Rainbird said.

Jules was smoking a Camel. 'Yeah.'

'You understand the concept of mental domination?'

'Yeah.'

'You understand what happened to the two men in Ohio? The men that tried to take his daughter away?'

260

'I worked with George Waring,' Jules said evenly. 'That guy could burn water making tea.'

'In this man's outfit, that is not so unusual. I only need us to be clear. You'll need to be very quick.'

'Yeah, okay.'

'He's had a whole winter to rest, this guy. If he gets time to give you a shot, you're a good candidate to spend the next three years of your life in a padded room, thinking you're a bird or a turnip or something.'

'All right.'

'All right what?'

'I'll be quick. Give it a rest, John.'

'There's a good chance that they will come out together,' Rainbird said, ignoring him. 'You'll be around the corner of the porch, out of sight of the door where they'll come out. You wait for me to take the girl. Her father will go to her. You'll be behind him. Get him in the neck.'

'Sure.'

'Don't screw this up, Don.'

Jules smiled briefly and smoked. 'No,' he said.

3

The suitcases were packed. Charlie had put on her coat and her snowpants. Andy shrugged into his own jacket, zipped it, and picked up the suitcases. He didn't feel good, not at all good. He had the jumps. One of his hunches.

'You feel it, too, don't you?' Charlie asked. Her small face was pale and expressionless.

Andy nodded reluctantly.

'What do we do?'

'We hope the feeling's a little early,' he said, although in his heart he didn't think it was so. 'What else can we do?'

'What else can we do?' she echoed.

She came to him then and lifted her arms to be picked

up, something he could not remember her doing for a long time – maybe two years. It was amazing how time got by, how quickly a child could change, change in front of your eyes with an unobtrusiveness that was nearly terrible.

He put the suitcases down and picked her up and hugged her. She kissed his cheek and then hugged him again, very tightly.

'Are you ready?' he asked, setting her down.

'I guess so,' Charlie said. She was close to tears again. 'Daddy . . . I won't make fires. Not even if they come before we can get away.'

'Yes,' he said. 'That's all right, Charlie. I understand that.'

'I love you, Dad.'

He nodded. 'I love you too, kiddo.'

Andy went to the door and opened it. For a moment the sunlight was so bright that he could see nothing at all. Then his pupils contracted and the day cleared before him, bright with melting snow. To his right was Tashmore Pond, dazzling, jaggedly irregular patches of blue water showing between the floating chunks of ice. Straight ahead were pine woods. Through them he could barely see the green shingled roof of the next camp, free of snow at last.

The woods were still, and Andy's feeling of disquiet intensified. Where was the birdsong that had greeted their mornings ever since the winter temperatures had begun to moderate? There was none today . . . only the drip of snow melting from the branches. He found himself wishing desperately that Granther had put in a phone out here. He had to restrain an urge to shout *Who's there?* at the top of his lungs. But that would only frighten Charlie more.

'Looks fine,' he said. 'I think we're still ahead of them . . . if they're coming at all.'

'That's good,' she said colorlessly.

'Let's hit the road, kid,' Andy said, and thought for the

hundredth time, *What else is there to do?* and thought again how much he hated them.

Charlie came across the room to him, past the drainer full of dishes they had washed that morning after breakfast. The entire cottage was the way they had found it, spick-and-span. Granther would have been pleased.

Andy slipped an arm around Charlie's shoulders and gave her one more brief hug. Then he picked up the suitcases and they stepped out into the early spring sunshine together.

4

John Rainbird was halfway up a tall spruce one hundred and fifty yards away. He was wearing lineman's spikes on his feet and a lineman's belt held him firmly against the trunk of the tree. When the cabin door opened, he threw the rifle to his shoulder and seated it firmly. Total calm fell over him in a reassuring cloak. Everything became start-lingly clear in front of his one good eye. When he lost his other eye, he had suffered a blurring of his depth of perception, but at moments of extreme concentration, like this one, his old, clear seeing came back to him; it was as if the ruined eye could regenerate itself for brief periods.

It was not a long shot, and he would not have wasted a moment's worry if it had been a bullet he was planning to put through the girl's neck – but he was dealing with something far more clumsy, something that jumped the risk element by a factor of ten. Fixed inside the barrel of this specially modified rifle was a dart tipped with an ampul of Orasin, and at this distance there was always a chance it might tumble or veer. Luckily, the day was almost without wind.

If it is the will of the Great Spirit and of my ancestors,

Rainbird prayed silently, *guide my hands and my eye that the shot may be true.*

The girl came out with her father by her side – Jules was in it, then. Through the telescopic sight the girl looked as big as a barn door. The parka was a bright blue blaze against the weathered boards of the cabin. Rainbird had a moment to note the suitcases in McGee's hands, to realize they were just in time after all.

The girl's hood was down, the tab of her zipper pulled up only to her breastbone, so that the coat spread open slightly at the throat. The day was warm, and that was in his favor, too.

He tightened down on the trigger and sighted the crosshairs on the base of her throat.

If it is the will—

He squeezed the trigger. There was no explosion, only a hollow *phut!* and a small curl of smoke from the rifle's breech.

5

They were on the edge of the steps when Charlie suddenly stopped and made a strangled swallowing noise. Andy dropped the suitcases immediately. He had heard nothing, but something was terribly wrong. Something about Charlie had changed.

'Charlie? *Charlie?*'

He stared at her. She stood as still as a statue, incredibly beautiful against the bright snowfield. Incredibly small. And suddenly he realized what the change was. It was so fundamental, so awful, that he had not been able to grasp it at first.

What appeared to be a long needle was sticking out of Charlie's throat just below the Adam's apple. Her mittened hand groped for it, found it, twisted it to a new and grotesque, upward-jutting angle. A thin trickle of blood began to flow from the wound and down the side of her throat. A flower of blood, small and delicate, stained the collar of her shirt and just touched the edging of fake fur that bordered the zipper of her parka.

'*Charlie!*' he screamed. He leaped forward and grabbed her arm just as her eyes rolled up and she pitched outward. He let her down to the porch, crying her name over and over. The dart in her throat twinkled brightly in the sun. Her body had the loose, boneless feel of a dead thing. He held her, cradled her, and looked out at the sunshiny woods that seemed so empty – and where no birds sang.

'*Who did it?*' he screamed? '*Who did it? Come out where I can see you!*'

Don Jules stepped around the corner of the porch. He was wearing Adidas tennis sneakers. He held the .22 in one hand.

'*Who shot my daughter?*' Andy screamed. Something in his throat vibrated painfully with the force of his scream. He held her to him, so terribly loose and boneless inside her warm blue parka. His fingers went to the dart and pulled it out, starting a fresh trickle of blood.

Get her inside, he thought. *Got to get her inside.*

Jules approached him and shot him in the back of the neck, much as the actor Booth had once shot a President. For a moment Andy jerked upward on his knees, holding Charlie even more tightly against him. Then he collapsed forward over her.

Jules looked at him closely, then waved the men out of the woods.

'Nothing to it,' he said to himself as Rainbird came toward the cabin, wading through the sticky, melting snow of late March. 'Nothing to it. What was all the fuss about?'

The Blackout

1

The chain of events that ended in such destruction and loss of life began with a summer storm and the failure of two generators.

The storm came on August 19, almost five months after Andy and Charlie were taken at Granther's camp in Vermont. For ten days the weather had been sticky and still. That August day, the thunderheads began to pile up shortly after noon, but nobody who worked on the grounds of the two handsome antebellum homes which faced each other across the rolling expanse of green lawn and manicured flowerbeds believed that the thunderheads were telling the truth – not the groundsmen astride their Lawnboys, not the woman who was in charge of computer subsections A–E (as well as the computer-room coffeemaker), who took one of the horses and cantered it lovingly along the well-kept bridle paths during her lunch hour, certainly not Cap, who ate a hero sandwich in his air-conditioned office and went right on working on next year's budget, oblivious of the heat and humidity outside.

Perhaps the only person in the Shop compound at Longmont that day who thought it really would rain was the man who had been named for the rain. The big Indian drove in at twelve-thirty, prefatory to clocking in at one. His bones, and the shredded hollow where his left eye had been, ached when rain was on the way.

He was driving a very old and rusty Thunderbird with a *D* parking sticker on the windshield. He was dressed in orderly's whites. Before he got out of the car, he put on an embroidered eyepatch. He wore it when he was on the job, because of the girl, but only then. It bothered him. It was only the patch that made him think about the lost eye.

There were four parking lots inside the Shop enclave. Rainbird's personal car, a new yellow Cadillac that ran on diesel fuel, bore an *A* sticker. *A* was the VIP parking lot, located beneath the southernmost of the two plantation houses. An underground tunnel-and-elevator system connected the VIP lot directly with the computer room, the situation rooms, the extensive Shop library and newsrooms, and, of course, the Visitors' Quarters – a nondescript name for the complex of laboratories and nearby apartments where Charlie McGee and her father were being kept.

The *B* lot was for second-echelon employees; it was farther away. *C* parking lot was for secretaries, mechanics, electricians, and the like; it was farther away still. *D* lot was for unskilled employees – spear carriers, in Rainbird's own terms. It was almost half a mile from anything, and always filled with a sad and motley collection of Detroit rolling iron only a step and a half away from the weekly demo derby at Jackson Plains, the nearby stock-car track.

The bureaucratic pecking order, Rainbird thought, locking his wreck of a T-bird and tilting his head up to look at the thunderheads. The storm was coming. It would arrive around four o'clock, he reckoned.

He began to walk toward the small Quonset hut set tastefully back in a grove of sugarpines where low-level employees, Class Vs and VIs, punched in. His whites flapped around him. A gardener putted by him on one of the Groundskeeping Department's dozen or so riding lawnmowers. A gaily colored sun parasol floated above the seat. The gardener took no notice of Rainbird; that was also part of the bureaucratic pecking order. If you were a Class IV, a Class V became invisible. Not even Rainbird's

268

half-destroyed face caused much comment; like every other government agency, the Shop hired enough vets to look good. Max Factor had little to teach the U.S. government about good cosmetics. And it went without saying that a vet with some visible disability – a prosthetic arm, a motorized wheelchair, a scrambled face – was worth any three vets who looked 'normal.' Rainbird knew men who had had their minds and spirits mauled as badly as his own face had been in the Vietnam traveling house party, men who would have been happy to find a job clerking in a Piggly Wiggly. But they just didn't look right. Not that Rainbird had any sympathy for them. In fact, he found the whole thing rather funny.

Nor was he recognized by any of the people he now worked with as a former Shop agent and hatchet man; he would have sworn to that. Until seventeen weeks ago, he had been only a shadow shape behind his yellow Cadillac's polarized windshield, just someone else with an *A* clearance.

'Don't you think you're going overboard with this a bit?' Cap had asked. 'The girl has no connection with the gardeners or the steno pool. You're only onstage with her.'

Rainbird shook his head. 'All it would take is a single slip. One person to mention, just casually, that the friendly orderly with the messed-up face parks his car in the VIP lot and changes to his whites in the executive washroom. What I am trying to build here is a sense of trust, that trust to be based on the idea that we're both outsiders – both freaks, if you will – buried in the bowels of the KGB's American branch.'

Cap hadn't liked that; he didn't like anyone taking cheap shots at the Shop's methods, particularly in this case, where the methods were admittedly extreme.

'Well, you're sure doing one hell of a job,' Cap had answered.

And to that there was no satisfactory answer, because in fact, he *wasn't* doing a hell of a job. The girl had not done so much as light a match in all the time she had been here. And the same could be said for her father, who had demonstrated not the slightest sign of any mental-domination ability, if the ability still existed within him. More and more they were coming to doubt that it did.

The girl fascinated Rainbird. The first year he had been with the Shop, he had taken a series of courses not to be found in any college curriculum – wiretapping, car theft, unobtrusive search, a dozen others. The only one that had engaged Rainbird's attention fully was the course in safecracking, taught by an aging burglar named G. M. Rammaden. Rammaden had been sprung from an institution in Atlanta for the specific purpose of teaching this craft to new Shop agents. He was supposed to be the best in the business, and Rainbird would not have doubted that, although he believed that by now he was almost Rammaden's equal.

Rammaden, who had died three years ago (Rainbird had sent flowers to his funeral – what a comedy life could sometimes be!), had taught them about Skidmore locks, about square-door boxes, about secondary locking devices that can permanently freeze a safe's tumblers if the combination dial is knocked off with a hammer and chisel; he had taught them about barrel boxes, and niggerheads, and cutting keys; the many uses of graphite; how you could take a key impression with a Brillo pad and how to make bathtub nitroglycerine and how to peel a box from the back, one layer at a time.

Rainbird had responded to G. M. Rammaden with a cold and cynical enthusiasm. Rammaden had said once that safes were like women: given the tools and the time, any box could be opened. There were, he said, tough cracks and easy cracks, but no impossible cracks.

This girl was tough.

At first they had had to feed Charlie intravenously just to keep her from starving herself to death. After a while she began to understand that not eating was gaining her nothing but a lot of bruises on the insides of her elbows, and she began to eat, not with any enthusiasm but simply because using her mouth was less painful.

She read some of the books that were given her – leafed through them, at any rate – and would sometimes turn on the color TV in her room only to turn it off again a few minutes later. She had watched a local movie presentation of *Black Beauty* all the way through in June, and she had sat through *The Wonderful World of Disney* once or twice. That was all. On her weekly reports the phrase 'sporadic aphasia' had begun to crop up more and more often.

Rainbird had looked the term up in a medical dictionary and understood it at once – because of his own experiences as Indian and warrior, he understood it perhaps better than the doctors themselves. Sometimes the girl ran out of words. She would simply stand there, not a bit upset, her mouth working soundlessly. And sometimes she would use a totally out-of-context word, apparently without realizing it at all. 'I don't like this dress, I'd rather have the hay one.' Sometimes she would correct herself absently – 'I mean the *green* one' – but more often it would simply pass unnoticed.

According to the dictionary, aphasia was forgetfulness caused by some cerebral disorder. The doctors had immediately begun monkeying with her medication. Orasin was changed to Valium with no appreciable change for the better. Valium and Orasin were tried together, but an unforeseen interaction between the two had caused her to cry steadily and monotonously until the dose wore off. A brand-new drug, a combination of tranquilizer and light hallucinogenic, was tried and seemed to help for a while.

Then she had begun to stutter and broke out in a light rash. Currently she was back on Orasin, but she was being monitored closely in case the aphasia got worse.

Reams had been written about the girl's delicate psychological condition and about what the shrinks called her 'basic fire conflict,' a fancy way of saying that her father had told her not to and the Shop people were telling her to go ahead . . . all of it complicated by her guilt over the incident at the Manders farm.

Rainbird bought none of it. It wasn't the drugs, it wasn't being locked up and watched constantly, it wasn't being separated from her father.

She was just tough, that was all.

She had made up her mind somewhere along the line that she wasn't going to cooperate, no matter what. The end. Toot finnee. The psychiatrists could run around showing her inkblots until the moon was blue, the doctors could play with her medication and mutter in their beards about the difficulty of successfully drugging an eight-year-old girl. The papers could pile up and Cap could rave on.

And Charlie McGee would simply go on toughing it out.

Rainbird sensed it as surely as he sensed the coming of rain this afternoon. And he admired her for it. She had the whole bunch of them chasing their tails, and if it was left up to them they would still be chasing their tails when Thanksgiving and then Christmas rolled around. But they wouldn't chase their tails forever, and this more than anything worried John Rainbird.

Rammaden, the safecracker, had told an amusing story about two thieves who had broken into a supermarket one Friday night when they knew a snowstorm had kept the Wells Fargo truck from arriving and taking the heavy end-of-the-week receipts to the bank. The safe was a barrel box. They tried to drill out the combination dial with no success. They had tried to peel it but had been totally unable to bend back a corner and get a start. Finally they had blown it. That was a total success. They blew that barrel wide open, so wide open in fact that all the money inside had been totally destroyed. What was left had looked like the shredded money you sometimes see in those novelty pens.

'The point is,' Rammaden had said in his dry and wheezing voice, 'those two thieves didn't beat the safe. The whole game is beating the safe. You don't beat the safe unless you can take away what was in it in usable condition, you get my point? They overloaded it with soup. They killed the money. They were assholes and the safe beat them.'

Rainbird had got the point.

There were better than sixty college degrees in on this, but it still came down to safecracking. They had tried to drill the girl's combination with their drugs; they had enough shrinks to field a softball team, and these shrinks were all doing their best to resolve the 'basic fire conflict'; and all that particular pile of horseapples boiled down to was that they were trying to peel her from the back.

Rainbird entered the small Quonset hut, took his time card from the rack, and punched in. T. B. Norton, the shift supervisor, looked up from the paperback he was reading.

'No overtime for punching in early, Injun.'

'Yeah?' Rainbird said.

'Yeah.' Norton stared at him challengingly, full of the grim, almost holy assurance that so often goes with petty authority.

Rainbird dropped his eyes and went over to look at the bulletin board. The orderlies' bowling team had won last night. Someone wanted to sell '2 good used washing machine's.' An official notice proclaimed that ALL W-I

THROUGH W-6 WORKERS MUST WASH HANDS BEFORE LEAVING THIS OFFICE.

'Looks like rain,' he said over his shoulder to Norton.

'Never happen, Injun,' Norton said. 'Why don't you blow? You're stinking the place up.'

'Sure, boss,' Rainbird said. 'Just clockin in.'

'Well next time clock in when you're spozed to.'

'Sure, boss,' Rainbird said again, going out, sparing one glance at the side of Norton's pink neck, the soft spot just below the jawbone. Would you have time to scream, boss? Would you have time to scream if I stuck my forefinger through your throat at that spot? Just like a skewer through a piece of steak . . . boss.

He went back out into the muggy heat. The thunderheads were closer now, moving slowly, bowed down with their weight of rain. It was going to be a hard storm. Thunder muttered, still distant.

The house was close now. Rainbird would go around to the side entrance, what had once been the pantry, and take C elevator down four levels. Today he was supposed to wash and wax all the floors in the girl's quarters; it would give him a good shot. And it wasn't that she was unwilling to talk with him; it wasn't that. It was just that she was always so damned distant. He was trying to peel the box in his own way, and if he could get her to *laugh*, just once get her to laugh, to share a joke with him at the Shop's expense, it would be like prying up that one vital corner. It would give him a place to set his chisel. Just that one laugh. It would make them insiders together, it would make them a committee in secret session. Two against the house.

But so far he hadn't been able to get that one laugh, and Rainbird admired her for that more than he could have said.

Rainbird put his ID card in the proper slot and then went down to the orderlies' station to grab a cup of coffee before going on. He didn't want coffee, but it was still early. He couldn't afford to let his eagerness show; it was bad enough that Norton had noticed and commented on it.

He poured himself a slug of mud from the hotplate and sat down with it. At least none of the other nerds had arrived yet. He sat down on the cracked and sprung gray sofa and drank his coffee. His blasted face (and Charlie had shown nothing but the most passing interest in that) was calm and impassive. His thoughts ran on, analyzing the situation as it now stood.

The staff on this were like Rammaden's green safecrackers in the supermarket office. They were handling the girl with kid gloves now, but they weren't doing it out of any love for the girl. Sooner or later they would decide that the kid gloves were getting them nowhere, and when they ran out of 'soft' options, they would decide to blow the safe. When they did, Rainbird was almost sure that they would 'kill the money,' in Rammaden's pungent phrase.

Already he had seen the phrase 'light shock treatments' in two of the doctors' reports – and one of the doctors had been Pynchot, who had Hockstetter's ear. He had seen a contingency report that had been couched in such stultifying jargon that it was nearly another language. Translated, what it boiled down to was a lot of strongarm stuff: if the kid sees her dad in enough pain, she'll break. What Rainbird thought the kid might do if she saw her dad hooked up to a Delco battery and doing a fast polka with his hair on end was to go calmly back to her room, break a waterglass, and eat the pieces.

But you couldn't tell them that. The Shop, like the FBI and CIA, had a long history of killing the money. If you can't get what you want with foreign aid, go in there with some Thompsons and gelignite and assassinate the bastard. Put some cyanide gas in Castro's cigars. It was crazy, but you couldn't tell them that. All they could see were RESULTS, glittering and blinking like some mythical Vegas jackpot. So they killed the money and stood there with a bunch of useless green scraps sifting through their fingers and wondered what the hell had happened.

Now other orderlies began to drift in, joking, smacking each other on the fat part of the arm, talking about the strikes they made and the spares they converted the night before, talking about women, talking about cars, talking about getting shitfaced. The same old stuff that went on even unto the end of the world, hallelujah, amen. They steered clear of Rainbird. None of them liked Rainbird. He didn't bowl and he didn't want to talk about his car and he looked like a refugee from a Frankenstein movie. He made them nervous. If one of them had smacked him on the heavy part of the arm, Rainbird would have put him in traction.

He took out a sack of Red Man, a Zig-Zag paper, and made a quick cigarette. He sat and smoked and waited for it to be time to go down to the girl's quarters.

All things taken together, he felt better, more alive, than he had in years. He realized this and was grateful to the girl. In a way she would never know of, she had given him back his life for a while – the life of a man who feels things keenly and hopes for things mightily; which is to say, a man with vital concerns. It was good that she was tough. He would get to her eventually (tough cracks and easy cracks, but no impossible cracks); he would make her do her dance for them, for whatever that was worth; when the dance was done he would kill her and look into her eyes, hoping to catch that spark of understanding, that message, as she crossed over into whatever there was.

In the meantime, he would live.

He crushed his cigarette out and got up, ready to go to work.

3

The thunderheads built up and up. By three o'clock, the skies over the Longmont complex were low and black. Thunder rolled more and more heavily, gaining assurance, making believers out of the people below. The grounds-keepers put away their mowers. The tables on the patios of the two homes were taken in. In the stables, two hostlers tried to soothe nervous horses that shifted uneasily at each ominous thud from the skies.

The storm came around three-thirty; it came as suddenly as a gunslinger's draw and with all-out fury. It started as rain, then quickly turned to hail. The wind blew from west to east and then suddenly shifted around to exactly the opposite direction. Lightning flashed in great blue-white strokes that left the air smelling like weak gasoline. The winds began to swirl counterclockwise, and on the evening weathercasts there was film of a small tornado that had just skirted Longmont Center and had torn the roof off a shopping-center Fotomat in passing.

The Shop weathered most of the storm well. Two windows were driven in by hail, and the windstorm picked up a low picket fence surrounding a quaint little gazebo on the far side of the duckpond and threw it sixty yards, but that was the extent of the damage (except for flying branches and some ruined flowerbeds – more work for the groundskeeping force). The guard dogs ran between the inner and outer fences crazily at the height of the storm, but they calmed down quickly as it began to slack off.

The damage was done by the electrical storm that came after the hail, rain, and wind. Parts of eastern Virginia were

277

without power until midnight as a result of lightning strikes on the Rowantree and Briska power stations. The area served by the Briska station included Shop headquarters.

In his office, Cap Hollister looked up in annoyance as the lights went off and the solid, unobtrusive hum of the air conditioner wound down to nothing. There were perhaps five seconds of shadowy semi-darkness caused by the power outage and the heavy stormclouds – long enough for Cap to whisper 'Goddam!' under his breath and wonder what the hell had happened to their backup electrical system.

He glanced out the window and saw lightning flickering almost continuously. That evening one of the guardhouse sentries would tell his wife that he had seen an electrical fireball that looked as big as two serving platters bouncing from the weakly charged outer fence to the more heavily charged inner fence and back again.

Cap reached for the phone to find out about the power – and then the lights came on again. The air conditioner took up its hum, and instead of reaching for the phone, Cap reached for his pencil.

Then the lights went out again.

'Shit!' Cap said. He threw the pencil down and picked up the phone after all, daring the lights to come on again before he had the chance to chew someone's ass. The lights declined the dare.

The two graceful homes facing each other across the rolling lawns – and all of the Shop complex underneath – were served by the Eastern Virginia Power Authority, but there were two backup systems powered by diesel generators. One system served the 'vital functions' – the electrical fence, the computer terminals (a power failure can cost unbelievable amounts of money in terms of computer time), and the small infirmary. A second system served the lesser functions of the complex – lights, air conditioning, elevators, and all of that. The secondary system was built to 'cross' – that is, to come in if the primary system showed signs of overloading – but the primary system would not cross if the secondary system began to overload. On August 19, both systems overloaded. The secondary system crossed when the primary system began to overload, just as the power-system architects had planned (although in truth, they had never planned for the primary system to overload in the first place), and as a result, the primary system operated for a full seventy seconds longer than the secondary system. Then the generators for both systems blew, one after the other, like a series of firecrackers. Only these firecrackers had cost about eighty thousand dollars each.

Later, a routine inquiry had brought back the smiling and benign verdict of 'mechanical failure,' although a more accurate conclusion would have been 'greed and venality.' When the backup generators had been installed in 1971, a senator privy to the acceptable-low-bid figures on that little operation (as well as sixteen million dollars' worth of other Shop construction) had tipped his brother-in-law, who was an electrical-engineering consultant. The consultant had decided he could quite handily come in under the lowest bid by cutting a corner here and there.

It was only one favor in an area that lives on favors and under-the-table information, and it was notable only because it was the first link in the chain that led to the final destruction and loss of life. The backup system had been used only piecemeal in all the years since it had been constructed. In its first major test, during the storm that knocked out the Briska power station, it failed completely. By then, of course, the electrical-engineering consultant had gone onward and upward; he was helping to build a multimillion-dollar beach resort at Coki Beach, on St Thomas.

The Shop didn't get its power back until the Briska station came on line again . . . which is to say, at the same time the rest of eastern Virginia got its juice back – around midnight.

By then, the next links had already been forged. As a result of the storm and the blackout, something tremendous had happened to both Andy and Charlie McGee, although neither of them had the slightest idea of what had happened to the other.

After five months of stasis, things had begun to roll onward again.

4

When the power went off, Andy McGee was watching *The PTL Club* on TV. The PTL stood for 'Praise the Lord.' On one of the Virginia stations, *The PTL Club* seemed to run continuously, twenty-four hours a day. This was probably not the case, but Andy's perceptions of time had become so screwed up it was hard to tell.

He had put on weight. Sometimes – more often when he was straight – he would catch a glimpse of himself in the mirror and think of Elvis Presley and the way the man had softly ballooned near the end of his life. At other times, he would think of the way a tomcat that had been 'fixed' would sometimes get fat and lazy.

He wasn't fat yet, but he was getting there. In Hastings Glen, he had weighed himself on the bathroom scale in the Slumberland Motel and had come in at one-sixty-two. These days he was tipping the scales at about one-ninety. His cheeks were fuller, and he had the suggestion of a double chin and what his old high-school gym teacher used to call (with utter contempt) 'man-tits.' And more than a suggestion of a gut. There was not much exercise – or much urge to exercise while in the grip of a solid Thorazine high – and the food was very good.

He did not worry about his weight when he was high, and that was most of the time. When they were ready to make some more of their fruitless tests, they would iron him out over an eighteen-hour period, a doctor would test his physical reactions, an EEG would be taken to make sure his brainwaves were nice and sharp, and then he would be taken into a testing cubicle, which was a small white room with drilled-cork paneling.

They had began, back in April, with human volunteers. They told him what to do and told him that if he did anything overenthusiastic – like striking someone blind, for instance – that he would be made to suffer. An undertone to this threat was that he might not suffer alone. This threat struck Andy as an empty one; he didn't believe that they would really harm Charlie. She was their prize pupil. He was very much the B feature on the program.

The doctor in charge of testing him was a man named Herman Pynchot. He was in his late thirties and perfectly ordinary except for the fact that he grinned too much. Sometimes all that grinning made Andy nervous. Occasionally an older doctor named Hockstetter would drop by, but mostly it was Pynchot.

Pynchot told him as they approached the first test that there was a table in the small testing room. On this table was a bottle of grape Kool-Aid, labeled INK, a fountain pen in a stand, a pad of notepaper, a pitcher of water, and two glasses. Pynchot told him that the volunteer would have no idea that there was anything other than ink in the ink bottle. Pynchot further told Andy that they would be grateful if he would 'push' the volunteer into pouring himself a glass of water, then dumping a goodish quantity of the 'ink' into it, and then quaffing the whole mess.

'Neat,' Andy said. He himself had not been feeling so

neat. He missed his Thorazine and the peace that it brought.

'Very neat,' Pynchot said. 'Will you do it?'

'Why should I?'

'You'll get something in return. Something nice.'

'Be a good rat and you get the cheese,' Andy said. 'Right?'

Pynchot shrugged and grinned. His smock was screamingly neat; it looked as if it might have been tailored by Brooks Brothers.

'All right,' Andy said. 'I give up. What's my prize for making this poor sucker drink ink?'

'Well, you can go back to taking your pills, for one thing.'

Suddenly it was a little hard to swallow, and he wondered if Thorazine was addicting, and if it was, if the addiction was psychological or physiological. 'Tell me, Pynchot,' he said. 'How does it feel to be a pusher? Is that in the Hippocratic oath?'

Pynchot shrugged and grinned. 'You also get to go outdoors for a while,' he said. 'I believe you've expressed an interest in that?'

Andy had. His quarters were nice – so nice you could sometimes almost forget they were nothing but a padded jail cell. There were three rooms plus a bath; there was a color TV equipped with Home Box Office, where a new choice of three recent films appeared each week. One of the munchkins – possibly it had been Pynchot – must have pointed out that there was no use taking away his belt and giving him only Crayolas to write with and plastic spoons to eat with. If he wanted to commit suicide, there was just no way they could stop him. If he pushed hard enough and long enough, he would simply blow his brain like an old tire.

So the place had all the amenities, even extending to a

microwave oven in the kitchenette. It was all done in decorator colors, there was a thick shag rug on the living-room floor, the pictures were all good prints. But for all of that, a dog turd covered with frosting is not a wedding cake; it is simply a frosted dog turd, and none of the doors leading out of this tasteful little apartment had doorknobs on the inside. There were small glass loopholes scattered here and there around the apartment – the sort of loopholes you see in the doors of hotel rooms. There was even one in the bathroom, and Andy had calculated that they provided sightlines to just about anyplace in the apartment. TV monitoring devices was Andy's guess, and probably equipped with infrared as well, so you couldn't even jerk off in relative privacy.

He wasn't claustrophobic, but he didn't like being closed up for long periods of time. It made him nervous, even with the drugs. It was a low nervousness, usually evidenced by long sighs and periods of apathy. He had indeed asked to go out. He wanted to see the sun again, and green grass.

'Yes,' he said softly to Pynchot. 'I have expressed an interest in going out.'

But he didn't get to go out.

The volunteer was nervous at first, undoubtedly expecting Andy to make him stand on his head and cluck like a chicken or something equally ridiculous. He was a football fan. Andy got the man, whose name was Dick Albright, to bring him up to date on the previous season – who had made it to the playoffs and how they went, who had won the Super Bowl.

Albright kindled. He spent the next twenty minutes reliving the entire season, gradually losing his nervousness. He was up to the lousy reffing that had allowed the Pats to triumph over the Dolphins in the AFC championship game when Andy said, 'Have a glass of water, if you want. You must be thirsty.'

Albright glanced up at him. 'Yeah, I am kinda thirsty. Say . . . am I talkin too much? Is it screwin up their tests, do you think?'

'No, I don't think so,' Andy said. He watched Dick Albright pour himself a glass of water from the pitcher.

'You want some?' Albright asked.

'No, I'll pass,' Andy said, and suddenly gave a hard push. 'Have some ink in it, why don't you?'

Albright looked up at him, then reached for the bottle of 'ink.' He picked it up, looked at it, and put it back down again. 'Put *ink* in it? You must be crazy.'

Pynchot grinned as much after the test as before it, but he was not pleased. Not pleased at all. Andy was not pleased either. When he had pushed out at Albright there had been none of that sideslipping sensation . . . that curious feeling of *doubling* that usually accompanied the push. And no headache. He had concentrated all of his will toward suggesting to Albright that putting ink in his water would be a perfectly reasonable thing to do, and Albright had made a perfectly reasonable reply: that Andy was nuts. In spite of all the pain it had caused him, he had felt a touch of panic at the thought the talent might have deserted him.

'Why do you want to keep it under wraps?' Pynchot asked him. He lit a Chesterfield and grinned. 'I don't understand you, Andy. What *good* does it do you?'

'For the tenth time,' Andy had replied, 'I wasn't holding back. I wasn't faking. I pushed him as hard as I could. Nothing happened, that's all.' He wanted his pill. He felt depressed and nervous. All the colors seemed too bright, the light too strong, voices too loud. It was better with the pills. With the pills, his useless outrage over what had happened and his loneliness for Charlie and his worry over what might be happening to her – these things faded back and became manageable.

'I'm afraid I don't believe that,' Pynchot said, and grinned. 'Think it over, Andy. We're not asking you to make someone walk off a cliff or shoot himself in the head. I guess you didn't want that walk as badly as you thought you did.'

He stood up as if to go.

'Listen,' Andy said, unable to keep the desperation entirely out of his voice, 'I'd like one of those pills.'

'Would you?' Pynchot said. 'Well, it might interest you to know that I'm lightening your dosage . . . just in case it's the Thorazine that's interfering with your ability.' His grin bloomed anew. 'Of course, if your ability suddenly came back . . .'

'There are a couple of things you should know,' Andy told him. 'First, the guy was nervous, expecting something. Second, he wasn't all that bright. It's a lot harder to push old people and people with low or low-normal IQs. Bright people go easier.'

'Is that so?' Pynchot said.

'Yes.'

'Then why don't you push me into giving you a pill right now? My tested IQ is one-fifty-five.'

Andy had tried – with no results at all.

Eventually he had got his walk outside, and eventually they had increased the dosage of his medication again as well – after they became convinced that he really wasn't faking, that he was, in fact, trying desperately hard to use the push, with no success at all. Quite independently of each other, both Andy and Dr Pynchot began to wonder if he hadn't tipped himself over permanently in the run that had taken him and Charlie from New York to Albany County Airport to Hastings Glen, if he hadn't simply used the talent up. And both of them wondered if it wasn't some kind of psychological block. Andy himself came to believe that either the talent was really gone or it was simply a

285

defense mechanism: his mind refusing to use the talent because it knew it might kill him to do so. He hadn't forgotten the numb places on his cheek and neck, and the bloodshot eye.

Either way, it amounted to the same thing – a big goose-egg. Pynchot, his dreams of covering himself with glory as the first man to get provable, empirical data on psychic mental domination now flying away, came around less and less often.

The tests had continued through May and June – first more volunteers and then totally unsuspecting test subjects. Using the latter was not precisely ethical, as Pynchot was the first to admit, but some of the first tests with LSD hadn't been precisely ethical, either. Andy marveled that by equating these two wrongs in his mind, Pynchot seemed to come out the other side feeling that everything was okay. It didn't matter, because Andy had no success pushing any of them.

A month ago, just after the Fourth of July, they had begun testing him with animals. Andy protested that pushing an animal was even more impossible than trying to push a stupid person, but his protests cut zero ice with Pynchot and his team, who were really only going through the motions of a scientific investigation at this point. And so once a week Andy found himself sitting in a room with a dog or a cat or a monkey, feeling like a character from an absurdist novel. He remembered the cab driver who had looked at a dollar bill and had seen a five hundred. He remembered the timid executives he had managed to tip gently in the direction of more confidence and assertiveness. Before them, in Port City, Pennsylvania, there had been the Weight-Off program, the classes attended mostly by lonely fat housewives with an addiction to Snackin' Cakes, Pepsi-Cola, and anything between two slices of bread. These were things that filled up the emptiness of their lives a little. That had simply been a matter of pushing a little bit, because most of them had really wanted to lose weight. He had helped them do that. He thought also of what had happened to the two Shop ramrods who had taken Charlie.

He *had* been able to do it, but no more. It was hard even to remember exactly what it had felt like. So he sat in the room with dogs that lapped his hand and cats that purred and monkeys that moodily scratched their asses and sometimes showed their teeth in apocalyptic, fang-filled grins that were obscenely like Pynchot's grins, and of course none of the animals did anything unusual at all. And later on he would be taken back to his apartment with no doorknobs on the doors and there would be a blue pill in a white dish on the counter in the kitchenette and in a little while he would stop feeling nervous and depressed. He would start feeling pretty much okay again. And he would watch one of the Home Box Office movies – something with Clint Eastwood, if he could get it – or perhaps *The PTL Club*. It didn't bother him so much that he had lost his talent and become a superfluous person.

5

On the afternoon of the big storm, he sat watching *The PTL Club*. A woman with a beehive hairdo was telling the host how the power of God had cured her of Bright's disease. Andy was quite fascinated with her. Her hair gleamed under the studio lighting like a varnished table-leg. She looked like a time traveler from the year 1963. That was one of the fascinations *The PTL Club* held for him, along with the shameless carny pitches for money in the name of God. Andy would listen to these pitches delivered by hard-faced young men in expensive suits and think, bemused, of how Christ had driven the moneychangers from the temple. And *all* the people on *PTL* looked like time travelers from 1963.

The woman finished her story of how God had saved her from shaking herself to pieces. Earlier in the program an actor who had been famous in the early 1950s had told how God had saved him from the bottle. Now the woman with the beehive hairdo began to cry and the once-famous actor embraced her. The camera dollied in for a close-up. In the background, the PTL Singers began to hum. Andy shifted in his seat a little. It was almost time for his pill.

In a dim sort of way he realized that the medication was only partially responsible for the peculiar changes that had come over him in the last five months, changes of which his soft weight gain was only an outward sign. When the Shop had taken Charlie away from him, they had knocked the one solid remaining prop out from under his life. With Charlie gone – oh, she was undoubtedly somewhere near, but she might as well have been on the moon – there seemed to be no reason for holding himself together.

On top of that, all the running had induced a nervous kind of shellshock. He had lived on the tightrope for so long that when he had finally fallen off, total lethargy had been the result. In fact, he believed he had suffered a very quiet sort of nervous breakdown. If he *did* see Charlie, he wasn't even sure she would recognize him as the same person, and that made him sad.

He had never made any effort to deceive Pynchot or cheat on the tests. He did not really think that doing so would rebound on Charlie, but he would not have taken even the most remote chance of that happening. And it was easier to do what they wanted. He had become passive. He had screamed the last of his rage on Granther's porch, as he cradled his daughter with the dart sticking out of her neck. There was no more rage left in him. He had shot his wad.

That was Andy McGee's mental state as he sat watching TV that August 19 while the storm walked the hills outside. The *PTL* host made a donations pitch and then introduced a gospel trio. The trio began to sing, and suddenly the lights went out.

The TV also went, the picture dwindling down to a bright speck. Andy sat in his chair, unmoving, not sure just what had happened. His mind had just enough time to register the scary totality of the dark, and then the lights went on again. The gospel trio reappeared, singing 'I Got a Telephone Call from Heaven and Jesus Was on the Line.' Andy heaved a sigh of relief, and then the lights went out again.

He sat there, gripping the arms of the chair as if he would fly away if he let go. He kept his eyes desperately fixed on the bright speck of light from the TV even after he knew it was gone and he was only seeing a lingering after-image . . . or wishful thinking.

It'll be back on in a second or two, he told himself. *Secondary generators somewhere. You don't trust to house current to run a place like this.*

Still, he was scared. He suddenly found himself recalling the boys'-adventure stories of his childhood. In more than one of them, there had been an incident in some cave with the lights or candles blown out. And it seemed that the author would always go to great lengths to describe the dark as 'palpable' or 'utter' or 'total.' There was even that tried-and-true old standby 'the living dark,' as in 'The living dark engulfed Tom and his friends.' If all of this had been meant to impress the nine-year-old Andy McGee, it hadn't done. As far as he was concerned, if he wanted to be 'engulfed by the living dark,' all he had to do was go into his closet and put a blanket along the crack at the bottom of the door. Dark was, after all, dark.

Now he realized that he had been wrong about that; it

wasn't the only thing he'd been wrong about as a kid, but it was maybe the last one to be discovered. He would just as soon have forgone the discovery, because dark *wasn't* dark. He had never been in a dark like this one in his life. Except for the sensation of the chair beneath his butt and under his hands, he could have been floating in some lightless Lovecraftian gulf between the stars. He raised one hand and floated it in front of his eyes. And although he could feel the palm lightly touching his nose, he couldn't see it.

He took the hand away from his face and gripped the arm of the chair with it again. His heart had taken on a rapid and thready beat in his chest. Outside, someone called out hoarsely, 'Richie! Where the fuck areya?' and Andy cringed back in his chair as if he had been threatened. He licked his lips.

It'll be back on in just a second or two now, he thought, but a scared part of his mind that refused to be comforted by mere rationalities asked: *How long is a second or two, or a minute or two, in total darkness? How do you measure time in total darkness?*

Outside, beyond his 'apartment,' something fell over and someone screamed in pain and surprise. Andy cringed back again and moaned shakily. He didn't like this. This was no good.

Well, if it takes them longer than a few minutes to fix it – to reset the breakers or whatever – they'll come and let me out. They'll have to.

Even the scared part of his mind – the part that was only a short distance away from gibbering – recognized the logic of this, and he relaxed a little. After all, it was just the *dark*; that's all it was – just the absence of light. It wasn't as if there were *monsters* in the dark, or anything like that.

He was very thirsty. He wondered if he dared get up and go get a bottle of ginger ale out of the fridge. He decided he could do it if he was careful. He got up, took two shuffling steps forward, and promptly barked his shin on the edge of the coffee table. He bent and rubbed it, eyes watering with pain.

This was like childhood, too. They had played a game called 'blind man'; he supposed all kids did. You had to try to get from one end of the house to the other with a bandanna or something over your eyes. And everyone else thought it was simply the height of humor when you fell over a hassock or tripped over the riser between the dining room and the kitchen. The game could teach you a painful lesson about how little you actually remembered about the layout of your supposedly familiar house and how much more you relied upon your eyes than your memory. And the game could make you wonder how the hell you'd live if you went blind.

But I'll be all right, Andy thought. *I'll be all right if I just take it slow and easy.*

He moved around the coffee table and then began to shuffle his way slowly across the open space of the living room with his hands out in front of him. It was funny how threatening open space could feel in the dark. *Probably the lights'll come on right now and I can have a good laugh at myself. Just have a good l—*

'Ow!'

His outstretched fingers struck the wall and bent back painfully. Something fell – the picture of the barn and hayfield after the style of Wyeth that hung near the kitchen door, he guessed. It swished by him, sounding ominously like a whickering sword blade in the dark, and clattered to the floor. The sound was shockingly loud.

He stood still, holding his aching fingers, feeling the throb of his barked shin. He was cotton-mouthed with fear.

'Hey!' he shouted. 'Hey, don't forget about me, you guys!'

He waited and listened. There was no answer. There were still sounds and voices, but they were farther away now. If they got much farther away, he would be in total silence.

Forgotten all about me, he thought, and his fright deepened.

His heart was racing. He could feel cold sweat on his arms and brow, and he found himself remembering the time at Tashmore Pond when he had gone out too deep, got tired and begun to thrash and scream, sure he was going to die . . . but when he put his feet down the bottom was there, the water only nipple high. Where was the bottom now? He licked at his dry lips, but his tongue was dry, too.

'*HEY!*' he shouted at the top of his lungs, and the sound of terror in his voice terrified him even more. He had to get hold of himself. He was within arm's length of total panic now, just bulling around mindlessly in here and screaming at the top of his lungs. All because someone had blown a fuse.

Oh goddammit all anyway, why'd it have to happen when it was time for my pill? If I had my pill I'd be all right. I'd be okay then. Christ it feels like my head's full of broken glass—

He stood there, breathing heavily. He had aimed for the kitchen door, had gone off course and run into the wall. Now he felt totally disoriented and couldn't even remember if that stupid barn picture had been hung to the right or left of the doorway. He wished miserably that he had stayed in his chair.

'Get hold,' he muttered aloud. 'Get hold.'

It was not *just* panic, he recognized that. It was the pill that was now overdue, the pill on which he had come to depend. It just wasn't fair that this had happened when his pill was due.

'Get hold,' he muttered again.

Ginger ale. He had got up to get ginger ale and he was going to by-God get it. He had to fix on something. That's all it came down to, and ginger ale would do as well as anything else.

He began to move again, toward the left, and promptly fell over the picture that had come off the wall.

Andy screamed and went down, pinwheeling his arms wildly and fruitlessly for balance. He struck his head hard and screamed again.

Now he was very frightened. Help me, he thought. Somebody help me, bring me a candle, for Christ's sake, something, I'm scared—

He began to cry. His fumbling fingers felt thick wetness on the side of his head – blood – and he wondered with numb terror how bad it was.

'*Where are you people?*' he screamed. There was no answer. He heard – or thought he heard – a single faraway shout, and then there was silence. His fingers found the picture he had tripped over and he threw it across the room, furious at it for hurting him. It struck the end table beside the couch, and the now-useless lamp that stood there fell over. The lightbulb exploded with a hollow sound, and Andy cried out again. He felt the side of his head. More blood there now. It was crawling over his cheek in little rivulets.

Panting, he began to crawl, one hand out to feel the wall. When its solidity abruptly ended in blankness, he drew in both his breath and his hand, as if he expected something nasty to snake out of the blackness and grab him. A little *whhh!* sound sucked in past his lips. For just one second the totality of childhood came back and he could hear the whisper of trolls as they crowded eagerly toward him.

'Just the kitchen door, for fuck's sake,' he muttered raggedly. 'That's all.'

He crawled through it. The fridge was to the right and he began to bear that way, crawling slowly and breathing fast, his hands cold on the tile.

Somewhere overhead, on the next level, something fell over with a tremendous clang. Andy jerked up on his knees. His nerve broke and he lost himself. He began to scream *'Help! Help! Help!'* over and over until he was hoarse. He had no idea how long he might have screamed there, on his hands and knees in the black kitchen.

At last he stopped and tried to get hold of himself. His hands and arms were shaking helplessly. His head ached from the thump he had given it, but the flow of blood seemed to have stopped. That was a little reassuring. His throat felt hot and flayed from all his screaming, and that made him think of the ginger ale again.

He began to crawl once more, and he found the refrigerator with no further incident. He opened it (ridiculously expecting the interior light to come on with its familiar frosty-white glow) and fumbled around in the cool dark box until he found a can with a ringtab on top. Andy shut the fridge door and leaned against it. He opened the can and swilled half the ginger ale at a draft. His throat blessed him for it.

Then a thought came and his throat froze.

The place is on fire, his mind told him with spurious calmness. *That's why no one's come to get you out. They're evacuating. You, now . . . you're expendable.*

This thought brought on an extremity of claustrophobic terror that was beyond panic. He simply cringed back against the refrigerator, his lips pulled back from his teeth in a grimace. The strength went out of his legs. For a moment, he even imagined he could smell smoke, and heat seemed to rush over him. The soda can slipped from his fingers and gurgled its contents out onto the floor, wetting his pants.

Andy sat in the wetness, moaning.

6

John Rainbird thought later that things could not have worked better if they had planned it . . . and if those fancy psychologists had been worth a tin whistle in a high wind, they *would* have planned it. But as it happened, it was only the lucky happenstance of the blackout's occurring when it did that allowed him to finally get his chisel under one corner of the psychological steel that armored Charlie McGee. Luck, and his own inspired intuition.

He let himself into Charlie's quarters at three-thirty, just as the storm was beginning to break outside. He pushed a cart before him that was no different from the ones most hotel and motel maids push as they go from room to room. It contained clean sheets and pillow slips, furniture polish, a rug-shampoo preparation for spot stains. There was a floor bucket and a mop. A vacuum cleaner was clipped to one end of the cart.

Charlie was sitting on the floor in front of the couch, wearing a bright blue Danskin leotard and nothing else. Her long legs were crossed in a lotuslike position. She sat that way a great deal. An outsider might have thought she was stoned, but Rainbird knew better. She was still being lightly medicated, but now the dosage was little more than a placebo. All of the psychologists were in disappointed agreement that she meant what she said about never lighting fires again. The drugs had originally been meant to keep her from burning her way out, but now it seemed sure that she wasn't going to do that . . or anything else.

295

'Hi, kid,' Rainbird said. He unclipped the vacuum cleaner.

She glanced over at him but didn't respond. He plugged the vacuum in, and when he started it, she got up gracefully and went into the bathroom. She shut the door.

Rainbird went on vacuuming the rug. He had no plan in mind. It was a case of looking for small signs and signals, picking up on them, and following them. His admiration for the girl was unalloyed. Her father was turning into a fat, apathetic pudding, the psychologists had their own terms for it – 'dependency shock,' and 'loss of identity,' and 'mental fugue,' and 'mild reality dysfunction' – but what it all came down to was he had given up and could now be canceled out of the equation. The girl hadn't done that. She had simply hidden herself. And Rainbird never felt so much like an Indian as he did when he was with Charlie McGee.

He vacuumed and waited for her to come out – maybe. He thought she was coming out of the bathroom a little more frequently now. At first she had always hidden there until he was gone. Now sometimes she came out and watched him. Perhaps she would today. Perhaps not. He would wait. And watch for signs.

7

Charlie sat in the bathroom with the door shut. She would have locked it if she could. Before the orderly came to clean the place, she had been doing some simple exercises she had found in a book. The orderly came to keep it orderly. Now the toilet seat felt cold under her. The white light from the fluorescents that ringed the bathroom mirror made everything seem cold, and too bright.

At first there had been a live-in 'companion,' a woman

of about forty-five. She was supposed to be 'motherly,' but the 'motherly companion' had hard green eyes with small flecks in them. The flecks were like ice. These were the people who had killed her real mother; now they wanted her to live here with the 'motherly companion.' Charlie told them she didn't want the 'motherly companion.' They smiled. Then Charlie stopped talking, and she didn't say another word until the 'motherly companion' left, taking her green ice-chip eyes with her. She had made a deal with that man Hockstetter: she would answer his questions, and his alone, if he would get that 'motherly companion' out. The only companion she wanted was her father, and if she couldn't have him, she would be alone.

In many ways she felt that the last five months (they told her it was five months; it didn't feel like anything) had been a dream. There was no way to mark time, faces came and went with no memories attached to them, disembodied as balloons, and food had no particular taste. She felt like a balloon herself sometimes. She felt as if she were floating. But in a way, her mind told her with perfect certitude, it was fair. She was a murderer. She had broken the worst of the Ten Commandments and was surely damned to hell.

She thought about this at night, with the lights turned down low so that the apartment itself seemed like a dream. She saw it all. The men on the porch wearing their crowns of flame. The cars exploding. The chickens catching fire. The smell of burning that was always the smell of smoldering stuffing, the smell of her teddy bear.

(and she had liked it)

That was it; that was the trouble. The more she had done it the more she had liked it; the more she had done it the more she had been able to feel the power, a living thing, getting stronger and stronger. It was like a pyramid standing upside down, standing on its tip, and the more you did it the harder it got to stop it. It *hurt* to stop it

(and it was fun)

and so she was never going to do it again. She would die in here before she did it again. Maybe she even wanted to die in here. The idea of dying in a dream wasn't scary at all.

The only two faces that weren't totally dissociated were Hockstetter's and that of the orderly who came to clean her apartment every day. Charlie had asked him once why he had to come every day, since she wasn't messy.

John – that was his name – had taken a scrungy old pad from his back pocket and a cheap ballpoint pen from his breast pocket. He said 'That's just my job, kid.' And on the paper he wrote *Because they're full of shit, why else?*

She had almost giggled but had stopped herself in time by thinking of men with crowns of fire, men who smelled like smoldering teddy bears. Giggling would have been dangerous. So she simply pretended that she hadn't seen the note or didn't understand it. The orderly's face was a mess. He wore an eyepatch. She felt sorry for him and once she had almost asked him what happened – if he had been in a car accident or something – but that would have been even more dangerous than giggling at his note. She didn't know why, but she felt that in every fiber.

His face was very horrible to look at, but he seemed pleasant enough, and his face was no worse than the face of little Chuckie Eberhardt back in Harrison. Chuckie's mother had been frying potatoes when Chuckie was three and Chuckie had pulled the pan of hot fat off the stove all over himself and had almost died. Afterward the other kids sometimes called him Chuckie Hamburger and Chuckie Frankenstein, and Chuckie would cry. It was mean. The other kids didn't seem to understand that a thing like that could happen to any kid. When you were three you didn't have much in the smarts department.

John's face was all ripped up, but that didn't scare her.

It was Hockstetter's face that scared her, and his face – except for the eyes – was as ordinary as anyone else's. His eyes were even worse than the eyes of the 'motherly companion.' He was always using them to pry at you. Hockstetter wanted her to make fires. He asked her again and again. He took her to a room, and sometimes there would be crumpled-up pieces of newspaper and sometimes there would be little glass dishes filled with oil and sometimes there would be other things. But for all the questions, and all the fake sympathy, it always came down to the same thing: Charlie, set this on fire.

Hockstetter scared her. She sensed that he had all sorts of . . . of

(things)

that he could use on her to make her light fires. But she wouldn't. Except she was scared that she would. Hockstetter would use anything. He didn't play fair, and one night she had had a dream, and in this dream she had set Hockstetter on fire and she had awakened with her hands stuffed into her mouth to keep back a scream.

One day, in order to postpone the inevitable request, she had asked when she could see her father. It had been much on her mind, but she hadn't asked, because she knew what the answer would be. But on this day she was feeling specially tired and low-spirited, and it had just slipped out.

'Charlie, I think you know the answer to that,' Hockstetter had said. He pointed to the table in the little room. There was a steel tray on the table and it was filled with heaps of curly woodshavings. 'If you'll light that, I'll take you to your father right away. You can be with him in two minutes.' Beneath his cold, watching eyes, Hockstetter's mouth spread wide in a just-pals sort of grin. 'Now, what say?'

'Give me a match,' Charlie had answered, feeling the tears threaten. 'I'll light it.'

'You can light it just by thinking about it. You know that.'

'No. I can't. And even if I could, I wouldn't. It's wrong.'

Hockstetter looked at her sadly, the just-pals smile fading. 'Charlie, why do you hurt yourself like this? Don't you want to see your dad? He wants to see you. He told me to tell you it was all right.'

And then she *did* cry, she cried hard and long, because she did want to see him, not a minute of any day went by without her thoughts turning to him, without missing him, without wanting to feel his solid arms around her. Hockstetter watched her cry and there was no sympathy in his face, no sorrow or kindness. There was, however, careful calculation. Oh, she hated him.

That had been three weeks ago. Since then she had stubbornly not mentioned her father, although Hockstetter had dangled him before her constantly, telling her that her father was sad, that her father said it was okay to make fires, and worst of all, that her father had told Hockstetter that he guessed Charlie didn't love him anymore.

She looked at her pale face in the bathroom mirror and listened to the steady whine of John's vacuum cleaner. When he finished that, he would change her bed. Then he would dust. Then he would be gone. Suddenly she didn't want him to be gone, she wanted to listen to him talk.

At first she had always gone into the bathroom and stayed in there until he was gone, and once he had turned off the vacuum cleaner and knocked on the bathroom door, calling worriedly: 'Kid? You all right? You ain't sick, are you?'

His voice was so kind – and kindness, simple kindness, was so hard to come by in here – that she had had to struggle to keep her voice calm and cool because the tears were threatening again. 'Yes . . . I'm okay.'

She waited, wondering if he would try to take it further, try to get inside her like the others did, but he had simply gone away and started his vacuum up again. In a way she had been disappointed.

Another time he had been washing the floor and when she came out of the bathroom, he had said, without looking up, 'Watch out for that wet floor, kid, you don't want to break your arm.' That was all, but again she had been nearly surprised into tears – it was concern, so simple and direct it was unconscious.

Just lately she had been coming out of the bathroom to watch him more and more. To watch him . . . and to listen to him. He would ask her questions sometimes, but they were never threatening ones. Still, most times she wouldn't answer, just on general principles. It didn't stop John. He would talk to her anyway. He would talk about his bowling scores, about his dog, about how his TV got broken and it would be a couple of weeks before he could get it fixed because they wanted so much for those little tiny tubes.

She supposed he was lonely. With a face like his, he probably didn't have a wife or anything. She liked to listen to him because it was like a secret tunnel to the outside. His voice was low, musical, sometimes wandering. It was never sharp and interrogative, like Hockstetter's. He required no reply, seemingly.

She got off the toilet seat and went to the door, and that was when the lights went out. She stood there, puzzled, one hand on the doorknob, her head cocked to one side. It immediately came to her that this was some sort of trick. She could hear the dying whine of John's vacuum cleaner and then he said, 'Well, what the *Christ?*'

Then the lights came back on. Still Charlie didn't come out. The vacuum cleaner cycled back up again. Footsteps approached the door and John said, 'Did the lights go out in there for a second?'

'Yes.'

'It's the storm, I guess.'

'What storm?'

'Looked like it was going to storm when I came to work. Big thunderheads.'

Looked like it was going to storm. Outside. She wished she could go outside and see the big thunderheads. Smell that funny way the air got before a summer storm. It got a rainy, wet smell. Everything looked gr—

The lights went out again.

The vacuum died. The darkness was total. Her only connection with the world was her hand on the brushed-chrome doorknob. She began to tap her tongue thoughtfully against her upper lip.

'Kid?'

She didn't answer. A trick? A storm, he had said. And she believed that. She believed John. It was surprising and scary to find that she believed what someone had told her, after all this time.

'Kid?' It was him again. And this time he sounded . . . frightened.

Her own fear of the dark, which had only begun to creep up on her, was sublimated in his.

'John, what's the matter?' She opened the door and groped in front of her. She didn't go out, not yet. She was afraid of tripping over the vacuum cleaner.

'What happened?' Now there was a beat of panic in his voice. It scared her. 'Where's the lights?'

'They went out,' she said. 'You said . . . the storm . . .'

'I can't stand the dark,' he said. There was terror in his voice and a kind of grotesque apology. 'You don't understand. I can't . . . I got to get out. . . .' She heard him make a sudden blundering rush across the living room,

302

and then there was a loud and frightening crash as he fell over something – the coffee table, most likely. He cried out miserably and that frightened her even more.

'John? John! Are you all right?'

'I got to get out!' he screamed. 'Make them let me out, kid!'

'What's wrong?'

There was no answer, not for a long time. Then she heard a low, choked sound and understood that he was crying.

'Help me,' he said then, and Charlie stood in the bathroom doorway, trying to decide. Part of her fear had already dissolved into sympathy, but part of it remained questioning, hard and bright.

'Help me, oh somebody help me,' he said in a low voice, so low it was as if he expected no one to hear or heed. And that decided her. Slowly she began to feel her way across the room toward him, her hands held out in front of her.

8

Rainbird heard her coming and could not forbear a grin in the dark – a hard, humorless grin that he covered with the palm of his hand, in case the power should come back on at that precise instant.

'John?'

He made a voice of strained agony through his grin. 'I'm sorry, kid. I just . . . it's the dark. I can't stand the dark. It's like the place where they put me after I was captured.'

'Who put you?'

'The Cong.'

She was closer now. The grin left his face and he began to put himself into the part. *Scared. You're scared because the Cong put you in a hole in the ground after one of their mines*

blew most of your face off . . . and they kept you there . . . and
now you need a friend.

In a way, the part was a natural. All he had to do was
make her believe that his extreme excitement at this
unexpected chance was extreme fear. And of course he *was*
afraid -- afraid of blowing it. This made the shot from the
tree with the ampul of Orasin look like child's play. Her
intuitions were deadly sharp. Nervous perspiration was
flowing off him in rivers.

'Who are the Cong?' she asked, very close now. Her
hand brushed lightly past his face and he clutched it. She
gasped nervously.

'Hey, don't be scared,' he said. 'It's just that—'

'You . . . that hurts. You're hurting me.'

It was exactly the right tone. She was scared too, scared
of the dark and scared of him . . . but worried about him,
too. He wanted her to feel she had been clutched by a
drowning man.

'I'm sorry, kid.' He loosened his grip but didn't let go.
'Just . . . can you sit beside me?'

'Sure.' She sat down, and he jumped at the mild thud of
her body coming down on the floor. Outside, far away,
someone hollered something to someone else.

'Let us out!' Rainbird screamed immediately. 'Let us
out! Hey, let us out! People in here!'

'Stop it,' Charlie said, alarmed. 'We're okay . . . I mean,
aren't we?'

His mind, that overtuned machine, was clicking along at
high speed, writing the script, always three or four lines
ahead, enough to be safe, not enough to destroy hot
spontaneity. Most of all he wondered just how long he had,
how long before the lights went back on. He cautioned
himself not to expect or hope for too much. He had got his
chisel under the edge of the box. Anything else would be
gravy.

'Yeah, I guess we are,' he said. 'It's just the dark, that's all. I don't even have a fucking match or— Aw, hey, kid, I'm sorry. That just slipped out.'

'That's okay,' Charlie said. 'Sometimes my dad says that word. Once when he was fixing my wagon out in the garage he hit his hand with the hammer and said it five or six times. Other ones, too.' This was by far the longest speech she had ever made in Rainbird's presence. 'Will they come and let us out pretty soon?'

'They can't until they get the power back on,' he said, miserable on the outside, gleeful on the inside. 'These doors, kid, they've all got electric locks. They're built to lock solid if the power goes off. They've got you in a fuh— they've got you in a cell, kid. It looks like a nice little apartment, but you might as well be in jail.'

'I know,' she said quietly. He was still holding her hand tightly but she didn't seem to mind as much now. 'You shouldn't say it, though. I think they listen.'

They! Rainbird thought, and a hot triumphant joy flashed through him. He was faintly aware that he had not felt such intensity of emotion in ten years. *They! She's talking about they!*

He felt his chisel slip farther under the corner of the box that was Charlie McGee, and he involuntarily squeezed her hand again.

'Ow!'

'Sorry, kid,' he said, letting off. 'I know damn well they listen. But they ain't listening now, with the power off. Oh kid, I don't like this, I gotta get out of here!' He began to tremble.

'Who are the Cong?'

'You don't know? . . . No, you're too young, I guess. It was the war, kid. The war in Vietnam. The Cong were the bad guys. They wore black pajamas. In the jungle. You know about the Vietnam war, don't you?'

305

She knew about it . . . vaguely.

'We were on patrol and we walked into an ambush,' he said. That much was the truth, but this was where John Rainbird and the truth parted company. There was no need to confuse her by pointing out that they had all been stoned, most of the grunts smoked up well on Cambodian red, and their West Point lieutenant, who was only one step away from the checkpoint between the lands of sanity and madness, on the peyote buttons that he chewed whenever they were out on patrol. Rainbird had once seen this looey shoot a pregnant woman with a semiautomatic rifle, had seen the woman's six-month fetus ripped from her body in disintegrating pieces; that, the looey told them later, was known as a West Point Abortion. So there they were, on their way back to base, and they had indeed walked into an ambush, only it had been laid by their own guys, even more stoned than they were, and four guys had been blown away. Rainbird saw no need to tell Charlie all of this, or that the Claymore that had pulverized half his face had been made in a Maryland munitions plant.

'There were only six of us that got out. We ran. We ran through the jungle and I guess I went the wrong way. Wrong way? Right way? In that crazy war you didn't know which way was the right way because there weren't any real lines. I got separated from the rest of my guys. I was still trying to find something familiar when I walked over a land mine. That's what happened to my face.'

'I'm very sorry,' Charlie said.

'When I woke up, *they* had me,' Rainbird said, now off into the never-never land of total fiction. He had actually come to in a Saigon army hospital with an IV drip in his arm. 'They wouldn't give me any medical treatment, nothing like that, unless I answered their questions.'

Now carefully. If he did it carefully it would come right; he could feel it.

His voice rose, bewildered and bitter. 'Questions, all the time questions. They wanted to know about troop movements . . . supplies . . . light-infantry deployment . . . everything. They never let up. They were always at me.'

'Yes,' Charlie said fervently, and his heart gladdened.

'I kept telling them I didn't know anything, couldn't tell them anything, that I was nothing but a lousy grunt, just a number with a pack on its back. They didn't believe me. My face . . . the pain . . . I got down on my knees and begged for morphine . . . they said after . . . after I told them I could have the morphine. I could be treated in a good hospital . . . after I told them.'

Now Charlie's grip was the one that was tightening. She thought about Hockstetter's cool gray eyes, of Hockstetter pointing at the steel tray filled with curly woodshavings. *I think you know the answer . . . if you light that, I'll take you to see your father right away. You can be with him in two minutes.* Her heart went out to this man with the badly wounded face, this grown man who was afraid of the dark. She thought she could understand what he had been through. She knew his pain. And in the dark she began to cry silently for him, and in a way the tears were also for herself . . . all the unshed tears of the last five months. They were tears of pain and rage for John Rainbird, her father, her mother, herself. They burned and scourged.

The tears were not silent enough to go unheard by Rainbird's radar ears. He had to struggle to suppress another smile. Oh yes, the chisel was well-planted. Tough cracks and easy cracks, but no impossible cracks.

'They just never believed me. Finally they threw me into a hole in the ground, and it was always dark. There was a little . . . a room, I guess you'd say, with roots sticking out of the earth walls . . . and sometimes I could see a little sunlight about nine feet up. They'd come – their commandant, I guess he was – and he'd ask me if I was

307

ready to talk yet. He said I was turning white down there, like a fish. That my face was getting infected, that I'd get gangrene in my face and then it would get into my brain and rot it and make me crazy and then I'd die. He'd ask me if I'd like to get out of the dark and see the sun again. And I'd plead with him . . . I'd beg . . . I'd swear on my mother's name that I didn't know anything. And then they'd laugh and put the boards back and cover them up with dirt. It was like being buried alive. The dark . . . like this . . .'

He made a choked sound in his throat and Charlie squeezed his hand tighter to show him that she was there.

'There was the room and there was a little tunnel about seven feet long. I had to go down to the end of the tunnel to . . . you know. And the air was bad and I kept thinking I'm going to smother down here in the dark, I'm going to choke on the smell of my own sh—' He groaned. 'I'm sorry. This is nothing to tell a kid.'

'That's all right. If it makes you feel better, it's all right.'

He debated, and then decided to go just a little further.

'I was down there for five months before they exchanged me.'

'What did you eat?'

'They threw down rotted rice. And sometimes spiders. Live spiders. Great big ones - tree spiders, I guess. I'd chase after them in the dark, you know, and kill them and eat them.

'Oh, *gross!*'

'They turned me into an animal,' he said, and was quiet for a moment, breathing loudly. 'You got it better than me, kid, but it comes down to pretty much the same thing. A rat in a trap. You think they'll get the lights on pretty soon?'

She didn't say anything for a long time, and he was

coldly afraid that he had gone too far. Then Charlie said, 'It doesn't matter. We're together.'

'All right,' he said, and then in a rush: 'You won't tell, will you? They'd fire me for the way I been talking. I need this job. When you look the way I do, you need a good job.'

'No, I won't tell.'

He felt the chisel slip smoothly in another notch. They had a secret between them now.

He was holding her in his hands.

In the dark, he thought how it would be to slip his hands around her neck. That was the final object in view, of course – not their stupid tests, their playground games. Her . . . and then perhaps himself. He liked her, he really did. He might even be falling in love with her. The time would come when he would send her over, looking carefully into her eyes all the time. And then, if her eyes gave him the signal he had looked for so long, perhaps he would follow her. Yes. Perhaps they would go into the real darkness together.

Outside, beyond the locked door, eddies of confusion passed back and forth, sometimes near, sometimes far away.

Rainbird mentally spat on his hands and then went back to work on her.

9

Andy had no idea that they hadn't come to get him out because the power failure had automatically locked the doors. He sat in a half-swoon of panic for some unknown time, sure the place was burning down, imagining the smell of smoke. Outside, the storm had cleared and late afternoon sunshine was slanting down toward dusk.

Quite suddenly Charlie's face came into his mind, as clearly as if she had been standing there in front of him.

(*she's in danger charlie's in danger*)

It was one of his hunches, the first he'd had since that last day in Tashmore. He thought he had lost that along with the push, but apparently that was not so, because he had never had a hunch clearer than this one – not even on the day Vicky was killed.

Did that mean the push was still there, too? Not gone at all, but only hiding?

(*charlie's in danger!*)

What sort of danger?

He didn't know. But the thought, the fear, had brought her face clearly in front of him, outlined on this darkness in every detail. And the image of her face, her wide-set blue eyes and fine-spun blond hair, brought guilt like a twin . . . except that guilt was too mild a word for what he felt; it was something like horror that he felt. He had been in a craze of panic ever since the lights went out, and the panic had been completely for himself. It had never even occurred to him that Charlie must be in the dark, too.

No, they'll come and get her out, they probably came and got her out long ago. Charlie's the one they want. Charlie's their meal ticket.

That made sense, but he still felt that suffocating surety that she was in some terrible danger.

His fear for her had the effect of sweeping the panic for himself away, or at least of making it more manageable. His awareness turned outward again and became more objective. The first thing he became aware of was that he was sitting in a puddle of ginger ale. His pants were wet and tacky with it, and he made a small sound of disgust.

Movement. Movement was the cure for fear.

He got on his knees, felt for the overturned Canada Dry can, and batted it away. It went clink-rolling across the tiled floor. He got another can out of the fridge; his mouth was still dry. He pulled the tab and dropped it down into the can and then drank. The ringtab tried to escape into his mouth and he spat it back absently, not pausing to reflect that only a little while ago, that alone would have been excuse enough for another fifteen minutes of fear and trembling.

He began to feel his way out of the kitchen, trailing his free hand along the wall. This level was entirely quiet now, and although he heard an occasional faraway call, there seemed to be nothing upset or panicky about the sound. The smell of smoke had been a hallucination. The air was a bit stale because all the convectors had stopped when the power went off, but that was all.

Instead of crossing the living room, Andy turned left and crawled into his bedroom. He felt his way carefully to the bed, set his can of ginger ale on the bedtable, and then undressed. Ten minutes later he was dressed in fresh clothes and feeling much better. It occurred to him that he had done all of this with no particular trouble, whereas after the lights went out, crossing the living room had been like crossing a live minefield.

(*charlie – what's wrong with charlie?*)

But it wasn't really a feeling that something was *wrong* with her, just a feeling that she was in danger of something happening. If he could see her, he could ask her what—

He laughed bitterly in the dark. Yes, right. And pigs will whistle, beggars will ride. Might as well wish for the moon in a mason jar. Might as well—

For a moment his thoughts stopped entirely, and then moved on – but more slowly, and with no bitterness.

Might as well wish to think businessmen into having more self-confidence.

Might as well wish to think fat ladies thin.

Might as well wish to blind one of the goons who had kidnapped Charlie.

Might as well wish for the push to come back.

His hands were busy on the bedspread, pulling it, kneading it, feeling it – the mind's need, nearly unconscious, for some sort of constant sensory input. There was no sense in hoping for the push to come back. The push was gone. He could no more push his way to Charlie than he could pitch for the Reds. It was gone.

(*is it!*)

Quite suddenly he wasn't sure. Part of him – some very deep part – had maybe just decided it didn't buy his conscious decision to follow the path of least resistance and give them whatever they wanted. Perhaps some deep part of him had decided not to give up.

He sat feeling the bedspread, running his hands over and over it.

Was that true, or only wishful thinking brought on by one sudden and unprovable hunch? The hunch itself might have been as false as the smoke he'd thought he smelled, brought on by simple anxiety. There was no way to check the hunch, and there was certainly no one here to push.

He drank his ginger ale.

Suppose the push *had* come back. That was no universal cure-all; he of all people knew that. He could give a lot of little pushes or three or four wallopers before he tipped himself over. He might get to Charlie, but he didn't have a snowflake's chance in hell of getting them out of here. All he would succeed in doing was pushing himself into the grave via a brain hemorrhage (and as he thought of this, his fingers went automatically to his face, where the numb spots had been).

Then there was the matter of the Thorazine they had been feeding him. The lack of it – the lateness of the dose due when the lights had gone out – had played a large part in his panic, he knew. Even now, feeling more in control of himself, he *wanted* that Thorazine and the tranquil, coasting feeling it brought. At the beginning, they had kept him off the Thorazine for as long as two days before testing him. The result had been constant nervousness and a low depression like thick clouds that never seemed to let up . . . and back then he hadn't built up a heavy thing, as he had now.

'Face it, you're a junky,' he whispered.

He didn't know if that was true or not. He knew that there were physical addictions like the one to nicotine, and to heroin, which caused physical changes in the central nervous system. And then there were psychological addictions. He had taught with a fellow named Bill Wallace who got very, very nervous without his three or four Cokes a day, and his old college buddy Quincey had been a potato-chip freak – but he had to have an obscure New England brand, Humpty Dumpty; he claimed no other kind satisfied. Andy supposed those qualified as psychological addictions. He didn't know if his craving for his pill was physical or psychological; he only knew that he needed it, he really *needed* it. Just sitting here and thinking about the blue pill in the white dish had him cotton-mouthed all over again. They no longer kept him without the drug for forty-eight hours before testing him, although whether that was because they felt he couldn't go that long without getting the screaming meemies or because they were just going through the motions of testing, he didn't know.

The result was a cruelly neat, insoluble problem; he couldn't push if he was full of Thorazine, and yet he simply didn't have the will to refuse it (and, of course, if they *caught* him refusing it, that would open a whole new can of worms for them, wouldn't it? – real night-crawlers). When they brought him the blue pill in the white dish after this was over, he would take it. And little by little, he would work his way back to the calmly apathetic steady state he had been in when the power went off. All of this was just a spooky little side-trip. He would be back to watching *PTL Club* and Clint Eastwood on Home Box Office soon enough, and snacking too much out of the always-well-stocked fridge. Back to putting on weight.

(*charlie, charlie's in danger, charlie's in all sorts of trouble, she's in a world of hurt*)

If so, there was nothing he could do about it.

And even if there was, even if he could somehow conquer the monkey on his back and get them out of here – pigs will whistle and beggars will ride, why the hell not? – any ultimate solution concerning Charlie's future would be as far away as ever.

He lay back on his bed, spread-eagled. The small department of his mind that now dealt exclusively with Thorazine continued to clamor restlessly.

There were no solutions in the present, and so he drifted into the past. He saw himself and Charlie fleeing up Third Avenue in a kind of slow-motion nightmare, a big man in a scuffed cord jacket and a little girl in red and green. He saw Charlie, her face strained and pale, tears running down her cheeks after she had got all the change from the pay phones at the airport . . . she got the change and set some serviceman's shoes on fire.

His mind drifted back even further to the storefront in Port City, Pennsylvania, and Mrs Gurney. Sad, fat Mrs Gurney, who had come into the Weight-Off office in a green pantsuit, clutching at the carefully lettered slogan that had actually been Charlie's idea. *You Will Lose Weight or We Will Buy Your Groceries for the Next Six Months.*

Mrs Gurney, who had borne her truck-dispatcher husband four children between 1950 and 1957, and now the children were grown and they were disgusted with her, and her husband was disgusted with her, and he was seeing another woman, and she could understand that because Stan Gurney was still a good-looking, vital, virile man at fifty-five, and she had slowly gained one hundred and sixty pounds over the years since the second-to-last child had left for college, going from the one-forty she had weighed at marriage to an even three hundred pounds. She had come in, smooth and monstrous and desperate in her green pantsuit, and her ass was nearly as wide as a bank president's desk. When she looked down into her purse to find her checkbook, her three chins became six.

He had put her in a class with three other fat women. There were exercises and a mild diet, both of which Andy had researched at the Public Library; there were mild pep talks, which he billed as 'counseling' – and every now and then there was a medium-hard push.

Mrs Gurney had gone from three hundred to two-eighty to two-seventy, confessing with mixed fear and delight that she didn't seem to want second helpings anymore. The second helping just didn't seem to taste good. Before, she had always kept bowls and bowls of snacks in the refrigerator and doughnuts in the breadbox, and two or three Sara Lee cheesecakes in the freezer for watching TV at night, but now she somehow . . . well, it sounded almost crazy, but . . . she kept *forgetting* they were there. And she had always heard that when you were dieting, snacks were all you *could* think of. It certainly hadn't been this way, she said, when she tried Weight Watchers.

The other three women in the group had responded eagerly in kind. Andy merely stood back and watched them, feeling absurdly paternal. All four of them were astounded and delighted by the commonality of their experience. The toning-up exercises, which had always seemed so boring and painful before, now seemed almost pleasant. And then there was this weird compulsion to *walk*. They all agreed that if they hadn't walked a good bit by the end of the day, they felt somehow ill at ease and restless. Mrs Gurney confessed that she had got into the habit of walking downtown and back every day, even though the round trip was more than two miles. Before, she had always taken the bus, which was surely the sensible thing to do, since the stop was right in front of her house.

But the one day she had taken it – because her thigh muscles did ache *that* much – she had got to feeling so uneasy and restless that she had got off at the second stop. The others agreed. And they all blessed Andy McGee for it, sore muscles and all.

Mrs Gurney had dropped to two-fifty at her third weigh-in, and when her six-week course ended, she was down to two hundred and twenty-five pounds. She said her husband was stunned at what had happened, especially after her failure with countless dieting programs and fads. He wanted her to go see a doctor; he was afraid she might have cancer. He didn't believe it was possible to lose seventy-five pounds in six weeks by natural means. She showed him her fingers, which were red and callused from taking in her clothes with needle and thread. And then she threw her arms around him (nearly breaking his back) and wept against his neck.

His alumni usually came back, just as his more successful college students usually came back at least once, some to say thanks, some merely to parade their success before him – to say, in effect, Look here, the student has outraced the teacher . . . something that was hardly as uncommon as they seemed to think, Andy sometimes thought.

But Mrs Gurney had been one of the former. She had come back to say hello and thanks a lot only ten days or so before Andy had begun to feel nervous and watched in Port City. And before the end of that month, they had gone on to New York City.

Mrs Gurney was still a big woman; you noticed the

startling difference only if you had seen her before – like one of those before-and-after ads in the magazines. When she dropped in that last time, she was down to a hundred and ninety-five pounds. But it wasn't her exact weight that mattered, of course. What mattered was that she was losing weight at the same measured rate of six pounds a week, plus or minus two pounds, and she would go on losing at a decreasing rate until she was down to one hundred and thirty pounds, plus or minus ten pounds. There would be no explosive decompression, and no lingering hangover of food horror, the sort of thing that sometimes led to *anorexia nervosa*. Andy wanted to make some money, but he didn't want to kill anyone doing it.

'You ought to be declared a national resource for what you're doing,' Mrs Gurney had declared, after telling Andy that she had effected a rapprochement with her children and that her relations with her husband were improving. Andy had smiled and thanked her, but now, lying on his bed in the darkness, growing drowsy, he reflected that that was pretty close to what had happened to him and Charlie: they had been declared national resources.

Still, the talent was not all bad. Not when it could help a Mrs Gurney.

He smiled a little.

And smiling, slept.

10

He could never remember the details of the dream afterward. He had been looking for something. He had been in some labyrinthine maze of corridors, lit only by dull red trouble lights. He opened doors on empty rooms and then closed them again. Some of the rooms were littered with balls of crumpled paper and in one there was an overturned table lamp and a fallen picture done in the

317

style of Wyeth. He felt that he was in some sort of installation that had been shut down and cleared out in one hell of a tearing hurry.

And yet he had at last found what he was looking for. It was . . . what? A box? A chest? It was terribly heavy, whatever it was, and it had been marked with a white-stenciled skull and crossbones, like a jar of rat poison kept on a high cellar shelf. Somehow, in spite of its weight (it had to weigh at least as much as Mrs Gurney), he managed to pick it up. He could feel all his muscles and tendons pulling taut and hard, yet there was no pain.

Of course there isn't, he told himself. *There's no pain because it's a dream. You'll pay for it later. You'll have the pain later.*

He carried the box out of the room where he had found it. There was a place he had to take it, but he didn't know what or where it was—

You'll know it when you see it, his mind whispered.

So he carried the box or chest up and down endless corridors, its weight tugging painlessly at his muscles, stiffening the back of his neck; and although his muscles didn't hurt, he was getting the beginnings of a headache.

'*The brain is a muscle,* his mind lectured, and the lecture became a chant like a child's song, a little girl's skipping rhyme: *The brain is a muscle that can move the world. The brain is a muscle that can move*—

Now all the doors were like subway doors, bulging outward in a slight curve, fitted with large windows; all these windows had rounded corners. Through these doors (if they were doors) he saw a confusion of sights. In one room Dr Wanless was playing a huge accordion. He looked like some crazed Lawrence Welk with a tin cup full of pencils in front of him and a sign around his neck that read THERE ARE NONE SO BLIND AS THOSE WHO WILL NOT SEE. Through another window he could see a girl in a white caftan flying through the air, screaming, careering off the walls, and Andy hurried past that one quickly.

Through another he saw Charlie and he became convinced again that this was some sort of pirate dream – buried treasure, yo-ho-ho and all of that – because Charlie appeared to be talking with Long John Silver. This man had a parrot on his shoulder and an eyepatch over one eye. He was grinning at Charlie with a kind of smarmy false friendship that made Andy nervous. As if in confirmation of this, the one-eyed pirate slipped an arm around Charlie's shoulders and cried hoarsely, 'We'll do 'em yet, kid!'

Andy wanted to stop there and knock on the window until he attracted Charlie's attention – she was staring at the pirate as if hypnotized. He wanted to make sure she saw through this strange man, to make sure she understood that he wasn't what he seemed.

But he couldn't stop. He had this damned

(*box? chest?*)

to

(???)

to what? Just what the hell was he supposed to do with it?

But he would know when it was time.

He went past dozens of other rooms – he couldn't remember all of the things he saw – and then he was in a long blank corridor that ended in a blank wall. But not entirely blank; there was something in the exact center of it, a big steel rectangle like a mail slot.

Then he saw the word that had been stamped on it in raised letters, and understood.

DISPOSAL, it read.

And suddenly Mrs Gurney was beside him, a slim and pretty Mrs Gurney with a shapely body and trim legs that looked made for dancing all night long, dancing on a terrace until the stars went pale in the sky and dawn rose in the east like sweet music. You'd never guess, he thought, bemused, that her clothes were once made by Omar the Tentmaker.

He tried to lift the box, but couldn't. Suddenly it was just too heavy. His headache was worse. It was like the black horse, the riderless horse with the red eyes, and with dawning horror he realized it was loose, it was somewhere in this abandoned installation, and it was coming for him, thudding, thudding—

'I'll help you,' Mrs Gurney said. 'You helped me; now I'll help you. After all, you are the national resource, not me.'

'You look so pretty,' he said. His voice seemed to come from far away, through the thickening headache.

'I feel like I've been let out of prison,' Mrs Gurney responded. 'Let me help you.'

'It's just that my head aches—'

'Of course it does. After all, the brain is a muscle.'

Did she help him, or did he do it himself? He couldn't remember. But he could remember thinking that he understood the dream now, it was the push he was getting rid of, once and for all, the push. He remembered tipping the box against the slot marked DISPOSAL, tipping it up, wondering what it would look like when it came out, this thing that had sat inside his brain since his college days. But it wasn't the push that came out; he felt both surprise and fear as the top opened. What spilled into the chute was a flood of blue pills, *his* pills, and he was scared, all right; he was, in the words of Granther McGee, suddenly scared enough to shit nickels.

'No!' he shouted.

'Yes,' Mrs Gurney answered firmly. 'The brain is a muscle that can move the world.'

Then he saw it her way.

It seemed that the more he poured the more his head

ached, and the more his head ached the darker it got, until there was no light, the dark was total, it was a living dark, someone had blown all the fuses somewhere and there was no light, no box, no dream, only his headache and the riderless horse with the red eyes coming on and coming on.

Thud, thud, thud . . .

11

He must have been awake a long time before he actually realized he was awake. The total lack of light made the exact dividing line hard to find. A few years before, he had read of an experiment in which a number of monkeys had been put into environments designed to muffle all their senses. The monkeys had all gone crazy. He could understand why. He had no idea how long he had been sleeping, no concrete input except—

'Oww, Jesus!'

Sitting up drove two monstrous bolts of chromium pain into his head. He clapped his hands to his skull and rocked it back and forth, and little by little the pain subsided to a more manageable level.

No concrete sensory input except this rotten headache. I must have slept on my neck or something, he thought. I must have—

No. Oh, no. He knew this headache, knew it well. It was the sort of headache he got from a medium-to-hard push . . . harder than the ones he had given the fat ladies and shy businessmen, not quite as hard as the ones he had given the fellows at the turnpike rest stop that time.

Andy's hands flew to his face and felt it all over, from brow to chin. There were no spots where the feeling trailed away to numbness. When he smiled, both corners of his mouth went up just as they always had. He wished to God for a light so he could look into his own eyes in the bathroom mirror to see if either of them showed that telltale blood sheen. . . .

Push? Pushing?

That was ridiculous. Who was there to push?

Who, except—

His breath slowed to a stop in his throat and then resumed slowly.

He had thought of it before but had never tried it. He thought it would be like overloading a circuit by cycling a charge through it endlessly. He had been scared to try it.

My pill, he thought. *My pill is overdue and I want it, I really want it, I really need it. My pill will make everything all right.*

It was just a thought. It brought on no craving at all. The idea of taking a Thorazine had all the emotional gradient of *please pass the butter*. The fact was, except for the rotten headache, he felt pretty much all right. And the fact also was he had had headaches a lot worse than this – the one at the Albany airport, for instance. This one was a baby compared to that.

I've pushed myself, he thought, amazed.

For the first time he could really understand how Charlie felt, because for the first time he was a little frightened by his own psi talent. For the first time he really understood how little he understood about what it was and what it could do. Why had it gone? He didn't know. Why had it come back? He didn't know that either. Did it have something to do with his intense fear in the dark? His sudden feeling that Charlie was being threatened (he had a ghostly memory of the piratical one-eyed man and then it floated away, gone) and his own dismal self-loathing at the way he had forgotten her? Possibly even the rap on the head he had taken when he fell down?

He didn't know; he knew only that he had pushed himself.

The brain is a muscle that can move the world.

It suddenly occurred to him that while he was giving little nudges to businessmen and fat ladies, he could have become a one-man drug-rehabilitation center, and he was seized in a shivery ecstasy of dawning supposition. He had gone to sleep thinking that a talent that could help poor fat Mrs Gurney couldn't be all bad. What about a talent that could knock the monkey off the back of every poor junkie in New York City? What about *that*, sports fans?

'Jesus,' he whispered. 'Am I really clean?'

There was no craving. Thorazine, the image of the blue pill on the white plate – that thought had become unmistakably neutral.

'I am clean,' he answered himself.

Next question: could he stay clean?

But he had no more than asked himself that one when other questions flooded in. Could he find out exactly what was happening to Charlie? He had used the push on himself in his sleep, like a kind of autohypnosis. Could he use it on others while awake? The endlessly, repulsively grinning Pynchot, for instance? Pynchot would know what was happening to Charlie. Could he be made to tell? Could he maybe even get her out of here after all? Was there a way to do that? And if they did get out, what then? No more running, for one thing. That was no solution. There had to be a place to go.

For the first time in months he felt excited, hopeful. He began to try scraps of plan, accepting, rejecting, questioning. For the first time in months he felt at home in his own head, alive and vital, capable of action. And above all else, there was this: if he could fool them into believing two things – that he was still drugged and that he was still

323

incapable of using his mental-domination talent, he might – he just might have a chance of doing – doing *something*.

He was still turning it all over restlessly in his mind when the lights came back on. In the other room, the TV began spouting that same old Jesus-will-take-care-of-your-soul-and-we'll-take-care-of-your-bank-book jive.

The eyes, the electric eyes! They're watching you again, or soon will be. . . . Don't forget that!

For one moment, everything came home to him – the days and weeks of subterfuge that would surely lie ahead if he was to have any chance at all, and the near certainty that he would be caught at some point. Depression waved in . . . but it brought no craving for the pill with it, and that helped him to catch hold of himself.

He thought of Charlie, and that helped more.

He got up slowly from the bed and walked into the living room. 'What happened?' he cried loudly. 'I was scared! Where's my medication? Somebody bring me my medication!'

He sat down in front of the TV, his face slack and dull and heavy.

And behind that vapid face, his brain – that muscle that could move the world – ticked away faster and faster.

12

Like the dream her father had had at the same time, Charlie McGee could never remember the details of her long conversation with John Rainbird, only the high spots. She was never quite sure how she came to pour out the story of how she came to be here, or to speak of her intense loneliness for her father and her terror that they would find some way to trick her into using her pyrokinetic ability again.

Part of it was the blackout, of course, and the knowledge

that *they* weren't listening. Part of it was John himself, he had been through so much, and he was so pathetically afraid of the dark and of the memories it brought of the terrible hole those 'Congs' had put him in. He had asked her, almost apathetically, why they had locked her up, and she had begun talking just to distract his mind. But it had quickly become more than that. It began to come out faster and faster, everything she had kept bottled up, until the words were tumbling out all over one another, helter-skelter. Once or twice she had cried, and he held her clumsily. He was a sweet man . . . in many ways he reminded her of her father.

'Now if they find out you know all of that,' she said, 'they'll probably lock you up, too. I shouldn't have told.'

'They'd lock me up, all right,' John said cheerfully. 'I got a D clearance, kid. That gives me clearance to open bottles of Johnson's Wax and that's about all.' He laughed. 'We'll be all right if you don't let on that you told me, I guess.'

'I won't,' Charlie said eagerly. She had been a little uneasy herself, thinking if John told, they might use him on her like a lever. 'I'm awful thirsty. There's icewater in the refrigerator. You want some?'

'Don't leave me,' he said immediately.

'Well, let's go together. We'll hold hands.'

He appeared to think about this. 'All right,' he said.

They shuffled across to the kitchen together, hands gripped tightly.

'You'd better not let on, kid. Especially about this. Heap-big Indian afraid of the dark. The guys'd laugh me right out of this place.'

'They wouldn't laugh if they knew—'

'Maybe not. Maybe so.' He chuckled a little. 'But I'd just as soon they never found out. I just thank God you was here, kid.'

She was so touched that her eyes filled again and she had to struggle for control of herself. They reached the fridge, and she located the jug of icewater by feel. It wasn't icy cold anymore, but it soothed her throat. She wondered with fresh unease just how long she had talked, and didn't know. But she had told . . . everything. Even the parts she had meant to hold back, like what had happened at the Manders farm. Of course, the people like Hockstetter knew, but she didn't care about them. She did care about John . . . and his opinion of her.

But she had told. He would ask a question that somehow pierced right to the heart of the matter, and . . . she had told, often with tears. And instead of more questions and cross-examination and mistrust, there had been only acceptance and calm sympathy. He seemed to understand the hell she had been through, maybe because he had been through hell himself.

'Here's the water,' she said.

'Thanks.' She heard him drink, and then it was placed back in her hands. 'Thanks a lot.'

She put it away.

'Let's go back in the other room,' he said. 'I wonder if they'll ever get the lights back on.' He was impatient for them to come on now. They had been off more than seven hours, he guessed. He wanted to get out of here and think about all of this. Not what she had told him – he knew all of that – but how to use it.

'I'm sure they'll be on soon,' Charlie said.

They shuffled their way back to the sofa and sat down.

'They haven't told you anything about your old man?'

'Just that he's all right,' she said.

'I'll bet I could get in to see him,' Rainbird said, as if this idea had just occurred to him.

'You could? You really think you could?'

'I could change with Herbie someday. See him. Tell him

326

you're okay. Well, not tell him but pass him a note or something.'

'Oh, wouldn't that be dangerous?'

'It would be dangerous to make a business of it, kid. But I owe you one. I'll see how he is.'

She threw her arms around him in the dark and kissed him. Rainbird gave her an affectionate hug. In his own way, he loved her, now more than ever. She was his now, and he supposed he was hers. For a while.

They sat together, not talking much, and Charlie dozed. Then he said something that woke her up as suddenly as completely as a dash of cold water in the face.

'Shit, you ought to light their damn fires, if you can do it.'

Charlie sucked her breath in, shocked, as if he had suddenly hit her.

'I *told* you,' she said. 'It's like letting a . . . a wild animal out of a cage. I promised myself I'd never do it again. That soldier at the airport . . . and those men at that farm . . . I killed them . . . burned them *up*!' Her face was hot, burning, and she was on the verge of tears again.

'The way you told it, it sounded like self-defense.'

'Yes, but that's no excuse to—'

'It also sounded like maybe you saved your old man's life.'

Silence from Charlie. But he could feel trouble and confusion and misery coming off her in waves. He hastened on, not wanting her to remember right now that she had come very close to killing her father as well.

'As for that guy Hockstetter, I've seen him around. I saw guys like him in the war. Every one of them a ninety-day wonder, King Shit of Turd Mountain. If he can't get what he wants from you one way, he'll try some other way.'

'That's what scares me the most,' she admitted in a low voice.

'Besides, there's one guy who could use a hotfoot.'

Charlie was shocked, but giggled hard – the way a dirty joke could sometimes make her laugh harder just because it was so bad to tell them. When she was over her giggles, she said: 'No, I won't light fires. I promised myself. It's bad and I won't.

It was enough. It was time to stop. He felt that he could keep going on pure intuition, but he recognized that it might be a false feeling. He was tired now. Working on the girl had been every bit as exhausting as working on one of Rammaden's safes. It would be too easy to go on and make a mistake that could never be undone.

'Yeah, okay. I guess you're right.'

'You really will see my dad?'

'I'll try, kid.'

'I'm sorry you got stuck in here with me, John. But I'm awful glad, too.'

'Yeah.'

They talked of inconsequential things, and she put her head on his arm. He felt that she was dozing off again -- it was very late now -- and when the lights went on about forty minutes later, she was fast asleep. The light in her face made her stir and turn her head into his darkness. He looked down thoughtfully at the slender willow stem of her neck, the tender curve of her skull. So much power in that small, delicate cradle of bone. Could it be true? His mind still rejected it, but his heart felt it was so. It was a strange and somehow wonderful feeling to find himself so divided. His heart felt it was true to an extent they wouldn't believe, true perhaps to the extent of that mad Wanless's ravings.

He picked her up, carried her to her bed, and slipped her between the sheets. As he pulled them up to her chin, she stirred half awake.

He leaned over impulsively and kissed her. 'Goodnight, kid.'

'Goodnight, Daddy,' she said in a thick, sleeping voice. Then she rolled over and became still.

He looked down at her for several minutes longer, then went back into the living room. Hockstetter himself came bustling in ten minutes later.

'Power failure,' he said. 'Storm. Damn electronic locks, all jammed. Is she—'

'She'll be fine if you keep your goddam voice down,' Rainbird said in a low voice. His huge hands pistoned out, caught Hockstetter by the lapels of his white lab coat, and jerked him forward, so that Hockstetter's suddenly terrified face was less than an inch from his own. 'And if you ever behave as if you know me in here again, if you ever behave toward me as if I am anything but a D-clearance orderly, I'll kill you, and then I'll cut you into pieces, and Cuisinart you, and turn you into catmeat.'

Hockstetter spluttered impotently. Spit bubbled at the corners of his lips.

'Do you understand? I'll kill you.' He shook Hockstetter twice.

'I-I-I un-un-understand.'

'Then let's get out of here,' Rainbird said, and shoved Hockstetter, pale and wide-eyed, out into the corridor.

He took one last look around and then wheeled his cart out and closed the self-locking door behind him. In the bedroom, Charlie slept on, more peacefully than she had in months. Perhaps years.

Small Fires,
Big Brother

1

The violent storm passed. Time passed – three weeks of it. Summer, humid and overbearing, still held sway over eastern Virginia, but school was back in session and lumbering yellow school buses trundled up and down the well-kept rural roads in the Longmont area. In not-too-distant Washington, D.C., another year of legislation, rumor, and innuendo was beginning, marked with the usual freak-show atmosphere engendered by national television, planned information leaks, and overmastering clouds of bourbon fumes.

None of that made much of an impression in the cool, environmentally controlled rooms of the two antebellum houses and the corridors and levels honeycombed beneath. The only correlative might have been that Charlie McGee was also going to school. It was Hockstetter's idea that she be tutored, and Charlie had balked, but John Rainbird had talked her into it.

'What hurt's it gonna do?' he asked. 'There's no sense in a smart girl like you getting way behind. Shit – excuse me, Charlie – but I wish to God sometimes that I had more than an eighth-grade education. I wouldn't be moppin floors now – you can bet your boots on that. Besides, it'll pass the time.'

So she had done it – for John. The tutors came: the young man who taught English, the older woman who taught mathematics, the younger woman with the thick glasses who began to teach her French, the man in the wheelchair who taught science. She listened to them, and she supposed she learned, but she had done it for John.

On three occasions John had risked his job to pass her father notes, and she felt guilty about that and hence was more willing to do what she thought would please John. And he had brought her news of her dad -- that he was well, that he was relieved to know Charlie was well too, and that he was cooperating with their tests. This had distressed her a little, but she was now old enough to understand -- a little bit, anyway -- that what was best for her might not always be best for her father. And lately she had begun to wonder more and more if John might know best about what was right for her. In his earnest, funny way (he was always swearing and then apologizing for it, which made her giggle), he was very persuasive.

He had not said anything about making fires for almost ten days after the blackout. Whenever they talked of these things, they did it in the kitchen, where he said there were no 'bugs,' and they always talked in low voices.

On that day he had said, 'You thought any more about that fire business, Charlie?' He always called her Charlie now instead of 'kid.' She had asked him to.

She began to tremble. Just thinking about making fires had this effect on her since the Manders farm. She got cold and tense and trembly; on Hockstetter's reports this was called a 'mild phobic reaction.'

'I told you,' she said. 'I can't do that. I won't do that.'

'Now, can't and won't aren't the same thing,' John said. He was washing the floor -- but very slowly, so he could talk to her. His mop swished. He talked the way cons talk in prison, barely moving his lips.

Charlie didn't reply.

'I just had a couple of thoughts on this,' he said. 'But if

you don't want to hear them — if your head's really set – I'll just shut up.'

'No, that's okay,' Charlie said politely, but she did really wish he would shut up, not talk about it, not even think about it, because it made her feel bad. But John had done so much for her . . . and she desperately didn't want to offend him or hurt his feelings. She needed a friend.

'Well, I was just thinking that they must know how it got out of control at that farm,' he said. 'They'd probably be really careful. I don't think they'd be apt to test you in a room full of paper and oily rags, do you?'

'No, but—'

He raised one hand a little way off his mop. 'Hear me out, hear me out.'

'Okay.'

'And they sure know that was the only time you caused a real — what's it? – a conflagration. Small fires, Charlie. That's the ticket. Small fires. And if something did happen — which I doubt, cause I think you got better control over yourself than you think you do — but say something *did* happen. Who they gonna blame, huh? They gonna blame you? After the fuckheads spent half a year twisting your arm to do it? Oh hell, I'm sorry.'

The things he was saying scared her, but still she had to put her hands to her mouth and giggle at the woebegone expression on his face.

John smiled a little too, then shrugged. 'The other thing I was thinkin is that you can't learn to control something unless you practice it and practice it.'

'I don't care if I ever control it or not, because I'm just not going to do it.'

'Maybe or maybe not,' John said stubbornly, wringing out his mop. He stood it in the corner, then dumped his soapy water down the sink. He began to run a bucket of fresh to rinse with. 'You might get *surprised* into using it.'

333

'No, I don't think so.'

'Or suppose you got a bad fever sometime. From the flu or the croup or, hell, I dunno, some kind of infection.' This was one of the few profitable lines Hockstetter had given him to pursue. 'You ever have your appendix out, Charlie?'

'No-ooo . . .'

John began to rinse the floor.

'My brother had his out, but it went bust first and he almost died. That was cause we were reservation Indians and nobody gave a – nobody cared much if we lived or died. He got a high fever, a hundred and five, I guess, and he went ravin right off his head, sayin horrible curses and talkin to people who weren't there. Do you know he thought our father was the Angel of Death or somethin, come to carry him off, and he tried to stick im with a knife that was on his bedside table there? I told you this story, didn't I?'

'No,' Charlie said, whispering now not to keep from being overheard but out of horrified fascination. 'Really?'

'Really,' John affirmed. He squeezed the mop out again. 'It wasn't his fault. It was the fever that did it. People are apt to say or do anything when they're delirious. *Anything.*'

Charlie understood what he was saying and felt a sinking fear. Here was something she had never even considered.

'But if you had control of this pyro-whatsis . . .'

'How could I have control of it if I was delirious?'

'Just because you *do.*' Rainbird went back to Wanless's original metaphor, the one that had so disgusted Cap almost a year ago now. 'It's like toilet-training, Charlie. Once you get hold of your bowels and bladder, you're in control for good. Delirious people sometimes get their beds all wet from sweat, but they rarely piss the bed.'

Hockstetter had pointed out that this was not invariably true, but Charlie wouldn't know that.

'Well, anyway, all I mean is that if you got *control*, don't you see, you wouldn't have to worry about this anymore. You'd have it licked. But to get control you have to practice and practice. The same way you learned to tie your shoes, or to make your letters in kinnygarden.'

'I . . . I just don't want to make fires! And I won't! I *won't!*'

'There, I went and upset you,' John said, distressed. 'I sure didn't mean to do that. I'm sorry, Charlie. I won't say no more. Me and my big fat mouth.'

But the next time she brought it up herself.

It was three or four days later, and she had thought over the things he had said very carefully . . . and she believed that she had put her finger on the one flaw. 'It would just never end,' she said. 'They'd always want more and more and more. If you only knew the way they *chased* us, they *never* give up. Once I started they'd want bigger fires and then even bigger ones and then bonfires and then . . . I don't know . . . but I'm afraid.'

He admired her again. She had an intuition and a native wit that was incredibly sharp. He wondered what Hockstetter would think when he, Rainbird, told him that Charlie McGee had an extremely good idea what their top-secret master plan was. All of their reports on Charlie theorized that pyrokinesis was only the centerpiece of many related psionic talents, and Rainbird believed that her intuition was one of them. Her father had told them again and again that Charlie had *known* Al Steinowitz and the others were coming up to the Manders farm even before they had arrived. That was a scary thought. If she should ever get one of her funny intuitions about *his* authenticity . . . well, they said hell had no fury like a woman scorned, and if half of what he believed about Charlie was true, then she was perfectly capable of manufacturing hell, or a reasonable facsimile. He might suddenly find himself getting very hot. It added a certain spice to the proceedings . . . a spice that had been missing for too long.

'Charlie,' he said, 'I'm not sayin you should do any of these things for *free*.'

She looked at him, puzzled.

John sighed. 'I don't hardly know how to put it to you,' he said. 'I guess I love you a little. You're like the daughter I never had. And the way they're keeping you cooped up here, not letting you see your daddy and all, never getting to go out, missing all the things other little girls have . . . it just about makes me *sick*.'

Now he allowed his good eye to blaze out at her, scaring her a little.

'You could get all kinds of things just by going along with them . . . and attaching a few strings.'

'Strings,' Charlie said, utterly mystified.

'Yeah! You could get them to let you go outside in the sun, I bet. Maybe even into Longmont to shop for things. You could get out of this goddam box and into a regular house. See other kids. And—'

'And see my father?'

'Sure, that, too.' But that was one thing that was never going to happen, because if the two of them put their information together they would realize that John the Friendly Orderly was just too good to be true. Rainbird had never passed along a single message to Andy McGee. Hockstetter thought it would be running a risk for no gain, and Rainbird, who thought Hockstetter a total bleeding asshole about most things, agreed.

It was one thing to fool an eight-year-old kid with fairy stories about there being no bugs in the kitchen and about how they could talk in low voices and not be overheard, but it would be quite another thing to fool the girl's father with the same fairy story, even though he was hooked through the bag and back. McGee might not be hooked enough to miss the fact that they were now doing little more than playing Nice Guy and Mean Guy with Charlie, a technique police departments have used to crack criminals for hundreds of years.

So he maintained the fiction that he was taking her messages to Andy just as he was maintaining so many other fictions. It was true that he saw Andy quite often, but he saw him only on the TV monitors. It was true that Andy was cooperating with their tests, but it was also true that he was tipped over, unable to push a kid into eating a Popsicle. He had turned into a big fat zero, concerned only with what was on the tube and when his next pill was going to arrive, and he never asked to see his daughter anymore. Meeting her father face to face and seeing what they had done to him might stiffen her resistance all over again, and he was very close to breaking her now; she *wanted* to be convinced now. No, all things were negotiable except that. Charlie McGee was never going to see her father again. Before too long, Rainbird surmised, Cap would have McGee on a Shop plane to the Maui compound. But the girl didn't need to know that, either.

'You really think they'd let me see him?'

'No question about it,' he responded easily. 'Not at first, of course; he's their ace with you, and they know it. But if you went to a certain point and then said you were going to cut them off unless they let you see him—' He let it dangle there. The bait was out, a big sparkling lure dragged through the water. It was full of hooks and not good to eat anyway, but that was something else this tough little chick didn't know.

She looked at him thoughtfully. No more was said about it. That day.

Now, about a week later, Rainbird abruptly reversed his field. He did this for no concrete reason, but his own intuition told him he could get no further by advocacy. It was time to beg, as Br'er Rabbit had begged Br'er Fox not to be thrown into that briar patch.

'You remember what we was talkin about?' He opened the conversation. He was waxing the kitchen floor. She was pretending to linger over her selection of a snack from the fridge. One clean, pink foot was cocked behind the other so he could see the sole – a pose that he found curiously evocative of mid-childhood. It was somehow pre-erotic, almost mystic. His heart went out to her again. Now she looked back over her shoulder at him doubtfully. Her hair, done up in a ponytail, lay over one shoulder.

'Yes,' she said. 'I remember.'

'Well, I been thinkin, and I started to ask myself what makes me an expert on givin advice,' he said. 'I can't even float a thousand-dollar bank loan for a car.'

'Oh, John, that doesn't mean anything—'

'Yes it does. If I knew something, I'd be one of those guys like that Hockstetter. College-educated.'

With great disdain she replied, 'My daddy says any fool can buy a college education somewhere.'

In his heart, he rejoiced.

2

Three days after that, the fish swallowed the lure.

Charlie told him that she had decided to let them make their tests. She would be careful, she said. And she would make *them* be careful, if they didn't know how. Her face was thin and pinched and pale.

'Don't you do it,' John said, 'unless you've thought it all out.'

'I've tried,' she whispered.

'Are you doing it for them?'

'*No!*'

'Good! Are you doing it for you?'

'Yes. For me. And for my father.'

'All right,' he said. 'And Charlie – make them play it your way. Understand me? You've shown them how tough you can be. Don't let them see a weak streak now. If they see it, they'll use it. Play tough. You know what I mean?'

'I . . . think so.'

'They get something, you get something. Every time. No freebies.' His shoulders slumped a bit. The fire went out of his eye. She hated to see him this way, looking depressed and defeated. 'Don't let them treat you like they treated me. I gave my country four years of my life and one eye. One of those years I spent in a hole in the ground eating bugs and running a fever and smelling my own shit all the time and picking lice out of my hair. And when I got out they said thanks a lot, John, and put a mop in my hand. They stole from me, Charlie. Get it? Don't let them do that to you.'

'I get it,' she said solemnly.

He brightened a little, then smiled. 'So when's the big day?'

'I'm seeing Dr Hockstetter tomorrow. I'll tell him I've decided to cooperate . . . a little. And I'll . . . I'll tell him what *I* want.'

'Well, just don't ask for too much at first. It's just like the carny at the midway, Charlie. You got to show em some flash before you take their cash.'

She nodded.

'But you show them who's in the saddle, right? Show them who's boss.'

'Right.'

He smiled more broadly. 'Good kid!' he said.

Hockstetter was furious.

'What the *hell* sort of game are you playing?' he shouted at Rainbird. They were in Cap's office. He dared to shout, Rainbird thought, because Cap was here to play referee. Then he took a second look at Hockstetter's hot blue eyes, his flushed cheeks, his white knuckles, and admitted that he was probably wrong. He had dared to make his way through the gates and into Hockstetter's sacred garden of privilege. The shaking-out Rainbird had administered after the blackout ended was one thing; Hockstetter had lapsed dangerously and had known it. This was something else altogether. He thought.

Rainbird only stared at Hockstetter.

'You've carefully set it up around an impossibility! You know damned well she isn't going to see her father! "They get something, you get something," ' Hockstetter mimicked furiously. 'You fool!'

Rainbird continued to stare at Hockstetter. 'Don't call me a fool again,' he said in a perfectly neutral voice. Hockstetter flinched . . . but only a little.

'Please, gentlemen,' Cap said wearily. 'Please.'

There was a tape recorder on his desk. They had just finished listening to the conversation Rainbird had had with Charlie that morning.

'Apparently Dr Hockstetter had missed the point that he and his team are finally going to get *something*,' Rainbird said. 'Which will improve their store of practical knowledge by one hundred percent, if my mathematics are correct.'

'As the result of a totally unforeseen accident,' Hockstetter said sullenly.

'An accident you people were too shortsighted to manufacture for yourselves,' Rainbird countered. 'Too busy playing with your rats, maybe.'

'Gentlemen, that's enough!' Cap said. 'We're not here to indulge in a lot of recriminations; that is not the purpose of this meeting.' He looked at Hockstetter. 'You're going to get to play ball,' he said. 'I must say you show remarkably little gratitude.'

Hockstetter muttered.

Cap looked at Rainbird. 'All the same, I also think you took your role of *amicus curiae* a little bit too far in the end.'

'Do you think so? Then you still don't understand.' He looked from Cap to Hockstetter and then back to Cap again. 'I think both of you have shown an almost paralyzing lack of understanding. You've got two child psychiatrists at your disposal, and if they are an accurate representation of the caliber of that field, there are a lot of disturbed kids out there who have got big-time trouble.'

'Easy to say,' Hockstetter said. 'This—'

'You just don't understand how *smart* she is,' Rainbird cut him off. 'You don't understand how . . . how adept she is at seeing the causes and effects of things. Working with her is like picking your way through a minefield. I pointed out the carrot-and-stick idea to her because she would have thought of it herself. By thinking of it for her, I've shored up the trust she has in me . . . in effect, turned a disadvantage into an advantage.'

Hockstetter opened his mouth. Cap held up one hand and then turned to Rainbird. He spoke in a soft, placatory tone that he used with no one else . . . but then, no one else was John Rainbird. 'That doesn't alter the fact that you seem to have limited how far Hockstetter and his people can go. Sooner or later she's going to understand that her ultimate request – to see her father – is not going to be granted. We're all in agreement that to allow that might close off her usefulness to us forever.'

'Right on,' Hockstetter said.

341

'And if she's as sharp as you say,' Cap said, 'she's apt to make the ungrantable request sooner rather than later.'

'She'll make it,' Rainbird agreed, 'and that will end it. For one thing, she'd realize as soon as she saw him that I was lying all along about his condition. That would lead her to the conclusion that I had been shilling for you guys all along. So it becomes entirely a question of how long you can keep her going.'

Rainbird leaned forward.

'A couple of points. First, you've both got to get used to the idea that she's simply not going to light fires for you *ad infinitum*. She's a human being, a little girl who wants to see her father. She's not a lab rat.'

'We've already—' Hockstetter began impatiently.

'No. No, you haven't. It goes back to the very basis of the reward system in experimentation. The carrot and the stick. By lighting fires, Charlie thinks she's holding the carrot out to you and that she will eventually lead you – and herself – to her father. But we know differently. In truth, her father is the carrot, and we are leading her. Now a mule will plow the whole south forty trying to get that carrot dangling in front of his eyes, because a mule is stupid. *But this little girl isn't.*'

He looked at Cap and Hockstetter.

'I keep saying that. It is like pounding a nail into oak – oak of the first cutting. Hard going, don't you know; you both seem to keep forgetting. Sooner or later she's going to wise up and tell you to stick it. Because she isn't a mule. Or a white lab rat.'

And you want her to quit, Cap thought with slow loathing. You want her to quit so you can kill her.

'So you start with that one basic fact,' Rainbird continued. 'That's Go. Then you start thinking of ways to prolong her cooperation as long as possible. Then, when it's over, you write your report. If you got enough data, you get

342

rewarded with a big cash appropriation. You get to eat the carrot. Then you can start injecting a bunch of poor, ignorant slobs with your witch's brew all over again.'

'You're being insulting,' Hockstetter said in a shaking voice.

'It beats the terminal stupids,' Rainbird answered.

'How do you propose to prolong her cooperation?'

'You'll get some mileage out of her just by granting small privileges,' Rainbird said. 'A walk on the lawn. Or . . . every little girl loves horses. I'll bet you could get half a dozen fires out of her just by having a groom lead her around the bridle paths on one of those stable nags. That ought to be enough to keep a dozen paper pushers like Hockstetter dancing on the head of a pin for five years.'

Hockstetter pushed back from the table. 'I don't have to sit here and listen to this.'

'Sit down and shut up,' Cap said.

Hot blood slammed into Hockstetter's face and he looked ready to fight; it left as suddenly as it had come and he looked ready to cry. Then he sat down again.

'You let her go into town and shop,' Rainbird said. 'Maybe you arrange for her to go to Seven Flags over Georgia and ride the roller-coaster. Maybe even with her good friend John the orderly.'

'You seriously think just those things—' Cap began.

'No, I don't. Not for long. Sooner or later it will get back to her father. But she's only human. She wants things for herself as well. She'll go quite aways down the road you want her to go down just by rationalizing it to herself, telling herself she's showing you the flash before grabbing the cash. But eventually it's going to get back to dear old Dads, yes. She's no sellout, that one. She's tough.'

'And that's the end of the trolley-car ride,' Cap said thoughtfully. 'Everybody out. The project ends. This

343

phase of it, anyway.' In many ways, the prospect of an end in sight relieved him tremendously.

'Not right there, no,' Rainbird said, smiling his mirthless smile. 'We have one more card up our sleeve. One more very large carrot when the smaller ones play out. Not her father – not the grand prize – but something that will keep her going yet a while longer.'

'And what would that be?' Hockstetter asked.

'You figure it out,' Rainbird said, still smiling, and said no more. Cap might, in spite of how far he had come unraveled over the last half year or so. He had more smarts on half power than most of his employees (and all the pretenders to his throne) had on full power. As for Hockstetter, he would never see it. Hockstetter had risen several floors past his level of incompetency, a feat more possible in the federal bureaucracy than elsewhere. Hockstetter would have trouble following his nose to a shit-and-cream-cheese sandwich.

Not that it mattered if any of them figured out what the final carrot (the Game Carrot, one might say) in this little contest was; the results would still be the same. It was going to put him comfortably in the driver's seat one way or the other. He might have asked them: *Who do you think her father is now that her father isn't there?*

Let them figure it out for themselves. If they could.

John Rainbird went on smiling.

4

Andy McGee sat in front of his television set. The little amber Home Box Office pilot light glowed in the square gadget on top of the TV. On the screen, Richard Dreyfuss was trying to build the Devil's Butte in his living room. Andy watched with a calm and vapid expression of

344

pleasure. Inside he was boiling with nervousness. Today was the day.

For Andy, the three weeks since the blackout had been a period of almost unbearable tension and strain interwoven with bright threads of guilty exhilaration. He could understand simultaneously how the Russian KGB could inspire such terror and how George Orwell's Winston Smith must have enjoyed his brief period of crazy, furtive rebellion. He had a secret again. It gnawed and worked in him, as all grave secrets do within the minds of their keepers, but it also made him feel whole and potent again. He was putting one over on them. God knew how long he would be able to continue or if it would come to anything, but right now he was *doing* it.

It was almost ten in the morning and Pynchot, that eternally grinning man, was coming at ten. They would be going for a walk in the garden to 'discuss his progress.' Andy intended to push him . . . or to at least try. He might have made the effort before this, except for the TV monitors and the endless bugging devices. And the wait had given him time to think out his line of attack and probe it again and again for weak spots. He had, in fact, rewritten parts of the scenario in his mind many times.

At night, lying in bed in the dark, he had thought over and over again: *Big Brother is watching. Just keep telling yourself that, keep it foremost in your mind. They've got you locked up right in the forebrain of Big Brother, and if you really expect to help Charlie, you've got to keep on fooling them.*

He was sleeping less than he ever had in his life, mostly because he was terrified of talking in his sleep. Some nights he lay wakeful for hours, afraid even to toss and turn in case they should wonder why a drugged man should be so restless. And when he did sleep it was thin, shot with strange dreams (often the Long John Silver figure, the one-

345

eyed pirate with the pegleg, recurred in these and easily broken.

Slipping the pills was the easiest part, because they believed he wanted them. The pills came four times a day now, and there had been no more tests since the blackout. He believed they had given up, and that was what Pynchot wanted to tell him today on his walk.

Sometimes he would cough the pills out of his mouth into his cupped hand and put them in food scraps he would later scrape down the garbage disposal. More went down the toilet. Still others he had pretended to take with ginger ale. He spat the pills into the half-empty cans to dissolve and then let them stand, as if forgotten. Later he would turn them down the sink.

God knew he was no professional at this, and presumably the people who were monitoring him were. But he didn't think they were monitoring him very closely anymore. If they were, he would be caught. That was all.

Dreyfuss and the woman whose son had been taken for a ride by the saucer people were scaling the side of Devil's Butte when the buzzer that marked the breaking of the door circuit went off briefly. Andy didn't let himself jump.

This is it, he told himself again.

Herman Pynchot came into the living room. He was shorter than Andy but very slender; there was something about him that had always struck Andy as slightly effeminate, although it was nothing you could put your finger on. Today he was looking extremely reet and compleat in a thin gray turtleneck sweater and a summerweight jacket. And of course he was grinning.

'Good morning, Andy,' he said.

'Oh,' Andy said, and then paused, as if to think. 'Hello, Dr Pynchot.'

'Do you mind if I turn this off? We ought to go for our walk, you know.'

'Oh.' Andy's brow furrowed, then cleared. 'Sure. I've seen it three or four times already. But I like the ending. It's pretty. The UFOs take him away, you know. To the stars.'

'Really,' Pynchot said, and turned off the TV. 'Shall we go?'

'Where?' Andy asked.

'Our walk,' Herman Pynchot said patiently. 'Remember?'

'Oh,' Andy said. 'Sure.' He got up.

5

The hall outside Andy's room was wide and tile-floored. The lighting was muted and indirect. Somewhere not far away was a communications or computer center; people strolled in with keypunch cards, out with swatches of printouts, and there was the hum of light machinery.

A young man in an off-the-rack sport coat – the essence of government agent – lounged outside the door of Andy's apartment. There was a bulge under his arm. The agent was a part of the standard operating procedure, but as he and Pynchot strolled, he would fall behind them, watching but out of earshot. Andy thought he would be no problem.

The agent fell in behind them now as he and Pynchot strolled to the elevator. Andy's heartbeat was now so heavy it felt as if it were shaking his entire ribcage. But without seeming to, he was watching everything closely. There were perhaps a dozen unmarked doors. Some of them he had seen standing open on other walks up this corridor – a small, specialized library of some kind, a photocopying room in another – but about many of them he simply had no idea. Charlie might be behind any one of them right now . . . or in some other part of the installation entirely.

They got into the elevator, which was big enough to

accommodate a hospital gurney. Pynchot produced his keys, twisted one of them in the keyway, and pushed one of the unmarked buttons. The doors closed and the elevator rose smoothly. The Shop agent lounged at the back of the car. Andy stood with his hands in the pockets of his Lee Riders, a slight, vapid smile on his face.

The elevator door opened on what had once been a ballroom. The floor was polished oak, pegged together. Across the wide expanse of the room, a spiral staircase made a graceful double twist on its way to the upper levels. To the left, French doors gave on to a sunny terrace and the rock garden beyond it. From the right, where heavy oak doors stood half open, came the clacking sound of a typing pool, putting out that day's two bales of paperwork.

And from everywhere came the smell of fresh flowers.

Pynchot led the way across the sunny ballroom, and as always Andy commented on the pegged-together floor as if he had never noticed it before. They went through the French doors with their Shop-shadow behind them. It was very warm, very humid. Bees buzzed lazily through the air. Beyond the rock garden were hydrangea, forsythia, and rhododendron bushes. There was the sound of riding lawnmowers making their eternal rounds. Andy turned his face up to the sun with a gratitude that wasn't feigned.

'How are you feeling, Andy?' Pynchot asked.

'Good. Good.'

'You know, you've been here almost half a year now,' Pynchot said in an isn't-it-amazing-how-the-time-flies-when-you're-having-a-good-time tone of mild surprise. They turned right, onto one of the graveled paths. The smell of honeysuckle and sweet sassafras hung in the still air. On the other side of the duckpond, near the other house, two horses cantered lazily along.

'That long,' Andy said.

'Yes, it is a long time,' Pynchot said, grinning. 'And

348

we've decided that your power has . . . diminished, Andy. In fact, you know we've had no appreciable results at all.'

'Well, you keep me drugged all the time,' Andy said reproachfully. 'You can't expect me to do my best if I'm stoned.'

Pynchot cleared his throat but did not point out that Andy had been totally clean for the first three series of tests and all three had been fruitless.

'I mean, I've done my best, Dr Pynchot. I've *tried*.'

'Yes, yes. Of course you have. And we think – that is, *I* think – that you deserve a rest. Now, the Shop has a small compound on Maui, in the Hawaii chain, Andy. And I have a six-month report to write very soon. How would you like it' – Pynchot's grin broadened into a game-show host's leer and his voice took on the tones of a man about to offer a child an incredible treat – 'how would you like it if I recommended that you be sent there for the immediate future?'

And the immediate future might be two years, Andy thought. Maybe five. They would want to keep an eye on him in case the mental-domination ability recurred, and maybe as an ace in the hole in case some unforeseen difficulty with Charlie cropped up. But in the end, he had no doubt that there would be an accident or an overdose or a 'suicide.' In Orwell's parlance, he would become an unperson.

'Would I still get my medication?' Andy asked.

'Oh, of course,' Pynchot said.

'Hawaii . . .' Andy said dreamily. Then he looked around at Pynchot with what he hoped was an expression of rather stupid cunning. 'Probably Dr Hockstetter won't let me go. Dr Hockstetter doesn't like me. I can tell.'

'Oh, he does,' Pynchot assured him. 'He does like you, Andy. And in any case, you're my baby, not Dr Hockstetter's. I assure you, he'll go along with what I advise.'

'But you haven't written your memorandum on the subject yet,' Andy said.

'No, I thought I'd talk to you first. But, really, Hockstetter's approval is just a formality.'

'One more series of tests might be wise,' Andy said, and pushed out lightly at Pynchot. 'Just for safety's sake.'

Pynchot's eyes suddenly fluttered in a strange way. His grin faltered, became puzzled, and then faded altogether. Now Pynchot was the one who looked drugged, and the thought gave Andy a vicious kind of satisfaction. Bees droned in the flowers. The scent of new-cut grass, heavy and cloying, hung in the air.

'When you write your report, suggest one more series of tests,' Andy repeated.

Pynchot's eyes cleared. His grin came splendidly back. 'Of course, this Hawaii thing is just between us for the time being,' he said. 'When I write my report, I will be suggesting one more series of tests. I think it might be wise. Just for safety's sake, you know.'

'But after that I might go to Hawaii?'

'Yes,' Pynchot said. 'After that.'

'And another series of tests might take three months or so?'

'Yes, about three months.' Pynchot beamed on Andy as if he were a prize pupil.

They were nearing the pond now. Ducks sailed lazily across its mirror surface. The two men paused by it. Behind them, the young man in the sport coat was watching a middle-aged man and woman cantering along side by side on the far side of the pond. Their reflections were broken only by the long, smooth glide of one of the white ducks. Andy thought the couple looked eerily like an ad for mail-order insurance, the kind of ad that's always falling out of your Sunday paper and into your lap— or your coffee.

There was a small pulse of pain in his head. Not bad at all. But in his nervousness he had come very close to pushing Pynchot much harder than he had to, and the young man might have noticed the results of that. He didn't seem to be watching them, but Andy wasn't fooled.

'Tell me a little about the roads and the countryside around here,' he said quietly to Pynchot, and pushed out lightly again. He knew from various snatches of conversation that they were not terribly far from Washington, D.C., but nowhere as close as the CIA's base of operations in Langley. Beyond that he knew nothing.

'Very pretty here,' Pynchot said dreamily, 'since they've filled the holes.'

'Yes, it is nice,' Andy said, and lapsed into silence. Sometimes a push triggered an almost hypnotic trace memory in the person being pushed – usually through some obscure association – and it was unwise to interrupt whatever was going on. It could set up an echo effect, and the echo could become a ricochet, and the ricochet could lead to . . . well, to almost anything. It had happened to one of his Walter Mitty businessmen, and it had scared the bejesus out of Andy. It had turned out okay, but if friend Pynchot suddenly got a case of the screaming horrors, it would be anything but okay.

'My wife loves that thing,' Pynchot said in that same dreamy voice.

'What's that?' Andy asked. 'That she loves?'

'Her new garbage disposer. It's very . . .'

He trailed off.

'Very pretty,' Andy suggested. The guy in the sport coat had drifted a little closer and Andy felt a fine sweat break on his upper lip.

'Very pretty,' Pynchot agreed, and looked vaguely out at the pond.

The Shop agent came closer still, and Andy decided he might have to risk another push . . . a very small one. Pynchot was standing beside him like a TV set with a blown tube.

The shadow picked up a small chunk of wood and tossed it in the water. It struck lightly and ripples spread, shimmering. Pynchot's eyes fluttered.

'The country is very pretty around here,' Pynchot said. 'Quite hilly, you know. Good riding country. My wife and I ride here once a week, if we can get away. I guess Dawn's the closest town going west . . . southwest, actually. Pretty small. Dawn's on Highway Three-oh-one. Gether's the closest town going east.'

'Is Gether on a highway?'

'Nope. Just on a little road.'

'Where does Highway Three-oh-one go? Besides Dawn?'

'Why, all the way up to D.C., if you go north. Most of the way to Richmond, if you go south.'

Andy wanted to ask about Charlie now, had planned to ask about Charlie, but Pynchot's reaction had scared him a little. His association of *wife*, *holes*, *pretty*, and – very strange! – *garbage disposer* had been peculiar and somehow disquieting. It might be that Pynchot, although accessible, was nevertheless not a good subject. It might be that Pynchot was a disturbed personality of some sort, tightly corseted into an appearance of normality while God knew what forces might be delicately counterbalanced underneath. Pushing people who were mentally unstable could lead to all sorts of unforeseen results. If it hadn't been for the shadow he might have tried anyway (after all that had happened to him, he had damn few compunctions about messing with Herman Pynchot's head), but now he was afraid to. A psychiatrist with the push might be a great boon to mankind . . . but Andy McGee was no shrink.

Maybe it was foolish to assume so much from a single trace-memory reaction; he had got them before from a good many people and very few of them had freaked out. But he didn't trust Pynchot. Pynchot smiled too much.

A sudden cold and murderous voice spoke from deep inside

him, from some well sunk far into his subconscious: *Tell him to go home and commit suicide. Then push him. Push him hard.*

He thrust the thought away, horrified and a little sickened.

'Well,' Pynchot said, looking around, grinning. 'Shall we returnez-vous?'

'Sure,' Andy said.

And so he had begun. But he was still in the dark about Charlie.

6

INTERDEPARTMENTAL MEMO

From   Herman Pynchot
To   Patrick Hockstetter
Date   September 12
Re   Andy McGee

I've been over all of my notes and most of the tapes in the last three days, and have spoken to McGee. There is no essential change in the situation since we last discussed it 9/5, but for the time being I'd like to put the Hawaii idea on hold if there is no big objection (as Captain Hollister himself says, 'it's only money'!).

The fact is, Pat, I believe that a final series of tests might be wise – just for safety's sake. After that we might go ahead and send him to the Maui compound. I believe that a final series might take three months or so.

Please advise before I start the necessary paperwork.

Herm

INTERDEPARTMENTAL
MEMO

From   P. H.
To   Herm Pynchot
Date   September 13
Re   Andy McGee

I don't get it! The last time we all got together we agreed – you as much as any of us – that McGee was as dead as a used fuse. You can only hesitate so long at the bridge, you know!

If you want to schedule another series of tests – an *abbreviated* series, then be my guest. We're starting with the girl next week, but thanks to a good deal of inept interference from a certain source, I think it likely that her cooperation may not last long. While it does, it might not be a bad idea to have her father around . . . as a 'fire-extinguisher'???

Oh yes – it may be 'only money,' but it is the taxpayer's money, and levity on that subject is rarely encouraged, Herm. *Especially* by Captain Hollister. Keep it in mind.

Plan on having him for 6 to 8 weeks at most, unless you get results . . . and if you do, I'll personally eat your Hush Puppies.

Pat

8

   'Son-of-a-fucking-bitch,' Herm Pynchot said aloud as he finished reading this memorandum. He reread the third paragraph: here was Hockstetter, Hockstetter who owned a completely restored 1958 Thunderbird, spanking *him* about money. He crumpled up the memo and threw it at the wastebasket and leaned back in his swivel chair. Two months at most! He didn't like that. Three would have been more like it. He really felt that—

Unbidden and mysterious, a vision of the garbage-disposal unit he had installed at home rose in his mind. He didn't like that, either. The disposal unit had somehow got into his mind lately, and he didn't seem to be able to get it out. It came to the fore particularly when he tried to deal with the question of Andy McGee. The dark hole in the center of the sink was guarded by a rubber diaphragm . . . vaginal, that . . .

He leaned farther back in his chair, dreaming. When he came out of it with a start, he was disturbed to see that almost twenty minutes had gone by. He drew a memo form toward him and scratched out a note to that dirty bird Hockstetter, eating the obligatory helping of crow about his ill-advised 'it's only money' comment. He had to restrain himself from repeating his request for three months (and in his mind, the image of the disposer's smooth dark hole rose again). If Hockstetter said two, it was two. But if he did get results with McGee, Hockstetter was going to find two size-nine Hush Puppies sitting on his desk blotter fifteen minutes later, along with a knife, a fork, and a bottle of Adolph's Meat Tenderizer.

He finished the note, scrawled *Herm* across the bottom, and sat back, massaging his temples. He had a headache.

In high school and in college, Herm Pynchot had been a closet transvestite. He liked to dress up in women's clothes because he thought they made him look . . . well, very pretty. His junior year in college, as a member of Delta Tau Delta, he had been discovered by two of his fraternity brothers. The price of their silence had been a ritual humiliation, not much different from the pledge hazing that Pynchot himself had participated in with high good humor.

At two o'clock in the morning, his discoverers had spread trash and garbage from one end of the fraternity kitchen to the other and had forced Pynchot, dressed only in ladies' panties, stockings and garter belt, and a bra stuffed with toilet paper, to clean it all up and then wash the floor, under constant threat of discovery: all it would have taken was another frat 'brother' wandering down for an early-morning snack.

The incident had ended in mutual masturbation, which, Pynchot supposed, he should have been grateful for – it was probably the only thing that caused them to really keep their promise. But he had dropped out of the frat, terrified and disgusted with himself – most of all because he had found the entire incident somehow exciting. He had never 'cross-dressed' since that time. He was not gay. He had a lovely wife and two fine children and that proved he was not gay. He hadn't even thought of that humiliating, disgusting incident in years. And yet—

The image of the garbage disposal, that smooth black hole faced with rubber, remained. And his headache was worse.

The echo set off by Andy's push had begun. It was lazy and slow-moving now; the image of the disposal, coupled with the idea of being very pretty, was still an intermittent thing.

But it would speed up. Begin to ricochet.

Until it became unbearable.

9

'No,' Charlie said. 'It's wrong.' And she turned around to march right out of the small room again. Her face was white and strained. There were dark, purplish dashes under her eyes.

'Hey, whoa, wait a minute,' Hockstetter said, putting out his hands. He laughed a little. 'What's wrong, Charlie?'

'Everything,' she said. 'Everything's wrong.'

Hockstetter looked at the room. In one corner, a Sony TV camera had been set up. Its cords led through the pressed-cork wall to a VCR in the observation room next door. On the table in the middle of the room was a steel tray loaded with woodchips. To the left of this was an electroencephalograph dripping wires. A young man in a white coat presided over this.

'That's not much help,' Hockstetter said. He was still smiling paternally, but he was mad. You didn't have to be a mind reader to know that; you had only to look in his eyes.

'You don't listen,' she said shrilly. 'None of you listen except—'

(*except John but you can't say that*)

'Tell us how to fix it,' Hockstetter said.

She would not be placated. 'If you *listened*, you'd know. That steel tray with the little pieces of wood, *that's* all right, but that's the only thing that is. The table's wood, that wall stuff, that's fluh-flammable . . . and so's that guy's clothes.' She pointed to the technician, who flinched a little.

'Charlie—'

'That camera is, too.'

'Charlie, that camera's—'

'It's plastic and if it gets hot enough it will explode and little pieces will go everywhere. And there's no water! I told you, I have to push it at water once it gets started. My father and my mother told me so. I have to push it at water to put it out. Or . . . or . . .'

She burst into tears. She wanted John. She wanted her father. More than anything, oh, more than *anything*, she didn't want to be here. She had not slept at all last night.

For his part, Hockstetter looked at her thoughtfully. The tears, the emotional upset . . . he thought those things made it as clear as anything that she was really prepared to go through with it.

'All right,' he said. 'All right, Charlie. You tell us what to do and we'll do it.'

'You're right,' she said. 'Or you don't get nothing.'

Hockstetter thought: *We'll get plenty, you snotty little bitch.*

As it turned out, he was absolutely right.

10

Late that afternoon they brought her into a different room. She had fallen asleep in front of the TV when they brought her back to her apartment – her body was still young enough to enforce its need on her worried, confused mind – and she'd slept for nearly six hours. As a result of that and a hamburger and fries for lunch, she felt much better, more in control of herself.

She looked carefully at the room for a long time.

The tray of woodchips was on a metal table. The walls were gray industrial sheet steel, unadorned.

Hockstetter said, 'The technician there is wearing an asbestos uniform and asbestos slippers.' He spoke down to her, still smiling his paternal smile. The EEG operator looked hot and uncomfortable. He was wearing a white cloth mask to avoid aspirating any asbestos fiber. Hockstetter pointed to a long, square pane of mirror glass set into the far wall. 'That's one-way glass. Our camera is behind it. And you see the tub.'

Charlie went over to it. It was an old-fashioned clawfoot tub and it looked decidedly out of place in these stark surroundings. It was full of water. She thought it would do.

'All right,' she said.

Hockstetter's smile widened. 'Fine.'

'Only you go in the other room there. I don't want to have to look at you while I do it.' Charlie stared at Hockstetter inscrutably. 'Something might happen.'

Hockstetter's paternal smile faltered a little.

11

'She was right, you know,' Rainbird said. 'If you'd listened to her, you could have got it right the first time.'

Hockstetter looked at him and grunted.

'But you still don't believe it, do you?'

Hockstetter, Rainbird, and Cap were standing in front of the one-way glass. Behind them the camera peered into the room and the Sony VCR hummed almost inaudibly. The glass was lightly polarized, making everything in the testing room look faintly blue, like scenery seen through the window of a Greyhound bus. The technician was hooking Charlie up to the EEG. A TV monitor in the observation room reproduced her brainwaves.

'Look at those alphas,' one of the technicians murmured. 'She's really jacked up.'

'Scared,' Rainbird said. 'She's really scared.'

'You believe it, don't you?' Cap asked suddenly. 'You didn't at first, but now you do.'

'Yes,' Rainbird said. 'I believe it.'

In the other room, the technician stepped away from Charlie. 'Ready in here.'

Hockstetter flipped a toggle switch. 'Go ahead, Charlie. When you're ready.'

Charlie glanced toward the one-way glass, and for an eerie moment she seemed to be looking right into Rainbird's one eye.

He looked back, smiling faintly.

12

Charlie McGee looked at the one-way glass and saw nothing save her own reflection . . . but the sense of eyes watching her was very strong. She wished John could be back there; that would have made her feel more at ease. But she had no feeling that he was.

She looked back at the tray of woodchips.

It wasn't a push; it was a *shove*. She thought about doing it and was again disgusted and frightened to find herself *wanting* to do it. She thought about doing it the way a hot and hungry person might sit in front of a chocolate ice-cream soda and think about gobbling and slurping it down. That was okay, but first you wanted just a moment to . . . to savor it.

That wanting made her feel ashamed of herself, and then she shook her head almost angrily. *Why shouldn't I want to do it? If people are good at things, they always want to do them. Like Mommy with her double-crostics and Mr Douray down the street in Port City, always making bread. When they had enough at his house, he'd make some for other people. If you're good at something, you want to do it . . .*

Woodchips, she thought a little contemptuously. *They should have given me something* hard.

13

The technician felt it first. He was hot and uncomfortable and sweaty in the asbestos clothing, and at first he thought that was all it was. Then he saw that the kid's alpha waves had taken on the high spike rhythm that is the hallmark of extreme concentration, and also the brain's signature of imagination.

The sense of heat grew – and suddenly he was scared.

14

'Something happening in there,' one of the technicians in the observation room said in a high, excited voice. 'Temperature just jumped ten degrees. Her alpha pattern looks like the fucking Andes—'

'There it goes!' Cap exclaimed. *There it goes!*' His voice vibrated with the shrill triumph of a man who has waited years for the one moment now at hand.

15

She *shoved* as hard as she could at the tray of woodchips. They did not so much burst into flames as explode. A moment later the tray itself flipped over twice, spraying chunks of burning wood, and clanged off the wall hard enough to leave a dimple in the sheet steel.

The technician who had been monitoring at the EEG cried out in fear and made a sudden, crazy dash for the door. The sound of his cry hurled Charlie suddenly back in time to the Albany airport. It was the cry of Eddie Delgardo, running for the ladies' bathroom with his army-issue shoes in flames.

She thought in sudden terror and exaltation, *Oh God it's gotten so much stronger!*

The steel wall had developed a strange, dark ripple. The room had become explosively hot. In the other room, the digital thermometer, which had gone from seventy degrees to eighty and then paused, now climbed rapidly past ninety to ninety-four before slowing down.

Charlie threw the firething at the tub; she was nearly panicked now. The water swirled, then broke into a fury of bubbles. In a space of five seconds, the contents of the tub went from cool to a rolling, steaming boil.

The technician had exited, leaving the testing-room door

heedlessly ajar. In the observation room there was a sudden, startled turmoil. Hockstetter was bellowing. Cap was standing gape-jawed at the window, watching the tubful of water boil. Clouds of steam rose from it and the one-way glass began to fog over. Only Rainbird was calm, smiling slightly, hands clasped behind his back. He looked like a teacher whose star pupil has used difficult postulates to solve a particularly aggravating problem.

(*back off!*)

Screaming in her mind.

(*back off! back off! BACK OFF!*)

And suddenly it was gone. Something disengaged, spun free for a second or two, and then simply stopped. Her concentration broke up and let the fire go. She could see the room again and feel the heat she had created bringing sweat to her skin. In the observation room, the thermo-meter crested at ninety-six and then dropped a degree. The wildly bubbling caldron began to simmer down – but at least half of its contents had boiled away. In spite of the open door, the little room was as hot and moist as a steam room.

16

Hockstetter was checking his instruments feverishly. His hair, usually combed back so neatly and tightly that it almost seemed to scream, had now come awry, sticking up in the back. He looked a bit like Alfalfa of *The Little Rascals*.

'Got it!' he panted. 'Got it, we got it all . . . it's on tape . . . the temperature gradient . . . did you see the water in that tub boil? . . . Jesus! . . . did we get the audio? . . . we did? . . . my *God*, did you see what she did?'

He passed one of his technicians, whirled back, and

grabbed him roughly by the front of his smock. 'Would you say there was any doubt that she *made* that happen?' he shouted.

The technician, nearly as excited as Hockstetter, shook his head. 'No doubt at all, Chief. None.'

'Holy God,' Hockstetter said, whirling away, distracted again. 'I would have thought . . . something . . . yes, something . . . but that tray . . . *flew* . . .'

He caught sight of Rainbird, who was still standing at the one-way glass with his hands crossed behind his back, that mild, bemused smile on his face. For Hockstetter, old animosities were forgotten. He rushed over to the big Indian, grabbed his hand, pumped it.

'We got it,' he told Rainbird with savage satisfaction. 'We got it all, it would be good enough to stand up in court! *Right up in the fucking Supreme Court!*'

'Yes, you got it,' Rainbird agreed mildly. 'Now you better send somebody along to get *her.*'

'Huh?' Hockstetter looked at him blankly.

'Well,' Rainbird said, still in his mildest tone, 'the guy that was in there maybe had an appointment he forgot about, because he left in one hell of an ass-busting rush. He left the door open, and your firestarter just walked out.'

Hockstetter gaped at the glass. The steaming effect had got worse, but there was no doubt that the room was empty except for the tub, the EEG, the overturned steel tray, and the flaming scatter of woodchips.

'One of you men go get her!' Hockstetter cried, turning around. The five or six men stood by their instruments and didn't move. Apparently no one but Rainbird had noticed that Cap had left as soon as the girl had.

Rainbird grinned at Hockstetter and then raised his eye to include the others, these men whose faces had suddenly gone almost as pale as their lab smocks.

'Sure,' he said softly. 'Which of you wants to go get the little girl?'

No one moved. It was amusing, really; it occurred to Rainbird that this was the way the politicians were going to look when they found out it was finally done, that the missiles were really in the air, the bombs raining down, the woods and cities on fire. It was so amusing he had to laugh . . . and laugh . . . and laugh.

17

'They're so beautiful,' Charlie said softly. 'It's all so beautiful.'

They were standing near the duckpond, not far from where her father and Pynchot had stood only a few days previously. This day was much cooler than that one had been, and a few leaves had begun to show color. A light wind, just a little too stiff to be called a breeze, ruffled the surface of the pond.

Charlie turned her face up to the sun and closed her eyes, smiling. John Rainbird, standing beside her, had spent six months on stockade duty at Camp Stewart in Arizona before going overseas, and he had seen the same expression on the faces of men coming out after a long hard bang inside.

'Would you like to walk over to the stables and look at the horses?'

'Oh yes, sure,' she said immediately, and then glanced shyly at him. 'That is, if you don't mind.'

'Mind? I'm glad to be outside, too. This is recess for me.'

'Did they assign you?'

'Naw,' he said. They began to walk along the edge of the pond toward the stables on the far side. 'They asked for volunteers. I don't think they got many, after what happened yesterday.'

'It scared them?' Charlie asked, just a little too sweetly.

'I guess it did,' Rainbird said, and he was speaking nothing but the truth. Cap had caught up with Charlie as she wandered down the hall and escorted her back to her apartment. The young man who had bolted his position at the EEG was now being processed for duty in Panama City. The staff meeting following the test had been a nutty affair, with the scientists at both their best and worst, blue-skying a hundred new ideas on one hand and worrying tiresomely – and considerably after the fact – about how to control her on the other hand.

It was suggested that her quarters be fireproofed, that a full-time guard be installed, that the drug series be started on her again. Rainbird had listened to as much of this as he could bear and then rapped hard on the edge of the conference table with the band of the heavy turquoise ring he wore. He rapped until he had the attention of everyone there. Because Hockstetter disliked him (and perhaps 'hated' would not have been too strong a word), his cadre of scientists also disliked him, but Rainbird's star had risen in spite of that. He had, after all, been spending a good part of each day with this human blowtorch.

'I suggest,' he had said, rising to his feet and glaring around at them benignly from the shattered lens of his face, 'that we continue exactly as we have been. Up until today you have been proceeding on the premise that the girl probably didn't have the ability which you all knew had been documented two dozen times over, and that if she did have it, it was a small ability, and if it wasn't a small ability, she would probably never use it again anyway. Now you know differently, and you'd like to upset her all over again.'

'That's not true,' Hockstetter said, annoyed. 'That is simply—'

'*It is true!*' Rainbird thundered at him, and Hockstetter shrank back in his chair. Rainbird smiled again at the faces around the table. 'Now. The girl is eating again. She has put on ten pounds and is no longer a scrawny shadow of what she should be. She is reading, talking, doing paint-by-the-numbers kits; she has asked for a dollhouse, which her friend the orderly has promised to try and get for her. In short, her frame of mind is better than it has been since she came here. Gentlemen, we are not going to start monkeying around with a fruitful status quo, are we?'

The man who had been monitoring the videotape equipment earlier had said hesitantly, 'But what if she sets that little suite of hers on fire?'

'If she was going to,' Rainbird said quietly, 'she would have done it already.' To that there had been no response.

Now, as he and Charlie left the edge of the pond and crossed toward the dark-red stables with their fresh piping of white paint, Rainbird laughed out loud. 'I guess you did scare them, Charlie.'

'But you're not scared?'

'Why should I be scared?' Rainbird said, and ruffled her hair. 'I only turn into a baby when it's dark and I can't get out.'

'Oh John, you don't have to be ashamed of that.'

'If you were going to light me up,' he said, rephrasing his comment of the night before, 'I guess you would've by now.'

She stiffened immediately. 'I wish you wouldn't . . . wouldn't even say things like that.'

'Charlie, I'm sorry. Sometimes my mouth gets ahead of my brains.'

They went into the stables, which were dim and fragrant.

366

Dusky sunlight slanted in, making mellow bars and stripes in which motes of haychaff danced with dreamy slowness.

A groom was currying the mane of a black gelding with a white blaze on its forehead. Charlie stopped, looking at the horse with delighted wonder. The groom looked around at her and grinned. 'You must be the young miss. They told me to be on the watch-out for you.'

'She's so *beautiful*,' Charlie whispered. Her hands trembled to touch that silky coat. One look in the horse's dark, calm, mellow eyes and she was in love.

'Well, it's a boy, actually,' the groom said, and tipped a wink at Rainbird, whom he had never seen before and didn't know from Adam. 'After a fashion, that is.'

'What's his name?'

'Necromancer,' the groom said. 'Want to pet him?'

Charlie drew hesitantly near. The horse lowered his head and she stroked him; after a few moments she spoke to him. It did not occur to her that she would light another half-dozen fires just to ride on him with John beside her . . . but Rainbird saw it in her eyes, and he smiled.

She looked around at him suddenly and saw the smile, and for a moment the hand she had been stroking the horse's muzzle with paused. There was something in that smile she didn't like, and she had thought she liked everything about John. She got feelings about most people and did not consider this much; it was part of her, like her blue eyes and her double-jointed thumb. She usually dealt with people on the basis of these feelings. She didn't like Hockstetter, because she felt that he didn't care for her anymore than he would care for a test tube. She was just an object to him.

But with John, her liking was based only on what he did, his kindness to her, and perhaps part of it was his disfigured face: she could identify and sympathize with him on that account. After all, why was she here if not because she was also a freak? Yet beyond that, he was one of those rare people – like Mr Raucher, the delicatessen owner in New York who often played chess with her daddy – who were for some reason completely closed to her. Mr Raucher was old and wore a hearing aid and had a faded blue number tattooed on his forearm. Once Charlie had asked her father if that blue number meant anything, and her daddy had told her – after cautioning her never to mention it to Mr Raucher – that he would explain it later. But he never had. Sometimes Mr Raucher would bring her slices of kielbasa which she would eat while watching TV.

And now, looking at John's smile, which seemed so strange and somehow disquieting, she wondered for the first time, *What are you thinking?*

Then such trifling thoughts were swept away by the wonder of the horse.

'John,' she said, 'what does "Necromancer" mean?'

'Well,' he said, 'so far as I know, it means something like "wizard," or "sorcerer." '

'Wizard. Sorcerer.' She spoke the words softly, tasting them as she stroked the dark silk of Necromancer's muzzle.

18

Walking back with her, Rainbird said: 'You ought to ask that Hockstetter to let you ride that horse, if you like him so much.'

'No . . . I couldn't . . .' she said, looking at him wide-eyed and startled.

'Oh, sure you could,' he said, purposely misunderstanding. 'I don't know much about geldings, but I know they're supposed to be gentle. He looks awful big, but I don't think he'd run away with you, Charlie.'

'No – I don't mean that. They just wouldn't let me.'

He stopped her by putting his hands on her shoulders.

'Charlie McGee, sometimes you're really dumb,' he said. 'You done me a good turn that time the lights went out, Charlie, and you kept it to yourself. So now you listen to me and I'll do you one. You want to see your father again?'

She nodded quickly.

'Then you want to show them that you mean business. It's like poker, Charlie. If you ain't dealin from strength . . . why, you just ain't dealin. Every time you light a fire for them, for one of their tests, you get something from them.' He gave her shoulders a soft shake. 'This is your uncle John talking to you. Do you hear what I'm sayin?'

'Do you really think they'd let me? If I asked?'

'If you *asked*? Maybe not. But if you *told* them, yeah. I hear them sometimes. You go in to empty their waste-baskets and ashtrays, they think you're just another piece of the furniture. That Hockstetter's just about wettin his pants.'

'Really?' She smiled a little.

'Really.' They began to walk again. 'What about you, Charlie? I know how scared of it you were before. How do you feel about it now?'

She was a long time answering. And when she did, it was in a more thoughtful and somehow adult tone than Rainbird had ever heard from her. 'It's different now,' she said. 'It's a lot stronger. But . . . I was more in control of it than I ever was before. That day at the farm' – she shivered a little and her voice dropped a little – 'it just . . . just got away for a little while. It . . . it went everywhere.' Her eyes darkened. She looked inside memory and saw chickens exploding like horrible living fireworks. 'But yesterday, when I told it to back off, it did. I said to myself, it's just going to be a small fire. And it was. It was like I let it out in a single straight line.'

'And then you pulled it back into yourself?'

369

'God, no,' she said, looking at him. 'I put it into the water. If I pulled it back into myself . . . I guess *I'd* burn up.'

They walked in silence for a while.

'Next time there has to be more water.'

'But you're not scared now?'

'Not as scared as I was,' she said, making the careful distinction. 'When do you think they'll let me see my dad?'

He put an arm around her shoulders in rough good comradeship.

'Give them enough rope, Charlie,' he said.

19

It began to cloud up that afternoon and by evening a cold autumn rain had begun to fall. In one house of a small and very exclusive suburb near the Shop complex – a suburb called Longmont Hills – Patrick Hockstetter was in his workshop, building a model boat (the boats and his restored T-bird were his only hobbies, and there were dozens of his whalers and frigates and packets about the house) and thinking about Charlie McGee. He was in an extremely good mood. He felt that if they could get another dozen tests out of her – even another ten – his future would be assured. He could spend the rest of his life investigating the properties of Lot Six . . . and at a substantial raise in pay. He carefully glued a mizzenmast in place and began to whistle.

In another house in Longmont Hills, Herman Pynchot was pulling a pair of his wife's panties over a gigantic erection. His eyes were dark and trancelike. His wife was at a Tupperware party. One of his two fine children was at a Cub Scout meeting and the other fine child was at an intramural chess tourney at the junior high school. Pynchot carefully hooked one of his wife's bras behind his back. It

370

hung limply on his narrow chest. He looked at himself in the mirror and thought he looked . . . well, very pretty. He walked out into the kitchen, heedless of the unshaded windows. He walked like a man in a dream. He stood by the sink and looked down into the maw of the newly installed Waste-King disposer. After a long, thoughtful time, he turned it on. And to the sound of its whirling, gnashing steel teeth, he took himself in hand and masturbated. When his orgasm had come and gone, he started and looked around. His eyes were full of blank terror, the eyes of a man waking from a nightmare. He shut off the garbage disposal and ran for the bedroom, crouching low as he passed the windows. His head ached and buzzed. What in the name of God was happening to him?

In yet a third Longmont Hills house – a house with a hillside view that the likes of Hockstetter and Pynchot could not hope to afford – Cap Hollister and John Rainbird sat drinking brandy from snifters in the living room. Vivaldi issued from Cap's stereo system. Vivaldi had been one of his wife's favorites. Poor Georgia.

'I agree with you,' Cap said slowly, wondering again why he had invited this man whom he hated and feared into his home. The girl's power was extraordinary, and he supposed extraordinary power made for strange bedfellows. 'The fact that she mentioned a "next time" in such an offhand way is extremely significant.'

'Yes,' Rainbird said. 'It appears we do indeed have a string to play out.'

'But it won't last forever.' Cap swirled his brandy, then forced himself to meet Rainbird's one glittering eye. 'I believe I understand how you intend to lengthen that string, even if Hockstetter does not.'

'Do you?'

'Yes,' Cap said, paused a moment, then added. 'It's dangerous to you.'

Rainbird smiled.

'If she finds out what side you're really on,' Cap said, 'you stand a good chance of finding out what a steak feels like in a microwave oven.'

Rainbird's smile lengthened into an unfunny shark's grin. 'And would you shed a bitter tear, Captain Hollister?'

'No,' Cap said. 'No sense lying to you about that. But for some time now — since before she actually went and did it — I've felt the ghost of Dr Wanless drifting around in here. Sometimes as close as my own shoulder.' He looked at Rainbird over the rim of his glass. 'Do you believe in ghosts, Rainbird?'

'Yes. I do.'

'Then you know what I mean. During the last meeting I had with him, he tried to warn me. He made a metaphor — let me see — John Milton at seven, struggling to write his name in letters that were legible, and that same human being growing up to write *Paradise Lost*. He talked about her . . . her potential for destruction.'

'Yes,' Rainbird said, and his eye gleamed.

'He asked me what we'd do if we found we had a little girl who could progress from starting fires to causing nuclear explosions to cracking the very planet open. I thought he was funny, irritating, and almost certainly mad.'

'But now you think he may have been right.'

'Let us say that I find myself wondering sometimes at three in the morning. Don't you?'

'Cap, when the Manhattan Project group exploded their first atomic device, no one was quite sure what would happen. There was a school of thought which felt that the chain reaction would never end — that we would have a miniature sun glowing in the desert out there even unto the end of the world.'

Cap nodded slowly.

'The Nazis were also horrible,' Rainbird said. 'The Japs were horrible. Now the Germans and the Japanese are nice and the Russians are horrible. The Muslims are horrible. Who knows who may become horrible in the future?'

'She's dangerous,' Cap said, rising restlessly. 'Wanless was right about that. She's a dead end.'

'Maybe.'

'Hockstetter says that the place where that tray hit the wall was rippled. It was sheet steel, but it rippled with the heat. The tray itself was twisted entirely out of shape. She smelted it. That little girl might have put out three thousand degrees of heat for a split second there.' He looked at Rainbird, but Rainbird was looking vaguely around the living room, as if he had lost interest. 'What I'm saying is that what you plan to do is dangerous for all of us, not just for you.'

'Oh yes,' Rainbird agreed complacently. 'There's a risk. Maybe we won't have to do it. Maybe Hockstetter will have what he needs before it becomes necessary to implement . . . uh, plan B.'

'Hockstetter's a type,' Cap said curtly. 'He's an information junkie. He'll never have enough. He could test her for two years and still scream we were too hasty when we . . . when we took her away. You know it and I know it, so let's not play games.'

'We'll know when it's time,' Rainbird said. '*I'll* know.'

'And then what will happen?'

'John the friendly orderly will come in,' Rainbird said, smiling a little. 'He will greet her, and talk to her, and make her smile. John the friendly orderly will make her feel happy because he's the only one who can. And when John feels she is at the moment of greatest happiness, he will strike her across the bridge of the nose, breaking it explosively and driving bone fragments into her brain. It will be quick . . . and I will be looking into her face when it happens.'

He smiled – nothing sharklike about it this time. The smile was gentle, kind . . . and *fatherly*. Cap drained his brandy. He needed it. He only hoped that Rainbird would indeed know the right time when it came, or they might all find out what a steak felt like in a microwave oven.

'You're crazy,' Cap said. The words escaped before he could hold them back, but Rainbird did not seem offended.

'Oh yes,' he agreed, and drained his own brandy. He went on smiling.

20

Big Brother. Big Brother was the problem.

Andy moved from the living room of his apartment to the kitchen, forcing himself to walk slowly, to hold a slight smile on his face – the walk and expression of a man who is pleasantly stoned out of his gourd.

So far he had succeeded only in keeping himself here, near Charlie, and finding out that the nearest road was Highway 301 and that the countryside was fairly rural. All of that had been a week ago. It had been a month since the blackout, and he still knew nothing more about the layout of this installation than he had been able to observe when he and Pynchot went for their walks.

He didn't want to push anyone down here in his quarters, because Big Brother was always watching and listening. And he didn't want to push Pynchot anymore, because Pynchot was cracking up – Andy was sure of it. Since their little walk by the duckpond, Pynchot had lost weight. There were dark circles under his eyes, as if he were sleeping poorly. He sometimes would begin speaking and then trail off, as if he had lost his train of thought . . . or as if it had been interrupted.

All of which made Andy's own position that much more precarious.

How long before Pynchot's colleagues noticed what was happening to him? They might think it nothing but nervous strain, but suppose they connected it with him? That would be the end of whatever slim chance Andy had of getting out of here with Charlie. And his feeling that Charlie was in big trouble had got stronger and stronger.

What in the name of Jesus Christ was he going to do about Big Brother?

He got a Welch's Grape from the fridge, went back to the living room, and sat down in front of the TV without seeing it, his mind working restlessly, looking for some way out. But when that way out came, it was (like the power blackout) a complete surprise. In a way, it was Herman Pynchot who opened the door for him: he did it by killing himself.

21

Two men came and got him. He recognized one of them from Manders's farm.

'Come on, big boy,' this one said. 'Little walk.'

Andy smiled foolishly, but inside, the terror had begun. Something had happened. Something bad had happened; they didn't send guys like this if it was something good. Perhaps he had been found out. In fact, that was the most likely thing. 'Where to?'

'Just come on.'

He was taken to the elevator, but when they got off in the ballroom, they went farther into the house instead of outside. They passed the secretarial pool, entered a smaller room where a secretary ran off correspondence on an IBM typewriter.

'Go right in,' she said.

They passed her on the right and went through a door into a small study with a bay window that gave a view of the duckpond through a screen of low alders. Behind an old-fashioned roll-top desk sat an elderly man with a sharp, intelligent face; his cheeks were ruddy, but from sun and wind rather than liquor, Andy thought.

He looked up at Andy, then nodded at the two men who had brought him in. 'Thank you. You can wait outside.'

They left.

The man behind the desk looked keenly at Andy, who looked back blandly, still smiling a bit. He hoped to God he wasn't overdoing it. 'Hello, who are you?' he asked.

'My name is Captain Hollister, Andy. You can call me Cap. They tell me I am in charge of this here rodeo.'

'Pleased to meet you,' Andy said. He let his smile widen a little. Inside, the tension screwed itself up another notch.

'I've some sad news for you, Andy.'

(*oh God no it's Charlie something's happened to Charlie*)

Cap was watching him steadily with those small, shrewd eyes, eyes caught so deeply in their pleasant nets of small wrinkles that you almost didn't notice how cold and studious they were.

'Oh?'

'Yes,' Cap said, and fell silent for a moment. And the silence spun out agonizingly.

Cap had fallen into a study of his hands, which were neatly folded on the blotter in front of him. It was all Andy could do to keep from leaping across the desk and throttling him. Then Cap looked up.

'Dr Pynchot is dead, Andy. He killed himself last night.'

Andy's jaw dropped in unfeigned surprise. Alternating waves of relief and horror raced through him. And over it all, like a boiling sky over a confused sea, was the realization that this changed everything . . . but how? *How?*

Cap was watching him. *He suspects. He suspects something. But are his suspicions serious or only a part of his job?*

A hundred questions. He needed time to think and he had no time. He would have to do his thinking on his feet.

'That surprises you?' Cap asked.

'He was my friend,' Andy said simply, and had to close his mouth to keep from saying more. This man would listen to him patiently; he would pause long after Andy's every remark (as he was pausing now) to see if Andy would plunge on, the mouth outracing the mind. Standard interrogation technique. And there were man-pits in these woods; Andy felt it strongly. It had been an echo, of course. An echo that had turned into a ricochet. He had pushed Pynchot and started a ricochet and it had torn the man apart. And for all of that, Andy could not find it in his heart to be sorry. There was horror . . . and there was a caveman who capered and rejoiced.

'Are you sure it was . . . I mean, sometimes an accident can look like—'

'I'm afraid it was no accident.'

'He left a note?'

(*naming me?*)

'He dressed up in his wife's underwear, went out into the kitchen, started up the garbage disposal, and stuck his arm into it.'

'Oh . . . my . . . *God.*' Andy sat down heavily. If there hadn't been a chair handy he would have sat on the floor. All the strength had left his legs. He stared at Cap Hollister with sick horror.

'You didn't have anything to do with that, did you, Andy?' Cap asked. 'You didn't maybe push him into it?'

'No,' Andy said. 'Even if I could still do it, why would I do a thing like that?'

'Maybe because he wanted to send you to the Hawaiians,' Cap said. 'Maybe you didn't want to go to Maui, because your daughter's here. Maybe you've been fooling us all along, Andy.'

And although this Cap Hollister was crawling around on top of the truth, Andy felt a small loosening in his chest. If Cap really thought he had pushed Pynchot into doing that, this interview wouldn't be going on between just the two of them. No, it was just doing things by the book; that was all. They probably had all they needed to justify suicide in Pynchot's own file without looking for arcane methods of murder. Didn't they say that psychiatrists had the highest suicide rate of any profession?

'No, that's not true at all,' Andy said. He sounded afraid, confused, close to blubbering. 'I *wanted* to go to Hawaii. I told him that. I think that's why he wanted to make more tests, because I wanted to go. I don't think he liked me in some ways. But I sure didn't have anything to do with . . . with what happened to him.'

Cap looked at him thoughtfully. Their eyes met for a moment and then Andy dropped his gaze.

'Well, I believe you, Andy,' Cap said. 'Herm Pynchot had been under a lot of pressure lately. It's a part of this life we live, I suppose. Regrettable. Add this secret transvestism on top of that, and, well, it's going to be hard on his wife. Very hard. But we take care of our own, Andy.' Andy could feel the man's eyes boring into him. 'Yes, we always take care of our own. That's the most important thing.'

'Sure,' Andy said dully.

There was a lengthening moment of silence. After a little bit Andy looked up, expecting to see Cap looking at him. But Cap was staring out at the back lawn and the alders and his face looked saggy and confused and old, the face of a man who has been seduced into thinking of other, perhaps happier, times. He saw Andy looking at him and a small wrinkle of disgust passed over his face and was

378

gone. Sudden sour hate flared inside Andy. Why shouldn't this Hollister look disgusted? He saw a fat drug addict sitting in front of him – or that was what he thought he saw. But who gave the orders? And what are you doing to my daughter, you old monster?

'Well,' Cap said. 'I'm happy to tell you you'll be going to Maui anyway, Andy – it's an ill wind that doesn't blow somebody good, or something like that, hmmm? I've started the paperwork already.'

'But . . . listen, you don't really think I had anything to do with what happened to Dr Pynchot, do you?'

'No, of course not.' That small and involuntary ripple of disgust again. And this time Andy felt the sick satisfaction that he imagined a black guy who has successfully tommed an unpleasant white must feel. But over this was the alarm brought on by that phrase *I've started the paperwork already.*

'Well, that's good. Poor Dr Pynchot.' He looked downcast for only a token instant and then said eagerly, 'When am I going?'

'As soon as possible. By the end of next week at the latest.'

Nine days at the outside! It was like a battering ram in his stomach.

'I've enjoyed our talk, Andy. I'm sorry we had to meet under such sad and unpleasant circumstances.'

He was reaching for the intercom switch, and Andy suddenly realized he couldn't let him do that. There was nothing he could do in his apartment with its cameras and listening devices. But if this guy really was the big cheese, this office would be as dead as a doornail: he would have the place washed regularly for bugs. Of course, he might have his own listening devices, but—

'Put your hand down,' Andy said, and pushed.

Cap hesitated. His hand drew back and joined its mate

379

on the blotter. He glanced out at the back lawn with that drifting, remembering expression on his face.

'Do you tape meetings in here?'

'No,' Cap said evenly. 'For a long time I had a voice-activated Uher-Five thousand – like the one that got Nixon in trouble – but I had it taken out fourteen weeks ago.'

'Why?'

'Because it looked like I was going to lose my job.'

'Why did you think you were going to lose your job?'

Very rapidly, in a kind of litany, Cap said: 'No production. No production. No production. Funds must be justified with results. Replace the man at the top. No tapes. No scandal.'

Andy tried to think it through. Was this taking him in a direction he wanted to go? He couldn't tell, and time was short. He felt like the stupidest, slowest kid at the Easter-egg hunt. He decided he would go a bit further down this trail.

'Why weren't you producing?'

'No mental-domination ability left in McGee. Permanently tipped over. Everyone in agreement on that. The girl wouldn't light fires. Said she wouldn't no matter what. People saying I was fixated on Lot Six. Shot my bolt.' He grinned. 'Now it's okay. Even Rainbird says so.'

Andy renewed the push, and a small pulse of pain began to beat in his forehead. 'Why is it okay?'

'Three tests so far. Hockstetter's ecstatic. Yesterday she flamed a piece of sheet steel. Spot temp over twenty thousand degrees for four seconds, Hockstetter says.'

Shock made the headache worse, made it harder to get a handle on his whirling thoughts. Charlie was lighting fires? What had they done to her? What, in the name of God?

He opened his mouth to ask and the intercom buzzed, jolting him into pushing much harder than he had to. For a moment, he gave Cap almost everything there was. Cap shuddered all over as if he had been whipped with an electric cattle prod. He made a low gagging sound and his ruddy face lost most of its color. Andy's headache took a quantum leap and he cautioned himself uselessly to take it easy; having a stroke in this man's office wouldn't help Charlie.

'Don't do that,' Cap whined. 'Hurts—'

'Tell them no calls for the next ten minutes,' Andy said. Somewhere the black horse was kicking at its stable door, wanting to get out, wanting to run free. He could feel oily sweat running down his cheeks.

The intercom buzzed again. Cap leaned forward and pushed the toggle switch down. His face had aged fifteen years.

'Cap, Senator Thompson's aide is here with those figures you asked for on Project Leap.'

'No calls for the next ten minutes,' Cap said, and clicked off.

Andy sat drenched in sweat. Would that hold them? Or would they smell a rat? It didn't matter. As Willy Loman had been so wont to cry, the woods were burning. Christ, what was he thinking of Willy Loman for? He was going crazy. The black horse would be out soon and he could ride there. He almost giggled.

'Charlie's been lighting fires?'

'Yes.'

'How did you get her to do that?'

'Carrot and stick. Rainbird's idea. She got to take walks outside for the first two. Now she gets to ride the horse. Rainbird thinks that will hold her for the next couple of weeks.' And he repeated, 'Hockstetter's ecstatic.'

'Who is this Rainbird?' Andy asked, totally unaware that he had just asked the jackpot question.

Cap talked in short bursts for the next five minutes. He

told Andy that Rainbird was a Shop hitter who had been horribly wounded in Vietnam, had lost an eye there (the one-eyed pirate in my dream, Andy thought numbly). He told Andy that it was Rainbird who had been in charge of the Shop operation that had finally netted Andy and Charlie at Tashmore Pond. He told him about the blackout and Rainbird's inspired first step on the road to getting Charlie to start lighting fires under test conditions. Finally, he told Andy that Rainbird's personal interest in all of this was Charlie's life when the string of deception had finally run itself out. He spoke of these matters in a voice that was emotionless yet somehow urgent. Then he fell silent.

Andy listened in growing fury and horror. He was trembling all over when Cap's recitation had concluded. Charlie, he thought. Oh, Charlie, Charlie.

His ten minutes were almost up, and there was still so much he needed to know. The two of them sat silent for perhaps forty seconds; an observer might have decided they were companionable older friends who no longer needed to speak to communicate. Andy's mind raced.

'Captain Hollister,' he said.

'Yes?'

'When is Pynchot's funeral?'

'The day after tomorrow,' Cap said calmly.

'We're going. You and I. You understand?'

'Yes, I understand. We're going to Pynchot's funeral.'

'I asked to go. I broke down and cried when I heard he was dead.'

'Yes, you broke down and cried.'

'I was very upset.'

'Yes, you were.'

'We're going to go in your private car, just the two of us. There can be Shop people in cars ahead and behind us, motorcycles on either side if that's standard operating procedure, *but we're going alone*. Do you understand?'

'Oh, yes. That's perfectly clear. Just the two of us.'

'And we're going to have a good talk. Do you also understand that?'

'Yes, a good talk.'

'Is your car bugged?'

'Not at all.'

Andy began to push again, a series of light taps. Each time he pushed, Cap flinched a little, and Andy knew there was an excellent chance that he might be starting an echo in there, but it had to be done.

'We're going to talk about where Charlie is being kept. We're going to talk about ways of throwing this whole place into confusion without locking all the doors the way the power blackout did. And we're going to talk about ways that Charlie and I can get out of here. Do you understand?'

'You're not supposed to escape,' Cap said in a hateful, childish voice. 'That's not in the scenario.'

'*It is now,*' Andy said, and pushed again.

'*Owwwww!*' Cap whined.

'Do you understand that?'

'Yes, I understand, don't, don't do that anymore, it hurts!'

'This Hockstetter – will he question my going to the funeral?'

'No, Hockstetter is all wrapped up in the little girl. He thinks of little else these days.'

'Good.' It wasn't good at all. It was desperation. 'Last thing, Captain Hollister. You're going to forget that we had this little talk.'

'Yes, I'm going to forget all about it.'

The black horse was loose. It was starting its run. *Take me out of here*, Andy thought dimly. *Take me out of here; the horse is loose and the woods are burning*. The headache came in a sickish cycle of thudding pain.

'Everything I've told you will occur naturally to you as your own idea.'

'Yes.'

Andy looked at Cap's desk and saw a box of Kleenex there. He took one of them and began dabbing at his eyes with it. He was not crying, but the headache had caused his eyes to water and that was just as good.

'I'm ready to go now,' he said to Cap.

He let go. Cap looked out at the alders again, thoughtfully blank. Little by little, animation came back into his face, and he turned toward Andy, who was wiping at his eyes a bit and sniffing. There was no need to overact.

'How are you feeling now, Andy?'

'A little better,' Andy said. 'But . . . you know . . . to hear it like that . . .'

'Yes, you were very upset,' Cap said. 'Would you like to have a coffee or something?'

'No, thanks. I'd like to go back to my apartment, please.'

'Of course. I'll see you out.'

'Thank you.'

22

The two men who had seen him up to the office looked at Andy with doubtful suspicion – the Kleenex, the red and watering eyes, the paternal arm that Cap had put around his shoulders. Much the same expression came into the eyes of Cap's secretary.

'He broke down and cried when he heard Pynchot was dead,' Cap said quietly. 'He was very upset. I believe I'll see if I can arrange for him to attend Herman's funeral with me. Would you like to do that, Andy?'

'Yes,' Andy said. 'Yes, please. If it can be arranged. Poor Dr Pynchot.' And suddenly he burst into real tears. The two men led him past Senator Thompson's bewildered, embarrassed aide, who had several blue-bound folders in his hands. They took Andy out, still weeping, each with a hand clasped lightly at his elbow. Each of them wore an expression of disgust that was very similar to Cap's — disgust for this fat drug addict who had totally lost control of his emotions and any sense of perspective and gushed tears for the man who had been his captor.

Andy's tears were real . . . but it was Charlie he wept for.

23

John always rode with her, but in her dreams Charlie rode alone. The head groom, Peter Drabble, had fitted her out with a small, neat English saddle, but in her dreams she rode bareback. She and John rode on the bridle paths that wove their way across the Shop grounds, moving in and out of the toy forest of sugarpines and skirting the duckpond, never doing more than an easy canter, but in her dreams she and Necromancer galloped together, faster and faster, through a real forest; they plunged at speed down a wild trail and the light was green through the interlaced branches overhead, and her hair streamed out behind her.

She could feel the ripple of Necromancer's muscles under his silky hide, and she rode with her hands twisted in his mane and whispered in his ear that she wanted to go faster . . . faster . . . faster.

Necromancer responded. His hooves were thunder. The path through these tangled, green woods was a tunnel, and from somewhere behind her there came a faint crackling and

(*the woods are burning*)

a whiff of smoke. It was a fire, a fire she had started, but there was no guilt — only exhilaration. They could outrace it. Necromancer could go anywhere, do anything. They would escape the forest-tunnel. She could sense brightness ahead.

'Faster. Faster.'

The exhilaration. The freedom. She could no longer tell where her thighs ended and Necromancer's sides began. They were one, fused, as fused as the metals she welded with her power when she did their tests. Ahead of them was a huge deadfall, a blowdown of white wood like a tangled cairn of bones. Wild with lunatic joy, she kicked at Necromancer lightly with her bare heels and felt his hindquarters bunch.

They leaped it, for a moment floating in the air. Her head was back; her hands held horsehair and she screamed – not in fear but simply because not to scream, to hold in, might cause her to explode. *Free, free, free . . . Necromancer, I love you.*

They cleared the deadfall easily but now the smell of smoke was sharper, clearer – there was a popping sound from behind them and it was only when a spark spiraled down and briefly stung her flesh like a nettle before going out that she realized she was naked. Naked and

(*but the woods are burning*)

free, unfettered, loose – she and Necromancer, running for the light.

'Faster,' she whispered. 'Faster, oh please.'

Somehow the big black gelding produced even more speed. The wind in Charlie's ears was rushing thunder. She did not have to breathe; air was scooped into her throat through her half-open mouth. Sun shone through these old trees in dusty bars like old copper.

And up ahead was the light – the end of the forest, open land, where she and Necromancer would run forever. The fire was behind them, the hateful smell of smoke, the feel of fear. The sun was ahead, and she would ride Necromancer all the way to the sea, where she would perhaps find her father and the two of them would live by pulling in nets full of shining, slippery fish.

'Faster!' she cried triumphantly. 'Oh, Necromancer, go *faster*, go *faster*, go—'

And that was when the silhouette stepped into the widening funnel of light where the woods ended, blocking the light in its own shape, blocking the way out. At first, as always in this dream, she thought it was her father, was *sure* it was her father, and her joy became almost hurtful . . . before suddenly transforming into utter terror.

She just had time to register the fact that the man was too big, too tall – and yet somehow familiar, dreadfully familiar, even in silhouette – before Necromancer reared, screaming.

Can horses scream? I didn't know they could scream—

Struggling to stay on, her thighs slipping as his hooves pawed at the air, and he wasn't screaming, he was whinnying, but it was a *scream* and there were other screaming whinnies somewhere behind her, *oh dear God*, she thought, *horses back there, horses back there and the woods are burning—*

Up ahead, blocking the light, that silhouette, that dreadful shape. Now it began to come toward her; she had fallen onto the path and Necromancer touched her bare stomach gently with his muzzle.

'Don't you hurt my horse!' she screamed at the advancing silhouette, the dream-father who was not her father. 'Don't you hurt the horses. Oh, please don't hurt the horses!'

But the figure came on and it was drawing a gun and that was when she awoke, sometimes with a scream, sometimes only in a shuddery cold sweat, knowing that she had dreamed badly but unable to remember anything save the mad, exhilarating plunge down the wooded trail and the smell of fire . . . these things, and an almost sick feeling of betrayal. . . .

And in the stable that day, she would touch Necromancer or perhaps put the side of her face against his warm shoulder and feel a dread for which she had no name.

Endgame

1

It was a bigger room.

Until last week, in fact, it had been the Shop's non-denominational chapel. The speed with which things were picking up could have been symbolized by the speed and ease with which Cap had rammed through Hockstetter's requests. A new chapel – not an odd spare room but a real chapel – was to be built at the eastern end of the grounds. Meanwhile, the remainder of the tests on Charlie McGee would be held here.

The fake wood paneling and the pews had been ripped out. Both flooring and walls had been insulated with asbestos batting that looked like steel wool and then covered over with heavy-guage tempered sheet steel. The area that had been the altar and the nave had been partitioned off. Hockstetter's monitoring instruments and a computer terminal had been installed. All of this had been done in a single week; work had begun just four days before Herman Pynchot ended his life in such grisly fashion.

Now, at two in the afternoon on an early October day, a cinderblock wall stood in the middle of the long room. To the left of it was a huge, low tank of water. Into this tank, which was six feet deep, had been dumped more than two thousand pounds of ice. In front of it stood Charlie McGee, looking small and neat in a blue denim jumper and red and black striped rugby socks. Blond pigtails tied off with small black velvet bows hung down to her shoulder blades.

'All right, Charlie,' Hockstetter's voice said over the intercom. Like everything else, the intercom had been hastily installed, and its reproduction was tinny and poor. 'We're ready when you are.'

The cameras filmed it all in living color. In these films, the small girl's head dips slightly, and for a few seconds nothing happens at all. Inset at the left of the film frame is a digital temperature readout. All at once it begins to move upward, from seventy to eighty to ninety. After that the figures jump up so rapidly that they are just a shifting reddish blur; the electronic temperature probe has been placed in the center of the cinderblock wall.

Now the film switches to slow motion; it is the only way that the entire action can be caught. To the men who watched it through the observation room's leaded-glass viewing ports, it happened with the speed of a gunshot.

In extreme slow motion, the cinderblock wall begins to smoke; small particles of mortar and concrete begin to jump lazily upward like popping corn. Then the mortar holding the blocks together can be observed to be *running*, like warm molasses. Then the bricks begin to crumble, from the center outward. Showers of particles, then clouds of them, blow back as the blocks explode with the heat. Now the digital heat sensor implanted in the center of this wall freezes at a reading of over seven thousand degrees. It freezes not because the temperature has stopped climbing but because the sensor itself has been destroyed.

Set around this testing room that used to be a chapel are eight huge Kelvinator air conditioners, all running at high speed, all pumping freezing air into the testing room. All eight kicked into operation as soon as the room's *overall* temperature passed ninety-five. Charlie had got very good at directing the stream of heat that somehow came from her at a single point, but as anyone who has ever burned his or her hand on a hot skillet handle knows, even so-called nonconductable surfaces will conduct heat – if there is enough heat to conduct.

With all eight of the industrial Kelvinators running, the temperature in the testing room should have been minus fifteen degrees Fahrenheit, plus or minus five degrees. Instead, the records show a continued climb, up over a hundred degrees, then a hundred and five, then a hundred and seven. But all of the sweat running down the faces of the observers cannot be accounted for by the heat alone.

Now not even extreme slow motion will give a clear picture of what is happening, but one thing is clear: as the cinderblocks continue to explode outward and backward, there can be no doubt that they are burning; these blocks are burning as briskly as newspapers in a fireplace. Of course, an eighth-grade science book teaches that *anything* will burn if it gets hot enough. But it is one thing to read such information and quite another to see cinderblock blazing with blue and yellow flame.

Then everything is obscured by a furious blowback of disintegrating particles as the whole wall vaporizes. The little girl makes a slow-motion half turn and a moment later the calm surface of the icy water in the tank is convulsed and boiling. And the heat in the room, which has crested at a hundred twelve, even with all eight air conditioners, it is as hot as a summer noontime in Death Valley), begins to go back.

There's one for the sweeper.

2

INTERDEPARTMENTAL
MEMO

From   Bradford Hyuck
To   Patrick Hockstetter

Date October 2
Re Telemetry, latest C. McGee Test #4

Pat – I've watched the films four times now and still can't believe it isn't some sort of special effects trick. Some unsolicited advice: When you get before the Senate subcommittee that's going to deal with the Lot Six appropriations and renewal plans, have your ducks in a row and do more than cover your ass – armor-plate it! Human nature being what it is, those guys are going to look at those films and have a hard job believing it isn't a flat-out shuck-and-jive.

To business: The readouts are being delivered by special messenger, and this memo should beat them by no more than two or three hours. You can read them over for yourself, but I'll briefly sum up our findings. Our conclusions can be summed up in two words: We're stumped. She was wired up this time like an astronaut going into space. You will note:

1. Blood pressure within normal parameters for a child of eight, and there's hardly a jog when that wall goes up like the Hiroshima bomb.
2. Abnormally high alpha wave readings: what we'd call her 'imagination circuitry' is well-engaged. You may or may not agree with Clapper and me that the waves are rather more even, suggesting a certain 'controlled imaginative dexterity' (Clapper's rather fulsome phrase, not mine). Could indicate she's getting in control of it and can manipulate the ability with greater precision. Practice, as they say, makes perfect. Or it may mean nothing at all.
3. All metabolic telemetry is within normal parameters – nothing strange or out of place. It's as if she was reading a good book or writing a class theme instead of creating what you say must have been upwards of 30,000 degrees of spot heat. To my mind the most fascinating (and frustrating!) information of all is the Beal-Searles CAT test. *Next to no caloric burn!* In case you've forgotten your physics – occupational hazard with you shrinks – a calorie is nothing but a unit of heat; the amount of heat necessary to raise

392

a gram of water one degree centigrade, to be exact. She burned maybe 25 calories during that little exhibition, what we would burn doing half a dozen sit-ups or walking twice around the building. But calories measure heat, damn it, *heat*, and what she's producing is heat . . . or is she? Is it coming *from* her or *through* her? And if it's the latter, where is it coming from? Figure that one out and you've got the Nobel Prize in your hip pocket! I'll tell you this: if our test series is as limited as you say it is, I'm positive we'll never find out.

Last word: Are you sure you *want* to continue these tests? Lately I just have to think about that kid and I start to get very antsy. I start thinking about things like pulsars and neutrinos and black holes and Christ knows what else. There are forces loose in this universe that we don't even know about yet, and some we can observe only at a remove of millions of light-years . . . and breathe a sigh of relief because of it. The last time I looked at that film I began to think of the girl as a crack – a chink, if you like – in the very smelter of creation. I know how that sounds, but I feel I would be remiss not to say it. God forgive me for saying this, with three lovely girls of my own, but I personally will breathe a sigh of relief when she's been neutralized.

If she can produce 30,000 degrees of spot heat without even trying, have you ever thought what might happen if she really set her mind to it?

Brad

3

'I want to see my father,' Charlie said when Hockstetter came in. She looked pale and wan. She had changed from her jumper into an old nightgown, and her hair was loose on her shoulders.

'Charlie—' he began, but anything he had been meaning to follow with was suddenly gone. He was deeply troubled by Brad Hyuck's memo and by the supporting telemetry readouts. The fact that Brad had trusted those final two paragraphs to print said much, and suggested more.

Hockstetter himself was scared. In authorizing the changeover of chapel to testing room, Cap had also authorized the installation of more Kelvinator air conditioners around Charlie's apartment – not eight but twenty. Only six had been installed so far, but after Test #4, Hockstetter didn't care if they were installed or not. He thought they could set up two hundred of the damned things and not impede her power. It was no longer a question of whether or not she could kill herself; it was a question of whether or not she could destroy the entire Shop installation if she wanted to – and maybe all of eastern Virginia in the bargain. Hockstetter now thought that if she wanted to do those things, she could. And the last stop on that line of reasoning was even scarier: only John Rainbird had an effective checkrein on her now. And Rainbird was nuts.

'I want to see my father,' she repeated.

Her father was at the funeral of poor Herman Pynchot. He attended with Cap, at the latter's request. Even Pynchot's death, as unrelated to anything going on here as it was, seemed to have cast its own evil pall over Hockstetter's mind.

'Well, I think that can be arranged,' Hockstetter said cautiously, 'if you can show us a little more—'

'I've shown you enough,' she said. 'I want to see my daddy.' Her lower lip trembled; her eyes had taken on a sheen of tears.

'Your orderly,' Hockstetter said, 'that Indian fellow, said you didn't want to go for a ride on your horse this morning after the test. He seemed worried about you.'

'It's not my horse,' Charlie said. Her voice was husky. 'Nothing here is mine. Nothing except my daddy and I . . .

394

want . . . to . . . *see him!*' Her voice rose to an angry, tearful shout.

'Don't get excited, Charlie,' Hockstetter said, suddenly frightened. Was it suddenly getting hotter in here, or was it just his imagination? 'Just . . . just don't get excited.'

Rainbird. This should have been Rainbird's job, goddammit.

'Listen to me, Charlie.' He smiled a wide, friendly smile. 'How would you like to go to Six Flags over Georgia? It's just about the neatest amusement park in the whole South, except maybe for Disney World. We'd rent the whole park for a day, just for you. You could ride the Ferris wheel, go in the haunted mansion, the merry-go-round—'

'I don't want to go to any amusement park, I just want to see my daddy. And I'm going to. I hope you hear me, because I'm going to!'

It *was* hotter.

'You're sweating,' Charlie said.

He thought of the cinderblock wall, exploding so fast you could see the flames only in slow motion. He thought of the steel tray flipping over twice as it flew across the room, spraying burning chunks of wood. If she flicked that power out at him, he would be a pile of ashes and fused bone almost before he knew what was happening to him.

Oh God please—

'Charlie, getting mad at me won't accomplish anyth—'

'Yes,' she said with perfect truth. 'Yes it will. And I'm mad at you, Dr Hockstetter. I'm really mad at you.'

'Charlie, please—'

'I want to see him,' she said again. 'Now go away. You tell them I want to see my father and then they can test me some more if they want. I don't mind. But if I don't see him, I'll make something happen. Tell them that.'

He left. He felt that he should say something more –

something that would redeem his dignity a little, make up a little for the fear

(*'you're sweating'*)

she had seen scrawled on his face – but nothing occurred. He left, and not even the steel door between him and her could completely ease his fear . . . or his anger at John Rainbird. Because Rainbird had foreseen this, and Rainbird had said nothing. And if he accused Rainbird of that, the Indian would only smile his chilling smile and ask who was the psychiatrist around here, anyway?

The tests had diminished her complex about starting fires until it was like an earthen dam that had sprung leaks in a dozen places. The tests had afforded her the practice necessary to refine a crude sledgehammer of power into something she could flick out with deadly precision, like a circus performer throwing a weighted knife.

And the tests had been the perfect object lesson. They had shown her, beyond a shadow of a doubt, who was in charge here.

She was.

4

When Hockstetter was gone, Charlie fell on the couch, her hands to her face, sobbing. Waves of conflicting emotion swept her · guilt and horror, indignation, even a kind of angry pleasure. But fear was the greatest of them all. Things had changed when she agreed to their tests; she feared things had changed forever. And now she didn't just *want* to see her father; she *needed* him. She needed him to tell her what to do next.

At first there had been rewards – walks outside with John, currying Necromancer, then riding him. She loved John and she loved Necromancer . . . if that stupid man could only have known how badly he had hurt her by saying Necromancer was hers when Charlie knew he never could be. The big gelding was only hers in her uneasy half-remembered dreams. But now . . . now . . . the tests themselves, the chance to use her power and feel it grow . . . *that* was starting to become the reward. It had become a terrible but compelling game. And she sensed she had barely scratched the surface. She was like a baby who has just learned how to walk.

She needed her father, she needed him to tell her what was right, what was wrong, whether to go on or to stop forever. If—

'If I *can* stop,' she whispered through her fingers.

That was the most frightening thing of all – no longer being sure that she *could* stop. And if she could not, what would that mean? Oh, what would that mean?

She began to cry again. She had never felt so dreadfully alone.

5

The funeral was a bad scene.

Andy had thought he would be okay; his headache was gone, and, after all, the funeral was only an excuse to be alone with Cap. He hadn't liked Pynchot, although in the end Pynchot had proved to be just a little too small to hate. His barely concealed arrogance and his unconcealed plea-sure at being on top of a fellow human being – because of those things and because of his overriding concern for Charlie, Andy had felt little guilt about the ricochet that he had inadvertently set up in Pynchot's mind. The ricochet that had finally torn the man apart.

The echo effect had happened before, but he had always had a chance to put things right again. It was something he had got pretty good at by the time he and Charlie had to run from New York City. There seemed to be land mines planted deep in almost every human brain, deep-seated fears and guilts, suicidal, schizophrenic, paranoid impulses – even murderous ones. A push caused a state of extreme suggestibility, and if a suggestion tended down one of those dark paths, it could destroy. One of his housewives in the Weight-Off program had begun to suffer frightening catatonic lapses. One of his businessmen had confessed a morbid urge to take his service pistol down from the closet and play Russian roulette with it, an urge that was somehow connected in his mind with a story by Edgar Allan Poe, 'William Wilson,' that he had read way back in high school. In both cases, Andy had been able to stop the echo before it sped up and turned into that lethal ricochet. In the case of the businessman, a quiet, sandy-haired, third-echelon bank officer, all it had taken was another push and the quiet suggestion that he had never read the Poe story at all. The connection – whatever it had been – was broken. The chance to break the echo had never come with Pynchot.

Cap talked restlessly of the man's suicide as they drove to the funeral through a cold, swishing autumn rain; he seemed to be trying to come to terms with it. He said he wouldn't have thought it possible for a man just to . . . to keep his arm in there once those blades had begun to chop and grind. But Pynchot had. Somehow Pynchot had. That was when the funeral started being bad for Andy.

The two of them attended only the graveside services, standing well back from the small group of friends and family, clustered under a bloom of black umbrellas. Andy discovered it was one thing to remember Pynchot's arrogance, the little-Caesar power-tripping of a small man who had no real power; to remember his endless and irritating nervous tic of a smile. It was quite another to look at his pallid, washed-out wife in her black suit and veiled hat, holding the hands of her two boys (the younger was about Charlie's age, and they both looked utterly stunned and out of it, as if drugged), knowing – as she must – that the friends and relatives must all know how her husband was found, dressed in her underwear, his right arm vaporized nearly to the elbow, sharpened like a living pencil, his blood splattered in the sink and on the Wood-Mode cabinets, chunks of his flesh—

Andy's gorge rose helplessly. He bent forward in the cold rain, struggling with it. The minister's voice rose and fell senselessly.

'I want to go,' Andy said. 'Can we go?'

'Yes, of course,' Cap said. He looked pale himself, old and not particularly well. 'I've been to quite enough funerals this year to hold me.'

They slipped away from the group standing around the fake grass, the flowers already drooping and spilling petals in this hard rain, the coffin on its runners over the hole in the ground. They walked side by side back toward the winding, graveled drive where Cap's economy-sized Chevy was parked near the rear of the funeral cortege. They walked under willows that dripped and rustled mysteriously. Three or four other men, barely seen, moved around them. Andy thought that he must know now how the President of the United States feels.

'Very bad for the widow and the little boys,' Cap said. 'The scandal, you know.'

'Will she . . . uh, will she be taken care of?'

'Very handsomely, in terms of money,' Cap said almost tonelessly. They were nearing the lane now. Andy could see Cap's orange Vega, parked on the verge. Two men were getting quietly into a Biscayne in front of it. Two more got into a gray Plymouth behind it. 'But nobody's going to be able to buy off those two little boys. Did you see their faces?'

Andy said nothing. Now he felt guilt; it was like a sharp sawblade working in his guts. Not even telling himself that his own position had been desperate would help. All he could do now was hold Charlie's face in front of him . . . Charlie and a darkly ominous figure behind her, a one-eyed pirate named John Rainbird who had wormed his way into her confidence so he could hasten the day when—

They got into the Vega and Cap started the engine. The Biscayne ahead pulled out and Cap followed. The Plymouth fell into place behind them.

Andy felt a sudden, almost eerie certainty that the push had deserted him again – that when he tried there would be nothing. As if to pay for the expression on the faces of the two boys.

But what else was there to do but try?

'We're going to have a little talk,' he said to Cap, and pushed. The push was there, and the headache settled in almost at once – the price he was going to have to pay for using it so soon after the last time. 'It won't interfere with your driving.'

Cap seemed to settle in his seat. His left hand, which had been moving toward his turnsignal, hesitated a moment and then went on. The Vega followed the lead car sedately between the big stone pillars and onto the main road.

'No, I don't think our little talk will interfere with my driving at all,' Cap said.

They were twenty miles from the compound; Andy had checked the odometer upon leaving and again upon arriving at the cemetery. A lot of it was over the highway Pynchot had told him about, 301. It was a fast road. He guessed he had no more than twenty-five minutes to arrange everything. He had thought of little else over the last two days and thought he had everything pretty well mapped out . . . but there was one thing he badly needed to know.

'How long can you and Rainbird ensure Charlie's co-operation, Captain Hollister?'

'Not much longer,' Cap said. 'Rainbird arranged things very cleverly so that in your absence, he's the only one really in control of her. The father surrogate.' In a low, almost chanting voice, he said, 'He's her father when her father isn't there.'

'And when she stops, she's to be killed?'

'Not immediately. Rainbird can keep her at it awhile longer.' Cap signaled his turn onto 301. 'He'll pretend we found out. Found out that they were talking. Found out that he was giving her advice on how to handle her . . . her problem. Found out he had passed notes to you.'

He fell silent, but Andy didn't need any more. He felt sick. He wondered if they had congratulated each other on how easy it was to fool a little kid, to win her affections in a lonely place and then twist her to their own purposes once they had earned her trust. When nothing else would work, just tell her that her only friend, John the orderly, was going to lose his job and maybe be prosecuted under the Official Secrets Act for presuming to be her friend. Charlie would do the rest on her own. Charlie would deal with them. She would continue to cooperate.

I hope I meet this guy soon. I really do.

But there was no time to think about that now . . . and if things went right, he would never have to meet Rainbird at all.

'I'm slated to go to Hawaii a week from today,' Andy said.

'Yes, that's right.'

'How?'

'By army transport plane.'

'Who did you contact to arrange that?'

'Puck,' Cap said immediately.

'Who's Puck, Captain Hollister?'

'Major Victor Puckeridge,' Cap said. 'At Andrews.'

'Andrews Air Force Base?'

'Yes, of course.'

'He's a friend?'

'We play golf.' Cap smiled vaguely. 'He slices.'

Wonderful news, Andy thought. His head was throbbing like a rotted tooth.

'Suppose you called him this afternoon and said you wanted to move that flight up by three days?'

'Yes?' Cap said doubtfully.

'Would that present a problem? A lot of paperwork?'

'Oh, no. Puck would slice right through the paperwork.' The smile reappeared, slightly odd and not really happy. 'He slices. Did I tell you that?'

'Yes. Yes, you did.'

'Oh. Good.'

The car hummed along at a perfectly legal fifty-five. The rain had mellowed to a steady mist. The windshield wipers clicked back and forth.

'Call him this afternoon, Cap. As soon as you get back.'

'Call Puck, yes. I was just thinking I ought to do that.'

'Tell him I've got to be moved on Wednesday instead of Saturday.'

Four days was not much time to recuperate – three weeks would have been more like it – but things were moving rapidly to a climax now. The endgame had begun. The fact was there, and Andy, out of necessity, recognized it. He wouldn't – couldn't – leave Charlie in the path of this Rainbird creature any longer than he had to.

'Wednesday instead of Saturday.'

'Yes. And then you tell Puck that you'll be coming along.'

'Coming along? I can't—'

Andy renewed the push. It hurt him, but he pushed hard. Cap jerked in his seat. The car swerved minutely on the road, and Andy thought again that he was practically begging to start up an echo in this guy's head.

'Coming along, yes. I'm coming along.'

'That's right,' Andy said grimly. 'Now – what sort of arrangements have you made about security?'

'No particular security arrangements,' Cap said. 'You're pretty much incapacitated by Thorazine. Also, you're tipped over and unable to use your mental-domination ability. It has become dormant.'

'Ah, yes,' Andy said, and put a slightly shaky hand to his forehead. 'Do you mean I'll be riding the plane alone?'

'No,' Cap said immediately, 'I believe I'll come along myself.'

'Yes, but other than the two of us?'

'There will be two Shop men along, partly to act as stewards and partly to keep an eye on you. SOP, you know. Protect the investment.'

'Only two operatives are scheduled to go with us? You're sure?'

'Yes.'

'And the flight crew, of course.'

'Yes.'

Andy looked out the window. They were halfway back now. This was the crucial part, and his head was already aching so badly that he was afraid he might forget something. If he did, the whole cardhouse would come tumbling down.

Charlie, he thought, and tried to hold on.

'Hawaii's a long way from Virginia, Captain Hollister. Will the plane make a refueling stop?'

'Yes.'

'Do you know where?'

'No.' Cap said serenely, and Andy could have punched him in the eye.

'When you speak to . . .' What was his name? He groped frantically in his tired, hurt mind and retrieved it. 'When you speak to Puck, find out where the plane will set down for refueling.'

'Yes, all right.'

'Just work it naturally into your conversation with him.'

'Yes, I'll find out where it's going to refuel by working it naturally into our conversation.' He glanced at Andy with thoughtful, dreamy eyes, and Andy found himself wondering if this man had given the order that Vicky be killed. There was a sudden urge to tell him to floor the accelerator pedal and drive into that oncoming bridge abutment. Except for Charlie. Charlie! his mind said. Hold on for Charlie. 'Did I tell you that Puck slices?' Cap said fondly.

'Yes. You did.' Think! Think, dammit! Somewhere near Chicago or Los Angeles seemed the most likely. But not at a civilian airport like O'Hare or L. A. International. The plane would refuel at an airbase. That in itself presented no problem to his rag of a plan – it was one of the few things that did not – as long as he could find out where in advance.

'We'd like to leave at three in the afternoon,' he told Cap.

'Three.'

'You'll see that this John Rainbird is somewhere else.'

'Send him away?' Cap said hopefully, and it gave Andy a chill to realize that Cap was afraid of Rainbird – quite badly afraid.

'Yes. It doesn't matter where.'

'San Diego?'

'All right.'

Now. Last lap. He was just going to make it; up ahead a green reflectorized sign pointed the way to the Longmont exit. Andy reached into the front pocket of his pants and pulled out a folded slip of paper. For the moment, he only held it in his lap, between first and second fingers.

'You're going to tell the two Shop guys who are going to Hawaii with us to meet us at the airbase,' he said. 'They're to meet us at Andrews. You and I will go to Andrews just as we are now.'

'Yes.'

Andy drew in a deep breath. 'But my daughter will be with us.'

'Her?' Cap showed real agitation for the first time. '*Her?* She's dangerous! She can't – we can't—'

'She wasn't dangerous until you people started playing with her,' Andy said harshly. 'Now she is coming with us and you are not to contradict me again, *do you understand that?*'

This time the car's swerve was more pronounced, and Cap moaned. 'She'll be coming with us,' he agreed. 'I won't contradict you anymore. That hurts. That hurts.'

But not as much as it hurts me.

Now his voice seemed to be coming from far away, through the blood-soaked net of pain that was pulling tighter and tighter around his brain. 'You're going to give her this,' Andy said, and passed the folded note to Cap. 'Give it to her today, but do it carefully, so that no one suspects.'

Cap tucked the note into his breast pocket. Now they were approaching the Shop; on their left were the double runs of electrified fence. Warning signs flashed past every fifty yards or so.

'Repeat back the salient points,' Andy said.

Cap spoke quickly and concisely – the voice of a man who had been trained in the act of recall since the days of his military-academy boyhood.

'I will arrange for you to leave for Hawaii on an army transport plane on Wednesday instead of Saturday. I will be coming with you; your daughter will also accompany us. The two Shop agents who will also be coming will meet

405

us at Andrews. I will find out from Puck where the plane will be refueling. I'll do that when I call him to change the flight date. I have a note to give your daughter. I'll give it to her after I finish talking to Puck, and I will do it in a way which will arouse no undue suspicion. And I will arrange to have John Rainbird in San Diego next Wednesday. I believe that covers the waterfront.'

'Yes,' Andy said, 'I believe it does.' He leaned back against the seat and closed his eyes. Jumbled fragments of past and present flew through his mind, aimlessly, jackstraws blown in the high wind. Did this really have a chance to work, or was he only buying death for both of them? They knew what Charlie could do now; they'd had firsthand experience. If it went wrong, they would finish their trip in the cargo bay of that army transport plane. In two boxes.

Cap paused at the guardbooth, rolled down his window, and handed over a plastic card, which the man on duty slipped into a computer terminal.

'Go ahead, sir,' he said.

Cap drove on.

'One last thing, Captain Hollister. You're going to forget all about this. You'll do each of the things we've discussed perfectly spontaneously. You'll discuss them with no one.'

'All right.'

Andy nodded. It wasn't all right, but it would have to do. The chances of setting up an echo here were extraordinarily high because he had been forced to push the man terribly hard and also because the instructions he had given Cap would go completely against the grain. Cap might be able to bring everything off simply by virtue of his position here. He might not. Right now Andy was too tired and in too much pain to care much.

He was barely able to get out of the car; Cap had to take

his arm to steady him. He was dimly aware that the cold autumn drizzle felt good against his face.

The two men from the Biscayne looked at him with a kind of cold disgust. One of them was Don Jules. Jules was wearing a blue sweatshirt that read U.S. OLYMPIC DRINKING TEAM.

Get a good look at the stoned fat man, Andy thought groggily. He was close to tears again, and his breath began to catch and hitch in his throat. You get a good look now, because if the fat guy gets away this time, he's going to blow this whole rotten cesspool right out of the swamp.

'There, there,' Cap said, and patted him on the shoulder with patronizing and perfunctory sympathy.

Just do your job, Andy thought, holding on grimly against the tears; he would not cry in front of them again, none of them. Just do your job, you son of a bitch.

6

Back in his apartment, Andy stumbled to his bed, hardly aware of what he was doing, and fell asleep. He lay like a dead thing for the next six hours, while blood seeped from a minute rupture in his brain and a number of brain cells grew white and died.

When he woke up, it was ten o'clock in the evening. The headache was still raging. His hands went to his face. The numb spots – one below his left eye, one on his left cheekbone, and one just below the jawbone – were back. This time they were bigger.

I can't push it much further without killing myself, he thought, and knew it was true. But he would hold on long enough to see this through, to give Charlie her chance, if he possibly could. Somehow he would hold on that long.

He went to the bathroom and got a glass of water. Then he lay down again, and after a long time, sleep returned.

His last waking thought was that Charlie must have read his note by now.

7

Cap Hollister had had an extremely busy day since getting back from Herm Pynchot's funeral. He had no more than got settled into his office when his secretary brought him an interdepartmental memo marked URGENT. It was from Pat Hockstetter. Cap told her to get him Vic Puckeridge on the phone and settled back to read the memo. I should get out more often, he thought; it aerates the brain cells or something. It had occurred to him on the ride back that there was really no sense waiting a whole week to ship McGee off to Maui; this Wednesday would be plenty late enough.

Then the memo captured his whole attention.

It was miles from Hockstetter's usual cool and rather baroque style; in fact, it was couched in nearly hysterical purple prose, and Cap thought with some amusement that the kid must have really hit Hockstetter with the chicken-stick. Hit him hard.

What it came down to was that Charlie had dug in her heels. It had come sooner than they had expected, that was all. Maybe – no, probably – even sooner than Rainbird had expected. Well, they would let it lie for a few days and then . . . then . . .

His train of thought broke up. His eyes took on a faraway, slightly puzzled cast. In his mind he saw a golf club, a five iron, whistling down and connecting solidly with a Spalding ball. He could hear that low, whistling *whhoooop* sound. Then the ball was gone, high and white against the blue sky. But it was slicing . . . slicing . . .

His brow cleared. What had he been thinking of? It wasn't like him to wander off the subject like that. Charlie had dug in her heels; that was what he had been thinking. Well, that was all right. Nothing to get bent out of shape about. They would let her alone for a while, until the weekend maybe, and then they could use Rainbird on her. She would light a lot of fires to keep Rainbird out of dutch.

His hand stole to his breast pocket and felt the small paper folded in there. In his mind he heard the soft swinging sound of a golf club again; it seemed to reverberate in the office. But now it was not a *whhoooop* sound. It was a quiet *sssssss*, almost the sound of a . . . a snake. That was unpleasant. He had always found snakes unpleasant, ever since earliest childhood.

With an effort, he swept all this foolishness about snakes and golf clubs from his mind. Perhaps the funeral had upset him more than he had thought.

The intercom buzzed and his secretary told him Puck was on line one. Cap picked up the phone and after some small talk asked Puck if there would be a problem if they decided to move the Maui shipment up from Saturday to Wednesday. Puck checked and said he saw no problem there at all.

'Say, around three in the afternoon?'

'No problem,' Puck repeated. 'Just don't move it up anymore, or we'll be in the bucket. This place is getting worse than the freeway at rush hour.'

'No, this is solid,' Cap said. 'And here's something else: I'm going along. But you keep that under your hat, okay?'

Puck burst into hearty baritone laughter. 'A little sun, fun, and grass skirts?'

'Why not?' Cap agreed. 'I'm escorting a valuable piece of cargo. I could justify myself in front of a Senate committee if I had to, I think. And I haven't had a real vacation since 1973. The goddamned Arabs and their oil bitched up the last week of that one.'

'I'll keep it to myself,' Puck agreed. 'You going to play

some golf while you're out there? I know of at least two great courses on Maui.'

Cap fell silent. He looked thoughtfully at the top of his desk, through it. The phone sagged away from his ear slightly.

'Cap? You there?'

Low and definite and ominous in this small, cozy study: *Sssssssssss—*

'Shit, I think we been cut off,' Puck muttered. 'Cap? Ca—'

'You still slicing the ball, old buddy?' Cap asked.

Puck laughed. 'You kidding? When I die, they're going to bury me in the fucking rough. Thought I lost you for a minute there.'

'I'm right here,' Cap said. 'Puck, are there snakes in Hawaii?'

Now it was Puck's turn to pause. 'Say again?'

'Snakes. Poisonous snakes.'

'I . . . gee, damn if I know. I can check it for you if it's important . . .' Puck's dubious tone seemed to imply that Cap employed about five thousand spooks to check just such things.

'No, that's okay,' Cap said. He held the telephone firmly against his ear again. 'Just thinking out loud, I guess. Maybe I'm getting old.'

'Not you, Cap. There's too much vampire in you.'

'Yeah, maybe. Thanks, goodbuddy.'

'No trouble at all. Glad you're getting away for a bit. Nobody deserves it more than you, after the last year you've put in.' He meant Georgia, of course; he didn't know about the McGees. Which meant, Cap thought wearily, that he didn't know the half of it.

He started to say good-bye and then added, 'By the way, Puck, where will that plane be stopping to refuel? Any idea?'

'Durban, Illinois,' Puck said promptly. 'Outside Chicago.'

Cap thanked him, said good-bye, hung up. His fingers went to the note in his pocket again and touched it. His eye fell on Hockstetter's memo. It sounded as if the girl had been pretty upset, too. Perhaps it wouldn't hurt if he went down and spoke to her, stroked her a little.

He leaned forward and thumbed the intercom.

'Yes, Cap?'

'I'll be going downstairs for a while,' he said. 'I should be back in thirty minutes or so.'

'Very good.'

He got up and left the study. As he did so, his hand stole to his breast pocket and felt the note there again.

8

Charlie lay on her bed fifteen minutes after Cap left, her mind in a total whirl of dismay, fear, and confused speculation. She literally didn't know what to think.

He had come at quarter of five, half an hour ago, and had introduced himself as Captain Hollister ('but please just call me Cap; everyone does'). He had a kindly, shrewd face that reminded her a little of the illustrations in *The Wind in the Willows*. It was a face she had seen somewhere recently, but she hadn't been able to place it until Cap jogged her memory. It had been he who had taken her back to her rooms after the first test, when the man in the white suit had bolted, leaving the door open. She had been so much in a fog of shock, guilt, and – yes – exhilarated triumph that it was really no wonder she hadn't been able to place his face. Probably she could have been escorted back to her apartment by Gene Simmons of Kiss without noticing it.

He talked in a smooth, convincing way that she immediately mistrusted.

He told her Hockstetter was concerned because she had declared the testing at an end until she saw her father. Charlie agreed that was so and would say no more, maintaining a stubborn silence . . . mostly out of fear. If you discussed your reasons for things with a smooth talker like this Cap, he would strip those reasons away one by one until it seemed that black was white and white black. The bare demand was better. Safer.

But he had surprised her.

'If that's the way you feel, okay,' he had said. The expression of surprise on her face must have been slightly comical, because he chuckled. 'It will take a bit of arranging, but—'

At the words 'a bit of arranging,' her face closed up again. 'No more fires,' she said. 'No more tests. Even if it takes you ten years to "arrange" it.'

'Oh, I don't think it will take that long,' he had said, not offended. 'It's just that I have people to answer to, Charlie. And a place like this runs on paperwork. But you don't have to light so much as a candle while I'm setting it up.'

'Good,' she said stonily, not believing him, not believing he was going to set anything up. 'Because I won't.'

'I think I ought to be able to arrange it . . . by Wednesday. Yes, by Wednesday, for sure.'

He had fallen suddenly silent. His head cocked slightly, as if he were listening to something just a bit too high-pitched for her to hear. Charlie looked at him, puzzled, was about to ask if he was all right, and then closed her mouth with a snap. There was something . . . something almost familiar about the way he was sitting.

'Do you really think I could see him on Wednesday?' she asked timidly.

'Yes, I think so,' Cap said. He shifted in his chair and

412

sighed heavily. His eye caught hers and he smiled a puzzled little smile . . . also familiar. Apropos of nothing at all, he said: 'Your dad plays a mean game of golf, I hear.'

Charlie blinked. So far as she knew, her father had never touched a golf club in his life. She got ready to say so . . . and then it came together in her mind and a dizzying burst of bewildered excitement ran through her.

(*Mr Merle! He's like Mr Merle!*)

Mr Merle had been one of Daddy's executives when they were in New York. Just a little man with light-blond hair and pink-rimmed glasses and a sweet, shy smile. He had come to get more confidence, like the rest of them. He worked in an insurance company or a bank or something. And Daddy had been very worried about Mr Merle for a while. It was a 'rick-o-shay.' It came from using the push. It had something to do with a story Mr Merle had read once. The push Daddy used to give Mr Merle more confidence made him remember that story in a bad way, a way that was making him sick. Daddy said the 'rick-o-shay' came from that story and it was bouncing around in Mr Merle's head like a tennis ball, only instead of finally stopping the way a bouncing tennis ball would, the memory of that story would get stronger and stronger until it made Mr Merle very sick. Only Charlie had got the idea that Daddy was afraid it might do more than make Mr Merle sick; he was afraid it might kill him. So he had kept Mr Merle after the others left one night and pushed him into believing he had never read that story at all. And after that, Mr Merle was all right. Daddy told her once that he hoped Mr Merle would never go to see a movie called *The Deer Hunter*, but he didn't explain why.

But before Daddy fixed him up, Mr Merle had looked like Cap did now.

She was suddenly positive that her father had pushed this man, and the excitement in her was like a tornado.

413

After hearing nothing about him except for the sort of general reports John sometimes brought her, after not seeing him or knowing where he was, it was in a strange way as if her father were suddenly in this room with her, telling her it was all right and that he was near.

Cap suddenly stood up. 'Well, I'll be going now. But I'll be seeing you, Charlie. And don't worry.'

She wanted to tell him not to go, to tell her about her dad, where he was, if he was okay . . . but her tongue was rooted to the bottom of her mouth.

Cap went to the door, then paused. 'Oh, almost forgot.' He crossed the room to her, took a folded piece of paper from his breast pocket, and handed it to her. She took it numbly, looked at it, and put it in her robe pocket. 'And when you're out riding that horse, you watch out for snakes,' he said confidentially. 'If a horse sees a snake, he is going to bolt. Every time. He'll—'

He broke off, raised a hand to his temple, and rubbed it. For a moment, he looked old and distracted. Then he shook his head a little, as if dismissing the thought. He bid her good-bye and left.

Charlie stood there for a long moment after he was gone. Then she took out the note, unfolded it, read what was written there and everything changed.

9

Charlie, love—

First thing: When you finish reading this, flush it down the toilet, okay?

Second thing: If everything goes the way I'm planning – the way I hope – we'll be out of here next Wednesday. The man who gave you this note is on our team, although he doesn't know he is . . . get it?

Third thing: I want you to be in the stables on Wednesday afternoon at one o'clock. I don't care how you do it - make another fire for them if that's what it takes. But be there.

Fourth, most important thing: *Don't trust this man John Rainbird*. This may upset you. I know you have trusted him. But he is a very dangerous man, Charlie. No way anyone's going to blame you for your trust in him - Hollister says he has been convincing enough to win an Academy Award. But know this: he was in charge of the men who took us prisoner at Granther's place. I hope this doesn't upset you too much, but knowing how you are, it probably will. It's no fun to find out that someone has been using you for his own purposes. Listen, Charlie: if Rainbird comes around - and he probably will - it is *very important* for him to think your feelings toward him haven't changed. He will be out of our way on Wednesday afternoon.

We are going to Los Angeles or Chicago, Charlie, and I think I know a way to arrange a press conference for us. I have an old friend named Quincey I'm counting on to help us, and I believe - I must believe - that he will come through for us if I can get in touch with him. A press conference would mean that the whole country would know about us. They may still want to keep us someplace, but we can be together. I hope you still want that as much as I do.

This wouldn't be so bad except that they want you to make fires for all the wrong reasons. If you have any doubts at all about running again, remember it is for the last time . . . and that it is what your mother would have wanted.

I miss you, Charlie, and love you lots.

Dad

10

John?
John in charge of the men that shot her and her father with tranquilizer darts?
John?

She rolled her head from side to side. The feeling of desolation in her, the heartbreak, seemed too great to be contained. There was no answer to this cruel dilemma. If she believed her father, she had to believe that John had been tricking her all along only to get her to agree to their tests. If she continued to believe in John, then the note she had crumpled and flushed down the toilet was a lie with her father's name signed to it. Either way, the hurt, the *cost*, was enormous. Was this what being grownup was about? Dealing with that hurt? That cost? If it was, she hoped she would die young.

She remembered looking up from Necromancer that first time and seeing John's smile . . . something in that smile that she didn't like. She remembered that she had never got any real feeling from him, as if he were closed off, or . . . or . . .

She tried to shunt the thought aside

(*or dead inside*)

but it would not be shunted.

But he wasn't *like* that. He *wasn't*. His terror in the blackout. His story about what those Cong had done to him. Could that be a lie? Could it, with the ruined map of his face to back up the tale?

Her head went back and forth on the pillow, back and forth, back and forth, in an endless gesture of negation. She did not want to think about it, did not, did not.

But couldn't help it.

Suppose . . . suppose they had made the blackout happen? Or suppose it had just happened . . . *and he had used it?*

(*NO! NO! NO! NO!*)

And yet her mind was now out of her conscious control, and it circled this maddening, horrifying patch of nettles with a kind of inexorable, cold determination. She was a bright girl, and she handled her chain of logic carefully, one bead at a time, telling it as a bitter penitent must tell the terrible beads of utter confession and surrender.

She remembered a TV show she had seen once, it had been on *Starsky and Hutch*. They put this cop into jail in the same cell with this bad guy who knew all about a robbery. They had called the cop pretending to be a jailbird a 'ringer.'

Was John Rainbird a ringer?

Her father said he was. And why would her father lie to her?

Who do you believe in? John or Daddy? Daddy or John?

No, no, no, her mind repeated steadily, monotonously . . . and to no effect. She was caught in a torture of doubt that no eight-year-old girl should have to stand, and when sleep came, the dream came with it. Only this time she saw the face of the silhouette, which stood to block the light.

11

'All right, what is it?' Hockstetter asked grumpily.

His tone indicated that it had better be pretty goddam good. He had been home watching James Bond on the Sunday Night Movie when the phone rang and a voice told him that they had a potential problem with the little girl. Over an open line, Hockstetter didn't dare ask what the problem was. He just went as he was, in a pair of paint-splattered jeans and a tennis shirt.

He had come frightened, chewing a Rolaid to combat the boil of sour acid in his stomach. He had kissed his wife good-bye, answering her raised eyebrows by saying it was a slight problem with some of the equipment and he would be right back. He wondered what she would say if she knew the 'slight problem' could kill him at any moment.

Standing here now, looking into the ghostly infrared

monitor they used to watch Charlie when the lights were out, he wished again that this was over and the little girl out of the way. He had never bargained for this when the whole thing was just an academic problem outlined in a series of blue folders. The truth was the burning cinderblock wall; the truth was spot temperatures of thirty thousand degrees or more; the truth was Brad Hyuck talking about whatever forces fired the engine of the universe; and the truth was that he was very scared. He felt as if he were sitting on top of an unstable nuclear reactor.

The man on duty, Neary, swung around when Hockstetter came in. 'Cap came down to visit her around five,' he said. 'She turned her nose up at supper. Went to bed early.'

Hockstetter looked into the monitor. Charlie was tossing restlessly on top of her bed, fully dressed. 'She looks like maybe she's having a nightmare.'

'One, or a whole series of them,' Neary said grimly. 'I called because the temperature in there has gone up three degrees in the last hour.'

'That's not much.'

'It is when a room's temperature-controlled the way that one is. Not much doubt that she's doing it.'

Hockstetter considered this, biting on a knuckle.

'I think someone should go in there and wake her up,' Neary said, finally drifting down to the bottom line.

'Is that what you got me down here for?' Hockstetter cried. 'To wake up a kid and give her a glass of warm milk?'

'I didn't want to exceed my authority,' Neary said stonily.

'No.' Hockstetter said, and had to bite down on the rest of the words. The little girl would have to be wakened if the temperature went much higher, and there was always a chance that if she was frightened enough, she might strike out at the first person she saw upon waking. After all, they had been busy removing the checks and balances on her pyrokinetic ability and had been quite successful.

'Where's Rainbird?' he asked.

Neary shrugged. 'Whipping his weasel in Winnipeg, for all I know. But as far as she's concerned, he's off duty. I think she'd be pretty suspicious if he showed up n—'

The digital thermometer inset on Neary's control board flicked over another degree, hesitated, and then flicked over two more in quick succession.

'Somebody's *got* to go in there,' Neary said, and now his voice was a bit unsteady. 'It's seventy-four in there now. What if she blows sky-high?'

Hockstetter tried to think what to do, but his brain seemed frozen. He was sweating freely now, but his mouth had gone as dry as a woolly sock. He wanted to be back home, tipped back in his La-Z-Boy, watching James Bond go after SMERSH or whatever the hell it was. He didn't want to be here. He didn't want to be looking at the red numbers under the little square of glass, waiting for them to suddenly blur upward in tens, thirties, hundreds, as they had when the cinderblock wall—

Think! he screamed at himself. *What do you do? What do you—*

'She just woke up,' Neary said softly.

They both stared intently at the monitor. Charlie had swung her legs over onto the floor and was sitting with her head down, her palms on her cheeks, her hair obscuring her face. After a moment she got up and went into the bathroom, face blank, eyes mostly closed – more asleep than awake, Hockstetter guessed.

Neary flicked a switch and the bathroom monitor came on. Now the picture was clear and sharp in the light of the fluorescent bar. Hockstetter expected her to urinate, but Charlie just stood inside the door, looking at the toilet.

'Oh Mother of Mary, look at that,' Neary murmured.

The water in the toilet bowl had begun to steam slightly. This went on for more than a minute (one-twenty-one in Neary's log), and then Charlie went to the toilet, flushed it, urinated, flushed it again, drank two glasses of water, and went back to bed. This time her sleep seemed easier, deeper. Hockstetter glanced at the thermometer and saw it had dropped four degrees. As he watched, it dropped another degree, to sixty-nine – just one degree above the suite's normal temperature.

He remained with Neary until after midnight. 'I'm going home to bed. You'll get this written up, won't you?'

'That's what I get paid for,' Neary said stolidly.

Hockstetter went home. The next day he wrote a memo suggesting that any further gains in knowledge that further testing might provide ought to be balanced against the potential hazards, which in his opinion were growing too fast for comfort.

12

Charlie remembered little of the night. She remembered being hot, getting up, getting rid of the heat. She remembered the dream but only vaguely – a sense of freedom

(up ahead was the light – the end of the forest, open land where she and Necromancer would ride forever)

mingled with a sense of fear and a sense of loss. It had been his face, it had been John's face, all along. And perhaps she had known it. Perhaps she had known that

(the woods are burning don't hurt the horses o please don't hurt the horses)

all along.

When she woke up the next morning, her fear, confusion, and desolation had begun their perhaps inevitable change into a bright, hard gem of anger.

He better be out of the way on Wednesday, she thought. *He just better. If it's true about what he did, he better not come near me or Daddy on Wednesday.*

13

Late that morning Rainbird came in, rolling his wagon of cleaning products, mops, sponges, and rags. His white orderly's uniform flapped softly around him.

'Hi, Charlie,' he said.

Charlie was on the sofa, looking at a picture book. She glanced up, her face pale and unsmiling in that first moment . . . cautious. The skin seemed stretched too tightly over her cheekbones. Then she smiled. But it was not, Rainbird thought, her usual smile.

'Hello, John.'

'You don't look so great this morning, Charlie, you should forgive me for sayin.'

'I didn't sleep very well.'

'Oh yeah?' He knew she hadn't. That fool Hockstetter was almost foaming at the mouth because she'd popped the temperature five or six degrees in her sleep. 'I'm sorry to hear that. Is it your dad?'

'I guess so.' She closed her book and stood up. 'I think I'll go and lie down for a while. I just don't feel like talking or anything.'

'Sure. Gotcha.'

He watched her go, and when the bedroom door had clicked shut, he went into the kitchen to fill his floorbucket. Something about the way she had looked at him. The smile. He didn't like it. She'd had a bad night, yes, okay. Everyone has them from time to time, and the next morning you snap at your wife or stare right through the paper or whatever. Sure. But . . . something inside had begun to jangle an alarm. It had been weeks since she had looked at him that way. She hadn't come to him this morning, eager and glad to see him, and he didn't like that, either. She had kept her own space today. It disturbed him. Maybe it was just the aftermath of a bad night, and maybe the bad dreams of the night before had just been caused by something she ate, but it disturbed him all the same.

And there was something else nibbling at him: Cap had been down to see her late yesterday afternoon. He had never done that before.

Rainbird set down his bucket and hooked the mop squeegee over its rim. He dunked the mop, wrung it out, and began to mop the floor in long, slow strokes. His mauled face was calm and at rest.

Have you been putting a knife in my back, Cap? Figure you've got enough? Or maybe you just went chickenshit on me.

If that last was true, then he had badly misjudged Cap. Hockstetter was one thing. Hockstetter's experience with Senate committees and subcommittees was almost zilch; a piddle here and a piddle there. Corroborative stuff. He could allow himself the luxury of indulging his fear. Cap couldn't. Cap would know there was no such thing as sufficient evidence, especially when you were dealing with something as potentially explosive (pun *certainly* intended) as Charlie McGee. And it wasn't just funding Cap would be asking for; when he got before that closed session, the most dread and mystic of all bureaucratic phrases would fall from his lips: *long-term funding.* And in the background, lurking unspoken but potent, the implication of eugenics. Rainbird guessed that in the end, Cap would find it impossible to avoid having a group of senators down here to watch Charlie perform. Maybe they should be allowed

422

to bring their kids, Rainbird thought, mopping and rinsing. Better than the trained dolphins at Sea World.

Cap would know he needed all the help he could get.

So why had he come to see her last night? Why was he rocking the boat?

Rainbird squeezed his mop and watched dirty gray water run back into the bucket. He looked through the open kitchen door at the closed door of Charlie's bedroom. She had shut him out and he didn't like that.

It made him very, very nervous.

14

On that early October Monday night, a moderate wind-storm came up from the Deep South, sending black clouds flying raggedly across a full moon that lolled pregnantly just above the horizon. The first leaves fell, rattling across the neatly manicured lawns and grounds for the indefatigable corps of groundskeepers to remove in the morning. Some of them swirled into the duckpond, where they floated like small boats. Autumn had come to Virginia again.

In his quarters, Andy was watching TV and still getting over his headache. The numb spots on his face had diminished in size but had not disappeared. He could only hope he would be ready by Wednesday afternoon. If things worked as he had planned, he could keep the number of times he would have to actively push to a bare minimum. If Charlie had got his note, and if she was able to meet him at the stables across the way . . . then *she* would become his push, his lever, his weapon. Who was going to argue with him when he had the equivalent of a nuclear rifle in his possession?

Cap was at home in Longmont Hills. As on the night Rainbird had visited him, he had a snifter of brandy, and music was coming from the stereo at low volume. Chopin tonight. Cap was sitting on the couch. Across the room, leaning below a pair of van Gogh prints, was his old and scuffed golf bag. He had fetched it from the basement, where a rickrack of sports equipment had built up over the twelve years he had lived here with Georgia, while not on assignment somewhere else in the world. He had brought the golf bag into the living room because he couldn't seem to get golf off his mind lately. Golf, or snakes.

He had brought the golf bag up meaning to take out each of the irons and his two putters and look them over, touch them, see if that wouldn't ease his mind. And then one of the irons had seemed to . . . well, it was funny (ridiculous, in fact), but one of the irons had seemed to *move*. As if it wasn't a golf club at all but a snake, a poison snake that had crawled in there—

Cap dropped the bag against the wall and scuttled away. Half a glass of brandy had stopped the minute shakes in his hands. By the time he finished the glass, he might be able to tell himself they had never trembled at all.

He started the glass on its way to his mouth and then halted. There it was again! Movement . . . or just a trick of his eyes?

Trick of his eyes, most definitely. There were no snakes in his damned golf bag. Just clubs he hadn't been using enough lately. Too busy. And he was a pretty good golfer, too. No Nicklaus or Tom Watson, hell no, but he could keep it on the course. Not always slicing, like Puck. Cap didn't like to slice the ball, because then you were in the rough, the tall grass, and sometimes there were—

Get hold of yourself. Just get hold of yourself. Is you still the Captain or is you ain't?

The trembling was back in his fingers again. What had done this. What in God's name had done this? Sometimes it seemed that there was an explanation, a perfectly reasonable one – something, perhaps, that someone had said and he just . . . couldn't remember. But at other times

(*like now Jesus Christ like now*)

it felt as if he were on the verge of a nervous breakdown. It felt as if his brain was being pulled apart like warm taffy by these alien thoughts he couldn't get rid of.

(*is you the Captain or is you ain't?*)

Cap suddenly threw his brandy glass into the fireplace, where it shattered like a bomb. A strangled sound – a sob – escaped his tight throat like something rotten that had to be sicked up whatever the miserable cost. Then he made himself cross the room (and he went at a drunken, stiltlike lurch), grab the strap of his golf bag (again something seemed to move and shift in there . . . to *shifffft* . . . and *hissssss*) and slip it over his shoulder. He hauled it back into the shadow-draped cavern of the cellar, going on nothing but guts, drops of sweat perched huge and clear on his forehead. His face was frozen in a grimace of fear and determination.

Nothing there but golf clubs, nothing there but golf clubs, his mind chanted over and over again, and at every step of the way he expected something long and brown, something with beady black eyes and small sharp fangs dripping poison, to slither out of the bag and jab twin hypos of death into his neck.

Back in his own living room he felt much better. Except for a nagging headache, he felt much better.

He could think coherently again.

Almost.

He got drunk.

And in the morning he felt better again.

For a while.

15

Rainbird spent that windy Monday night gathering information. Disturbing information. First he went in and talked to Neary, the man who had been watching the monitors when Cap paid his visit to Charlie the night before.

'I want to see the videotapes,' Rainbird said.

Neary didn't argue. He set Rainbird up in a small room down the hall with the Sunday tapes and a Sony deck complete with close-up and freeze-frame features. Neary was glad to be rid of him and only hoped that Rainbird wouldn't be coming back and wanting something else. The girl was bad enough. Rainbird, in his own reptilian way, was somehow worse.

The tapes were three-hour Scotch jobs, marked from 0000 to 0300 and so on. Rainbird found the one with Cap on it and watched it four times, not moving except to rewind the tape at the point where Cap said, 'Well, I'll be going now. But I'll be seeing you, Charlie. And don't worry.'

But there was plenty in that tape that worried John Rainbird.

He didn't like the way Cap looked. He seemed to have got older; at times while he was talking to Charlie he seemed to lose the thread of what he was saying, like a man on the edge of senility. His eyes had a vague, bemused look that was uncannily similar to the look Rainbird associated with the onset of combat fatigue, which a comrade-in-arms had once aptly dubbed The Brain Squitters and Trots.

I think I ought to be able to arrange it . . . by Wednesday. Yes, by Wednesday, for sure.

Now why in the name of God had he said that?

Setting up an expectation like that in the kid's mind was

the surest way Rainbird could think of to blow further testing right out of the water. The obvious conclusion was that Cap was playing his own little game – intriguing in the best Shop tradition.

But Rainbird didn't believe it. Cap didn't look like a man engaged in an intrigue. He looked like a man who was profoundly fucked up. That remark about Charlie's father playing golf, for instance. That had come right out of left field. It bore on nothing they had said before and nothing they said afterward. Rainbird toyed briefly with the idea that it was some sort of code phrase, but that was patently ridiculous. Cap knew that everything that went on in Charlie's rooms was monitored and recorded, subject to almost constant review. He was capable of disguising a trip phrase better than that. A remark about golf. It just hung there, irrelevant and puzzling.

And then there was the last thing.

Rainbird played it over and over. Cap pauses. *Oh, almost forgot.* And then he hands her something that she looks at curiously and then puts away in the pocket of her robe.

With Rainbird's finger on the buttons of the Sony VCR, Cap said *Oh, almost forgot* half a dozen times. He passed the thing to her half a dozen times. At first Rainbird thought it was a stick of gum, and then he used the freeze-frame and zoom gadgets. That convinced him that it was, very likely, a note.

Cap, what the fuck are you up to?

16

He spent the rest of that night and the early hours of Tuesday morning at a computer console, calling up every scrap of information he could think of on Charlie McGee, trying to make out some kind of pattern. And there was nothing. His head began to ache from eyestrain.

He was getting up to shut off the lights when a sudden thought, a totally off-the-wall connection, occurred to him. It had to do not with Charlie but with the portly, drugged-out cipher that was her father.

Pynchot. Pynchot had been in charge of Andy McGee, and last week Herman Pynchot had killed himself in one of the most grisly ways Rainbird could imagine. Obviously unbalanced. Crackers. Toys in the attic. Cap takes Andy to the funeral – maybe a little strange when you really stopped to think about it, but in no way remarkable.

The Cap starts to act a little weird – talking about golf and passing notes.

That's ridiculous. He's tipped over.

Rainbird stood with his hand on the light switches. The computer-console screen glowed a dull green, the color of a freshly dug emerald.

Who says he's tipped over? Him?

There was another strange thing here as well, Rainbird suddenly realized. Pynchot had given up on Andy, had decided to send him to the Maui compound. If there was nothing Andy could do that would demonstrate what Lot Six was capable of, there was no reason to keep him around at all . . . and it would be safer to separate him from Charlie. Fine. But then Pynchot abruptly changes his mind and decides to schedule another run of tests.

Then Pynchot decides to clean out the garbage disposal . . . while it's still running.

Rainbird walked back to the computer console. He paused, thinking, than tapped HELLO COMPUTER/ QUERY STATUS ANDREW MCGEE 14112/ FURTHER TESTING/MAUI INSTALLATION/Q4

PROCESS, the computer flashed. And a moment later: HELLO RAINBIRD/ANDREW MCGEE 14112 NO FURTHER TESTING/AUTHORIZATION/'STARLING'/ SCHEDULED DEPARTURE FOR MAUI 1500 HOURS

Rainbird glanced at his watch. October 9 was Wednesday. Andy was leaving Longmont for Hawaii tomorrow afternoon. Who said so? Authorization Starling said so, and that was Cap himself. But this was the first Rainbird knew of it.

His fingers danced over the keys again.

QUERY PROBABILITY ANDREW MCGEE 14112/
SUPPOSED MENTAL DOMINATION ABILITY/
CROSS-REF HERMON PYNCHOT

He had to pause to look up Pynchot's code number in the battered and sweat-stained code book he had folded into his back pocket before coming down here.

14409 Q4

PROCESS, the computer replied, and then remained blank so long that Rainbird began to think that he had misprogrammed and would end up with nothing but a '609' for his trouble.

Then the computer flashed ANDREW MCGEE 14112/MENTAL DOMINATION PROBABILITY 35%/
CROSS-REF HERMAN PYNCHOT/BREAK

Thirty-five percent?

How was that possible?

All right, Rainbird thought. Let's leave Pynchot out of the goddam equation and see what happens.

He tapped out QUERY PROBABILITY ANDREW MCGEE 14112/SUPPOSED MENTAL DOMINATION ABILITY Q4

PROCESS, the computer flashed, and this time its response came within a space of fifteen seconds. ANDREW MCGEE 14112/MENTAL DOMINATION PROBABILITY 2%/BREAK

Rainbird leaned back and closed his good eye and felt a

kind of triumph through the sour thud in his head. He had asked the important questions backward, but that was the price humans paid for their intuitive leaps, leaps a computer knew nothing about, even though it had been programmed to say 'Hello,' 'Good-bye,' 'I am sorry [programmer's name],' 'That is too bad,' and 'Oh shit.'

The computer didn't believe there was much of a probability Andy had retained his mental-domination ability . . . until you added in the Pynchot factor. Then the percent jumped halfway to the moon.

He tapped QUERY WHY SUPPOSED MENTAL DOMINATION ABILITY ANDREW MCGEE 14112 (PROBABILITY) RISES FROM 2% to 35% WHEN CROSS-REFERENCED W/HERMAN PYNCHOT 14409 Q4

PROCESS, the computer answered, and then: HERMAN PYNCHOT 14409 ADJUDGED SUICIDE/ PROBABILITY TAKES INTO ACCOUNT ANDREW MCGEE 14112 MAY HAVE CAUSED SUICIDE/ MENTAL DOMINATION/BREAK

There it was, right here in the banks of the biggest and most sophisticated computer in the Western Hemisphere. Only waiting for someone to ask it the right questions.

Suppose I feed it what I suspect about Cap as a certainty? Rainbird wondered, and decided to go ahead and do it. He dragged out his code book again and looked up Cap's number.

FILE, he tapped. CAPTAIN JAMES HOLLISTER 16040/ATTENDED FUNERAL OF HERMAN PYNCHOT 14409 W/ANDREW MCGEE 14112 F4

FILED, the computer returned.

FILE, Rainbird tapped back. CAPTAIN JAMES HOLLISTER 16040/CURRENTLY SHOWING SIGNS OF GREAT MENTAL STRESS F4

609, the computer returned. It apparently didn't know 'mental stress' from 'Shinola.'

430

'Bite my bag,' Rainbird muttered, and tried again.

FILE/CAPTAIN JAMES HOLLISTER 16040/ CURRENTLY BEHAVING COUNTER TO DIRECTIVES REF CHARLENE MCGEE 14111 F4

FILED

'File it, you whore,' Rainbird said. 'Let's see about this.' His fingers went back to the keys.

QUERY PROBABILITY ANDREW MCGEE 14112/ SUPPOSED MENTAL DOMINATION ABILITY/ CROSS-REF HERMAN PYNCHOT 14409/CROSS-REF CAPTAIN JAMES HOLLISTER 16040 Q4

PROCESS, the computer showed, and Rainbird sat back to wait, watching the screen. Two percent was too low. Thirty-five percent was still not betting odds. But—

The computer now flashed this: ANDREW MCGEE 14112/MENTAL DOMINATION PROBABILITY 90%/CROSS-REF HERMAN PYNCHOT 14409/ CROSS-REF CAPTAIN JAMES HOLLISTER 16040 BREAK

Now it was up to ninety percent. And those *were* betting odds.

And two other things that John Rainbird would have bet on were, one, that what Cap handed to the girl was indeed a note to Charlie from her father and, two, that it contained some sort of escape plan.

'You dirty old son of a bitch,' John Rainbird murmured – not without admiration.

Pulling himself to the computer again, Rainbird tapped

600 GOODBYE COMPUTER 600

604 GOODBYE RAINBIRD 604

Rainbird turned off the keyboard and began to chuckle.

17

Rainbird went back to the house where he was staying and fell asleep with his clothes on. He woke up just after noon on Tuesday and called Cap to tell him he wouldn't be in that afternoon. He had come down with a bad cold, possibly the onset of the grippe, and he didn't want to chance passing it on to Charlie.

'Hope that won't keep you from going to San Diego tomorrow,' Cap said briskly.

'San Diego?'

'Three files,' Cap said. 'Top secret. I need a courier. You're it. Your plane leaves from Andrews at oh-seven-hundred tomorrow.'

Rainbird thought fast. This was more of Andy McGee's work. McGee knew about him. Of course he did. That had been in the note to Charlie, along with whatever crazy escape plan McGee had concocted. And that explained why the girl had acted so strangely yesterday. Either going to Herman Pynchot's funeral or coming back, Andy had given Cap a good hard shove and Cap had spilled his guts about everything. McGee was scheduled to fly out of Andrews tomorrow afternoon; now Cap told him that he, Rainbird, was going tomorrow morning. McGee was using Cap to get him safely out of the way first. He was—

'Rainbird? Are you there?'

'I'm here,' he said. 'Can you send someone else? I feel pretty punky, Cap.'

'No one I trust as well as you,' Cap replied. 'This stuff is dynamite. We wouldn't want . . . any snake in the grass to . . . to get it.'

'Did you say "snakes"?' Rainbird asked.

'Yes! Snakes!' Cap fairly screamed.

McGee had pushed him, all right, and some sort of slow-motion avalanche was going on inside of Cap Hollister.

Rainbird suddenly had the feeling – no, the intuitive certainty– that if he refused Cap and just kept hammering away, Cap would blow up . . . the way Pynchot had blown up.

Did he want to do that?

He decided he did not.

'All right,' he said. 'I'll be on the plane. Oh-seven-hundred. And all the goddam antibiotics I can swallow. You're a bastard, Cap.'

'I can prove my parentage beyond a shadow of a doubt,' Cap said, but the badinage was forced and hollow. He sounded relieved and shaky.

'Yeah, I'll bet.'

'Maybe you'll get in a round of golf while you're out there.'

'I don't play—' Golf. He had mentioned golf to Charlie as well – golf and snakes. Somehow those two things were part of the weird merry-go-round McGee had set in motion in Cap's brain. 'Yeah, maybe I will,' he said.

'Get to Andrews by oh-six-thirty,' Cap said, 'and ask for Dick Folsom. He's Major Puckeridge's aide.'

'All right,' Rainbird said. He had no intention of being anywhere near Andrews Air Force Base tomorrow. 'Good-bye, Cap.'

He hung up, then sat on the bed. He pulled on his old desert boots and started planning.

18

HELLO COMPUTER/QUERY STATUS JOHN RAIN-BIRD 14222/ANDREW AFB (DC) TO SAN DIEGO (CA) FINAL DESTINATION/Q9

HELLO CAP/STATUS JOHN RAINBIRD14222/ANDREWS (DC) TO SAN DIEGO (CA) FINAL DESTINATION/LEAVES ANDREWS AFB 0700 HRS EST/STATUS OK/BREAK

Computers are children, Rainbird thought, reading this message. He had simply punched in Cap's new code – which Cap would have been stunned to know he had – and as far as the computer was concerned, he was Cap. He began to whistle tunelessly. It was just after sunset, and the Shop moved somnolently along the channels of routine.

FILE TOP SECRET
CODE PLEASE
CODE 19180
CODE 19180, the computer returned. READY TO FILE TOP SECRET

Rainbird hesitated only briefly and then tapped FILE/JOHN RAINBIRD 14222/ANDREWS (DC) TO SAN DIEGO (CA) FINAL DESTINATION/ CANCEL/CANCEL/CANCEL F9 (19180)
FILED

Then, using the code book, Rainbird told the computer whom to inform of the cancellation: Victor Puckeridge and his aide, Richard Folsom. These new instructions would be in the midnight telex to Andrews, and the plane on which he was to hitch a ride would simply take off without him. No one would know a thing, including Cap.

600 GOODBYE COMPUTER 600
604 GOODBYE CAP 604

Rainbird pushed back from the keyboard. It would be perfectly possible to put a stop to the whole thing tonight, of course. But that would not be conclusive. The computer would back him up to a certain degree, but computer probabilities do not butter any bread. Better to stop them after the thing had begun, with everything hanging out. More amusing, too.

The whole thing was amusing. While they had been watching the girl, the man had regained his ability or had successfully hidden it from them all along. He was likely ditching his medication. Now he was running Cap as well, which means that he was only one step away from running the organization that had taken him prisoner in the first place. It really was quite funny; Rainbird had learned that endgames often were.

He didn't know exactly what McGee had planned, but he could guess. They would go to Andrews, all right, only Charlie would be with them. Cap could get her off the Shop grounds without much trouble – Cap and probably no one else on earth. They would go to Andrews, but not to Hawaii. It might be that Andy had planned for them to disappear into Washington, D.C. Or maybe they would get off the plane at Durban and Cap would be programmed to ask for a staff car. In that case it would be Shytown they would disappear into – only to reappear in screaming Chicago *Tribune* headlines a few days later.

He had played briefly with the idea of not standing in their way at all. That would be amusing, too. He guessed that Cap would end up in a mental institution, raving about golf clubs and snakes in the grass, or dead by his own hand. As for the Shop: might as well imagine what would happen to an anthill with a quart jar of nitroglycerine planted beneath it. Rainbird guessed that no more than five months after the press got its first whiff of the Strange Ordeal of the Andrew McGee Family, the Shop would cease to exist. He felt no fealty to the Shop and never had. He was his own man, crippled soldier of fortune, copper-skinned angel of death, and the status quo here didn't mean bullrag in a pasture to him. It was not the Shop that owned his loyalty at this point.

It was Charlie.

The two of them had an appointment. He was going to look into her eyes, and she was going to look into his . . . and it might well be that they would step out together, in flames. The fact that he might be saving the world from some almost unimaginable armageddon by killing her had not played a part in his calculations, either. He owed the world no more fealty than he did the Shop. It was the world as much as the Shop that had cast him rootless from a closed desert society that might have been his only salvation . . . or, lacking that, have turned him into a harmless Sterno-guzzling Injun Joe pumping gas at a 76 station or selling fake kachina dolls at a shitty little roadside stand somewhere along the highway between Flagstaff and Phoenix.

But Charlie, Charlie!

They had been locked in a long waltz of death since that endless night of darkness during the power blackout. What he had only suspected that early morning in Washington when he had done Wanless had developed into an irrefutable certainty: the girl was his. But it would be an act of love, not of destruction, because the converse was almost certainly true as well.

It was acceptable. In many ways he wanted to die. And to die at her hands, in her flames, would be an act of contrition . . . and possibly of absolution.

Once she and her father were together again, she would become a loaded gun . . . no, a loaded flamethrower.

He would watch her and he would let the two of them get together. What would happen then? Who knew?

And wouldn't knowing spoil the fun?

19

That night Rainbird went to Washington and found a hungry lawyer who worked late hours. To this lawyer he gave three hundred dollars in small bills. And in the lawyer's office, John Rainbird neatened his few affairs in order to be ready for the next day.

436

Firestarter

1

At six o'clock on Wednesday morning, Charlie McGee got up, took off her nightgown, and stepped into the shower. She washed her body and her hair, then turned the water to cold and stood shivering under the spray for a minute more. She toweled dry and then dressed carefully – cotton underpants, silk slip, dark-blue knee socks, her denim jumper. She finished by putting on her scuffed and comfortable loafers.

She hadn't thought she would be able to sleep at all last night; she had gone to bed full of fear and nervous excitement. But she had slept. And dreamed incessantly not of Necromancer and the run through the woods but of her mother. That was peculiar, because she didn't think of her mother as often as she used to; at times her face seemed misty and distant in her memory, like a faded photograph. But in her dreams of last night, her mother's face – her laughing eyes, her warm, generous mouth – had been so clear that Charlie might last have seen her just the day before.

Now, dressed and ready for the day, some of the unnatural lines of strain had gone out of her face and she seemed calm. On the wall beside the door leading into the kitchenette there was a call button and a speaker grille set into a brushed-chrome plate just below the light switch. She pressed the button now.

'Yes, Charlie?'

She knew the owner of the voice only as Mike. At seven

o'clock – about half an hour from now – Mike went off and Louis came on. 'I want to go out to the stables this afternoon,' she said, 'and see Necromancer. Will you tell someone?'

'I'll leave a note for Dr Hockstetter, Charlie.'

'Thank you.' She paused, just for a moment. You got to know their voices. Mike, Louis, Gary. You got pictures of how they must look in your mind, the way you got pictures of how the DJs you heard on the radio must look. You got to like them. She suddenly realized that she would almost certainly never talk to Mike again.

'Was there something else, Charlie?'

'No, Mike. Have . . . have a good day.'

'Why, thank you, Charlie.' Mike sounded both surprised and pleased. 'You too.'

She turned on the TV and tuned to a cartoon show that came on every morning over the cable. Popeye was inhaling spinach through his pipe and getting ready to beat the sauce out of Bluto. One o'clock seemed an age away.

What if Dr Hockstetter said, she couldn't go out?

On the TV screen, they were showing a cutaway view of Popeye's muscles. There were about sixteen turbine engines in each one.

He better not say that. He better not. Because I'm going. One way or the other, I'm going.

2

Andy's rest hadn't been as easy or as healing as his daughter's. He had tossed and turned, sometimes dozing, then starting out of the doze just as it began to deepen because the terrible leading edge of some nightmare touched his mind. The only one he could remember was Charlie staggering down the aisle between the stalls in the

438

stable, her head gone and red-blue flames spouting from her neck instead of blood.

He had meant to stay in bed until seven o'clock, but when the digital face of the clock beside the bed got to 6:15, he could wait no longer. He swung out and headed for the shower.

Last night at just past nine, Pynchot's former assistant, Dr Nutter, had come in with Andy's walking papers. Nutter, a tall, balding man in his late fifties, was bumbling and avuncular. Sorry to be losing you; hope you enjoy your stay in Hawaii; wish I was going with you, ha-ha; please sign this.

The paper Nutter wanted him to sign was a list of his few personal effects (including his keyring, Andy noticed with a nostalgic pang). He would be expected to inventory them once in Hawaii and initial another sheet that said that they had, indeed, been returned. They wanted him to sign a paper concerning his personal effects after they had murdered his wife, chased him and Charlie across half the country, and then kidnapped and held them prisoner: Andy found that darkly hilarious and Kafkaesque. *I sure wouldn't want to lose any of those keys*, he thought, scrawling his signature; *I might need one of them to open a bottle of soda with sometime, right, fellows?*

There was also a carbon of the Wednesday schedule, neatly initialed by Cap at the bottom of the page. They would be leaving at twelve-thirty, Cap picking Andy up at his quarters. He and Cap would proceed toward the eastern checkpoint, passing Parking Area C, where they would pick up an escort of two cars. They would then drive to Andrews and board the plane at approximately fifteen hundred hours. There would be one stop for refueling – at Durban Air Force Base, near Chicago.

All right, Andy thought. *Okay.*

He dressed and began to move about the apartment,

packing his clothes, shaving tackle, shoes, bedroom slippers. They had provided him with two Samsonite suitcases. He remembered to do it all slowly, moving with the careful concentration of a drugged man.

After he found out about Rainbird from Cap, his first thought had been a hope that he would meet him: it would be such a great pleasure to push the man who had shot Charlie with the tranquilizer dart and later betrayed her in even more terrible fashion, to put his gun to his temple and pull the trigger. But he no longer wanted to meet Rainbird. He wanted no surprises of any kind. The numb spots on his face had shrunk to pinpricks, but they were still there – a reminder that if he had to overuse the push, he would very likely kill himself.

He only wanted things to go off smoothly.

His few things were packed all too soon, leaving him with nothing to do but sit and wait. The thought that he would be seeing his daughter again soon was like a small coal of warmth in his brain.

To him too one o'clock seemed an age away.

3

Rainbird didn't sleep at all that night. He arrived back from Washington around five-thirty A.M., garaged his Cadillac, and sat at his kitchen table drinking cup after cup of coffee. He was waiting for a call from Andrews, and until that call came, he would not rest easy. It was still theoretically possible for Cap to have found out what he had done with the computer. McGee had messed up Cap Hollister pretty well, but it still did not pay to underestimate.

Around six-forty-five, the telephone rang. Rainbird set his coffee cup down, rose, went into the living room, and answered it. 'Rainbird here.'

'Rainbird? This is Dick Folsom at Andrews. Major Puckeridge's aide.'

'You woke me up, man,' Rainbird said. 'I hope you catch crabs as big as orange crates. That's an old Indian curse.'

'You've been scrubbed,' Folsom said. 'I guess you knew.'

'Yes, Cap called me himself last night.'

'I'm sorry,' Folsom said. 'It's standard operating procedure, that's all.'

'Well, you operated in standard fashion. Can I go back to sleep now?'

'Yeah. I envy you.'

Rainbird uttered the obligatory chuckle and hung up. He went back into the kitchen, picked up his coffee cup, went to the window, looked out, saw nothing.

Floating dreamily through his mind was the Prayer for the Dead.

4

Cap did not arrive in his office that morning until almost ten-thirty, an hour and a half later than usual. He had searched his small Vega from stem to stern before leaving the house. He had become sure during the night that the car was infested with snakes. The search had taken him twenty minutes – the need to make sure there were no rattlers or copperheads (or something even more sinister and exotic) nesting in the darkness of the trunk, dozing on the fugitive warmth of the engine block, curled up in the glove compartment. He had pushed the glove-compartment button with a broomhandle, not wanting to be too close in case some hissing horror should leap out at him, and when a map of Virginia tumbled out of the square hole in the dash, he had nearly screamed.

Then, halfway to the Shop, he had passed the Greenway

Golf Course and had pulled over onto the shoulder to watch with a dreamy sort of concentration as the golfers played through the eighth and ninth. Every time one of them sliced into the rough, he was barely able to restrain a compulsion to step out of the car and yell for them to beware of snakes in the tall grass.

At last the blare of a ten-wheeler's airhorn (he had parked with his lefthand wheels still on the pavement) had startled him out of his daze and he drove on.

His secretary greeted him with a pile of overnight telex cables, which Cap simply took without bothering to shuffle through them to see if there was anything hot enough to demand immediate attention. The girl at the desk was going over a number of requests and messages when she suddenly looked up at Cap curiously. Cap was paying no attention to her at all. He was gazing at the wide drawer near the top of her desk with a bemused expression on his face.

'Pardon me,' she said. She was still very much aware of being the new girl, even after all these months, of having replaced someone Cap had been close to. And perhaps had been sleeping with, she had sometimes speculated.

'Hmmmm?' He looked around at her at last. But the blankness did not leave his eyes. It was somehow shocking . . . like looking at the shuttered windows of a house reputed to be haunted.

She hesitated, then plunged. 'Cap, do you feel all right? You look . . . well, a little white.'

'I feel fine,' he said, and for a moment he was his old self, dispelling some of her doubts. His shoulders squared, his head came up, and the blankness left his eyes. 'Anybody who's going to Hawaii ought to feel fine, right?'

'Hawaii?' Gloria said doubtfully. It was news to her.

'Never mind these now,' Cap said, taking the message forms and interdepartmental memos and stuffing them all together with the telex cables. 'I'll look at them later. Anything happening with either of the McGees?'

'One item,' she said. 'I was just getting to it. Mike Kellaher says she asked to go out to the stable this afternoon and see a horse—'

'Yes, that's fine,' Cap said.

'—and she buzzed back a little later to say she'd like to go out at quarter of one.'

'Fine, fine.'

'Will Mr Rainbird be taking her out?'

'Rainbird's on his way to San Diego,' Cap said with unmistakable satisfaction. 'I'll send a man to take her over.'

'All right. Will you want to see the . . .' She trailed off. Cap's eyes had wandered away from her and he appeared to be staring at the wide drawer again. It was partway open. It always was, per regulations. There was a gun in there. Gloria was a crack shot, just as Rachel before her had been.

'Cap, are you sure there's nothing wrong?'

'Ought to keep that shut,' Cap said. 'They like dark places. They like to crawl in and hide.'

'They?' she asked cautiously.

'Snakes,' Cap said, and marched into his office.

5

He sat behind his desk, the cables and messages in an untidy litter before him. They were forgotten. Everything was forgotten now except snakes, golf clubs, and what he was going to do at quarter of one. He would go down and see Andy McGee. He felt strongly that Andy would tell him what to do next. He felt strongly that Andy would make everything all right.

Beyond quarter of one this afternoon, everything in his life was a great funneling darkness.

He didn't mind. It was sort of a relief.

6

At quarter of ten, John Rainbird slipped into the small monitoring room near Charlie's quarters. Louis Tranter, a hugely fat man whose buttocks nearly overflowed the chair he sat in, was watching the monitors. The digital thermometer read a steady sixty-eight degrees. He looked over his shoulder when the door opened and his face tightened at the sight of Rainbird.

'I heard you were leaving town,' he said.

'Scrubbed,' Rainbird said. 'And you never saw me this morning at all, Louis.'

Louis looked at him doubtfully.

'You never saw me,' Rainbird repeated. 'After five this afternoon I don't give a shit. But until then, you never saw me. And if I hear you did, I'm going to come after you and cut me some blubber. Can you dig it?'

Louis Tranter paled noticeably. The Hostess Twinkie he had been eating dropped from his hand onto the slanted steel panel that housed the TV monitors and microphone pickup controls. It rolled down the slant and tumbled to the floor unheeded, leaving a trail of crumbs behind. Suddenly he wasn't a bit hungry. He had heard this guy was crazy, and now he was seeing that what he had heard was certainly true.

'I can dig it,' he said, whispering in the face of that weird grin and glittering one-eyed stare.

'Good,' Rainbird said, and advanced toward him. Louis shrank away from him, but Rainbird ignored him altogether for the moment and peered into one of the monitors. There was Charlie, looking pretty as a picture in her blue jumper. With a lover's eye, Rainbird noted that she had not braided her hair today; it lay loose and fine and lovely over her neck and shoulders. She wasn't doing anything but sitting on the sofa. No book. No TV. She looked like a woman waiting for a bus.

Charlie, he thought admiringly, *I love you. I really do.*

'What's she got going for today?' Rainbird asked.

'Nothing much,' Louis said eagerly. He was, in fact, nearly babbling. 'Just going out at quarter of one to curry that horse she rides. We're getting another test out of her tomorrow.'

'Tomorrow, huh?'

'Yep.' Louis didn't give a tin shit about the tests one way or the other, but he thought it would please Rainbird, and maybe Rainbird would leave.

He seemed to be pleased. His grin reappeared.

'She's going out to the stables at quarter of one, huh?'

'Yeah.'

'Who's taking her? Since I'm on my way to San Diego?'

Louis uttered a highpitched, almost female giggle to show that this piece of wit was appreciated.

'Your buddy there. Don Jules.'

'He's no buddy of mine.'

'No, course he isn't,' Louis agreed quickly. 'He . . . he thought the orders were a little funny, but since they came right from Cap—'

'Funny? What did he think was funny about them?'

'Well, just to take her out and leave her there. Cap said the stable boys would keep an eye on her. But they don't know from nothing. Don seemed to think it would be taking a helluva—'

'Yeah, but he doesn't get paid to think. Does he, fatty?' He slapped Louis on the shoulder, hard. It made a sound like a minor thunderclap.

'No, course he doesn't,' Louis came back smartly. He was sweating now.

'See you later,' Rainbird said, and went to the door again.

'Leaving?' Louis was unable to disguise his relief.

Rainbird paused with his hand on the doorknob and looked back. 'What do you mean?' he said. 'I was never here.'

'No sir, never here,' Louis agreed hastily.

Rainbird nodded and slipped out. He closed the door behind him. Louis stared at the closed door for several seconds and then uttered a great and gusty sigh of relief. His armpits were humid and his white shirt was stuck to his back. A few moments later he picked up his fallen Twinkie, brushed it off, and began to eat it again. The girl was still sitting quietly, not doing anything. How Rainbird – *Rainbird* of all people – had got her to like him was a mystery to Louis Tranter.

7

At quarter to one, an eternity after Charlie had awakened, there was a brief buzz at her door, and Don Jules came in, wearing a baseball warmup jacket and old cord pants. He looked at her coldly and without much interest.

'C'mon,' he said.

Charlie went with him.

8

That day was cool and beautiful. At twelve-thirty Rainbird strolled slowly across the still-green lawn to the low, L-shaped stable with its dark-red paint – the color of drying blood – and its brisk white piping. Overhead, great fair-weather clouds marched slowly across the sky. A breeze tugged at his shirt.

If dying was required, this was a fine day for it.

446

Inside the stable, he located the head groom's office and went in. He showed his ID with its A-rating stamp.

'Yes, sir?' Drabble said.

'Clear this place,' Rainbird said. 'Everyone out. Five minutes.'

The groom did not argue or bumble, and if he paled a bit, his tan covered it. 'The horses too?'

'Just the people. Out the back.'

Rainbird had changed into fatigues – what they had sometimes called gook-shooters in Nam. The pants pockets were large, deep, and flapped. From one of these he now took a large handgun. The head groom looked at it with wise, unsurprised eyes. Rainbird held it loosely, pointed at the floor.

'Is there going to be trouble, sir?'

'There may be,' Rainbird said quietly. 'I don't really know. Go on, now, old man.'

'I hope no harm will come to the horses,' Drabble said.

Rainbird smiled then. He thought, *So will she.* He had seen her eyes when she was with the horses. And this place, with its bays of loose hay and its lofts of baled hay, with its dry wood all about, was a tinderbox with NO SMOKING signs posted everywhere.

It was a thin edge.

But, as the years had drawn on and he had become more and more careless of his life, he had walked thinner ones.

He walked back to the big double doors and looked out. No sign of anyone just yet. He turned away and began to walk between the stall doors, smelling the sweet, pungent, nostalgic aroma of horse.

He made sure all of the stalls were latched and locked.

He went back to the double doors again. Now someone was coming. Two figures. They were still on the far side of the duckpond, five minutes' walk away. Not Cap and Andy McGee. It was Don Jules and Charlie.

447

Come to me, Charlie, he thought tenderly. *Come to me now*.

He glanced around at the shadowed upper lofts for a moment and then went to the ladder – simple wooden rungs nailed to a support beam – and began to climb with lithe ease.

Three minutes later, Charlie and Don Jules stepped into the shadowed, empty coolness of the stable. They stood just inside the doors for a moment as their eyes adjusted to the dimness. The .357 Mag in Rainbird's hand had been modified to hold a silencer of Rainbird's own construction; it crouched over the muzzle like a strange black spider. It was not, as a matter of fact, a very silent silencer: it is nearly impossible to completely quiet a big handgun. When – if – he pulled the trigger, it would utter a husky bark the first time, a low report the second time, and then it would be mostly useless. Rainbird hoped not to have to use the gun at all, but now he brought it down with both hands and leveled it so that the silencer covered a small circle on Don Jules's chest.

Jules was looking around carefully.

'You can go now,' Charlie said.

'Hey!' Jules said, raising his voice and paying no attention to Charlie. Rainbird knew Jules. A book man. Follow each order to the letter and nobody could put you in hack. Keep your ass covered at all times. 'Hey, groom! Somebody! I got the kid here!'

'You can go now,' Charlie said again, and once more Jules ignored her.

'Come on,' he said, clamping a hand over Charlie's wrist. 'We got to find somebody.'

A bit regretfully, Rainbird prepared to shoot Don Jules. It could be worse; at least Jules would die by the book, and with his ass covered.

'I *said* you could go now,' Charlie said, and suddenly

448

Jules let go of her wrist. He didn't just let go; he pulled his hand away, the way you do when you've grabbed hold of something hot.

Rainbird watched this interesting development closely.

Jules had turned and was looking at Charlie. He was rubbing his wrist, but Rainbird was unable to see if there was a mark there or not.

'You get out of here,' Charlie said softly.

Jules reached under his coat and Rainbird once more prepared to shoot him. He wouldn't do it until the gun was clear of Jules's jacket and his intention to march her back to the house was obvious.

But the gun was only partway out when he dropped it to the barnboard floor with a cry. He took two steps backward, away from the girl, his eyes wide.

Charlie made a half turn away, as if Jules no longer interested her. There was a faucet protruding from the wall halfway up the long side of the *L*, and beneath it was a bucket half full of water.

Steam began to rise lazily from the bucket.

Rainbird didn't think Jules noticed that; his eyes were riveted on Charlie.

'Get out of here, you bastard,' she said, 'or I'll burn you up. I'll fry you.'

John Rainbird raised Charlie a silent cheer.

Jules stood looking at her, indecisive. At this moment, with his head down and slightly cocked, his eyes moving restlessly from side to side, he looked ratlike and dangerous. Rainbird was ready to back her play if she had to make one, but he hoped Jules would be sensible. The power had a way of getting out of control.

'Get out right now,' Charlie said. 'Go back where you came from. I'll be watching to see that you do. *Move! Get out of here!*'

The shrill anger in her voice decided him.

'Take it easy,' he said. 'Okay. But you got nowhere to go, girl. You got nothing but a hard way to go.'

As he spoke he was easing past her, then backing toward the door.

'I'll be watching,' Charlie said grimly. 'Don't you even turn around, you . . . you turd.'

Jules went out. He said something else, but Rainbird didn't catch it.

'Just *go!*' Charlie cried.

She stood in the double doorway, back to Rainbird, in a shower of drowsy afternoon sunlight, a small silhouette. Again his love for her came over him. This was the place of their appointment, then.

'Charlie,' he called down softly.

She stiffened and took a single step backward. She didn't turn around, but he could feel the sudden recognition and fury flooding through her, although it was visible only in the slow way that her shoulders came up.

'Charlie,' he called again. 'Hey, Charlie.'

'You!' she whispered. He barely caught it. Somewhere below him, a horse nickered softly.

'It's me,' he agreed. 'Charlie, it's been me all along.'

Now she did turn and swept the long side of the stable with her eyes. Rainbird saw her do this, but she didn't see him; he was behind a stack of bales, well out of sight in the shadowy second loft.

'Where are you?' she rasped. 'You tricked me! It was you! My daddy says it was you that time at Granther's!' Her hand had gone unconsciously to her throat, where he had laid in the dart. '*Where are you?*'

Ah, Charlie, wouldn't you like to know?

A horse whinnied; no quiet sound of contentment this, but one of sudden sharp fear. The cry was taken up by another horse. There was a heavy double thud as one of the thoroughbreds kicked at the latched door of his stall.

450

'*Where are you?*' she screamed again, and Rainbird felt the temperature suddenly begin to rise. Directly below him, one of the horses – Necromancer, perhaps – whinnied loudly, and it sounded like a woman screaming.

9

The door buzzer made its curt, rasping cry, and Cap Hollister stepped into Andy's apartment below the north plantation house. He was not the man he had been a year before. That man had been elderly but tough and hale and shrewd; that man had possessed a face you might expect to see crouching over the edge of a duck blind in November and holding a shotgun with easy authority. This man walked in a kind of distracted shamble. His hair, a strong iron gray a year ago, was now nearly white and baby-fine. His mouth twitched infirmly. But the greatest change was in his eyes, which seemed puzzled and somehow childlike; this expression would occasionally be broken by a shooting sideways glance that was suspicious and fearful and almost cringing. His hands hung loosely by his sides and the fingers twitched aimlessly. The echo had become a ricochet that was now bouncing around his brain with crazy, whistling, deadly velocity.

Andy McGee stood to meet him. He was dressed exactly as he had been on that day when he and Charlie had fled up Third Avenue in New York with the Shop sedan trailing behind them. The cord jacket was torn at the seam of the left shoulder now, and the brown twill pants were faded and seat-shiny.

The wait had been good for him. He felt that he had been able to make his peace with all of this. Not understanding, no. He felt he would never have that, even if he and Charlie somehow managed to beat the fantastic odds and get away and go on living. He could find no fatal flaw in his own character on which to blame this royal balls-up, no sin of the father that needed to be expiated upon his daughter. It wasn't wrong to need two hundred dollars or to participate in a controlled experiment, anymore than it was wrong to want to be free. *If I could get clear*, he thought, *I'd tell them this: teach your children, teach your babies, teach them well, they say they know what they are doing, and sometimes they do, but mostly they lie.*

But it was what it was, *n'est-ce pas?* One way or another they would at least have a run for their money. But that brought him no feeling of forgiveness or understanding for the people who had done this. In finding peace with himself, he had banked the fires of his hate for the faceless bureaucretins who had done this in the name of national security or whatever it was. Only they weren't faceless now: one of them stood before him, smiling and twitching and vacant. Andy felt no sympathy for Cap's state at all.

You brought it on yourself, chum.

'Hello, Andy,' Cap said. 'All ready?'

'Yes,' Andy said. 'Carry one of my bags, would you?'

Cap's vacuity was broken by one of those falsely shrewd glances. 'Have you checked them?' he barked. 'Checked them for snakes?'

Andy pushed – not hard. He wanted to save as much as he could for an emergency. 'Pick it up,' he said, gesturing at one of the two suitcases.

Cap walked over and picked it up. Andy grabbed the other one.

'Where's your car?'

'It's right outside,' Cap said. 'It's been brought around.'

'Will anyone check on us?' What he meant was *Will anyone try to stop us?*

'Why would they?' Cap asked, honestly surprised. 'I'm in charge.'

452

Andy had to be satisfied with that. 'We're going out,' he said, 'and we're going to put these bags in the trunk—'

'Trunk's okay,' Cap broke in. 'I checked it this morning.'

'—and then we're going to drive around to the stable and get my daughter. Any questions?'

'No,' Cap said.

'Fine. Let's go.'

They left the apartment and walked to the elevator. A few people moved up and down the hall on their own errands. They glanced cautiously at Cap and then looked away. The elevator took them up to the ballroom and Cap led the way down a long front hall.

Josie, the redhead who had been on the door the day Cap had ordered Al Steinowitz to Hastings Glen, had gone on to bigger and better things. Now a young, prematurely balding man sat there, frowning over a computer-programming text. He had a yellow felt-tip pen in one hand. He glanced up as they approached.

'Hello, Richard,' Cap said. 'Hitting the books?'

Richard laughed. 'They're hitting me is more like it.' He glanced at Andy curiously. Andy looked back noncommittally.

Cap slipped his thumb into a slot and something thumped. A green light shone on Richard's console.

'Destination?' Richard asked. He exchanged his felt-tip for a ball-point. It hovered over a small bound book.

'Stable,' Cap said briskly. 'We're going to pick up Andy's daughter and they are going to escape.'

'Andrews Air Force Base,' Andy countered, and pushed. Pain settled immediately into his head like a dull meat cleaver.

' 'Andrews AFB,' Richard agreed, and jotted it into the book, along with the time. 'Have a good day, gentlemen.'

They went out into breezy October sunshine. Cap's Vega was drawn up on the clean white crushed stone of the circular driveway. 'Give me your keys,' Andy said. Cap handed them over, Andy opened the trunk, and they stowed the luggage. Andy slammed the trunk and handed the keys back. 'Let's go.'

Cap drove them on a loop around the duckpond to the stables. As they went, Andy noticed a man in a baseball warmup jacket running across to the house they had just left, and he felt a tickle of unease. Cap parked in front of the open stable doors.

He reached for the keys and Andy slapped his hand lightly. 'No. Leave it running. Come on.' He got out of the car. His head was thudding, sending rhythmic pulses of pain deep into his brain, but it wasn't too bad yet. Not yet.

Cap got out, then stood, irresolute. 'I don't want to go in there,' he said. His eyes shifted back and forth wildly in their sockets. 'Too much dark. They like the dark. They hide. They bite.'

'There are no snakes,' Andy said, and pushed out lightly. It was enough to get Cap moving, but he didn't look very convinced. They walked into the stable.

For one wild, terrible moment Andy thought she wasn't there. The change from the light to shadow left his eyes momentarily helpless. It was hot and stuffy in here, and something had upset the horses; they were whinnying and kicking at their stalls. Andy could see nothing.

'Charlie?' he called, his voice cracked and urgent. '*Charlie?*'

'Daddy!' she called, and gladness shot through him – gladness that turned to dread when he heard the shrill fear in her voice. 'Daddy, don't come in! Don't come—'

'I think it's a little late for that,' a voice said from somewhere overhead.

10

'Charlie,' the voice had called down softly. It was somewhere overhead, but where? It seemed to come from everywhere.

The anger had gusted through her – anger that was fanned by the hideous unfairness of it, the way that it never ended, the way they had of being there at every turn, blocking every lunge for escape. Almost at once she felt *it* start to come up from inside her. *It* was always so much closer to the surface now . . . so much more eager to come bursting out. Like with the man who had brought her over. When he drew his gun, she had simply made it hot so he would drop it. He was lucky the bullets hadn't exploded right inside it.

Already she could feel the heat gathering inside her and beginning to radiate out as the weird battery or whatever it was turned on. She scanned the dark lofts overhead but couldn't spot him. There were too many stacks of bales. Too many shadows.

'I wouldn't, Charlie.' His voice was a little louder now, but still calm. It cut through the fog of rage and confusion.

'You ought to come down here?' Charlie cried loudly. She was trembling. 'You ought to come down before I decide to set everything on fire! I can do it!'

'I know you can,' the soft voice responded. It floated down from nowhere, everywhere. 'But if you do, you're going to burn up a lot of horses, Charlie. Can't you hear them?'

She could. Once he had called it to her attention, she could. They were nearly mad with fear, whinnying and battering at their latched doors. Necromancer was in one of those stalls.

Her breath caught in her throat. Again she saw the

trench of fire running across the Manders yard and the chickens exploding.

She turned toward the bucket of water again and was now badly frightened. The power was trembling on the edge of her ability to control it, and in another moment

(*back off!*)

it was going to blow loose

(*!BACK OFF!*)

and just go sky high.

(*!!BACK OFF, BACK OFF, DO YOU HEAR ME, BACK OFF!!*)

This time the half-full bucket did not just steam; it came to an instant, furious boil. A moment later the chrome faucet just over the bucket twisted twice, spun like a propeller, and then blew off the pipe jutting from the wall. The fixture flew the length of the stable like a rocket payload and caromed off the far wall. Water gushed from the pipe. Cold water; she could *feel* its coldness. But moments after the water spurted out it turned to steam and a hazy mist filled the corridor between the stalls. A coiled green hose that hung on a peg next to the pipe had fused its plastic loops.

(*BACK OFF!*)

She began to get control of it again and pull it down. A year ago she would have been incapable of that; the thing would have had to run its own destructive course. She was able to hold on better now . . . ah, but there was so much more to control!

She stood there, shivering.

'What more do you want?' she asked in a low voice. 'Why can't you just let us go?'

A horse whinnied, high and frightened. Charlie understood exactly how it felt.

'No one thinks you can just be let go,' Rainbird's quiet voice answered. 'I don't think even your father thinks so.

456

You're dangerous, Charlie. And you know it. We could let you go and the next men that grabbed you might be Russians, or North Koreans, maybe even the Heathen Chinese. You may think I'm kidding, but I'm not.'

'That's not my fault!' she cried.

'No,' Rainbird said meditatively. 'Of course it isn't. But it's all bullshit anyway. I don't care about the Z factor, Charlie. I never did, I only care about you.'

'*Oh, you liar!*' Charlie screamed shrilly. 'You tricked me, pretended to be something you weren't—'

She stopped. Rainbird climbed easily over a low pile of bales, then sat down on the edge of the loft with his feet dangling down. The pistol was in his lap. His face was like a ruined moon above her.

'Lied to you? No. I mixed up the truth, Charlie, that's all I ever did. And I did it to keep you alive.'

'Dirty liar,' she whispered, but was dismayed to find that she *wanted* to believe him; the sting of tears began behind her eyes. She was so tired and she wanted to believe him, wanted to believe he had liked her.

'You weren't testing,' Rainbird said. 'Your old man wasn't testing, either. What were they going to do? Say "Oh, sorry, we made a mistake" and put you back on the street? You've seen these guys at work, Charlie. You saw them shoot that guy Manders in Hastings Glen. They pulled out your own mother's fingernails and then k—'

'*Stop it!*' she screamed in agony, and the power stirred again, restlessly close to the surface.

'No, I won't,' he said. 'Time you had the truth, Charlie. I got you going. I made you important to them. You think I did it because it's my job? The fuck I did. They're assholes. Cap, Hockstetter, Pynchot, that guy Jules who brought you over here – they're all assholes.'

She stared up at him, as if hypnotized by his hovering face. He was not wearing his eyepatch, and the place where his eye had been was a twisted, slitted hollow, like a memory of horror.

'I didn't lie to you about this,' he said, and touched his face. His fingers moved lightly, almost lovingly, up the scars gored in the side of his chin to his flayed cheek to the burned-out socket itself. 'I mixed up the truth, yeah. There was no Hanoi Rathole, no Cong. My own guys did it. Because they were assholes, like these guys.'

Charlie didn't understand, didn't know what he meant. Her mind was reeling. Didn't he know she could burn him to a crisp where he sat?

'None of this matters,' he said. 'Nothing except you and me. We've got to get straight with each other, Charlie. That's all I want. To be straight with you.'

And she sensed he was telling the truth – but that some darker truth lay just below his words. There was something he wasn't telling.

'Come on up,' he said, 'and let's talk this out.'

Yes, it was like hypnosis. And, in a way, it was like telepathy. Because even though she understood the shape of that dark truth, her feet began to move toward the loft ladder. It wasn't talking that he was talking about. It was ending. Ending the doubt, the misery, the fear . . . ending the temptation to make ever bigger fires until some awful end came of it. In his own twisted, mad way, he was talking about being her friend in a way no one else could be. And . . . yes, part of her wanted that. Part of her wanted an ending and a release.

So she began to move toward the ladder, and her hands were on the rungs when her father burst in.

11

'*Charlie?*' he called, and the spell broke.

Her hands left the rungs and terrible understanding spilled through her. She turned toward the door and saw him standing there. Her first thought

(*daddy you got fat!*)

passed through her mind and was gone so quickly she barely had a chance to recognize it. And fat or not, it was he; she would have known him anywhere, and her love for him spilled through her and swept away Rainbird's spell like mist. And the understanding was that whatever John Rainbird might mean to her, he meant only death for her father.

'Daddy!' she cried. 'Don't come in!'

A sudden wrinkle of irritation passed over Rainbird's face. The gun was no longer in his lap; it was pointed straight at the silhouette in the doorway.

'I think it's a little late for that,' he said.

There was a man standing beside her daddy. She thought it was that man they all called Cap. He was just standing there, his shoulders slumped as if they had been broken.

'Come in,' Rainbird said, and Andy came. 'Now stop.'

Andy stopped. Cap had followed him, a pace or two behind, as if the two of them were tied together. Cap's eyes shifted nervously back and forth in the stable's dimness.

'I know you can do it,' Rainbird said, and his voice became lighter, almost humorous. 'In fact, you can both do it. But, Mr McGee . . . Andy? May I call you Andy?'

'Anything you like,' her father said. His voice was calm.

'Andy, if you try using what you've got on me, I'm going to try to resist it just long enough to shoot your daughter. And, of course, Charlie, if you try using what you've got on me, who knows what will happen?'

Charlie ran to her father. She pressed her face against the rough wale of his corduroy jacket.

'Daddy, Daddy,' she whispered hoarsely.

'Hi, cookie,' he said, and stroked her hair. He held her, then looked up at Rainbird. Sitting there on the edge of the loft like a sailor on a mast, he was the one-eyed pirate of Andy's dream to the life. 'So what now?' he asked Rainbird. He was aware that Rainbird could probably hold them here until the fellow he had seen running across the lawn brought back help, but somehow he didn't think that was what this man wanted.

Rainbird ignored his question. 'Charlie?' he said.

Charlie shuddered beneath Andy's hands but did not turn around.

'Charlie,' he said again, softly, insistently. 'Look at me, Charlie.'

Slowly, reluctantly, she turned around and looked up at him.

'Come on up here,' he said, 'like you were going to do. Nothing has changed. We'll finish our business and all of this will end.'

'No, I can't allow that,' Andy said, almost pleasantly. 'We're leaving.'

'Come up, Charlie,' Rainbird said, 'or I'm going to put a bullet into your father's head right now. You can burn me, but I'm betting I can pull this trigger before it happens.'

Charlie moaned deep in her throat like a hurt animal.

'Don't move, Charlie,' Andy said.

'He'll be fine,' Rainbird said. His voice was low, rational, persuasive. 'They'll send him to Hawaii and he'll be fine. You choose, Charlie. A bullet in the head for him or the golden sands there on Kalami Beach. Which is it going to be? You choose.'

Her blue eyes never leaving Rainbird's one, Charlie took a trembling step away from her father.

'Charlie!' he said sharply. 'No!'

'It'll be over,' Rainbird said. The barrel of the pistol was unwavering; it never left Andy's head. 'And that's what you want, isn't it? I'll make it gentle and I'll make it clean. Trust me, Charlie. Do it for your father and do it for yourself. Trust me.'

She took another step. And another.

'No,' Andy said. 'Don't listen to him, Charlie.'

But it was as if he had given her a reason to go. She walked to the ladder again. She put her hands on the rung just above her head and then paused. She looked up at Rainbird, and locked her gaze with his.

'Do you promise he'll be all right?'

'Yes,' Rainbird said, but Andy felt it suddenly and completely: the force of the lie . . . all his lies.

I'll have to push her, he thought with dumb amazement. *Not him, but her.*

He gathered himself to do it. She was already standing on the first rung, her hands grasping the next one over her head.

And that was when Cap – they had all forgotten him – began to scream.

12

When Don Jules got back to the building Cap and Andy had left only minutes before, he was so wild-looking that Richard, on door duty, grasped the gun inside his drawer.

'What—' he began.

'The alarm, the alarm!' Jules yelled.

'Do you have auth—'

'I've got all the authorization I need, you fucking twit! The girl! The girl's making a break for it!'

On Richard's console there were two simple combination-type dials, numbered from one to ten. Flustered, Richard dropped his pen and set the lefthand dial to a little past seven. Jules came around and set the righthand dial just past one. A moment later a low burring began to come from the console, a sound that was being repeated all over the Shop compound.

Groundskeepers were turning off their mowers and running for sheds where rifles were kept. The doors to the rooms where the vulnerable computer terminals were slid closed and locked. Gloria, Cap's secretary, produced her own handgun. All available Shop agents ran toward loudspeakers to await instructions, unbuttoning coats to free weapons. The charge in the outer fence went from its usual mild daytime tickle to killing voltage. The Dobermans in the run between the two fences heard the buzzing, sensed the change as the Shop geared up to battle status, and began to bark and leap hysterically. Gates between the Shop and the outside world slid shut and locked automatically. A bakery truck that had been servicing the commissary had its rear bumper chewed off by one sliding gate, and the driver was lucky to escape electrocution.

The buzz seemed endless, subliminal.

Jules grabbed the mike from Richard's console and said, 'Condition Bright Yellow. I say again, Condition Bright Yellow. No drill. Converge on stables; use caution.' He searched his mind for the code term assigned to Charlie McGee and couldn't come up with it. They changed the fucking things by the day, it seemed. 'It's the girl, and she's using it! Repeat, she's using it!'

13

Orv Jamieson was standing underneath the loudspeaker in the third-floor lounge of the north house, holding The Windsucker in one hand. When he heard Jules's message, he sat down abruptly and holstered it.

'Uh-uh,' he said to himself as the three others he had been shooting eight ball with ran out. 'Uh-uh, not me, count me out.' The others could run over there like hounds on a hot scent if they wanted to. They had not been at the Manders farm. They had not seen this particular third-grader in action.

What OJ wanted more than anything at that point in time was to find a deep hole and pull it over him.

14

Cap Hollister had heard very little of the three-way conversation between Charlie, her father, and Rainbird. He was on hold, his old orders completed, no new ones yet issued. The sounds of the talk flowed meaninglessly over his head and he was free to think of his golf game, and snakes, and nine irons, and boa constrictors, and mashies, and timber rattlers, and niblicks, and pythons big enough to swallow a goat whole. He did not like this place. It was full of loose hay that reminded him of the way the rough on a golf course smelled. It had been in the hay that his brother had been bitten by a snake when Cap himself was only three, it wasn't a very dangerous snake, but his big brother had *screamed*, he had *screamed*, and there had been the smell of hay, the smell of clover, the smell of timothy, and his big brother was the strongest, bravest boy in the world but now he was *screaming*, big, tough, nine-year-old Leon Hollister was *screaming* 'Go get *Daddy!*' and tears were running down his cheeks as he held his puffing leg between his hands and as three-year-old

Cap Hollister turned to do what his brother said, terrified and blubbering, it had slithered over his *foot*, his own *foot*, like deadly green water – and later the doctor had said the bite wasn't dangerous, that the snake must have bitten something else only a little while before and exhausted its poison sac, but Lennie thought he was *dying* and everywhere had been the sweet summer smell of grass and the hoppers were jumping, making their eternal *rickety-rickety* sound and spitting tobacco juice ('Spit and I'll let you go' had been the cry in those long-ago Nebraska days); good smells, good sounds, golf-course smells and sounds, and the *screaming* of his brother and the dry, scaly feel of the snake, looking down and seeing its flat, triangular head, its black eyes . . . the snake had slithered across Cap's foot on its way back into the high grass . . . back into the rough, you might say . . . and the smell had been like this . . . and he didn't like this place.

Four irons and adders and putters and copperheads—

Faster and faster now the ricochet bounded back and forth, and Cap's eyes moved vacuously around the shadowy stable while John Rainbird confronted the McGees. Eventually his eyes fixed upon the partially fused green plastic hose by the burst waterpipe. It hung in coils on its peg, still partially obscured by the last of the drifting steam.

Terror flashed up in him suddenly, as explosive as flames in an old blowdown. For a moment the terror was so great that he could not even breathe, let alone cry a warning. His muscles were frozen, locked.

Then they let go. Cap drew in a great lungful of breath in a convulsive, heaving lurch and let out an earsplitting, sudden scream. '*Snake! SNAKE! SNAAAYYYKE!*'

He did not run away. Even reduced as he was, it wasn't in Cap Hollister to run. He lurched forward like a rusty automaton and seized a rake that was leaning against the wall. It was a snake and he would beat it and break it and crush it. He would . . . would . . .

He would save Lennie!

He rushed at the partially fused hose, brandishing the rake.

Then things happened very fast.

15

The agents, most of them armed with handguns, and the gardeners, most of them with rifles, were converging on the low L-shaped stable in a rough circle when the screaming began. A moment later there was a heavy thudding sound and what might have been a muffled cry of pain. Only a second later there was a low ripping sound, then a muted report that was surely a silenced revolver.

The circle around the stable paused and then began to move inward once more.

16

Cap's scream and sudden dash for the rake only broke Rainbird's concentration for a moment, but a moment was enough. The gun jerked away from Andy's head toward Cap; it was an instinctive movement, the quick and alert shift of a hunting tiger in the jungle. And so it was that his keen instincts betrayed him and caused him to tumble off the thin edge he had walked so long.

Andy used the push just as quickly and just as instinctively. When the gun jerked toward Cap, he called up to Rainbird, 'Jump!' and pushed harder than he ever had in his life. The pain that ripped through his head like splintering shards of shrapnel was sickening in its force, and he felt something *give*, finally and irrevocably.

Blowout, he thought. The thought was thick and sludgy. He staggered back. The entire left side of his body had gone numb. His left leg no longer wanted to hold him.

it finally came it's a blowout damn thing finally let go

Rainbird pushed himself away from the edge of the overhead loft with one hard thrust of his arms. His face was almost comically surprised. He held onto his gun; even when he hit the floor badly and sprawled forward with a broken leg, he held onto the gun. He could not stifle a cry of pain and bewilderment, but he held onto the gun.

Cap had reached the green hose and was beating it wildly with the rake. His mouth worked, but no sound came out – only a fine spray of spit.

Rainbird looked up. His hair had fallen over his face. He jerked his head to flip it out of his line of sight. His one eye glimmered. His mouth was drawn down in a bitter line. He raised the gun and pointed it at Andy.

'No!' Charlie screamed. 'No!'

Rainbird fired, and smoke belched from the vents of the silencer. The bullet dug bright, fresh splinters beside Andy's lolling head. Rainbird braced one arm on the floor and fired again. Andy's head snapped viciously to the right, and blood flew from the left side of his neck in a flood.

'*No!*' Charlie screamed again, and clapped her hands to her face. '*Daddy! Daddy!*'

Rainbird's hand slid out from under him; long splinters whispered into the palm of his hand.

'Charlie,' he murmured. 'Charlie, look at me.'

17

They ringed the outside of the stable now and paused, uncertain of just how to handle this.

'The girl,' Jules said. 'We rub her—'

'*No!*' the girl screamed from inside, as if she had heard what Jules had planned. Then '*Daddy! Daddy!*'

Then there was another report, this one much louder, and a sudden, vicious flash that made them shade their eyes. A wave of heat rolled out of the open stable doors, and the men standing in front reeled back from it.

Smoke came next, smoke and the red glimmer of fire.

Somewhere inside that infant hell, horses began to scream.

18

Charlie ran for her father, her mind in a horrified whirl, and when Rainbird spoke, she did turn toward him. He was sprawled on his belly, trying to steady the gun with both hands.

Incredibly, he was smiling.

'There,' he croaked. 'So I can see your eyes. I love you, Charlie.'

And he fired.

The power leaped crazily out of her, totally out of control. On its way to Rainbird, it vaporized the chunk of lead that otherwise would have buried itself in her brain. For a moment it seemed that a high wind was rippling Rainbird's clothes – and those of Cap behind him – and that nothing else was happening. But it was not just clothes that were rippling; it was the flesh itself, rippling, running like tallow, and then being hurled off bones that were already charring and blackening and flaming.

There was a soundless flashgun sizzle of light that momentarily blinded her; she saw no more but could hear the horses in their stalls, going mad with fear . . . and she could smell smoke.

The horses! The horses! she thought, groping in the dazzle before her eyes. It was her dream. It was changed, but it was here. And suddenly, momentarily, she was back in the Albany airport, a little girl who had been two inches shorter and ten pounds lighter and ever so much more innocent, a little girl with a shopping bag scavenged from a wastecan,

467

going from phonebooth to phonebooth, shoving at them, the silver cascading out of the coin returns. . . .

She shoved now, almost blindly, groping with her mind for what she needed to do.

A ripple ran along the doors of the stalls that formed the *L*'s long side. The latches fell, smoking, to the board floor one after another, twisted out of shape by the heat.

The back of the stable had blown out in a tangle of smoking timbers and boards as the power passed Cap and Rainbird and bellowed onward, like something shot from a psychic cannon. The splintered shrapnel whistled for sixty yards or more in a widening fan, and those Shop agents who had been standing in its path might as well have been hit with a broadside blast of hot grapeshot. A fellow by the name of Clayton Braddock was nearly decapitated by a whirling slice of barnboard siding. The man next to him was cut in two by a beam that came whirling through the air like a runaway propeller. A third had an ear clipped off by a smoking chunk of wood and was not aware of it for nearly ten minutes.

The skirmish line of Shop agents dissolved. Those who could not run crawled. Only one man kept his position even momentarily. This was George Sedaka, the man who, in the company of Orv Jamieson, had hijacked Andy's letters in New Hampshire. Sedaka had only been laying over at the Shop compound before going on to Panama City. The man who had been on Sedaka's left was now lying on the ground, groaning. The man on Sedaka's right had been the unfortunate Clayton Braddock.

Sedaka himself was miraculously untouched. Splinters and hot shrapnel had flown all around him. A baling hook, sharp-edged and lethal, had buried itself in the earth less than four inches from his feet. It glowed a dull red.

The back of the stable looked as if half a dozen sticks of dynamite had gone off there. Tumbled, burning beams framed a blackened hole that was perhaps twenty-five feet

468

across. A large compost heap had absorbed the bulk of Charlie's extraordinary force when it made its explosive exit; it was now in flames, and what remained of the rear of the stable was catching.

Sedaka could hear horses whinnying and screaming inside, could see the lurid red-orange gleam of fire as the flames raced into the lofts full of dry hay. It was like looking through a porthole into Sheol.

Sedaka suddenly decided he wanted no more of this.

It was a little heavier than sticking up unarmed mailmen on back-country roads.

George Sedaka reholstered his pistol and took to his heels.

19

She was still groping, unable to grasp all that had happened. *'Daddy!'* she screamed. *'Daddy! Daddy!'*

Everything was blurred, ghostly. The air was full of hot, choking smoke and red flashes. The horses were still battering at their stall doors, but now the doors, latchless, were swinging open. Some of the horses, at least, had been able to back out.

Charlie fell to her knees, feeling for her father, and the horses began to flash past her on their way out, little more than dim, dreamlike shapes. Overhead, a flaming rafter fell in a shower of sparks and ignited the loose hay in one of the lower bays. In the short side of the *L*, a thirty-gallon drum of tractor gas went up with a dull, coughing roar.

Flying hooves passed within scant inches of Charlie's head as she crawled with her hands out like a blind thing. Then one of the fleeing horses struck her a glancing blow and she fell backward. One of her hands found a shoe.

'Daddy?' she whimpered. 'Daddy?'

He was dead. She was sure he was dead. Everything was

dead; the world was flame; they had killed her mother and now they had killed her father.

Her sight was beginning to come back, but still everything was dim. Waves of heat pulsed over her. She felt her way up his leg, touched his belt, and then went lightly up his shirt until her fingers reached a damp, sticky patch. It was spreading. There she paused in horror, and she was unable to make her fingers go on.

'Daddy,' she whispered.

'Charlie?'

It was no more than a low, husky croak . . . but it was he. His hand found her face and tugged her weakly. 'Come here. Get . . . get close.'

She came to his side, and now his face swam out of the gray dazzle. The left side of it was pulled down in a grimace; his left eye was badly bloodshot, reminding her of that morning in Hastings Glen when they woke up in that motel.

'Daddy, look at this mess,' Charlie groaned, and began to cry.

'No time,' he said. 'Listen. Listen, Charlie!'

She bent over him, her tears wetting his face.

'This was coming, Charlie. . . . Don't waste your tears on me. But—'

'No! No!'

'Charlie, shut up!' he said roughly. 'They're going to want to kill you now. You understand? No . . . no more games. Gloves off.' He pronounced it 'glubs' from the corner of his cruelly twisted mouth. 'Don't let them, Charlie. And don't let them cover it up. Don't let them say . . . just a fire . . .'

He had raised his head slightly and now he lay back, panting. From outside, dim over the hungry crackle of the fire, came the faint and unimportant pop of guns . . . and once more the scream of horses.

'Daddy, don't talk . . . rest . . .'

'No. Time.' Using his right arm, he was able to get partway

470

up again to confront her. Blood trickled from both corners of his mouth. 'You have got to get away if you can, Charlie.' She wiped the blood away with the hem of her jumper. From behind, the fire baked into her. 'Get away if you can. If you have to kill the ones in your way, Charlie, do it. It's a war. Make them know they've been in a war.' His voice was failing now. 'You get away if you can, Charlie. Do it for me. Do you understand?'

She nodded.

Overhead, near the back, another rafter let go in a flaming Catherine wheel of orange-yellow sparks. Now the heat rushed out at them as if from an open furnace flue. Sparks lit on her skin and winked out like hungry, biting insects.

'Make it' – he coughed up thick blood and forced the words out – 'make it so they can never do anything like this again. Burn it down, Charlie. *Burn it all down.*'

'Daddy—'

'Go on, now. Before it all goes up.'

'I can't leave you,' she said in a shaking, helpless voice.

He smiled and pulled her even closer, as if to whisper in her ear. But instead he kissed her.

'—love you, Ch—' he said, and died.

20

Don Jules had found himself in charge by default. He held on as long as he could after the fire started, convinced that the little girl would run out into their field of fire. When it didn't happen – and when the men in front of the stables began to catch their first glimpse of what had happened to the men behind it – he decided he could wait no longer, not if he wanted to hold them. He began to move forward, and the others came with him . . . but their faces were tight and set. They no longer looked like men on a turkey shoot.

Then shadows moved rapidly inside the double doors. She

was coming out. Guns came up: two men fired before anything at all came out. Then—

But it wasn't the girl; it was the horses, half a dozen of them, eight, ten, their coats flecked with foam, their eyes rolling and white-rimmed, mad with fear.

Jules's men, on hair trigger, opened fire. Even those who had held back, seeing that horses rather than humans were leaving the stable, seemed unable to hold back once their colleagues had begun firing. It was a slaughter. Two of the horses pitched forward to their knees, one of them whinnying miserably. Blood flew in the bright October air and slicked the grass.

'*Stop!*' Jules bawled. '*Stop, dammit! Stop shooting the fucking horses!*'

He might as well have been King Canute giving orders to the tide. The men – afraid of something they could not see, hyped by the alarm buzzer, the Bright Yellow alert, the fire that was now pluming thick black smoke at the sky, and the heavy *ka-whummm!* of the exploding tractor-gas -- finally had moving targets to shoot at . . . and they were shooting.

Two of the horses lay dead on the grass. Another lay half on and half off the crushed-stone driveway, sides heaving rapidly. Three more, crazed with fear, veered to the left and made at the four or five men spread there. They gave way, still shooting, but one of the men tripped over his own feet and was trampled, screaming.

'*Quit it!*' Jules screamed. '*Quit it! Cease – cease firing! Goddammit, cease firing, you assholes!*'

But the slaughter went on. Men were reloading with strange, blank expressions on their faces. Many of them, like Rainbird, were veterans of the Vietnam war, and their faces wore the dull, twisted-rag expressions of men reliving an old nightmare at lunatic intensity. A few others had quit firing, but they were a minority. Five horses lay wounded or dead on the grass and in the driveway. A few others had run away, and Necromancer was among these, his tail waving like a battle flag.

'The girl!' someone screamed, pointing at the stable doors. '*The girl!*'

It was too late. The slaughter of the horses had barely ended and their attention was divided. By the time they swung back toward where Charlie stood with her head down, small and deadly in her denim jumper and dark-blue knee socks, the trenches of fire had already begun to radiate from her toward them, like strands of some deadly spider's web.

21

Charlie was submerged in the power again, and it was a relief.

The loss of her father, as keen and sharp as a stiletto, receded and became no more than a numb ache.

As always, the power drew her, like some fascinating and awful toy whose full range of possibilities still awaited discovery.

Trenches of fire raced across the grass toward the ragged line of men.

You killed the horses, you bastards, she thought, and her father's voice echoed, as if in agreement: *If you have to kill the ones in your way, Charlie, do it. It's a war. Make them know they've been in a war*.

Yes, she decided, she would make them know they had been in a war.

Some of the men were breaking and running now. She skewed one of the lines of fire to the right with a mild twist of her head and three of them were engulfed, their clothes becoming so many flaming rags. They fell to the ground, convulsed and screaming.

Something buzzed by her head, and something else

473

printed thin fire across her wrist. It was Jules, who had got another gun from Richard's station. He stood there, legs spread, gun out, shooting at her.

Charlie pushed out at him: one hard, pumping bolt of force.

Jules was thrown backward so suddenly and with such force that the wrecking ball of a great invisible crane might have struck him. He flew forty feet, not a man anymore but a boiling ball of fire.

Then they all broke and ran. They ran the way they had run at the Manders farm.

Good thing, she thought. *Good thing for you.*

She did not want to kill people. That had not changed. What had changed was that she'd kill them if she had to. If they stood in her way.

She began to walk toward the nearer of the two houses, which stood a little distance in front of a barn as perfect as the picture on a country calendar and facing its mate across the expanse of lawn.

Windows broke like gunshots. The ivy trellis climbing the east side of the house shuddered and then burst into arteries of fire. The paint smoked, then bubbled, then flamed. Fire ran up onto the roof like grasping hands.

One of the doors burst open, letting out the whooping, panicked bray of a fire alarm and two dozen secretaries, technicians, and analysts. They ran across the lawn toward the fence, veered away from the deaths of electricity and yapping, leaping dogs, and then milled like frightened sheep. The power wanted to go out toward them but she turned it away from them and onto the fence itself, making the neat chain-link diamonds droop and run and weep molten-metal tears. There was a low thrumming sound, a low-key *zapping* sound as the fence overloaded and then began to short out in segment after segment. Blinding purple sparks leaped up. Small fireballs began to jump from the top of the fence, and white porcelain conductors exploded like clay ducks in a shooting gallery.

The dogs were going mad now. Their coats stood out in crazy spikes and they raced back and forth like banshees between the inner and outer fences. One of them caromed into the spitting high-voltage fence and went straight up in the air, its legs splayed stiffly. It came down in a smoking heap. Two of its mates attacked it with savage hysteria.

There was no barn behind the house where Charlie and her father had been held, but there was a long, low, perfectly maintained building that was also red barnboard trimmed with white. This building housed the Shop motor pool. Now the wide doors burst open and an armored Cadillac limousine with government plates raced out. The sunroof was open and a man's head and torso poked through it. Elbows braced on the roof, he began to fire a light submachine gun at Charlie. In front of her, firm turf spun away in ragged digs and divots.

Charlie turned toward the car and let the power loose in that direction. The power was still growing; it was turning into something that was lithe yet ponderous, an invisible something that now seemed to be feeding itself in a spiraling chain reaction of exponential force. The limo's gas tank exploded, enveloping the rear of the car and shooting the tailpipe into the sky like a javelin. But even before that happened the head and torso of the shooter were incinerated, the car's windshield had blown in, and the limousine's special self-sealing tires had begun to run like tallow.

The car continued on through its own ring of fire, plowing out of control, losing its original shape, melting into something that looked like a torpedo. It rolled over twice and a second explosion shook it.

Secretaries were fleeing from the other house now, running like ants. She could have swept them with fire – and a part of her *wanted* to – but with an effort of her waning volition, she turned the power on the house itself, the house where the two of them had been kept against their will . . . the house where John had betrayed her.

She sent the force out, all of it. For just a moment it seemed that nothing at all was happening; there was a faint shimmer in the air, like the shimmer above a barbecue pit where the coals have been well banked . . . and then the entire house exploded.

The only clear image she was left with (and later, the testimony of the survivors repeated it several times) was that of the chimney of the house rising into the sky like a brick rocketship, seemingly intact, while beneath it the twenty-five-room house disintegrated like a little girl's cardboard playhouse in the flame of a blowtorch. Stone, lengths of board, planks, rose into the air and flew away on the hot dragon breath of Charlie's force. An IBM typewriter, melted and twisted into something that looked like a green steel dishrag tied in a knot, whirled up into the sky and crashed down between the two fences, digging a crater. A secretary's chair, the swivel seat whirling madly, was flung out of sight with the speed of a bolt shot from a crossbow.

Heat baked across the lawn at Charlie.

She looked around for something else to destroy. Smoke rose to the sky now from several sources – from the two graceful antebellum homes (only one of them still recognizable as a home now), from the stable, from what had been the limousine. Even out here in the open, the heat was becoming intense.

And still the power spun and spun, wanting to be sent out, *needing* to be sent out, lest it collapse back on its source and destroy it.

Charlie had no idea what unimaginable thing might eventually have happened. But when she turned back to the fence and the road leading out of the Shop compound, she saw people throwing themselves against the fence in a blind frenzy of panic. In some places the fence was shorted out and they had been able to climb over. The dogs had got one of them, a young woman in a yellow gaucho skirt who was screaming horribly. And as clearly as if he had still been alive and standing next to her, Charlie heard her father cry: *Enough, Charlie! It's enough! Stop while you still can!*

But could she?

Turning away from the fence, she searched desperately for what she needed, fending off the power at the same time, trying to hold it balanced and suspended. It began to scrawl directionless, crazy spirals across the grass in a widening pattern.

Nothing. Nothing except—

The duckpond.

22

OJ was getting out, and no dogs were going to stop him.

He had fled the house when the others began to converge on the stable. He was very frightened but not quite panicked enough to charge the electrified fence after the gates automatically slid shut on their tracks. He had watched the entire holocaust from behind the thick, gnarled trunk of an old elm. When the little girl shorted the fence, he waited until she had moved on a little way and turned her attention to the destruction of the house. Then he ran for the fence, The Windsucker in his right hand.

When one section of the fence was dead, he climbed over it and let himself down into the dog run. Two of them came for him. He grasped his right wrist with his left hand and shot them both. They were big bastards, but The Windsucker was bigger. They were all done eating Gravy Train, unless they served the stuff up in doggy heaven.

A third dog got him from behind, tore out the seat of his pants and a good chunk of his left buttock, knocked him to the ground. OJ turned over and grappled with it one-handed, holding The Windsucker with the other. He clubbed it with the butt of the gun, and then thrust forward with the muzzle when the dog came for his throat. The muzzle slid neatly between the Doberman's jaws and OJ pulled the trigger. The report was muffled.

'Cranberry sauce!' OJ cried, getting shakily to his feet. He began to laugh hysterically. The outer gate was not electrified any longer; even its weak keeper charge had shorted out. OJ tried to open it. Already other people were crowding and jouncing him. The dogs that were left had backed away, snarling. Some of the other surviving agents also had their guns out and were taking potshots at them. Enough discipline had returned so that those with guns stood in a rough perimeter around the unarmed secretaries, analysts and technicians.

OJ threw his whole weight against the gate. It would not open. It had locked shut along with everything else. OJ looked around, not sure what to do next. Sanity of a sort had returned; it was one thing to cut and run when you were by yourself and unobserved, but now there were too many witnesses around.

If that hellacious kid left any witnesses.

'You'll have to climb over it!' he shouted. His voice was lost in the general confusion. *'Climb over, goddammit!'* No response. They only crowded against the outer fence, their faces dumb and shiny with panic.

OJ grabbed a woman huddled against the gate next to him. *'Nooooo!'* she screamed.

'Climb, you cunt!' OJ roared, and goosed her to get her going. She began to climb.

Others saw her and began to get the idea. The inner fence was still smoking and spitting sparks in places; a fat man OJ recognized as one of the commissary cooks was holding onto roughly two thousand volts. He was jittering and jiving, his feet doing a fast boogaloo in the grass, his mouth open, his cheeks turning black.

Another one of the Dobermans lunged forward and tore a chunk from the leg of a skinny, bespectacled young man in a lab coat. One of the other agents snapped a shot at the dog, missed, and shattered the bespectacled young man's elbow. The young lab technician fell on the ground and began rolling around, clutching his elbow and screaming for the Blessed Virgin to help him. OJ shot the dog before it could tear the young man's throat out.

What a fuckup, he groaned inside. Oh dear God, what a fuckup.

Now there were maybe a dozen of them climbing the wide gate. The woman OJ had set in motion reached the top, tottered, and fell over on the outside with a strangled cry. She began to shriek immediately. The gate was high; it had been a nine-foot drop; she had landed wrong and broken her arm.

Oh Jesus Christ, what a fuckup.

Clawing their way up the gate, they looked like a lunatic's vision of training exercises at Marine bootcamp.

OJ craned back, trying to see the kid, trying to see if she was coming for them. If she was, the witnesses could take care of themselves; he was up over that gate and gone.

Then one of the analysts yelled, 'What in the name of *God*—'

The hissing sound rose immediately, drowning out his voice. OJ would say later that the first thing he thought of was his grandmother frying eggs, only this sound was a million times louder than that, as if a tribe of giants had all decided to fry eggs at once.

It swelled and grew, and suddenly the duckpond between the two houses was obscured in rising white steam. The whole pond, roughly fifty feet across and four feet deep at its center, was boiling.

For a moment OJ could see Charlie, standing about twenty yards from the pond, her back to those of them still struggling to get out, and then she was lost in the steam. The hissing sound went on and on. White fog drifted across the green lawn, and the bright autumn sun cast crazy arcs of rainbow in the cottony moisture. The cloud of steam billowed and drifted. Would-be escapees hung onto the fence like flies, their heads craned back over their shoulders, watching.

What if there isn't enough water? OJ thought suddenly. What if there isn't enough to put out her match or torch or whatever the hell it is? What happens then?

Orville Jamieson decided he didn't want to stick around to find out. He'd had enough of the hero bit. He jammed The Windsucker back into its shoulder holster and went up the gate at what was nearly a run. At the top he vaulted over neatly and landed in a flexed crouch near the woman who was still holding her broken arm and screaming.

'I advise you to save your breath and get the hell out of here,' OJ told her, and promptly took his own advice.

23

Charlie stood in her own world of white, feeding her power into the duckpond, grappling with it, trying to bring it down, to make it have done. Its vitality seemed endless. She had it under control now, yes; it fed smoothly into the pond as if through an invisible length of pipe. But what would happen if all the water boiled away before she could disrupt its force and disperse it?

No more destruction. She would let it fall back in on herself and destroy her before she allowed it to range out and begin feeding itself again.

(*Back off! Back off!*)

Now, at last, she could feel it losing some of its urgency,

its . . . its ability to stick together. It was falling apart Thick white steam everywhere, and the smell of laundries. The giant bubbling hiss of the pond she could no longer see.

(*!!BACK OFF!!*)

She thought dimly of her father again, and fresh grief sliced into her: dead; he was dead; the thought seemed to diffuse the power still more, and now, at last, the hissing noise began to fade. The steam rolled majestically past her. Overhead, the sun was a tarnished silver coin.

I changed the sun, she thought disjointedly, and then, *No – not really – it's the steam – the fog – it'll blow away—*

But with a sudden sureness that came from deep inside she knew that she *could* change the sun if she wanted to . . . in time.

The power was still growing.

This act of destruction, this apocalypse, had only approached its current limit.

The *potential* had hardly been tapped.

Charlie fell to her knees on the grass and began to cry, mourning her father, mourning the other people she had killed, even John. Perhaps what Rainbird had wanted for her would have been best, but even with her father dead and this rain of destruction on her head, she felt her response to life, a tough, mute grasping for survival.

And so, perhaps most of all, she mourned herself.

24

How long she sat on the grass with her head cradled in her arms she didn't know; as impossible as it seemed, she believed she might even have dozed. However long it was, when she came to herself she saw that the sun was brighter and a little more westerly in the sky. The steam of the boiling pond had been pulled to tatters by the light breeze and blown away.

Slowly, Charlie stood up and looked around.

The pond caught her eye first. She saw that it had been close . . . very close. Only puddles of water remained, flatly sheened with sunlight like bright glass gems set in the slick mud of the pond's bottom. Draggled lilypads and water-weeds lay here and there like corroded jewelry; already in places the mud was beginning to dry and crack. She saw a few coins in the mud, and a rusted thing that looked like a very long knife or perhaps a lawnmower blade. The grass all around the pond had been scorched black.

A deadly silence lay over the Shop compound, broken only by the brisk snap and crackle of the fire. Her father had told her to make them know they had been in a war, and what was left looked very much like an abandoned battleground. The stable, barn, and house on one side of the pond were burning furiously. All that remained of the house on the other side was smoky rubble; it was as if the place had been hit by a large incendiary bomb or a World War II V-rocket.

Blasted and blackened lines lay across the grass in all directions, making those idiot spiral patterns, still smoking. The armored limo had burned itself out at the end of a gouged trench of earth. It no longer resembled a car; it was only a meaningless hunk of junk.

The fence was the worst.

Bodies lay scattered along its inner perimeter, nearly half a dozen of them. In the space between there were two or three more bodies, plus a scattering of dead dogs.

As if in a dream, Charlie began walking in that direction.

Other people were moving on the lawn, but not many. Two of them saw her coming and shied away. The others seemed to have no conception of who she was and no knowledge that she had caused it all. They walked with the dreamy, portentous paces of shock-blasted survivors.

Charlie began to clamber up the inner fence.

482

'I wouldn't do that,' a man in orderly's whites called over conversationally. 'Dogs goan get you if you do that, girl.'

Charlie took no notice. The remaining dogs growled at her but did not come near; they, too, had had enough, it seemed. She climbed the outer gate, moving slowly and carefully, holding tight and poking the toes of her loafers into the diamond-shaped holes in the link. She reached the top, swung one leg over carefully, then the other. Then, moving with the same deliberation, she climbed down and, for the first time in half a year stepped onto ground that didn't belong to the Shop. For a moment she only stood there, as if in shock.

I'm free, she thought dully. *Free.*

In the distance, the sound of wailing sirens arose, drawing near.

The woman with the broken arm still sat on the grass, about twenty paces from the abandoned guardhouse. She looked like a fat child too weary to get up. There were white shock circles under her eyes. Her lips had a bluish tinge.

'Your arm,' Charlie said huskily.

The woman looked up at Charlie, and recognition came into her eyes. She began to scrabble away, whimpering with fear. 'Don't you come near me,' she hissed raggedly. 'All their tests! All their tests! I don't need no tests! You're a witch! A witch!'

Charlie stopped. 'Your arm,' she said. 'Please. Your arm. I'm sorry. Please?' Her lips were trembling again. It seemed to her now that the woman's panic, the way her eyes rolled, the way she unconsciously curled her lip up over her teeth – these were the worst things of all.

'Please!' she cried. 'I'm sorry! They killed my daddy!'

'Should have killed you as well,' the woman said, panting. 'Why don't you burn yourself up, if you're so sorry?'

Charlie took a step toward her and the woman moved away again, screaming as she fell over on her injured arm.

'Don't you come near me!'

And suddenly all of Charlie's hurt and grief and anger found its voice.

'*None of it was my fault!*' she screamed at the woman with the broken arm. '*None of it was my fault; they brought it on themselves, and I won't take the blame, and I won't kill myself! Do you hear me! Do you?*'

The woman cringed away, muttering.

The sirens were closer.

Charlie felt the power, surging up eagerly with her emotions.

She slammed it back down, made it gone.

(*and I won't do that either*)

She walked across the road, leaving the muttering, cringing woman behind. On the far side of the road was a field, thigh-high with hay and timothy, silver white with October, but still fragrant.

(*where am I going?*)

She didn't know yet.

But they were never going to catch her again.

Charlie Alone

1

The story appeared in fragments on the late television news that Wednesday night, but Americans were not greeted with the entire story until they rose the next morning. By then all the available data had been coordinated into what Americans really seem to mean when they say they want 'the news' – and what they really mean is 'Tell me a story' and make sure it has a beginning, a middle, and some kind of ending.

The story America got over its collective coffee cup, via *Today*, *Good Morning, America*, and *The CBS Morning News*, was this: There had been a terrorist firebomb attack at a top-secret scientific think tank in Longmont, Virginia. The terrorist group was not positively known yet, although three of them had already stepped forward to claim the credit – a group of Japanese Reds, the Khafadi splinter of Black September, and a domestic group who went by the rich and wonderful name of the Militant Midwest Weatherpeople.

Though no one was sure exactly who was behind the attack, the reports seemed quite clear on how it had been carried out. An agent named John Rainbird, an Indian and a Vietnam vet, had been a double agent who had planted the firebombs on behalf of the terrorist organization. He had either killed himself by accident or had committed suicide at the site of one of the firebombings, a stable. One source claimed that Rainbird had actually been overcome by heat and smoke while trying to drive the horses out of the burning stable; this occasioned the usual newscom irony about coldblooded terrorists who cared more for animals than they did for people. Twenty lives had been lost in the tragedy; forty-five people had been injured, ten of them seriously. The survivors had all been 'sequestered' by the government.

That was the story. The name of the Shop hardly surfaced at all. It was quite satisfactory.

Except for one dangling loose end.

2

'I don't care where she is,' the new head of the Shop said four weeks after the conflagration and Charlie's escape. Things had been in total confusion for the first ten days, when the girl might easily have been swept back into the Shop's net; they were still not back to normal. The new head sat behind a make-do desk; her own would not be delivered for another three days. 'And I don't care what she can do, either. She's an eight-year-old kid, not Superwoman. She can't stay out of sight long. I want her found and then I want her killed.'

She was speaking to a middle-aged man who looked like a small-town librarian. Needless to say, he was not.

He tapped a series of neat computer printouts on the head's desk. Cap's files had not survived the burning, but most of his information had been stored in the computer memory banks. 'What's the status of this?'

'The Lot Six proposals have been tabled indefinitely,' the head told him. 'It's all political, of course. Eleven old men, one young man, and three blue-haired old ladies who probably own stock in some Swiss goat-gland clinic . . . all of them with sweat under their balls about what would happen if the girl showed up. They—'

'I doubt very much if the senators from Idaho, Maine,

and Minnesota have any sweat under their balls,' the man who was not a librarian murmured.

The head shrugged it off. 'They're interested in Lot Six. Of course they are. I would describe the light as amber.' She began to play with her hair, which was long -- a shaggy, handsome dark auburn. ' "Tabled indefinitely" means until we bring them the girl with a tag on her toe.'

'We must be Salome,' the man across the desk murmured. 'But the platter is yet empty.'

'What the fuck are you talking about?'

'Never mind,' he said. 'We seem to be back to square one.'

'Not exactly,' the head replied grimly. 'She doesn't have her father to watch out for her anymore. She's on her own. And I want her found. Quickly.'

'And if she spills her guts before we can find her?'

The head leaned back in Cap's chair and laced her hands behind her neck. The man who was not a librarian eyed appreciatively the way her sweater pulled taut across the rounds of her breasts. Cap had never been like this.

'If she were going to spill her guts, I think she would have by now.' She leaned forward again, and tapped the desk calendar. 'November fifth,' she said, 'and nothing. Meantime, I think we've taken all the reasonable precautions. The *Times*, the Washington *Post*, the Chicago *Tribune* . . . we're watching all the majors, but so far, nothing.

'Suppose she decides to go to one of the minors? The Podunk *Times* instead of the New York *Times*? We can't watch every news organ in the country.'

'That is regrettably true,' the head agreed. 'But there has been nothing. Which means she has said nothing.'

'Would anyone really believe such a wild tale from an eight-year-old girl anyway?'

'If she lit a fire at the end of the story, I think that they might be disposed to,' the head answered. 'But shall I tell you what the computer says?' She smiled and tapped the sheets. 'The computer says there's an eighty-percent probability that we can bring the committee her dead body without lifting a finger . . . except to ID her.'

'Suicide?'

The head nodded. The prospect seemed to please her a great deal.

'That's nice,' the man who was not a librarian said, standing up. 'For my own part, I'll remember that the computer also said that Andrew McGee was almost certainly tipped over.'

The head's smile faltered a bit.

'Have a nice day, Chief,' the man who was not a librarian said, and strolled out.

3

On the same November day, a man in a flannel shirt, flannel pants, and high green boots stood chopping wood under a mellow white sky. On this mild day, the prospect of another winter still seemed distant; the temperature was an agreeable fifty degrees. The man's coat, which his wife had scolded him into wearing, hung over a fencepost. Behind him, stacked against the side of the old barn, was a spectacular drift of orange pumpkins – some of them starting to go punky now, sad to say.

The man put another log on the chopping block, slung the ax up, and brought it down. There was a satisfying thud, and two stove lengths fell to either side of the block. He was bending down to pick them up and toss them over with the others when a voice said from behind him: 'You got a new block, but the mark's still there, isn't it? It's still there.'

Startled, he turned around. What he saw caused him to step back involuntarily, knocking the ax to the ground, where it lay across the deep, indelible mark in the earth. At first he thought it was a ghost he was looking at, some gruesome specter of a child risen from the Dartmouth Crossing graveyard three miles up the road. She stood, pallid and dirty and thin in the driveway, her eyes hollow and glistening in their sockets, her jumper ragged and torn. A scrape mark skidded up her right arm almost to the elbow. It looked infected. There were loafers on her feet, or what had once been loafers; now it was hard to tell.

And then, suddenly, he recognized her. It was the little girl from a year ago; she had called herself Roberta, and she had a flamethrower in her head.

'Bobbi?' he said. 'My sainted hat, is that Bobbi?'

'Yes, it's still right there,' she repeated as if she had not heard him, and he suddenly realized what the glisten in her eyes was: she was weeping.

'Bobbi,' he said, 'honey, what's the matter? Where's your dad?'

'Still there,' she said a third time, and then collapsed forward in a faint. Irv Manders was barely able to catch her. Cradling her, kneeling in the dirt of his dooryard, Irv Manders began to scream for his wife.

4

Dr Hofferitz arrived at dusk and was in the back bedroom with the girl for about twenty minutes. Irv and Norma Manders sat in the kitchen, doing more looking at their supper than eating. Every now and then, Norma would look at her husband, not accusingly but merely questioningly, and there was the drag of fear, not in her eyes but around them – the eyes of a woman fighting a tension headache or perhaps low-back pain.

The man named Tarkington had arrived the day after the great burning; he had come to the hospital where Irv was being kept, and he had presented them with his card, which said only WHITNEY TARKINGTON   GOVERNMENT ADJUSTMENTS.

'You just want to get out of here,' Norma had said. Her lips were tight and white, and her eyes had that same look of pain they had now. She had pointed at her husband's arm, wrapped in bulky bandages; drains had been inserted, and they had been paining him considerably. Irv had told her he had gone through most of World War II with nothing much to show for it except a case of roaring hemorrhoids; it took being at home at his place in Hastings Glen to get shot up. 'You just want to get out,' Norma repeated.

But Irv, who had perhaps had more time to think, only said, 'Say what you have to, Tarkington.'

Tarkington had produced a check for thirty-five thousand dollars – not a government check but one drawn on the account of a large insurance company. Not one, however, that the Manderses did business with.

'We don't want your hush money,' Norma had said harshly, and reached for the call button over Irv's bed.

'I think you had better listen to me before you take any action you might regret later,' Whitney Tarkington had replied quietly and politely.

Norma looked at Irv, and Irv had nodded. Her hand fell away from the call button. Reluctantly.

Tarkington had a briefcase with him. Now he put it on his knees, opened it, and removed a file with the names MANDERS and BREEDLOVE written on the tab. Norma's eyes had widened, and her stomach began to twist and untwist. Breedlove was her maiden name. No one likes to see a government folder with his name on it; there is something terrible about the idea that tabs have been kept, perhaps secrets known.

Tarkington had talked for perhaps forty-five minutes in

490

a low, reasonable tone. He occasionally illustrated what he had to say with Xerox copies from the Manders/Breedlove file. Norma would scan these sheets with tight lips and then pass them on to Irv in his hospital bed.

We are in a national-security situation, Tarkington had said on that horrible evening. You must realize that. We don't enjoy doing this, but the simple fact is, you must be made to see reason. These are things you know very little about.

I know you tried to kill an unarmed man and his little girl, Irv had replied.

Tarkington had smiled coldly – a smile reserved for people who foolishly pretend to a knowledge of how the government works to protect its charges – and replied, You don't know what you saw or what it means. My job is not to convince you of that fact but only to try and convince you not to talk about it. Now, look here: this needn't be so painful. The check is tax-free. It will pay for repairs to your house and your hospital bills with a nice little sum left over. And a good deal of unpleasantness will be avoided.

Unpleasantness, Norma thought now, listening to Dr Hofferitz move around in the back bedroom and looking at her almost untouched supper. After Tarkington had gone, Irv had looked at her, and his mouth had been smiling, but his eyes had been sick and wounded. He told her: My daddy always said that when you was in a shit-throwing contest, it didn't matter how much you threw but how much stuck to you.

Both of them had come from large families. Irv had three brothers and three sisters; Norma had four sisters and one brother. There were uncles, nieces, nephews, and cousins galore. There were parents and grandparents, in-laws . . . and, as in every family, a few outlaws.

One of Irv's nephews, a boy named Fred Drew whom he

491

had met only three or four times, had a little pot garden growing in his backyard in Kansas, according to Tarkington's papers. One of Norma's uncles, a contractor, was up to his eyebrows in debt and shaky business ventures on the Gulf Coast of Texas; this fellow, whose name was Milo Breedlove, had a family of seven to support, and one whisper from the government would send Milo's whole desperate house of cards tumbling and put them all on the state, common bankrupts. A cousin of Irv's twice removed; he thought he had met her once but couldn't recall what she had looked like had apparently embezzled a small sum of money from the bank where she worked about six years ago. The bank had found out and had let her go, electing not to prosecute so as to avoid adverse publicity. She had made restitution over a period of two years and was now making a moderate success of her own beauty parlor in North Fork, Minnesota. But the statute of limitations had not run out and she could be federally prosecuted under some law or other having to do with banking practices. The FBI had a file on Norma's youngest brother, Don. Don had been involved with the SDS in the middle sixties and might have been briefly involved with a plot to firebomb a Dow Chemical Company office in Philadelphia. The evidence was not strong enough to stand up in court and Don had told Norma himself that when he got wind of what was going on, he had dropped the group, horrified, but a copy of the file forwarded to the division of the corporation he worked for would undoubtedly lose him his job.

It had gone on and on, Tarkington's droning voice in the closed, tight little room. He had saved the best for last. Irv's family's last name had been Mandroski when his great-grandparents came to America from Poland in 1888. They were Jews, and Irv himself was part Jewish, although there had been no pretension to Judaism in the family since the time of his grandfather, who had married a Gentile: the two of them had lived in happy agnosticism ever after. The blood had been further thinned when Irv's father had gone and done him likewise (as Irv himself had done, marrying Norma Breedlove, a sometime Methodist). But there were still Mandroskis in Poland, and Poland was behind the Iron Curtain, and if the CIA wanted to, they could set in motion a short chain of events that would end up making life very, very difficult for these relatives whom Irv had never seen. Jews were not loved behind the Iron Curtain.

Tarkington's voice ceased. He replaced his file, snapped his briefcase shut, put it between his feet again, and looked at them brightly, like a good student who has just given a winning recitation.

Irv lay against his pillow, feeling very weary. He felt Tarkington's eyes on him, and that he didn't particularly mind, but Norma's eyes were on him as well, anxious and questioning.

You haff relatives in the old country, yesss? Irv thought. It was such a cliché that it was funny, but he didn't feel like laughing at all, somehow. *How many removes before they're not your relatives anymore? Fourth-cousin remove? Sixth? Eighth? Christ on a sidecar. And if we stand up to this sanctimonious bastard and they ship those people off to Siberia, what do I do? Send them a postcard saying they're working in the salt mines because I picked up a little button and her daddy hitching on the road in Hastings Glen? Christ on a sidecar.*

Dr Hofferitz, who was nearly eighty, came slowly out of the back bedroom, brushing his white hair back with one gnarled hand. Irv and Norma, both glad to be jerked out of their memories of the past, looked around at him.

'She's awake,' Dr Hofferitz said, and shrugged. 'She's not in very good shape, your little ragamuffin, but she is in no danger, either. She has an infected cut on her arm and another on her back, which she says she got crawling under a barbed-wire fence to get away from "a pig that was mad at her." '

Hofferitz sat down at the kitchen table with a sigh, produced a pack of Camels, and lit one. He had smoked all his life, and, he had sometimes told colleagues, as far as he was concerned, the surgeon general could go fuck himself.

'Do you want something to eat, Karl?' Norma asked.

Hofferitz looked at their plates. 'No – but if I was to, it looks like you wouldn't have to dish up anything new,' he said dryly.

'Will she have to stay in bed for long?' Irv asked.

'Ought to have her down to Albany,' Hofferitz said. There was a dish of olives on the table and he took a handful. 'Observation. She's got a fever of a hundred and one. It's from the infection. I'll leave you some penicillin and some antibiotic ointment. Mostly what she needs to do is eat and drink and rest. Malnutrition. Dehydration.' He popped an olive into his mouth. 'You were right to give her that chicken broth, Norma. Anything else, she would have sicked it up, almost as sure as shooting. Nothing but clear liquids for her tomorrow. Beef broth, chicken broth, lots of water. And plenty of gin, of course; that's the best of those clear liquids.' He cackled at this old joke, which both Irv and Norma had heard a score of times before, and popped another olive into his mouth. 'I ought to notify the police about this, you know.'

'No,' Irv and Norma said together, and then they looked at each other, so obviously surprised that Dr Hofferitz cackled again.

'She's in trouble, ain't she?'

Irv looked uncomfortable. He opened his mouth, then closed it again.

'Got something to do with that trouble you had last year, maybe?'

This time Norma opened her mouth, but before she could speak, Irv said, 'I thought it was only gunshot wounds you had to report, Karl.'

'By law, by law,' Hofferitz said impatiently, and stubbed out his cigarette. 'But you know there's a spirit of the law as well as a letter, Irv. Here's a little girl and you say her name is Roberta McCauley and I don't believe that anymore than I believe a hog will shit dollar bills. She says she scraped her back open crawling under barbed wire, and I got to think that's a funny thing to have happen to you on the way to your relatives, even with gas as tight as it is. She says she don't remember much of the last week or so, and that I do believe. Who is she, Irv?'

Norma looked at her husband, frightened. Irv rocked back in his chair and looked at Dr Hofferitz.

'Yeah,' he said finally, 'she's part of that trouble from last year. That's why I called you, Karl. You've seen trouble, both here and back in the old country. You know what trouble is. And you know that sometimes the laws are only as good as the people in charge of them. I'm just saying that if you let out that little girl is here, it's going to mean trouble for a lot of people who haven't earned it. Norma and me, a lot of our kin . . . and her in there. And that's all I think I can tell you. We've known each other twenty-five years. You'll have to decide what you're going to do.'

'And if I keep my mouth shut,' Hofferitz said, lighting another cigarette, 'what are you going to do?'

Irv looked at Norma, and she looked back at him. After a moment she gave her head a bewildered little shake and dropped her eyes to her plate.

'I dunno,' Irv said quietly.

'You just gonna keep her like a parrot in a cage?' Hofferitz asked. 'This is a small town, Irv. I can keep my mouth shut, but I'm in the minority. Your wife and you belong to the church. To the Grange. People come and people go. Dairy inspectors gonna drop by to check your cows. Tax assessor's gonna drop by some fine day – that bald bastard – to reassess your buildings. What are you gonna do? Build her a room down cellar? Nice life for a kid, all right.'

Norma was looking more and more troubled.

'I dunno,' Irv repeated. 'I guess I have got to think on it some. I see what you're sayin . . . but if you knew the people that was after her . . .'

Hofferitz's eyes sharpened at this, but he said nothing.

'I got to think on it some. But will you keep quiet about her for the time being?'

Hofferitz popped the last of his olives into his mouth, sighed, stood up, holding onto the edge of the table. 'Yeah,' he said. 'She's stable. That V-Cillin will knock out the bugs. I'll keep my mouth shut, Irv. But you better think on it, all right. Long and hard. Because a kid ain't a parrot.'

'No,' Norma said softly. 'No, of course not.'

'Something strange about that kid,' Hofferitz said, picking up his black bag. 'Something damn funny about her. I couldn't see it and I couldn't put my finger on it . . . but I felt it.'

'Yeah,' Irv said. 'There's something strange about her, all right, Karl. That's why she's in trouble.'

He saw the doctor out into the warm and rainy November night.

5

After the doctor had finished probing and pressing with his old, gnarled, but wonderfully gentle hands, Charlie fell into a feverish but not unpleasant doze. She could hear their voices in the other room and understood that they

496

were talking about her, but she felt sure that they were only talking . . . not hatching plans.

The sheets were cool and clean; the weight of the crazy quilt was comforting on her chest. She drifted. She remembered the woman calling her a witch. She remembered walking away. She remembered hitching a ride with a vanful of hippies, all of them smoking dope and drinking wine, and she remembered that they had called her little sister and asked her where she was going.

'North,' she had replied, and that had caused a roar of approval.

After that she remembered very little until yesterday, and the hog that had charged her, apparently meaning to eat her. How she had got to the Manders farm, and why she had come here – whether it had been a conscious decision or something else – she could not remember.

She drifted. The doze deepened. She slept. And in her dream they were back in Harrison and she was starting up in her bed, her face wet with tears, screaming with terror, and her mother rushed in, auburn hair blinding and sweet in the morning light, and she had cried, 'Mommy, I dreamed you and Daddy were dead!' And her mother stroked her hot forehead with a cool hand and said, 'Shhh, Charlie, shhh. It's morning now, and wasn't that a silly dream?'

6

There was very little sleep for Irv and Norma Manders that night. They sat watching a succession of inane prime-time sitcoms, then the news, then the *Tonight* show. And every fifteen minutes or so Norma would get up, leave the living room quietly, and go to check on Charlie.

'How is she?' Irv asked around quarter of one.

'Fine. Sleeping.'

Irv grunted.

'Have you thought of it, Irv?'

'We've got to keep her until she's better,' Irv said. 'Then we'll talk to her. Find out about her dad. I can only see that far ahead.'

'If they come back—'

'Why should they?' Irv asked. 'They shut us up. They think they scared us—'

'They *did* scare me,' Norma said softly.

'But it wasn't right,' Irv replied, just as softly. 'You know that. That money . . . that "insurance money" . . . I never felt right about that, did you?'

'No,' she said, and shifted restlessly. 'But what Doc Hofferitz said is true, Irv. A little girl has got to have people . . . and she's got to go to school . . . and have friends . . . and . . . and—'

'You saw what she did that time,' Irv said flatly. 'That pyrowhatsis. You called her a monster.'

'I've regretted that unkind word ever since,' Norma said. 'Her father – he seemed like such a nice man. If only we knew where he was now.'

'He's *dead*,' a voice said from behind them, and Norma actually cried out as she turned and saw Charlie standing in the doorway, clean now and looking all the more pallid for that. Her forehead shone like a lamp. She floated in one of Norma's flannel nightgowns. 'My daddy is dead. They killed him and now there's nowhere I can go. Won't you please help me? I'm sorry. It's not my fault. I told them it wasn't my fault . . . I told them . . . but the lady said I was a witch . . . she said . . .' The tears were coming now, streaming down her cheeks, and Charlie's voice dissolved into incoherent sobs.

'Oh, honey, come here,' Norma said, and Charlie ran to her.

498

Dr Hofferitz came the next day and pronounced Charlie improved. He came two days after that and pronounced her much improved. He came over the weekend and pronounced her well.

'Irv, you decided what you're going to do?'

Irv shook his head.

Norma went to church by herself that Sunday morning, telling people that Irv had 'a touch of the bug.' Irv sat home with Charlie, who was still weak but able to get around inside the house now. The day before, Norma had bought her a lot of clothes – not in Hastings Glen, where such a purchase would have caused comment, but in Albany.

Irv sat beside the stove whittling, and after a while Charlie came and sat with him. 'Don't you want to know?' she said. 'Don't you want to know what happened after we took your car and left here?'

He looked up from his whittling and smiled at her. 'Figure you'll tell when you're ready, button.'

Her face, white, tense, and unsmiling, didn't change. 'Aren't you afraid of me?'

'Should I be?'

'Aren't you afraid I'll burn you up?'

'No, button. I don't think so. Let me tell you something. You're no little girl anymore. Maybe you ain't a big girl – you're someplace in the middle – but you're big enough. A kid your age – any kid – could get hold of matches if she wanted to, burn up the house or whatever. But not many do. Why would they want to? Why should you want to? A kid your age should be able to be trusted with a jackknife or a pack of matches if they're halfway bright. So, no. I ain't scared.'

At that Charlie's face relaxed; an expression of almost indescribable relief flowed across it.

'I'll tell you,' she said then. 'I'll tell you everything.' She began to speak and was still speaking when Norma returned an hour later. Norma stopped in the doorway, listening, then slowly unbuttoned her coat and took it off. She put her purse down. And still Charlie's young but somehow old voice droned, on and on, telling it, telling it all.

And by the time she was done, both of them understood just what the stakes were, and how enormous they had become.

9

Winter came with no firm decision made. Irv and Norma began to go to church again, leaving Charlie alone in the house with strict instructions not to answer the telephone if it rang and to go down the cellar if someone drove in while they were gone. Hofferitz's words, *like a parrot in a cage*, haunted Irv. He bought a pile of schoolbooks – in Albany – and took up teaching Charlie himself. Although she was quick, he was not particularly good at it. Norma was a little better. But sometimes the two of them would be sitting at the kitchen table, bent over a history or geography book, and Norma would look up at him with a question in her eyes . . . a question for which Irv had no answer.

The New Year came; February; March. Charlie's birthday. Presents bought in Albany. Like a parrot in a cage. Charlie did not seem entirely to mind, and in some ways, Irv reasoned to himself on nights when he couldn't sleep, perhaps it had been the best thing in the world for her, this period of slow healing, of each day taken in its slow winter course. But what came next? He didn't know.

There was the day in early April after a drenching two-day rain when the damned kindling was so damp he couldn't get the kitchen stove lit.

'Stand back a second,' Charlie said, and he did, automatically, thinking she wanted to look at something in there. He felt something pass him in midair, something tight and hot, and a moment later the kindling was blazing nicely.

Irv stared around at her, wide-eyed, and saw Charlie looking back at him with a kind of nervous, guilty hope on her face.

'I helped you, didn't I?' she said in a voice that was not quite steady. 'It wasn't really bad, was it?'

'No,' he said. 'Not if you can control it, Charlie.'

'I can control the little ones.'

'Just don't do it around Norma, girl. She'd drop her teddies.'

Charlie smiled a little.

Irv hesitated and then said, 'For myself, anytime you want to give me a hand and save me messing around with that damned kindling, you go right ahead. I've never been any good at it.'

'I will,' she said, smiling more now. 'And I'll be careful.'

'Sure. Sure you will,' he said, and for just a moment he saw those men on the porch again, beating at their flaming hair, trying to put it out.

Charlie's healing quickened, but still there were bad dreams and her appetite remained poor. She was what Norma Manders called 'peckish.'

Sometimes she would wake up from these nightmares with shuddering suddenness, not so much pulled from sleep as ejected from it, like a fighter pilot from his plane. This happened to her one night during the second week of

April; at one moment she was asleep, and at the next she was wide awake in her narrow bed in the back room, her body coated with sweat. For a moment the nightmare remained with her, vivid and terrible (the sap was running freely in the maples now, and Irv had taken her with him that afternoon to change the buckets; in her dream they had been sapping again, and she had heard something behind and had looked back to see John Rainbird creeping up on them, flitting from tree to tree, barely visible; his one eye glittered with a baleful lack of mercy, and his gun, the one he had shot her daddy with, was in one hand, and he was gaining). And then it slipped away. Mercifully, she could remember none of the bad dreams for long, and she rarely screamed anymore upon awakening from them, frightening Irv and Norma into her room to see what was wrong.

Charlie heard them talking in the kitchen. She fumbled for the Big Ben on her dresser and brought it close to her face. It was ten o'clock. She had been asleep only an hour and a half.

'—going to do?' Norma asked.

It was wrong to eavesdrop, but how could she help it? And they were talking about her; she knew it.

'I don't know,' Irv said.

'Have you thought anymore about the paper?'

Papers, Charlie thought. *Daddy wanted to talk to the papers. Daddy said it would be all right then.*

'Which one?' Irv asked. 'The Hastings *Bugle*? They can put it right next to the A&P ad and this week's shows at the Bijou.'

'It was what her father was planning to do.'

'Norma,' he said. 'I could take her to New York City. I could take her to the *Times*. And what would happen if four guys pulled guns and started shooting in the lobby?'

Charlie was all ears now. Norma's footfalls crossed the

kitchen; there was the rattle of the teapot's lid, and what she said in reply was mostly lost under running water.

Irv said, 'Yeah, I think it might happen. And I tell you what might be even worse, as much as I love her. She might get the drop on *them*. And if it got out of control, like it did at that place where they kep her . . . well, there's pretty nearly eight million people in New York City, Norma. I just feel like I'm too old to take a risk like that.'

Norma's footfalls crossed back to the table again, the old flooring of the farmhouse creaking comfortably beneath them. 'But, Irv, listen to me now,' she said. Norma spoke carefully and slowly, as if she had been thinking this out carefully over a long period of time. 'Even a little paper, even a little weekly like the *Bugle*, they're hooked into those AP tickers. News comes from everyplace these days. Why, just two years ago a little paper in Southern California won the Pulitzer Prize for some news story, and they had a circulation of under fifteen hundred!'

He laughed, and Charlie suddenly knew he had taken her hand across the table. 'You've been studying on this, haven't you?'

'Yes I have, and there's no reason to laugh at me for it, Irv Manders! This is serious, a serious business! We're in a box! How long can we keep her here before somebody finds out? You took her sapping out in the woods just this afternoon—'

'Norma, I wasn't laughin at you, and the child has got to get out sometime—'

'Don't you think I know that? I didn't say no, did I? That's just it! A growing child needs fresh air, exercise. Got to have those things if you're going to have any appetite, and she's—'

'Peckish, I know.'

'Pale and peckish, that's right. So I didn't say no. I was glad to see you take her. But, Irv, what if Johnny Gordon

503

or Ray Parks had been out today and had just happened to drift over to see what you were doing, like they sometimes do?'

'Honey, they didn't.' But Irv sounded uneasy.

'Not this time! Not the time before! But Irv, it can't go on! We been lucky already, and you know it!'

Her footsteps crossed the kitchen again, and then there was the sound of tea being poured.

'Yeah,' Irv said. 'Yeah, I know we have. But   thanks, darlin.'

'Welcome,' she said, sitting down again. 'And never mind the buts, either. You know it only takes one person, or maybe two. It'll spread. It'll get *out*, Irv, that we got a little girl up here. Never mind what it's doing to her; what happens if it gets back to *them*?'

In the darkness of the back room, Charlie's arms rashed out in goosebumps.

Slowly, Irv answered her. 'I know what you're saying, Norma. We got to do something, and I keep going over and over it in my head. A little paper . . . well, it's not just *sure* enough. You know we've got to get this story out right if we're going to make that girl safe for the rest of her life. If she's going to be safe, a lot of people have got to know she exists and what she can do – isn't that right? A *lot* of people.'

Norma Manders stirred restlessly but said nothing.

Irv pressed on. 'We got to do it right for her, and we got to do it right for us. Because it could be our lives at stake, too. Me, I've already been shot once. I believe that. I love her like my own, and I know you do, too, but we got to be realists about it, Norma. She could get us killed.'

Charlie felt her face grow hot with shame . . . and with terror. Not for herself but for them. What had she brought on their house?

'And it's not just us or her. You remember what that

504

man Tarkington said. The files he showed us. It's your brother and my nephew Fred and Shelley, and—'

'—and all those people back in Poland,' Norma said.

'Well, maybe he was only bluffing about that. I pray to God he was. It's hard for me to believe anyone could get that low.'

Norma said grimly, 'They've been pretty low already.'

'Anyway,' Irv said, 'we know they'll follow through on as much as they can, the dirty bastards. The shit is going to fly. All I'm saying, Norma, is I don't want the shit to fly to no good purpose. If we're going to make a move, I want it to be a good one. I don't want to go to some country weekly and then have them get wind of it and squash it. They could do it. They could do it.'

'But what does that leave?'

'That,' Irv said heavily, 'is what I keep tryin to figure out. A paper or a magazine, but one they won't think of. It's got to be honest, and it ought to be nationwide. But most of all, it can't have any ties to the government or to the government's ideas.'

'You mean to the Shop,' she said flatly.

'Yeah. That's what I mean.' There was the soft sound of Irv sipping his tea. Charlie lay in her bed, listening, waiting.

. . . it could be our lives at stake, too . . . I've already been shot once . . . I love her like my own, and I know you do, too, but we got to be realists about it, Norma . . . she could get us killed.

(no please I)

(she could get us killed like she got her mother killed)

(no please please don't don't say that)

(like she got her daddy killed)

(please stop)

Tears rolled across her side-turned face, catching in her ears, wetting the pillowcase.

'Well, we'll think on it some more,' Norma said finally. 'There's an answer to this, Irv. Somewhere.'

'Yeah. I hope so.'

'And in the meantime,' she said, 'we just got to hope no one knows she's here.' Her voice suddenly kindled with excitement. 'Irv, maybe if we got a lawyer—'

'Tomorrow,' he said. 'I'm done in, Norma. And no one knows she's here yet.'

But someone did. And the news had already begun to spread.

10

Until he was in his late sixties, Dr Hofferitz, an inveterate bachelor, had slept with his longtime housekeeper, Shirley McKenzie. The sex part of it had slowly dried up: the last time, as well as Hofferitz could recall, had been about fourteen years before, and that had been something of an anomaly. But the two of them had remained close; in fact, with the sex gone, the friendship had deepened and had lost some of that tense prickliness that seems to be at the center of most sexual relationships. Their friendship had become of that platonic variety that seems to genuinely obtain only in the very young and in the very old of the opposite sex.

Still, Hofferitz held onto his knowledge of the Manderses' 'boarder' for better than three months. Then, one night in February, after three glasses of wine while he and Shirley (who had just that January turned seventy-five) were watching television, he told her the whole story, after swearing her to complete secrecy.

Secrets, as Cap could have told Dr Hofferitz, are even more unstable than U-235, and stability lessens proportionately as the secret is told. Shirley McKenzie kept the secret for almost a month before telling her best girlfriend,

Hortense Barclay. Hortense kept the secret for about ten days before telling *her* best girlfriend, Christine Traegger. Christine told her husband and her best friends (all three of them) almost immediately.

This is how the truth spreads in small towns; and by the night in April when Irv and Norma had their overheard conversation, a good deal of Hastings Glen knew that they had taken in a mysterious girl. Curiosity ran high. Tongues wagged.

Eventually the news reached the wrong pair of ears. A telephone call was made from a scrambler phone.

Shop agents closed in on the Manders farm for the second time on the last day of April; this time they came across the dawn fields through a spring mist, like horrific invaders from Planet X in their bright flame-resistant suits. Backing them up was a National Guard unit who didn't know what the fuck they were doing or why they had been ordered out to the peaceful little town of Hastings Glen, New York.

They found Irv and Norma Manders sitting stunned in their kitchen, a note between them. Irv had found it that morning when he arose at five o'clock to milk the cows. It was one line: *I think I know what to do now. Love, Charlie.*

She had eluded the Shop again -- but wherever she was, she was alone.

The only consolation was that this time she didn't have so far to hitch.

11

The librarian was a young man, twenty-six years old, bearded, long-haired. Standing in front of his desk was a little girl in a green blouse and bluejeans. In one hand she held a paper shopping bag. She was woefully thin, and the young man wondered what the hell her mother and father had been feeding her . . . if anything.

He listened to her question carefully and respectfully. Her daddy, she said, had told her that if you had a really hard question, you had to go to the library to find the answer, because at the library they knew the answers to almost all the questions. Behind them, the great lobby of the New York Public Library echoed dimly; outside, the stone lions kept their endless watch.

When she was done, the librarian recapitulated, ticking off the salient points on his fingers.

'Honest.'

She nodded.

'Big . . . that is, nationwide.'

She nodded again.

'No ties to the government.'

For the third time, the thin girl nodded.

'Do you mind my asking why?'

'I' – she paused – 'I have to tell them something.'

The young man considered for several moments. He seemed about to speak, then held up a finger and went and conferred with another librarian. He came back to the little girl and spoke two words.

'Can you give me an address?' she asked.

He found the address and then printed it carefully on a square of yellow paper.

'Thank you,' the girl said, and turned to go.

'Listen,' he said, 'when was the last time you had something to eat, kid? You want a couple of bucks for lunch?'

She smiled – an amazingly sweet and gentle smile. For a moment, the young librarian was almost in love.

'I have money,' she said, and opened the sack so he could see.

The paper bag was filled with quarters.

Before he could say anything else – ask her if she had taken a hammer to her piggybank, or what – she was gone.

12

The little girl rode the elevator up to the sixteenth floor of the skyscraper. Several of the men and women who rode with her looked at her curiously – just a small girl in a green blouse and bluejeans, holding a crumpled paper bag in one hand and a Sunkist orange in the other. But they were New Yorkers, and the essence of the New York character is to mind your own business and let other people mind theirs.

She got off the elevator, read the signs, and turned left. Double glass doors gave on a handsome reception area at the end of the hall. Written below the two words the librarian had spoken to her was this motto: 'All the News That Fits.'

Charlie paused outside a moment longer.

'I'm doing it, Daddy,' she whispered. 'Oh, I hope I'm doing it right.'

Charlie McGee tugged open one of the glass doors and went into the offices of *Rolling Stone*, where the librarian had sent her.

The receptionist was a young woman with clear gray eyes. She looked at Charlie for several seconds in silence, taking in the crumpled Shop and Save bag, the orange, the slightness of the girl herself: she was slender almost to the point of emaciation, but tall for a child, and her face had a kind of serene, calm glow. *She's going to be so beautiful*, the receptionist thought.

'What can I do for you, little sister?' the receptionist asked, and smiled.

'I need to see someone who writes for your magazine,'

509

Charlie said. Her voice was low, but it was clear and firm. 'I have a story I want to tell. And something to show.'

'Just like show-and-tell in school, huh?' the receptionist asked.

Charlie smiled. It was the smile that had so dazzled the librarian. 'Yes,' she said. 'I've been waiting for a long time.'

All Futura Books are available at your bookshop or newsagent, or can be ordered from the following address: Futura Books, Cash Sales Department, P.O. Box 11, Falmouth, Cornwall TR10 9EN.

Please send cheque or postal order (no currency), and allow 60p for postage and packing for the first book plus 25p for the second book and 15p for each additional book ordered up to a maximum charge of £1.90 in U.K.

B.F.P.O. customers please allow 60p for the first book, 25p for the second book plus 15p per copy for the next 7 books, thereafter 9p per book.

Overseas customers, including Eire, please allow £1.25 for postage and packing for the first book, 75p for the second book and 28p for each subsequent title ordered.